Keeping Up Appearances

Keeping Up Appearances

Elizabeth Stevens

SLEEPING DRAGON BOOKS

ADELAIDE

Sleeping Dragon Books

Keeping Up Appearances
by Elizabeth Stevens

Print ISBN: 978-0648264866
Digital ISBN: 978-0648264873

Cover art by: Izzie Duffield

For Emily,
because you are invaluable.

Contents

Chapter One

Today was the day. The day I finally told Jason how I felt. I'd remembered to put on my big girl undies, I'd chugged three cups of coffee to steel myself against the nerves that were threatening to make me hurl – although, all that actually served to do was make the butterflies beat a slightly more violent samba on my ribcage – and I'd rehearsed what I was going to say to him for the last twenty-four hours.

I was ready.

I could do this.

"You just go up to him and you say the words. The good words. The coherent words." I mumbled the world's least inspiring pep-talk to myself as I walked into the school building.

I would have had no idea if anyone was saying 'good morning' or about to throw eggs at me. I was too busy keeping an eye out for Jason as I walked towards his locker. I forced my hands to relax out of the white-knuckle fists they'd balled themselves into and to take a deep breath.

"You can do this," I muttered. "Nancy agreed it sounded fine. It's fine. You can–"

I stopped and felt someone run into the back of me. They said something distasteful, but I didn't hear what the exact words were as I was too busy having my heart ripped out of my chest and stomped on. I was pretty sure it was then set on fire for good measure and the ashes were scattered prettily on a vat of acid.

Somehow, despite all that torture, the damned thing was still managing to beat furiously in my chest. It got far too hot and suddenly the air seemed far too thin. An inconvenient lump formed in my throat.

I blinked, not believing what I was seeing. Surely, I was dreaming? I actually slapped my own cheek, but the image in front of me was still clear as day.

Seeing Jason and Nancy standing in front of his locker on a Monday morning was not an unexpected sight, it happened on a weekly basis. But seeing Jason and Nancy in front of his locker with his hands on her hips, their foreheads and noses touching, and making goo-goo eyes at each other? That was something I'd only ever seen in my nightmares.

And, the universe didn't seem to think that was enough to throw at me that morning.

My heart, too despondent even for theatrics, stuttered to a stop when he pressed a kiss to her lips. As far as kisses went, it was a simple thing; chaste and sweet and completely appropriate for the school hallway. But, I felt that nausea threatening again and I took an involuntary step forward as if that was going to make any difference. I managed to drag my eyes off them for long enough to look around. No one seemed at all concerned that Jason and Nancy were kissing in the hallway.

Which only meant one thing.

Well, no. Actually it meant a multitude of things.

But first and foremost, it meant that I was the last one to find out.

It also meant that the whole time I was going over my speech to Nancy in the last twenty-four hours – and she'd been telling me she thought it was great and building up my confidence and telling me I *had* to talk to him today – she'd been, what? Already…with him?

I felt sick and my eyes felt unusually hot and prickly.

Someone clapped me on the back and I looked over to see Nigel grinning at me. "JT and Nance finally got together at Teagan's! Pretty great, huh, Holl?" he asked, clapped me on the back again and walked off with a huge grin.

Teagan's party.

The party we'd boycotted on Saturday night because Teagan was one of the Bows and we hated them. Or at least, I'd thought we hated them and I thought we'd boycotted her party. Apparently, I'd been the only one sitting at home on a Saturday night crying at bad rom-com movies in my pyjamas and stuffing myself with chocolate.

I dragged my eyes back to Jason and Nancy and found them looking at me like the school hallway was the last place they'd ever have expected to see me, like we didn't meet at Jason's locker every morning and had been meeting at Jason's locker every morning since the third week of Year Eight.

Concern flooded Jason's deep sapphire eyes, but it was Nancy's reaction that really hit home. The expression on her face said more to me than words ever could; the conniving weasel knew how I felt about him. She'd known all these years how I felt about him.

It had never been lost on us that a guy with two female best friends could cause some issues as we grew up. That was the whole reason Nancy and I had always been honest about him. We had a pact that we'd always tell each other if we started or stopped

3

crushing on him – or in my case, fell totally, completely and irrevocably in love with him and wouldn't stop even when I was stone cold dead.

Nancy had crushed on him plenty over the years, and we'd always laughed about it. Each time, I'd reassured her that he wasn't mine and if she really liked him and he liked her, I'd step back – and, I'd meant it… At least, I'd wanted to mean it. But, she'd then always assured me that Jason wasn't her type (particularly when her type was secretly the King of the Bows and all around dropkick – hot, yes, but arsehole extraordinaire) and that she wouldn't get in my way.

And, then! Then, she'd spent all of the day before texting me back and forth about me talking to him about how I felt! So with all this in mind, it was a bit of an understatement to say seeing them and their unexpected PDA was a bit of a surprise.

I just… I just couldn't comprehend such…betrayal.

I'd been blindsided. I felt like I'd been kicked in the gut and it hurt worse than those period cramps where it feels like Alien is trying to rip its way out of your uterus.

I blinked and realised my eyes were tearing up.

So, yay. Betrayal with a healthy sprinkling of humiliation threatening as well.

Just what I needed on a Monday morning after three cups of coffee.

Jason took a step forwards as he ignored the person who called out hello to him, but I turned and pushed my way through the throng of kids. I could only hope I'd find somewhere quiet before my eyes decided to join in on the betrayal and embarrass me in front of a whole school full of merciless teenagers. Thankfully, most of those merciless teenagers were making for their first lessons so the hallways were emptying aggravatingly slowly.

I had no idea where I thought I was going or what I planned to do once I got there. But, where I found myself was not what I'd been expecting – even considering I wasn't thinking straight. I pushed open a door, turned a corner, and my hands ran smack into a naked chest along with my face. I pulled my face off the naked chest and looked around, realising I'd somehow found myself in the boys' locker room. Thank God it seemed like this half-naked body was the only other body in there.

"Of all the girls I expected to see in here, you were *not* on the list," a very recognisable voice said and I looked up to find the dark brown hair and pale cognac-coloured eyes belonging to the King of the Bows himself. But, the cocky smirk turned to a frown as he searched my face. "What's wrong?"

I blinked and a tear actually had the audacity to run down my face. I sniffed, looked up at the ceiling and tried surreptitiously to wipe under my eye. "Nothing's wrong. Why would anything be wrong?"

The smirk was back. "You're certainly not the first girl brought to tears by my body."

My tears were suddenly, magically drying up and I was starting to forget why they'd welled in the first place as I glared at him. "I imagine I'm not the first one scarred by the experience either," I replied flippantly.

He only laughed and rubbed his hand along his stupidly perfect jaw. "Can't say that's been the feedback so far. But, I'll take it on board," he said with a conceding nod.

I looked around and saw that we were indeed thankfully the only ones in there. The first bell rang and I mentally cursed my bad luck. I turned to leave, but he caught my arm. I would have turned

5

back to say something particularly scathing I'm sure, but my phone buzzed. I pulled it out of my pocket. But, at the sight of Jason's name on the caller ID, I hit ignore.

"Ah," he breathed. "You found out then."

Tears threatened again and I huffed a frustrated sigh in the hope I'd suddenly feel more angry than sad. Standing in the boys' locker room with a half-naked King of the Bows (who somehow knew the news of Jason and Nancy before me) wasn't making it all that much of a stretch; I at least remembered who we did and didn't hate, and who we were and were not loyal to.

"You almost say that like you care," I scoffed.

"About you? No. About that git fucking up? Yes."

I rolled my eyes and turned to him with a glare I certainly wasn't feeling. "How *is* it so many girls want you when you're such an arsehole?" I asked as though I genuinely cared.

He grinned at me with that easy manner he had. "Didn't you hear? I'm officially out of the game."

I looked him over. "You, dating?" I scoffed. "That's about as likely as getting snow this Christmas."

He barely supressed a shudder like the whole idea of dating was mortally disgusting to him. That, or maybe the guy had an aversion to snow. I certainly didn't think the risk to my sanity was worth asking for clarification.

"Ew. No. I'm currently in the market to turn girls *off* my charms. By your rave review, I assume it's working." He was smiling now like he thought he was some kind of genius.

"I *have* never nor *will* I ever want you," I answered. "So, I am hardly the control group for your whacko little experiment. Now, kindly get your hand off me. Some of us don't get concessions when they're late to class."

6

Being the star striker for the Maple Ridge Grammar soccer team, he was given a multitude of concessions; he got to skip class to do whatever sports people did, he could be late, miss tests, have easier assignments, be a complete shit to the teachers, and they all just wished him well for the next match – even when it wasn't winter terms.

"Why are you half-naked?" I blurted out, realising that I was staring at his shirtless torso – which, yes, was all right if you liked your guys fit, lean and cocky as sin.

He ran a hand nonchalantly through his hair. "I went to the gym. Thought the rest of the population might appreciate me showering before being stuck in heated classrooms all day."

I was unimpressed, quite frankly. "Who would have thought I'd live to see the day you thought about someone else's feelings?"

"Does my cock count? Because, I think about his feelings *a lot*."

I glared at him, wondering where he got the confidence to just say things like that. "You're not as charming as you think you are."

"I think, Holly, you'll find I am."

The second bell rang and I swore, which earned me a chuckle from the King of the Bows. "I wish I could say it was a pleasure," I told him as I went to leave.

"Let me throw my shirt on and I'll walk you to class."

I frowned as he disappeared behind some lockers, frozen by the totally cavalier way he'd said that. "What?"

I heard the door to a locker bang and he reappeared in his shirt and tie, with his satchel slung over his shoulder. Although, how 'in' your clothes are you really when they're still flapping open like you're about to be on the cover of GQ or something?

"Ready?" he asked as though I hadn't moved because I'd been waiting for him.

And, I could totally understand why he thought that; it totally looked like that. In reality, my brain had misfired trying to work out in what universe he would tell me to wait for him as though he expected I would and that I would then *be* waiting for him.

This one, apparently.

"Holly?" He laid a hand on my arm and I jumped.

"Yes, what?" I answered hurriedly.

He looked at me like I concerned him for a moment, but then he was back to his sarcastically casual self. "Shall we get you out of the boys' locker rooms? Or, did you want Coach to find you in here? I've got pull, but I don't know if I can get us out of detention for this one."

I glared at him and nodded. "You know this from experience, I assume."

He gave me a wry smirk that told me he did indeed know that from experience and pushed the door open for me to go first.

I walked out into the hallway and was annoyed to find students still milling about. And, they didn't fail to notice me walking out of the boys' locker rooms while the King of the Bows held the door open for me and he may as well still have been half-naked. Of course, he didn't care in the slightest that they were staring and nudging each other as we walked down the hallway like we'd just had the hook-up of the century. Then again, the two of us being seen in any vicinity not at loggerheads *was* likely to cause a commotion.

"We've got French now, yeah?" he asked absently as he wandered beside me.

"You're actually coming to class today? No emergency sports practice that will conveniently get you out of your vocab test?"

He snorted. "Not this morning, unfortunately." There was a

pause. "Wait, we have a vocab test?"

I turned to see him stopped, halfway through doing his buttons up, and him looking up at me through the hair hanging over his face like I'd just told him the powers that be had made soccer illegal *and* all the women in the world just died simultaneously.

I gave him a sickly sweet smile. "Yes. We do."

I had never seen panic cross his face before, but I took a singular pleasure in it then. By the way his eyes narrowed, he could tell and that pissed him off. I wish I could say I cared.

"So, a question. Where are you going to sit now that your two best friends are doing the nasty?" he asked slowly as though it was something we discussed every day. My step faltered and he bent his head towards mine as we walked along. "Or, do we not talk about that particular heartbreak?"

"Be thankful I'm not a naturally violent person," I huffed, although I would be happy to make an exception for this guy.

He chuckled. "I'll tell you what. You come sit by me, give that git loser something to think about, and I won't even cheat off your test."

"Wow. What an enticing offer," I replied, sarcasm-heavy. "Thanks. But, no thanks."

"You going to sit in that empty seat right up front?" he cajoled. I frowned. "I…"

And really – if I did that – how obvious would it be? If I sat by King Douche, at least it would be *less* obvious I was avoiding my (former?) best friend. Sitting next to someone was a just enough cause for not sitting next to someone else, wasn't it? I mean, it *was* the King of the Bows and our sworn enemy… But, the alternative was just so much less appealing.

He rearranged his shoulder strap as he strolled beside me.

9

"You've got about two metres to reconsider my offer, Holly…"

"I *can* sit wherever I like." And wherever I liked was preferably not next to the King of the Bows.

"Yes. But if I'm in on it, you can really stick it to git-face."

I glared at him on Jason's behalf, if only because I'd temporarily forgotten that Jason had just broken my heart. "Fine. Thank you," I accepted begrudgingly.

Just as we walked up to the classroom door, he took my hand completely casually like he did it all the time. I looked at in him surprise, but didn't have a chance to say anything as Madame Renoir let out a deep sigh.

"Late again?" she asked as though she hoped maybe he had *any* other explanation for what was happening.

"Sorry, last minute study. We, uh, got a little distracted," he answered her as he dragged me to his usual desk, and I was sure I heard him wink.

Meanwhile, I was willing my cheeks to not be as red as they felt and I didn't look at anyone, merely stared at our clasped hands in front of me and really couldn't comprehend that something so warm and weirdly comforting would be attached to the great arsehole who was pulling me along behind him.

"Study? So, we shall see an improvement on your test today?" Madame Renoir asked with a hint of teasing in her tone and I was sure there were mutterings going around the classroom.

He laughed as we sat down. "Not today. I only enlisted Holly's help last week. And, I've a bit to learn about studying according to her." There was that wink again. "Maybe next time, though."

"I look forward to it," she chuckled and I wondered how it was that he got away with speaking to people like he was doing them a favour by just existing. "Now class, before our test…"

10

As I put my books on the unfamiliar desk in front of me, I felt an arm around the back of my chair and he tucked a stray piece of hair behind my ear. I forced myself not to pull away so I didn't look even stupider than I already did.

"Well, that got a reaction," he whispered in my ear and I forced myself not to look at Jason to see exactly what kind of reaction it was.

Then, he kissed my cheek. As casual as you please!

I felt my cheeks flame and heard him chuckle as he pulled away. I watched him find an empty page in his exercise book as though he hadn't just made a very public display of affection with me.

I, Holly Aberdeen, had been kissed – albeit on the cheek – by Xander Bowen.

I felt like I needed a shower and an anti-bacterial scrub.

Chapter Two

Class continued on with not a lot of people paying attention to me sitting next to Xander past some staring and a little whispering.

I was sure I felt Jason staring at me in shock, but I couldn't look at him again. It wasn't even that hard not to; just the thought of now seeing the face I'd dreamt about for so long made my eyes hot. Especially when I couldn't stop picturing him kissing Nancy. At least, along with that thought, I also got angry with myself for reacting like such a pansy and that helped me keep the tears at bay.

When the bell finally rang, I grabbed up my stuff and swept out of the room before anyone could stop me. How I thought I'd be able to avoid Jason or Nancy for the rest of the day when I was stuck in this veritable prison, I don't know. But, I was going to take a red hot college try at it.

I hurried to my locker, heedless of whether people were or weren't staring. Given my luck, the whole school already knew about Xander's little stunt. But in reality, it would take at least until about half-way through Recess before *everyone* found out that Jason Thomas' best friend had been seen canoodling with his arch nemesis. I just had to hope that I could avoid all three of them until... Well, the end of time was preferable at this point.

My heart thudded painfully in my chest as I grabbed my next

books – as though putting off going to Math was going to help me face it when I finally got there. Finally, I slammed my locker closed and trudged to my classroom; this one I shared with Jason *and* Nancy.

When I got to the room, Jason was sitting on the window sill and Nancy was between his legs. They were whispering something as Amy called something out to Jason. As he looked up to reply to her, he saw me and Nancy turned as well. The three of us froze when they saw me, which annoyed the kids following me into the room. But, my heart just looked at them with tears pouring down its little face and motioned people go around us. I took a seat on the other side of the room and waited for the teacher, wondering how we'd got ourselves into this whole mess.

I mean, why was Jason feeling so awkward? As far as he knew, he'd hooked up with one of his best friends and just neglected to tell his oldest friend. How was that awkward for him? Other than the fact I couldn't think of a single time in over ten years that Jason and I had ever hid something from each other. Well, there was the topic of the raging crush I'd had on him for about ten years… But, aside from that!

Nancy bloody well better be feeling awkward; just yesterday she was encouraging me to declare my feelings for him… Like full on coaching me to use my best words and to smile prettily and not choke – she knew what I was like when it came to my crush for Jason. We'd gone through the exact speech like a hundred times and she'd told me she was sure he'd be reciprocal.

But, then how did she know?

What had they talked about behind my back?

Oh my God, what did *they talk about behind my back?*

Blood rushed to my cheeks as I wondered what she'd told him.

13

If she'd told him! Had they been off making out this whole time? Hiding the fact they were together the whole time? Only stopping their make out sessions long enough to laugh at me behind my back because of my stupid crush?

What else could it be?

Why hadn't they told me they'd hooked up?

Nancy had had plenty of time to tell me the day before.

Simple fact was; Jason must know everything. That had to be why they hadn't told me. Jason knew and Nancy knew and they couldn't tell me because they thought I'd make a scene.

Well you sort of did, you idiot.

Why else made sense?

I had never felt so embarrassed or ashamed and my cheeks reminded me of that fact hotly. I knew it wasn't my fault I'd fallen for Jason. But, maybe if I'd mooned over him less with Nancy, something – anything – would be different. They at least wouldn't have hidden it from me and then I could have expected it. Wouldn't have been completely sideswiped by it. Wouldn't have gone mega freak-out, back-away-swiftly over it.

Because I mean, what had they expected? Did they really think that they could date and I just wouldn't notice? Was I such a poor, unfortunate wretch that I was to be pitied and treated like some idiot? Did over ten years of friendship with Jason and five with Nancy mean nothing?

Okay, I was overreacting.

I knew that.

Rationally.

Shame that emotions don't often listen to reason then, isn't it?

I got through Math and Home Group in some kind of a blur, not really paying attention until someone knelt down beside me. I jumped as and I found my home group teacher, Mr Burnett, smiling at me like I was some defenceless, wounded animal who was stuck in the headlights and desperate to run. I guessed that was a fairly appropriate description of my heart at that moment.

"Morning, Holly," he said.

I swallowed. "Morning, Mr Burnett."

"You were a little distracted today. Everything okay?"

I looked around the classroom and saw the last few students walking out; Jason and Nancy were nowhere to be seen. "Uh, yeah. Fine. Just – you know – stuff."

He nodded and tapped on the desk. "Well, you know my door's always open if you ever need to talk."

I gave him what I hoped was a decent smile. "Thanks. Sure." I stood up hurriedly and he followed suit. "I'll see you after lunch."

He nodded again. "See you then."

I rushed out of the classroom into the bustling hallway. I'd made it halfway across the school when I realised I was heading automatically for our Lunch spot – yes, it was Recess, but calling it by different names would be far too ridiculous. I stopped in the middle of the hallway, wondering where the hell I was supposed to go now.

I mean, strictly speaking I wasn't *not* talking to Jason and Nancy… There was no reason why I shouldn't go and sit with our friendship group like I had every day since Year Eight. But… Well, it was just going to be weird and awkward and I really didn't think I could handle any of those conversations right now.

Selfish and cowardly? Yes. But, my heart was too bruised just then to–

My name floated over to me and I looked around. I saw Rachel frowning at Xander as he pulled books out of his locker.

"…you cannot be serious?" came the end of her sentence.

He flicked his hair out of his eyes and looked at her. "Do you have a point to make?"

"She's one of JT's minions." Rachel paused. "No. That would actually require him to acknowledge she existed. She's his groupie at best. Are we suddenly crossing lines, now?"

Well, if that wasn't a double slap in the face…

My heart shook its fist as her while my internal monologue tried and failed to come up with some decent comebacks that we all knew Rachel was never going to hear even if they had been somewhat less lame.

Like the Bows were even good enough for the likes of us!

"Call me Romeo," Xander drawled, sounding like he couldn't care less what Rachel thought.

But then – if Xander was King of the Bows – Rachel was Queen Bow and not because they were the top couple; neither Xander or Rachel were the sort of people to have the word 'couple' attached to them in any capacity, unless maybe it was 'hooked up with a couple of people last night'. She was just queen-bitch of the Bows. Supreme Lady Leader. The female Xander. Most Popular Bitch on Campus.

Did that make Nancy the Rachel equivalent now? Who would it have been if I'd been at Teagan's party? Was Nancy now Queen…? Wait, what did people even call us? If they're the Bows, we'd be the…?

Short segue, it may not have escaped your notice that Xander's last name was Bowen and he was unaffectionately labelled the King of the Bows. Well, the Bows started out as a term for the girls he hooked up with, but soon it grew to include the guys he hung out with as well until their clique was just known to the rest of the school as the Bows. They were top shit, popular, cool, everyone had secretly yearned to be one of them at least…five times in their lives. Not that Jason would ever admit it because he was Xander's opposing cool dude and had an image to maintain.

"I'm serious, Xand," Rachel said and I realised I was totally standing in the middle of the hallway eavesdropping. *Oh well, not stopping now.* "You can't be seen with her. She's one of his."

"Is there some kind of segregation I'm not aware of at this school?" he asked, sounding bored.

"Yes!" she cried vehemently. "And, you are *totally* aware of it!"

My God, did she just stamp her foot at him?

He rolled his eyes so far they rolled right over me. He did a double-take when he registered I was standing there and looked an awful lot like he was debating something as the corner of his mouth twitched. But, I couldn't have even begun to imagine what that could be, let alone had the mental capacity to spend on the years' long journey that figuring out his mind would be. He closed his locker and pulled his bag over his shoulder.

"Look Rach, you worry about your own poor life choices and leave me to mine, yeah?" he said as he touched her arm briefly and walked towards me.

I looked around in panic since it would look entirely like I was waiting for him.

Again.

And, people looked like they'd noticed. As they passed, kids looked between Xander and me as though there might have been some great gossip afoot.

At least it would look less like I'd been eavesdropping…

Xander, meanwhile, looked me up and down as he walked

towards me like he'd never seen me before and had been taken off-guard by my astounding beauty.

Cue heavy snorting; I'd never been beautiful. I could pull off the kind of adorable that's sweet and cute in five-year-olds, but by seventeen is just sort of underwhelming. Nancy was the pretty one, always had been. Even when I was going through the cute five-year-old phase, Nancy was like a proper little lady pretty; I'd seen the photographic evidence on numerous occasions.

So, it wasn't surprising that Jason had picked her really.

Xander didn't stop walking until he was so close to me that our ties brushed as he stared into my eyes like he had no better place to be. I gulped but my legs didn't seem to think my brain's suggestion of moving back was a very good one. I decided we'd be having words later...

"Oh, you waited for me?" he asked as one of his hands found their way to my waist, his eyes shining brightly like we were both in on something secret.

I glared at him rather more impressively than I'd managed earlier. "I was eavesdropping actually."

"I'm hurt, Holly," he teased, an annoying sparkle in those pale brown eyes.

"You were hoping I was waiting for you?" I sounded surprised because I was a little.

He ran his tongue along his teeth as the corner of his lip quirked and his eyes slid away from mine coquettishly. "I might not have hated the idea."

"Well, sorry to disappoint. But, think of this as me saving you from this weird obsession you suddenly have to slum it with the likes of JT's minion."

His eyes flashed back to mine, hardening somewhat. "Like you think any better of Rachel."

I shrugged. "I was just repeating what I heard."

He looked me up and down again. "Where are you going?"

I knew exactly what he meant.

"Jason hasn't screwed up again, so you needn't care." My eyes slid around the corridor as I answered; I took note of the people who noticed us and Rachel leaning against Xander's locker scowling at me like I'd personally offended her.

"If you hang out with me, I can guarantee he'll want you."

I looked back at Xander just in time to see him wink at me and I frowned at the obvious implication.

"Jason's a better man than you'll ever be."

Xander leant down so his lips were close to my ear. "*I* would never break your heart."

And with that, he planted a quick kiss to my cheek, gave me a cheeky little salute-wink combo, and sauntered off with his hands in his pants pockets. I watched him go until he'd disappeared, then I turned to find Rachel still glaring at me. I responded with a super intimidating awkward half-smile, shrugged half-questioningly and half-apologetically, and walked away.

I didn't know where I was going until I found myself in the library and decided that was as good a place to be as any.

Yes, I couldn't eat in there, but honestly I wasn't that hungry.

Would people miss me? Yes.

Would our friends wonder where I was? Yes.

Would they have absolutely any idea why I might suddenly not be talking to Jason and Nancy anymore and felt like complete and total crap? No.

There was absolutely no reason as far as I could see that they would have any idea what I was feeling – and, I suppose I only had myself to blame for that. In their eyes, Nancy and Jason dating would be better than Megan Gale offering them all free lap dances, or Chris Hemsworth letting them run around with Mjolnir for a while.

None of our friends could understand how Jason, Nancy and I were so close and he hadn't hooked up with one of us. Of course, they thought he and Nancy should hook up, and there were jokes on jokes on jokes about it. Jokes about me and Jason were rarer, but that may have been because I flushed and giggled like an overexcitable idiot while feverishly hoping he didn't realise I liked him – obviously I played my part a little *too* well. Nancy and her suave comebacks was much more entertaining fodder for their jokes.

I wandered through the stacks of the library, running my hands along the spines until I ran into a wall and decided to sit down. With very little else to do – particularly having found myself in the architecture section and zero interest in the subject – I pulled out my phone and found myself on Facebook.

And of course the first thing I saw in my feed was the post telling me that Jason and Nancy were now in a relationship. It was dated all of a few minutes ago and I could totally picture our friends crowding around them and teasing them mercilessly until they changed their statuses. Despite it only being a few minutes old and everyone standing centimetres apart, there were already a ton of likes and excitable comments.

My finger hovered over the 'Like' button.

I knew the friend in me should press it…

And had it been Nancy *or* Jason and anyone else in the history of the world, I wouldn't hesitate to press it. But, I just couldn't bring myself to do it. It had been all of twelve hours since Nancy had last told me that I should lay my cards out there and tell him how I felt. I just couldn't put what I felt into words anymore, let alone recognise half of it.

My mind span and the place where my heart was supposed to live was oddly numb and empty and heavy.

I pulled my knees up to my chest and leant my head on them.

I'd told myself I wasn't going to cry, but apparently I wasn't listening to that loser.

After all, the only guy she'd ever really liked had just given her the biggest, most definite pass-over known to man.

Chapter Three

I waded through the rest of the day, avoiding everyone.

I bet I looked like a right bitch to my friends, but I just couldn't face them asking me if I was happy for Jason and Nancy. And, if Nigel's reaction was anything to go by, I'd be grilled with question after question; whether I saw it coming, if I knew, was I in the middle this whole time just waiting for them to get together, had Jason asked me how to tell Nancy, had Nancy spent sleepovers wistfully planning their wedding, had I been wondering if I should just say something already?

I knew it was a dick move on my part, but I just couldn't face it or them with that feeling of betrayal weighing my heart down like it had been thrown to the fishes by a Mafioso.

So, I ignored everyone and they seemed to pretty easily and quickly get the memo that I didn't want to talk to them. We dealt with issues one way in our group; we ignored them until the person with the problem got over it because nine times out of ten it was a mountain out of a molehill – all of us had been guilty of it on numerous occasions over the years, me definitely included.

I went through the day watching Jason being Jason; people calling out to him in the hallways for a moment of his attention, smiling and laughing with the group as they hung onto his every word avidly like it was law, and just generally being the cool, popular guy he was as Nancy clung to him like she might lose him if she let go. When (read: if) Jason noticed me looking at him, he'd pause and throw me a pleading look and I knew he wanted to talk. At the sight of it, I almost forgot that heavy sense of betrayal. But, then Nancy would look at me with this indecipherable look on her face and I felt it all over again, totally raw. So, I made it to the bus without losing my resolve to stand stoic and tall, and pretending I was untouchable.

That resolve lasted until I got up to my bedroom and I fell face first on my bed, totally exhausted and not sure if I wanted to cry or not. My heart joined me in my exhausted flop and I was pretty sure it wasn't interested in getting up either, no matter how many times my phone went off. We both just lay there thinking of Jason's smile and the laughs we'd shared with him over the years.

So, that's where Mark found me God knew how long later.

I heard his chuckle just as I heard his knock on my door. "It's Monday, how hard could it have been?" he asked.

I mumbled unintelligibly into my doona and he laughed again.

"Of course. Couldn't have put it better myself."

I lifted my head long enough to say, "shut up," then realised that breathing was actually easier without my face in the blankets and I rolled over ungraciously onto my back and stared at the ceiling.

There was a pause in which I could picture him – without even feeling the need to look at him – trying to decide if this was something he wanted to get involved with or not.

"Is this period-related?" he asked hesitantly.

I snorted humourlessly. "Unless you equate the pain in my heart to the pain of my womb trying to kill me once a month, no."

He came in and dropped beside me, joining me in staring at the ceiling. "Okay. What's up, then?"

"And, if I said it *was* period-related?"

He sighed fatalistically. "Then I would lie here and listen anyway."

"You're getting soft in your old age," I said as I nudged him.

He huffed a laugh and nudged me back. "Yeah, because nineteen's ancient."

"You're risking your reputation here, buddy."

I felt him shrug. "I'd only do it for you."

I smiled then, feeling the best I had all day.

Mark was by all accounts a bit of a douche in his own right. But, I didn't pay much attention any of that. I didn't really care how many girls the rumours said he hooked up with or hearts he broke or stupid stunts he pulled, because when it came down to it he was my big brother and I loved him. He was all of about eighteen months older than me but we'd almost always got along pretty well. At school, he'd been Jason before Jason was.

Mark nudged me again. "So, come on. Tell me what's up. Did Nancy go get ice cream without you?" he teased in a baby voice.

I sighed deeply. "Something like that. If ice cream was dating Jason and without me was the whole school seemed to know before I did."

He sucked in a harsh breath, all joking aside. "Ouch. Sorry, Doll."

I tried to shrug it off and felt tears welling.

"Did you…?" He left the question hanging by a mile, but I knew what he was asking; there was very little about my life I didn't tell him.

I shook my head and wiped my burning eyes. "No. No, I found

out in plenty of time. Well," I amended, "in time."

"So, he doesn't know?"

I shrugged. "I don't know. They didn't see fit to tell me they'd hooked up on Saturday night and I only found out when I saw him kiss her at his locker this morning. I don't know what's going on."

"Well, it sounds like Nancy's been a total bitch and Jason's not much better," Mark said as he pulled himself to sitting. "You want to stuff ourselves full of Nutella?"

I shook my head again. "No, thanks. I have some homework to do."

"Hm…must be bad if you're turning down Nutella. Let me know if you change your mind. I can only justify breaking my diet if it's for you."

"Coach would kill me if I made you break your diet."

Mark laughed. "Yeah, well. What Coach doesn't know won't hurt him, will it?"

I sat up and smiled at him and he grinned right back at me.

Mark and I were obviously siblings; the similarities between us branded us as nothing less. We had the same mousy brown hair and vivid green eyes, although his were slightly darker than mine. We had the same shape nose and eyes and lips and we even smiled the same. He'd inherited a bit more height than me, but I took after Aunty Georgie that way. Not that I minded all that much; being as tall as Mark would have made me taller than Jason, and teenage boys seemed to have an issue with girls taller than them.

But, I think we've well established that teenage boys are stupid.

I nodded to Mark. "Okay. Maybe for dessert?"

His grin widened. "Oh, mix up a nice sauce for ice cream?"

I could almost feel the sugary goodness running through my veins and all my issues paled into an insignificance I could deal

25

with just then. "Yes."

He rubbed his hands. "Awesome! I suppose I'd best get to practice then… If you won't give me a reason to ditch," he added accusingly. "I'll see you for dinner."

He popped back into my room, kissed my hair and hurried out as I laughed, "Bye!"

I dragged my bag towards my feet and started pulling stuff out – books, binders, pencil case, water bottle – pretending it was an integral part of my homework process. Really, I just thought it was justifiable delay tactics. I mean, how was I supposed to know what homework I had to do if I didn't get everything out?

My phone blooped a couple more times but – on seeing it was Nancy – I ignored it and instead moved everything over to my desk and started up my laptop. I had some reading for English as well as a test on the poetry module in the next couple of weeks to study for. Psych had a statistics quiz early next term and all the help I could get in that department would be great – even with weeks to go. Maths had the usual few questions for the next day that I'd put off over the weekend. French was thankfully homework free that night. And, I had an essay due for History at the end of the week.

Plenty to keep me busy…

If my damned phone would stop blooping!

I unlocked it and looked at it. I had notifications from Nancy, Jason, Amy, Nigel, Jess, and…King Douche?

I opened Messenger and saw the string of new messages. I bypassed the ones from my friends – former friends? – and opened the one from Xander. There was nothing but a winky face. My fingers hovered over the keyboard, trying to decide if I wanted to reply to him or not.

I mean, I'd butt-messaged people before… But, Xander and I

weren't friends – on Facebook or in real life – so it would have been an exceptional butt-message for it to have come to me.

Eventually, I couldn't just leave it, so I settled for a

Holly Aberdeen:
You often stalk my FB page?

I watched my phone like an idiot as it just sat on my desk next to me, pretending I was reading my Psych textbook. Finally, it blooped again and I snatched it up as quickly as if Jason had just finally proclaimed his undying love for me.

Xander Bowen:
If u accepted my friend request, it wouldn't b stalking :P

Holly Aberdeen:
I can't accept, we're not friends.

Holly Aberdeen:
Now, if it was an enemy request? Well, that would be fine.

Xander Bowen:
Haha course it would.

Xander Bowen:
y don't we just call it an enemy request & not tell any1 otherwise?

Holly Aberdeen:
Can't.

Xander Bowen:
y not?

Holly Aberdeen:
I'm allergic to accepting any sort of request from people who don't use proper grammar.

Xander Bowen:

It's called text-speak.

Holly Aberdeen:
It's called lazy.

Xander Bowen:
Seriously?! How old r u?
I decided not to respond to that.
Eventually, he did.

Xander Bowen:
Fine!

Xander Bowen:
Holly, would you please accept my request?
See, I didn't even call it a 'friend' request...

Holly Aberdeen:
I see why you use shortcuts – you type slow, man.

Holly Aberdeen:
And, no. I think I like having you beg for it.

Xander Bowen:
I've never had to beg anyone for anything in my life and I don't plan to start now.
I believed that. Stories said, every girl was more than willing for anything he suggested.

Holly Aberdeen:
Then we shall be enemies in real life only
le sigh

Xander Bowen:
I'm not above...persuading you, though...
;)
I really wished I hadn't read that in the exact way he'd have

said that. Repulsive or not, it gave a girl a shiver.

Holly Aberdeen:

Lol, and how do you plan to do that?

Xander Bowen:

Just be my usual charming self.

Holly Aberdeen:

I thought we'd established you're not charming?

Holly Aberdeen:

Also, shouldn't you be at practice?

Xander was in the same club team as Mark, the practice to which Mark had alluded earlier. It was an unfortunate coincidence I happened to know where he was meant to be.

Xander Bowen:

*I wager the acceptance of my request that you'll find me charming by the end of term
:D*

Xander Bowen:

Who says I'm not?

Holly Aberdeen:

And, if I win?

Holly Aberdeen:

You're awfully chatty for a guy at practice.

How does El Captain feel about this?

Xander Bowen:

Then I'll punch the git for you.

Holly Aberdeen:

I feel like that's a reward for you...

Xander Bowen:

All right then. Whatever you want?

Xander Bowen:

*Also, we're taking a break. And, your
brother doesn't care. He's on his phone,
too.*

I was rewarded with a picture of Mark indeed on his phone on
the other side of the locker room. He was also mostly naked so I
tried to erase it from my memory as quickly as possible.
Thankfully, Xander sent another message so the picture moved far
enough up the screen that the scarring bits weren't visible anymore.

Xander Bowen:

*If you don't think I'm charming by the end
of term, then I will owe you whatever you
like.*

Holly Aberdeen:

*That's a dangerous wager. You that
cocky?*

Xander Bowen:

I am ;)

I snorted to myself, knowing full well he was referring to more
than one thing there. Then suddenly wondered why I found
anything about the King of the Bows humorous.

Holly Aberdeen:

And, who's judging?

Xander Bowen:

*I'm just cocky enough to trust you not to
lie to me, Holly.*

Holly Aberdeen:

*You're so cocky, you're going to trust me
to admit I lost?*

Xander Bowen:

You're just that trustworthy.

Holly Aberdeen:

You're just that delusional.

Xander Bowen:

Regardless, do we have a wager?

I was one hundred and twenty percent confident that there was absolutely no way I would ever find Xander Bowen charming. So, why not?

Holly Aberdeen:

I'd spit on my hand and shake yours, but that's a little hard online.

Xander Bowen:

I'll claim it tomorrow then.

Holly Aberdeen:

What makes you think I'll talk to you tomorrow?

Holly Aberdeen:

We've just talked more in the last ten minutes than we have in our entire lives.

Xander Bowen:

See, I'm charming ;)

Holly Aberdeen:

I think that's enough interaction to last me at least until...the intercol :P

Which was, conveniently, not until closer to the end of next term.

Xander Bowen:

I'll make you a side wager
– that you talk to me tomorrow.

Holly Aberdeen:

I'd take you up on that, but I think it's

unfair when I already know I'm going to
win :P

Xander Bowen:
We'll see.

Holly Aberdeen:
Bye, Xander.

Xander Bowen:
See you tomorrow :*

I closed the app and actually got into some study without getting too distracted. Putting my Messenger notifications on silent had helped, but it only meant that there were about thirty more waiting for me when I finally looked at my phone again.

I was torn. I sort of wanted to know what Nancy and Jason had to say. The rest were just my friends asking me if I was okay (or the usual group chat conversation which looked like it was full of 'Jason loves Nancy'). And I appreciated that, but I didn't want to go into my completely ridiculous freak out; now I was in it, I didn't know how to get out. But, I also didn't want them to know I'd read the messages and not replied. There was something worse about that somehow in my head.

I think we've established it can be a fairly strange place up there, though.

So, I was sticking to my guns.

I felt betrayed by my former two best friends, and I was going to continue avoiding the subject for as long as humanly possible. Of course, avoiding the issue meant not talking to them and not talking to the rest of our friends. I wasn't convinced I'd get away with it without looking like even more of a dick. But like I said, I had no idea how to get around it without talking to Jason and Nancy.

And, I honestly didn't think I could handle that like a civilised human being.

I might have been able to manage it like some kind of swamp monster; snot running everywhere while I balled my eyes out and screamed unintelligibly at them.

But, that somehow seemed worse than the ignoring them thing.

By the time I'd finished my more pressing homework and justified my actions to myself, my name was being called from downstairs. It was my dad and apparently it was dinner time. Well dinner I liked, my dad not so much – there wasn't anything inherently wrong with him, he just went with the whole friend-over-father parenting technique and honestly that lost him points; sometimes a kid just wanted some discipline, not a lax curfew or a beer with dinner.

But dinner with Dad also meant dinner with Mark, so that was a plus.

I wandered downstairs in half my uniform, having kicked off my shoes, untucked my shirt and loosened my tie. It felt an awful lot like one sock had fallen down and I resolved to wear stockings the rest of the winter terms so as to avoid looking like an idiot more than absolutely necessary.

"There you are, Dolly!"

Oh, good. Dad's girlfriend was over, too…

My eyes found Mark and I glared at him for not warning me Tammy was downstairs. I noticed his hair was still wet, so he must have gone late at practice and only just got back home; Mondays, the team did fitness and they usually elected to swim.

That explains the almost nudie shot from Xander.

"How was your day, Dolly?" Tammy gushed and I held back the retch that was usually my reaction to the way she always called

33

me Dolly; so sickeningly preppy and in every sentence she directed straight to me.

I hated it when she called me Dolly.

Dolly, or Doll, was a family nickname given to me by Mark when he was little because he'd been confused between Holly and dolly and there was something about me looking like a little doll; trust me, that phase didn't last long.

Tammy was new to the family and Mark and I were still supposed to be playing nice with her. We didn't have this problem with Mum; her beau was pretty cool and insisted we didn't pander to him because he had to earn our trust and affection. Tammy, though, was hands-on. Mum said it was because Tammy thought that was the best way to get to know us. I decided it was the best way for me to put my foot in my mouth and tell her to piss off.

Mark gave me a knowing smirk he tried to hide behind his beer and I stuck my tongue out at him.

"It was fine, thanks. Nothing to report."

"Your test was today wasn't it, Dolly?"

Mark barely hid a snicker under a cough.

"French vocab, yeah. We have them pretty regularly. You would have thought we'd have learnt it all by now, but…" I shrugged and gave her my best semblance of a smile. "Where's Doug?"

"Outside," Dad answered. "He and Vern found something to stick their noses in and have been busy ever since."

I frowned and looked towards the back of the house as though that was going to magically give me x-ray vision and I was going to see our goofy dog and equally weirdo cat; the cat had basically brought the dog up so he thought he was a cat, all thirty kilograms of him. Likewise, the cat had been brought up by Mum's dog so had some very dog-like moments. It was a shemozzle.

"He'll know it's dinner. He'll be in soon," Dad continued as he served up said dinner.

And, like clockwork, the dog door crashed open. Then the giant slobbering furball that was Doug came tearing inside followed by a daintily trotting Vern, tail stuck up in the air like a periscope. I'd been informed many times this was not normal cat behaviour, and it did not surprise me in the least if it was something Vern did.

I bent down and patted them. "Hey guys. How's your day been?"

I felt sort of terrible that I'd been so stuck in my own world that I'd ignored my two furry munchkins. I felt terrible about that and only mildly blasé about ignoring two people who had been my best friends for years. So, what did that say about me as a human being?

That I should stop analysing myself, I think.

I pulled myself off the floor and dropped into my seat next to Mark while Dad put the dinner on the table and Tammy sat across from me grinning like a Stepford wife. Actually, now that I'd drawn that comparison, it was sort of freaky; she even had the perfect blonde hair, the pearls…

I shook my head and smiled at her, hoping my weird train of thought hadn't been displayed loud and proud all over my face.

"So Mark, how was practice?" Dad began as we all started eating and I tried really hard to be a good daughter and be nice to everyone.

Chapter Four

I'd slept like shit and I was willing to bet I looked like shit.

Still, I walked into History on Tuesday morning with my head held high. And, if by high we here mean I stared at my shoes and sat in that lonely seat up the back that the other kids said was haunted, then yeah. Head held high.

I ignored everyone again all through lessons and home group.

Nancy didn't even bother trying to talk to me and she did a pretty good job at acting like I didn't even exist. But, a few of our other friends smiled at me nicely and Jason looked a little forlorn every time I accidentally caught his eye. Not quite forlorn enough to take his hands off Nancy's waist, though…

I found myself in the library again at Recess and sat in the same spot against the same wall I had the day before. Although why I did that, I wasn't sure; I still wasn't interested in architecture. Only, this time I managed not to cry or feel like my heart was going to pound out of my chest so that was a plus. I just leant my head back against the wall and didn't hate the moment of silence…

That was then rudely interrupted by a voice I could have done without.

"Well. *This* is incredibly sad."

I opened my mouth, but closed it again post-haste and frowned up at him.

"Are you actually not talking to me?" he laughed, seeming totally unfazed by it.

Like a small, petulant child, I got my phone out and messaged him.

Holly Aberdeen:
I said I wouldn't speak to you today, so
I'm not going to.

He shoved his hand in his pocket, pulled his phone out and unlocked it. As he read the message, his eyebrow quirked and the corner of his mouth went with it as he tried to supress a smile. When he looked back to me, I stuck my tongue out at him and that full smile flared to life.

I *supposed* I could see why girls fell over him…

"I think this counts," he said, waving his phone in my direction. "Does this mean I won?"

"I never agreed to your side wager, so no."

"Ah!" He pointed at me victoriously. "But, that was definite talking. So I *have* to have won, now."

I frowned again if only to stop the unfathomable smile that wanted to sneak in. "Still no. Besides, we didn't set terms."

"I'll give you my terms now. Come and hang out with me."

I felt my eyes widen so far I thought my eyeballs were going to roll lazily out of my head. "Sorry, you what now?"

He shrugged. "Come and hang out with me."

In what universe would I *ever* hang out with King Douche?

"And, why pray tell would I do such a thing? I'm not a Bow."

He scrubbed a hand along his jaw as he leant on the bookshelf to his right. "No, you're certainly not. And, *what* a message it would send to the git…"

My frown became more of a scowl. "I don't need to send him a message."

Although, I won't deny that a part of me felt like it, wanted to say yes; I felt like hanging out with Xander just to shove it back in Nancy's stupid face. It would also go a long way to shoving the proverbial 'it' in Jason's smarmy, gorgeous face.

He didn't want me? Well, I didn't want him either!

"You've thought about it, though," Xander said, interrupting my brain tantrum.

"I have not." And I hadn't, but I would now. *Thanks for nothing, King Douche.*

He grinned down at me. "If I was you, I would have thought of nothing else than showing him up."

I felt my eyes narrow as I looked up at him. Just how did he know about what I did or didn't feel about Jason? If Xander knew I'd been in love with Jason forever, that surely meant that Jason knew? How could King of the Bows know and Jason not?

"Sounds like a normal Tuesday for you. Don't you normally think of little else than sex, soccer and showing up Jason?"

He nodded as his eyes roved and he rearranged his bag on his shoulder. "Yeah, I suppose so."

"Let me guess. If you were me, you'd have hooked up with at least six people by now and shown him exactly what he's missing out on?"

Xander's eyes snapped back to me as his smirk widened. "Something like that. But, I'd think one would be commotion enough for Holly Aberdeen."

I rolled my eyes. "Well, yes. It's all relative, isn't it? You probably hook up with about six people every day, so you'd have to be with at least…eighteen to make a statement–"

"Whereas, you're with none. So one would be plenty."

There was a note of teasing in his voice that elicited a smile out of me, but I stamped it down quickly. Although, not quickly enough if the mischievous look on his face was anything to go by.

"How about you settle for hanging out with little old me?"

I shook my head. "No way. No way in hell am I *ever* hanging out with the Bows."

"Not even to hang out with me?" He pouted.

I couldn't help the small laugh that escaped. "No, not even for you. Sorry."

He shrugged. "All right. Different terms. How about you actually do that 'helping me with French' thing then?"

I gaped up at him, not sure how serious he was being. He was all Xander; languid and at ease, his face a mask of perfect nonchalance like nothing fazed him, and he knew he was stupidly good looking. As I stared at him, he raised his eyebrow as though he was waiting for me to answer.

"You're actually asking for me to help you with French?" I asked.

He scrubbed a hand over his jaw again. "Yep."

"Two questions."

"Shoot."

"Why?"

"Why what?"

"Are you failing or something?"

He scoffed. "One of those."

I crossed my arms. "Not really an answer, King Douche."

"What's your second question?"

I sighed, figuring I wouldn't get any more out of him. "Why me?"

"Three reasons. First, you're good at French. Second, I told Renoir you already were. Third, you can use it as an excuse to avoid the git whenever you like."

I scowled. "He's not a git."

"Isn't he, though?" Xander asked, his voice rising as he shrugged.

"No. He's–"

"Let's agree to disagree, shall we?"

We stared at each other in silence for a while, just assessing, evaluating.

Never in the seven or more years I'd known Xander Bowen had he been anything other than King Douche. Him and his Bows, we'd hated the lot of them because they were arrogant, conniving, mean, rude, just…douche-holes. I didn't think I'd ever spoken to him one on one as much in all those years as I had the last two days.

I jumped as the bell for the end of Recess rang above us and Xander seamlessly pushed off the shelf and took two steps towards me. His hands were outstretched to help me up like I was just totally going to take them, like we did it all the time.

Without even thinking – without even hesitating – I *did* take his hands and let him pull me up.

"Come on, Holly. Would it help if I said please?" he asked, smiling at me.

"I didn't realise you knew that word existed."

He huffed a laugh. "Please, Holly. I could really do with the help…?" He searched my eyes like he could find something that would make me say yes.

I thought about it; he *had* told Madame Renoir I was helping him already. So, bets were – when his grades hadn't picked up or whatever the problem was – I'd be the one in trouble because who

40

in their right mind would discipline the god that was Xander Bowen? He who could do no wrong in the eyes of the world. If he didn't improve, it was going to be my fault.

I sighed. "Fine."

A grin popped up on his face for a brief second then he kicked his head behind him. "Come on, Burnett won't be pleased if we're late."

"What's this 'we' you're talking about?" I asked as he started walking away.

He only let go of one of my hands so I was forced to follow as he pulled me along behind him by my other. "A killer team."

I rolled my eyes and tried to pull my hand from his. I just succeeded as we emerged from the stacks and I looked around guiltily as I noticed a couple of people might have seen. Farrah, a girl a bit younger than us I'd never talked to, certainly looked at me a moment longer than she usually would. I wiped my hand on my skirt and crossed my arms.

"There is no 'we', Xander."

"No, of course. We hate each other."

"Exactly."

We walked to English and I noticed Xander seemed in no hurry to walk any faster than me despite the fact his legs had to be something like eight times longer than mine. So, we arrived at the same time in a manner than could have meant we were walking together or meant we could have just happened to arrive at the same time. He fell back at the door, letting me go through first as he nodded to Greg over my head and they exchanged a greeting.

I was about to head to the chair I'd occupied the afternoon before, but I felt Xander's hand on my arm as he subtly pushed me towards his desk.

I looked back at him, but he could just as easily have been trying to move around me… Had his hand not lingered. As he talked to Greg, his eyes dropped to mine then he looked quickly over to his desk. I wanted to give him a talking to, but that would have looked ridiculous. So, I just frowned at him and he gave me a look as though asking me 'what?' in a very coquettish way.

Instead, I manoeuvred myself over to the empty desk I'd decided to call mine and dropped down against the wall. Two seconds later, Xander dropped next to me and Greg dropped into the chair next to him.

I looked around the room quickly and noticed that the other kids weren't sure whether it was something to be interested in or not. You could see the confusion on their faces like they were trying to decide for what possible reason King of the Bows had chosen to sit with JT's minion in her self-imposed exile. The fact Greg had sat with his king was definitely the least weird thing about the whole scenario.

I managed to ignore any and all looks from Jason and Nancy, so yay me.

As Mr Burnett called for silence and everyone sat down, I tried to forget I was sitting next to King Douche. As I tried to get into poetry, it was easier said than done. Quite aside from the fact that he radiated…something that starkly reminded me that the whole situation was weird, he was super unhelpful.

For example, part way through the lesson, I put my pen down for some reason and Xander flicked it onto the floor with a cheeky grin. I frowned at him and realised it had rolled under Jason's chair, which made me frown harder.

"You're lucky that wasn't my favourite pen!" I hissed.

"Lighten up," he replied, giving me a playful nudge.

I wanted to nudge him right out the window and off the balcony.

"Here," Greg whispered harshly, holding his pen out to me.

I looked at in surprise and he nodded at it, indicating I take it. Which I did. Slowly, in case it was going to bite me or something equally stupid. Greg gave me one of the most sincere smiles I think I'd ever seen on anyone and just turned to grab my pen from under Jason's chair like it was his and went back to making notes.

I felt Xander looking at me and looked right back at him.

"What?" I asked.

The corner of his lip quirked and he turned back to the board as though he didn't want me to see it. "Nothing."

He was thankfully less unhelpful through the rest of the lesson and Mr Burnett stopped me as I was leaving which meant Xander and Greg left without me.

When I got to the library, I squirrelled myself away among the mythology books (in case Xander came looking in architecture), pulled on my headphones, got out my Psych textbook, and vowed I'd get to next lesson late so Xander wouldn't be able to sit next to me.

By the time I got to school on Wednesday morning, I'd forgotten that I was trying to get to classes late in case Xander decided to sit with me. So, I was just quietly sitting at my desk in Psychology when Xander fell into the seat to my right still looking half asleep.

"Morning." He nodded without looking at me, his voice thick like he'd rolled out of bed not five minutes ago.

"Morning," I replied by instinct, looking him over. "Did your butler die or something?"

He rolled his head towards me like it was an effort and I realised he had stubble on his face. "What?" he asked, obviously confused.

I indicated at him, unable to remember a time he'd ever not been clean shaven. Not that I made a habit of looking at him close enough to tell, so who knew how often it actually happened.

"What's all this? Where's the with-it guy who goes to the gym before school?"

He looked down at himself slowly. "This sometimes happens." He scratched the left side of his jaw with his right hand. "I *am* human, you know."

"I wasn't aware royalty were human."

"Well, you learn something new every day." He threw me a cocky smirk that lit his eyes and told me he knew I'd been teasing him; I just hadn't realised I'd been teasing him. His voice was gravelly and I told my heart to stop sneaking peeks at him.

Not that I had to tell it off for long.

Because, just then Jason walked in. I didn't know how I knew, but it made me jump as I turned away from Xander and looked at Jason like I had something to be guilty for. Jason and his big blue eyes looked between me and Xander as though he'd walked in on something far more scandalous. And, just the thought of that made me blush, no doubt making me look even guiltier.

Nigel came in behind Jason, jostling him as he laughed about something. Knowing them, it was a continuation of a conversation they'd been having before school and I suspected had something to do with some new rumour. Jason gave Nigel what even I could tell was a half-hearted smile and response as his eyes didn't leave my face.

I cleared my throat and dropped my gaze to my notebook, leaning on my right elbow and raising my hand between Xander and me like a shield under the pretence of scratching the back of my head.

It was like I knew where Jason moved as he moved and likewise I felt Xander shifting in his seat. Still, Xander's voice in my ear was a surprise.

"Ignore the git, Holly."

I looked at him quickly and our noses bumped so I looked back down. "He's not–"

"Yes. He is."

I turned to stare at him and the vehement sincerity in his eyes softened, making them lose some of their glassiness.

"You sleep as well as me last night?" he asked gently.

I shifted away from him. Because the implication wasn't wrong. It wasn't just the previous night; I'd slept badly the last two nights, to say nothing of the hours I lay awake in nervous excitement on Sunday. My brain ran too fast but I couldn't catch anything that went through it, and my heart wallowed in its own tears. It wasn't so bad if I kept it busy, focussed on school work, talked with Mark, even Xander seemed like a decent occasional distraction when he messaged (read: annoyed) me. But, lying in bed trying to sleep wasn't working for me too well.

"I could use a drink," was the closest I'd come to admitting it.

He smirked. "Little early in the day for hard liquor isn't it? But, I'll play hooky with you if you want?" His voice was slowly losing that deep, gravelly effect that made my heart sit up and pay more attention than it should. But, it was still deep. Deeper than it really had any business being.

I looked away to hide my smile. "I meant caffeine."

"Sure you did."

I shook my head and didn't need to find a reason to not answer him, because the teacher walked in and got the lesson started. I was surprised to see that Xander actually seemed to know what he was doing. He was the most relaxed and laid back I'd ever seen him; making notes and following along with the lesson far more easily than I was.

"You're good at Psychology?" I whispered as Miss Phillips explained something at the front of the room.

He slid his eyes to me. "Can I not be good at something?"

"You're good a sport, I didn't expect you'd care about anything else."

"Who says I care about Psychology?" he asked as he flipped the page in the text book.

"What? You're actually doing what you should just because?"

He huffed a laugh. "I do what I should so I can do what I love."

I looked at him carefully and realised I knew what he meant; he needed decent grades to play soccer the way he did. Something about that didn't seem to add up to the Xander I knew. A guy who actually tried at school so he could be your typical bro-jock just didn't scream King Douche.

"So, you want to get a start on this French thing tomorrow?" I asked slowly.

He nodded as he wrote something down. "Sure. Lunch?"

"Sounds good."

"And, yeah. I'll help you out with Psych."

"I didn't ask."

"You didn't have to."

I covered my mouth to hide my smile, nibbling on my finger nail. As my eyes slid away, they fell on Jason. I could see he was sneaking looks at me as Nigel was asking his opinion on something and I felt incredibly uncomfortable. Psychology was one of the two

46

classes I had with Jason and without Nancy. There was something more vulnerable about him when he wasn't with Nancy, like he wanted to say something but didn't know how. I couldn't even begin to think about what it might have been, but the tension was thick between us.

Something touched my hand and I looked down to see Xander had slipped his fingers over mine so he was holding my hand. He rubbed the back of my hand twice with his thumb, then pulled away slowly and picked his pen back up. He did it all without taking his eyes off Miss Phillips at the front as she paced and waved her arm over something on the board.

It was only then I realised I'd tensed looking at Jason. And, that was only because the slightly comforting gesture from Xander had somehow helped me relax a little.

The bell rang for next lesson as I was pondering the ridiculousness of that.

"Okay, so I want you to finish reading chapter nine and answer the questions before Friday. We start stats next week!" Miss Phillips had to yell to be heard over us all packing up.

"I'll see you in English," Xander said, nudging me gently as he picked up his bag.

"Yeah. See you then," I answered without thinking, unable to stop myself wondering how I was suddenly so comfortable with him.

I guess I was shallow enough to take what I could get when I'd decided to be a dick and not speak to my friends. After all, had the tables been turned, Nancy would be acting totally comfortably with Xander. She'd be more than comfortable, she'd be hanging off him the way she'd been hanging off Jason since Monday morning. So, to get through this, all I had to do was what I always did; try to fit in and just think 'what would Nancy do?', although maybe with less of the climbing the King Douche man-mountain.

I grabbed my stuff, made it through home group, and passed a fairly uneventful Recess in the library as I did the Psych homework and tried not to fall asleep. I'd been okay when I'd woken up that morning. But, as the day was progressing, I was feeling more and more sleepy. Still, I was jolted out of my semi-dozing state when the bell went and I dragged myself to History.

I sat down and leant my chin in my hand, letting my eyes glass over as I enjoyed a semi-thoughtless moment when I finally didn't worry about anything but how tired I was. It was a welcome reprieve from my manic thoughts of the last few days.

I felt movement next to me but didn't move until someone slid a bottle in front of me. I blinked at said bottle in front of me, registering the brown liquid and red and white label but not getting much further than that. Turning, I looked to whoever belonged to the arm still attached to the bottle and found Greg sitting next to me with warm hazel eyes and a pleasant smile.

"What's that?" I asked him.

"Coke?" Greg replied uncertainly, looking like he suddenly wondered if there was something more to it than that.

"I know it's Coke. Why is it Coke?"

"I couldn't tell you." He frowned like he was thinking. "I think it had something to do with those plants you get cocaine from? But, that was all a little before my time."

I blinked again, not really sure what he was waffling about. "Why is it Coke in front of me?"

Greg obviously worked something out by the look on his face. "Oh! Compliments from King Douche." Here he gave a little mock-bow flourish with his hands. "It was the best he could do on short notice?" He shrugged like that was supposed to mean something to me.

I looked at the drink again. "Xander?"

He shrugged again. "I thought it was strange, too. But, the man said you needed caffeine, so…" Another flourish in the direction of the bottle. "Caffeine."

I decided not to question it.

By the time History was over, I had a pretty weird feeling that Greg was actually an okay sort of guy. I'd also finished the Coke.

So, when Greg and I walked into English and saw Xander sitting in one of the seats at the back, I tossed Xander the empty bottle. He caught it with a grin, waving it at me as Greg and I walked towards him.

"What's this for?" he asked.

"A thank you."

"What for?"

Greg sat on the seat furthest from Xander, leaving me with the choice to sit down between them or sit somewhere else. I decided not to choose yet.

"For making sure I didn't fall asleep today."

He shrugged, wearing the most adorable 'I know, I'm fabulous' smile. "That doesn't sound like something I'd do."

"No, it doesn't, does it?"

He looked me up and down. "You sitting?"

I opened my mouth and took hold of my bag strap. "I…"

I looked over at the empty desk and bit my lip. Then, my eyes locked with Nancy's as she walked in and everything in me plummeted; my heart, my stomach, my knees. Nancy looked me over and I felt like less than a bug under her gaze. I felt that slightly ill feeling in my stomach again. A hand took mine and I turned to see Xander looking up at me with a soft question, an offer. An offer that was looking mighty tantalising in the face of Nancy's expression.

Besides, Nancy would sit.

"Sitting... Yeah..." I said slowly as my knees buckled underneath me and I just managed to get the chair under my arse in time.

Xander kissed the back of my hand before letting it go and I ducked my head so no one would see me flushing bright red from sadness and anger as much as embarrassment at his actions.

Chapter Five

I was becoming one of those loner kids, the ones who wear their headphones in the corridors and slink around with their hands in their pockets. But, it was honestly the most comfortable just then. I didn't have to worry about people staring at me because I'd suddenly stopped hanging out with Jason and Nancy and our friends, or because I was suddenly on friendly-looking speaking terms with not only a Bow but also King Douche himself. If people were talking about me, I was blissfully unaware.

Shame then that my eyes still worked and had no problem seeing Nancy and Jason kissing in front of his locker as I walked past. My step faltered and I told my despondent heart to buck the hell up. If it ranted and railed much more, I was going to start crying in the hallway and neither of us wanted that. Already, I could feel the tears hot in my eyes and my lip threatened to quake. I bit it to keep it still and had just decided to keep walking when Jason looked up and his eyes found mine.

I couldn't decipher his look. I was feeling too much and trying to feel none of it. Was he apologetic? Was he angry with my behaviour? Was he rubbing my face in it? Did he not care about me at all now he had what he wanted?

I swallowed hard and took a deep breath as I took a step forward to keep walking. I could do this. I could get through life and get over this selfish heartache. It was all my fault anyway; I should have just told Jason how I felt ages ago. It wasn't his or Nancy's fault that I couldn't deal.

I tried to go back to being blissfully unaware.

So blissfully unaware even that someone managed to grab my arm and tug me gently towards a side corridor that lead to the bathrooms. My flailing elbow clocked them and I turned to see Xander holding his cheek as he looked at me half in annoyance and half in humour. I ripped off my headphones.

"What did you expect when you ambush people?" I hissed at him, sneaking a look out into the hallway where I couldn't tell if people were paying attention or not.

Jason was looking in our direction, as were a few other people. But, whether they'd seen King of the Bows drag me into the semi-dark corridor, I couldn't tell.

Xander chuckled. "Okay, fair enough. But, you do scream cute."

"I scream cute?" I asked, turning back to him. "What does that even mean?"

"Well, you gave this cute little yelp–"

"Of course I did, I thought I was being kidnapped!"

"Who the hell is going to kidnap you at school?"

"Are you saying I'm not kidnappable?" I asked, feeling highly insulted in my highly emotional state.

"Of course you're…kidnappable." He blinked away his look of confusion and shook his head. "That's ridiculous and not what I meant."

"For what did you attempt to kidnap me exactly, King Douche?"

As though he'd remembered something, he looked down at me and smiled softly. "Wanted to say hi."

"You wanted to..." My eyes narrowed. "Why?"

"Class notwithstanding, I assumed we weren't supposed to be seen together–"

"Xander, is there some reason your weird obsession with a JT minion is culminating in minor kidnapping, or can I get to class?" I huffed, in no mood for his...whatever he thought this was.

"I'll walk you. It's my free."

I frowned at him. "No, thanks."

He cupped my cheek gently. My frown deepened into a scowl and he pulled his hand away very slowly and very deliberately as his eyes widened in apology. I snuck a look around and saw that a couple of people walking past the opening to the corridor had probably seen, so I took a step away from him.

"Holly, are you okay?" he asked.

I looked back at him and sighed. "I'm fine. I need to get to class."

He looked like he wanted to press, but he only nodded. "We still on for lunch?"

"Yeah. I'll meet you in mythology. Unless you'll do better around sport?"

He flashed me a quick smile. "Mythology's fine. I'll see you later."

I nodded and looked him over suspiciously. I didn't know what was going through his head, but I could imagine it was nothing good.

"Yeah. I'll see you later," I replied before hanging my head and walking to class quickly in the hopes that no one would see me.

I got through Math relatively unscathed until I found myself cornered by Jess and Nigel as I was heading across the library at the start of Lunch.

"Holly!" Jess called and I looked around for her.

They'd obviously had their last lesson in the library and were still packing up. Jess smiled and Nigel waved at me. I looked around for Xander quickly, then gave them a terse smile and had little choice but to meet them in the middle of the walkway.

"Hey, you been okay?" Jess asked, looking over me like she was going to find evidence of me dying of cancer or something on my face.

I tried to give her a more sincere smile. "Yeah, fine. How about you?"

Jess nodded. "Yeah, good. Where have you been lately?"

"We've missed you," Nigel added with a bob of his head.

I looked around for Xander again and hoped I didn't look as guilty and shifty as I felt. "Uh, yeah… I've been…busy."

Xander stuck his head out of the stacks and gave me a humoured, questioning head tilt as he leant against the shelves casually. I felt my eyes go wide in the hopes that Jess and Nigel didn't notice that Xander was legitimately waiting for me this time. So of course, in reaction to my reaction, Jess turned around to see what I'd panicked about. Xander didn't take his eyes off me and Jess turned back to me with an eye roll.

"Is he on some quest to hook up in every place in the school?" Jess asked, disgusted with Xander the way I was supposed to be.

"He's probably looking for some poor nerdy virgin to deflower," Nigel said, rolling his own eyes.

"Farrah, maybe?" Jess asked.

Nigel snorted. "She could use a good deflowering, although I bet she'd just recite lines at you the whole time."

Jess laughed. "Oh, how good thee is," she teased in a high voice and I gave them a small smile.

"Make a guy lose his mojo, that would." Nigel paused. "I'm sure the King of the Bows would be up for the challenge, though."

Jess threw him one more glare and crossed her arms. "Such a douche." We didn't call him King Douche for nothing.

I nodded with a weak smile. "Yeah, totally."

"What are you doing here anyway?" Jess asked.

I tried to come up with something convincing. "Study?"

Nigel laughed. "You don't sound sure."

What would Nancy do?

My smile became slightly more believable. "I've got this History essay due tomorrow and it's not going well. So, you know how it is…" I petered off, hoping that was a good enough excuse.

"God, I feel you! Barely half way through the year, but it feels like there's not enough time to get everything done!" Jess cried.

I nodded again as my eyes slid to Xander. "Totally. Anyway, I'd best get on with it!"

"Are you coming back to sit with us when it's done?" Nigel asked and I really did believe they missed me. I just wasn't sure how many of the others – *cough* Nancy and Jason *cough* – were missing me, too.

I shrugged. "Why wouldn't I?" I gave a nervous laugh and hoped that didn't classify as lying.

Jess gave me a swift hug. "Awesome. We'll see you later."

I gave a weird little salute as they started walking away. "Yep, will do."

I hurried over to Xander. Just as I thought I'd got away with it, he saluted in the direction of behind me and I turned to see Jess looking back at him with a suspicious look. I rolled my eyes at him.

"Great, thank you."

He shrugged as he pushed himself off the shelf. "What?"

"Because my friends need to see me with you," I mumbled as I headed for the wall at the end of the aisle.

"Holly, if they were your friends they'd try harder to work out what was wrong and make you feel better."

"What would you know about friendship?" I asked as I fell onto the floor.

"More than the git, apparently." He dropped down beside me, his legs outstretched, and our shoulders bumped.

"Leave Jason out of this," I pleaded.

"Why? He was a total git."

"Don't you always think he's a git?"

"Yeah, but he's like a proper git now. You need to recruit someone else to expend all that unrequited passion on."

"What do you know about my unrequited passion?" I asked as I pulled my book out of my bag.

I felt him shrug. "More than–"

I brandished my textbook at him. "If you say 'the git, apparently' you'll meet my less jovial side."

"I didn't realise this *was* your jovial side. You need to work on that." He was completely deadpan.

"Let me guess, you think I should work on that by having a random hook up?"

"What better way?"

I scowled at him in disbelief. "Um, plenty."

"Name one."

"I don't have to justify myself to you, King Douche."

He leant towards me. "You wouldn't believe what a bit of skin on skin contact will do for you, Holly," he whispered in my ear. "A soft caress. A kiss to make your mind blissfully blank. A touch to set your skin on fire."

I swallowed hard but hid it well. "Some French to help you keep your grades up."

As he chuckled, his breath tickled my neck and I firmly chastised the way my heart twirled and goose bumps flared to life across my arms.

"Whatever you say, Holly."

So, we studied. And, I couldn't get the idea of a hook up out of my head.

It might not send the exact right message to Jason if I hooked up with someone, but it could make him jealous maybe? What better way to have him finally notice me than for me to be with someone else? Although, he'd had the opportunity to be jealous of me with someone else in the past and it hadn't worked. I suppose that might have been because my crush on Jason meant I hadn't really been into it in the past. Could I be into it now?

Who the hell would I even hook up with?

No one. It would be stupid to think I could make Jason finally notice me by hooking up with someone else. Although…what would Nancy do? She'd hook up with someone else.

"What happened to that other guy?" Xander asked after a while as though he could read my thoughts.

"What other guy?" I sighed and I turned the page.

"That guy you were dating…whenever it was."

"That's really not helping."

"I don't know. Like I keep track of who you date when."

"You seem to remember there was a guy." There'd only been one guy all year actually.

"I notice some things."

57

"Obviously nothing about French. Here." I pushed the book at him.

"Tell me about the guy first."

I rolled my eyes. "Matt and I broke up months ago."

"So, you can't date him again then?"

I looked up at him and frowned. "I'm going to deal with this like a mature human being. I'm not going to throw myself at someone else just because Jason–"

"Broke your heart."

"Okay. Stop that now," I snapped and elbowed him. "I'm fine."

I wasn't, but King Douche didn't need to know that. His suggestion was a tad too enticing, but I was going to keep telling myself that I wasn't going to stoop to ridiculously shallow and juvenile lows to make myself feel better. If Jason wanted Nancy, I just had to be a big girl and deal with it. I could get to a point where I supported them.

Eventually.

Well, him.

Maybe.

I hoped.

God, I really wasn't sure how I felt about Nancy at this point.

On a scale of Best Friends Forever to Arch Nemesis, where does 'encouraging you to declare your feelings for the person they're currently dating' fall?

"So, Matt's out–"

"Everyone's out!" I interrupted. "No one's in. Now, are you going to look at this French stuff or not? Madame Renoir will probably fail me if your marks don't go up."

"She won't–"

"Not doing this today, King Douche!" I snapped, dropping my

hands in my lap. "We both know everyone at this school tiptoes around you because you're captain of the soccer team and oh so dreamy and whatever else bullshit excuse they come up with. Madame Renoir is no exception. You told her I was helping you and there is no way she'll punish you if she doesn't have to, so that will fall on me. Can we just stop worrying about things that aren't important and do some damned study!"

I was breathing unnecessarily hard when my rant was done and I took a deep breath as I flushed hard.

"Your feelings *are* important, Holly. My feelings for him aside, the git did poorly."

Because of course Xander Bowen had a compassionate mode! What was one more topsy-turvy revelation for the week? And, King Douche in compassionate mode was just what I needed...

My heart looked up from its foetal position at him, but I told it not to fall for his act.

"There are no feelings. I don't have any feelings one way or another."

"Says the girl who ran straight into my arms on Monday crying."

"I wasn't crying and I didn't run into your arms—"

"Holly, you're the closest piece of action I've had in weeks. Do not take this away from me."

"And, it's all about you again."

"Well, you're not really letting me make it about you. So, it's gotta be about someone—"

"And don't give me that woe is me act. You're the one who's chosen to be celibate. You could have any girl in the school if you were really that desperate."

"But my goal average, Holly... Blue balls will do wonders for your focus."

"I doubt *your* blue balls would do anything for *my* focus…"

He huffed a laugh and I shot him a small smile, which he reciprocated.

His eyes were warm and I again wondered how in the hell I was so comfortable with the King of the Bows. Xander and I didn't know anything about each other aside from rumour and…well, what we saw on a daily basis, I guessed. We had nothing in common. We'd barely spoken to each other. And yet, I was sitting next to him like we did it all the time and exchanging un-witty banter with him.

"So, French, then…" he started as though he'd just realised the same and needed to ease whatever tension this was.

"French, then," I answered and we got back to work.

After Lunch, Greg sat with me in History again. He didn't seem to feel the need to say anything to me. He just sat by me, flashed me one of those sincere smiles and may have even hummed to himself for a little while.

After History, I had my free. So, I made for the bus to head home and actually finish my History essay.

Part way through my study, my phone blooped. When I looked down at it and saw the notification light blinking green. I unlocked it and saw a message from Xander.

Xander Bowen:
Voule vou coucher avec moi, ce soir? ;)
I snorted to myself as I shook my head.

Holly Aberdeen:
Pas dans un million d'années!
I put my phone down and went back to study until it blooped again.

Xander Bowen:

Pourqoui pas?

Xander Bowen:

(Also, are you very impressed with me?)

Holly Aberdeen:

I am very impressed you learnt how to work Google translate, yes.

Xander Bowen:

I might have known what it meant!

Holly Aberdeen:

Did you?

Xander Bowen:

No.

Holly Aberdeen:

I didn't think so.

Xander Bowen:

You never answered my question.

Holly Aberdeen:

What question?

Xander Bowen:

Why not?

Holly Aberdeen:

I do *not* have time to list every reason.

Xander Bowen:

Okay, one reason.

Holly Aberdeen:

Uh, the first thing that springs to mind is I'm not a Bow and you're gross.

Xander Bowen:

Strictly speaking, I think that's two things.

Holly Aberdeen:

Regardless.

Xander Bowen:

It would certainly make the git take notice... ;)

Well, because I needed that as an option running around my head!

Holly Aberdeen:

For the last time! I am not hooking up with anyone just because Jason and Nancy are...together. Let alone you.

Xander Bowen:

Doing the nasty, you mean.

Holly Aberdeen:

There has been no evidence of nasty.

Holly Aberdeen:

And, I don't recall asking your opinion.

Xander Bowen:

Friends offer their opinion anyway.

Holly Aberdeen:

We're not friends.

Xander Bowen:

We could be if you accepted my request.

Holly Aberdeen:

Oh yes!! Because *nothing's* real if it's not broadcast all over social media!

Xander Bowen:

Fine. But, we could be.

I paused. Did he mean in real life? Like we could actually be friends? Like the way I'd been friends with… Okay, maybe not Jason because I'd been in love with him for ten years. But, the way I was friends with Nigel?

I scoffed, not really seeing that ever happening.

Holly Aberdeen:

In what world?

Xander Bowen:

Where's the world that doesn't care?
Maybe I could meet you there?

I paused, ignoring a feeling that my heart very much wanted me to feel.

Holly Aberdeen:

That's actually kind of poetic.

Xander Bowen:

It should be. They're song lyrics.

I frowned and opened my browser. A couple of clicks later, I had the film clip for Busted's 'Meet You There' playing. It was actually a really lovely song.

Holly Aberdeen:

I didn't imagine you as the mushy song
type.

Xander Bowen:

There's a lot you don't know about me.

Holly Aberdeen:

Really? Who'd have thunked Xander
Bowen has hidden depths.

Xander Bowen:

Ah, now... I never said that. I just said there
were things you don't know about me.

Holly Aberdeen:

Okay, like what?

Xander Bowen:

It's hardly fair if I tell you something else
without reciprocation, don't you think?

Holly Aberdeen:

What is this, Silence of the Lambs?

Xander Bowen:

What?

Holly Aberdeen:

It's a movie...
Quid pro quo, Clarice...?
Ringing any bells?

Xander Bowen:

No, I know that. Great movie. I'm just surprised you know that.

Holly Aberdeen:

Why wouldn't I know that?

Xander Bowen:

Don't tell me little Holly likes horror films?

Holly Aberdeen:

Technically Thriller. But, so what if I do?

Xander Bowen:

Well, in the spirit of quid pro quo...

Xander Bowen:

I actually don't hate the DUFF.

I laughed so loudly that Doug whined from where he was lying on the floor.

"It's okay, bud. Sorry. Go back to sleep."

He padded over to me and I patted him absently while I replied to Xander.

Holly Aberdeen:

Seriously?

Xander Bowen:

Seriously.

Xander Bowen:

64

Double feature some time? ;)

I paused for a moment and was surprised by my answer. But, I'd hit send before I'd registered it, so there was no going back.

Holly Aberdeen:

Let me know when you find that world

that doesn't care...

Xander Bowen:

Deal.

Chapter Six

Mark wandered into the kitchen, stretching. "Why aren't you gone?" he asked as he yawned.

"Because I have a double free first," I answered as my phone blooped.

Xander Bowen:
Slacker :P

Oh. My. God. It was like the guy could read my mind half the time.

Holly Aberdeen:
Should have taken Math instead of PE :P

Xander Bowen:
And deprive the school of me in shorts?
Blasphemy!

I smiled to myself and turned off the screen.

"Oh! Has Dolly got a boyfriend?" Mark teased.

I frowned at him and his face fell.

"Sorry, Doll…"

I shrugged. "It's fine. I mean, I feel like my heart's been shredded. But, it's fine."

He came over and hugged me. "Oh, Doll. I mean, I knew you liked him. But, this…?"

I shook my head and let him comfort me. "I think it's Nancy

more than him? I don't know. I just got sideswiped by it. I mean, I was going to tell him. I was finally going to tell him. And, then…"

"I know. Are you okay? Can I do anything?"

I shook my head against his t-shirt. "No. Thanks though. I just need some time. I need to pull my head out of my arse and–"

"No, Dolly," Mark said forcefully. "No. If you need to step back, then you step back. That bitch should have been straight with you. Instead, she was setting you up to look like a complete tool in front of JT and probably the rest of the school. She's probably been planning this for years."

I pushed him away. "That's not fair."

"And, coaching you to finally tell him how you felt while she was dating him was?" Mark's voice rose in anger. "I know you guys were close for years, but that is not the way friends behave."

"She was probably confused. I mean, she didn't even like him. It probably just snuck up on her–"

"Holly, stop." Mark took my shoulders and stared into my eyes. "Did you ever stop to think that while you were being honest with her maybe she wasn't being honest with you?"

I opened and closed my mouth like an idiot fish. "No… She…"

"Okay. Maybe she was. Maybe she was and it did just sneak up on her. Maybe she knew all this time how you felt about him and denied her own feelings until they slapped her in the face. But maybe, Doll. Just maybe, that conniving bitch lulled you into a false sense of security and has always wanted to take Jason from you. Huh?"

I blinked. "No. She wouldn't–" I paused "Why would she…? Jason never liked me. That was the whole problem."

"I can't tell you if he liked you, liked you, Holly. But, he was always closer to you than he was to her. She's always been jealous–

"

"Mark, no–"

"Doll, yes. Nancy's always envied the relationship you and Jason had. Jason needed anything, wanted anything? You were the first person he went to because he knew you'd do it without question, without hesitation. He knew you'd drop everything for him–"

"Wait a minute. What are you saying?"

He shrugged. "Nothing. Just giving you something to think about."

"And, you thought this was supposed to make me feel better?"

He gave me that annoying lazy smirk like he thought he was being all older and wiser. "I thought maybe putting it into perspective might make you feel better. Maybe losing something you never really had might not have been such a blow."

"How does that…? No. Marco. No. That doesn't make me feel any better. Now I feel worse that I not only wasted my time on someone who was apparently never my friend but I've given her a mountain of leverage." I headed for the door. "No. Poorly done, Mark. Poorly done."

He gave me an apologetic smile. "I was just trying to help, Doll."

I frowned at him. "Yeah? Well next time you decide to help, maybe don't."

I snatched up my bag and headed for the bus stop in an even worse mood than I'd been in all week. I loved that Mark had tried to help and I knew – even if I hadn't liked what he'd said – that he'd meant well. But, he had so not done a very good job of it.

It was one thing assuming that Nancy had just been caught out. That something had happened at Teagan's on Saturday night totally out of the blue and she'd thought that's why I should tell him, and then maybe he'd asked her out after we'd talked… That was one thing. The idea that maybe Nancy had somehow planned all this, or at least planned for me to make a fool out of myself, was another and it kept banging around in the back of my head completely unhelpfully.

Thanks, Mark!

As I sat on the bus, my phone went off.

Xander Bowen:
You here for Recess?

Holly Aberdeen:
Does it matter?

Xander Bowen:
You okay?

Holly Aberdeen:
Why do you care?

Xander Bowen:
Wow. Hostile, much?

Holly Aberdeen:
Shouldn't you be in class?

Xander Bowen:
You're concern for my whereabouts seems to be becoming a thing.

Holly Aberdeen:
*your

Holly Aberdeen:
And, on the contrary. I'm wondering what's currently supposed to be keeping you from annoying me.

Xander Bowen:
Woah. Someone woke up on the wrong

side of the bed today! What is up your ass?

Holly Aberdeen:
None of your damned business.

Xander Bowen:
Holly, talk to me.

Holly Aberdeen:
Go for a jog or whatever it is you sport freaks do.

Xander Bowen:
Fucking Jesus, woman! What crawled up your ass and died to put you in this mood?

Holly Aberdeen:
ONLY THE LONGEST FRIENDSHIPS I'VE EVER HAD.

Holly Aberdeen:
You know, nothing important.

Xander Bowen:
Fuck.
You need caffeine when you get here?

Holly Aberdeen:
I don't need anything from you, King Douche.

Xander Bowen:
I'll meet you at your HG with caffeine.

Holly Aberdeen:
No. Thank you.

Xander Bowen:
Yes.

Holly Aberdeen:
Why?

Xander Bowen:

You sound like you need it.

Holly Aberdeen:
I don't want anything from you.

Xander Bowen:
Greg can be waiting if you have an aversion to me.

Holly Aberdeen:
I always have an aversion to you.

Xander Bowen:
Okay, okay, woman! Greg will be waiting.

Holly Aberdeen:
Leave me alone!

Xander Bowen:
If that's what you want.

Xander Bowen:
I'll be here if you

Xander Bowen:
I'm here, Holly.

My fingers hovered over the keyboard and I realised my eyes were hot with unshed tears. I tried to swallow away the lump that had formed in my throat. Mark's words about Nancy were swimming around my head and my conversation with Xander had taken my mind off it. But, only because I'd been projecting my anger at Nancy on him.

Weirdly, I didn't want Xander to leave me alone. It was completely stupid and unnecessary and I had no idea why my instinct was to send Xander what I did next.

Holly Aberdeen:
Caffeine would be great.
Thanks.

His reply was seconds later, but I didn't feel the need to

reprimand him for wasting his time in what was supposed to be his favourite class.

Xander Bowen:

:D I'll see you at your HG.

Holly Aberdeen:

Where's your class now?

Xander Bowen:

Why?

Holly Aberdeen:

No reason.

Xander Bowen:

Second oval.

Why?

I hopped off the bus and headed for the second oval.

Xander Bowen:

Holly?

Xander Bowen:

Your little face bubble is at the bottom of the chat.

Xander Bowen:

I know you're reading these...

As I stopped at the edge of the oval, I saw him in the middle of his class, looking at his phone. He was wearing one of those hideous PE bibs over his uniform shirt and Greg yelled at him. I watched as Xander frowned and slipped his phone back into his pocket and went back to play. I wrapped my arms around myself and watched their lesson.

A few minutes later, Greg looked up and gave me a smile and a wave. I waved back. My eyes slid to Xander and I saw him follow Greg's gaze. As he saw me, that cocky smirk lit his face and he gave me a single nod in greeting. My return smile was completely unbidden and I looked down while I got control over it.

At the end of their lesson, Greg jogged over to me. When it looked like he wasn't going to stop until he hugged me, I laughed and took a step back.

"Oh, no! Sweaty boys are not my thing," I said as I shook my head and held up my hands against him.

"I'm not that bad!" Greg chuckled.

Xander arrived beside him and gave me another one of those smirks. I furiously told my heart it was nothing and it should calm the hell down.

"Hi." Xander nodded again, doing a far better job of holding the lines against his full-blown smile.

Oh. My. God. Why was I suddenly flustered? "Hi."

"I didn't have time to go to the machine," Xander said, throwing a look to Greg like somehow he wouldn't be able to hear our conversation.

"Is this a continuation of why he was *not* paying attention all lesson?" Greg asked, obviously interested.

I nodded noncommittally. "I might have yelled at him."

Greg snorted. "What's new?"

I smiled at him. "Well, we do hate each other."

"You do. King of the Bows and JT's best girl are definitely enemies."

Xander elbowed Greg in the side as I looked at the exchange in surprise.

"Best girl? I think he's dating his best girl," I answered, pretending it didn't shred my poor heart all over again to be reminded of that and the fact the whole school knew it.

Greg grinned. "No, he's– Ow!" he yelled as Xander elbowed him again.

I looked between them and wondered what Greg had been about to say.

"I'll, uh, meet you at your room at Recess with that caffeine, yeah?" Xander asked, wiping the guilty look off his face.

I nodded slowly and it dawned on me just how messed up my life had become this week. Here I was, planning to meet up with the King of the Bows for caffeine of all things. Meeting up to study was...weird but acceptable. Running into each other in the hallway or him choosing to sit with me for unfathomable reasons in class was also weird...but acceptable. But...this...

"How about we cram some study in at Recess? Will that make you feel better?" Xander asked, once again like he could read my mind.

"Sure. Library?"

Xander sighed dramatically. "What is your obsession with that place?"

"What is your obsession with the JT minion?" I shot back.

"Touché, man," Greg chuckled as he nudged Xander.

I got the feeling Greg didn't care one bit that Xander was suddenly hanging around me or that we were talking or whatever it was we were doing; Xander just was, so Greg was more than happy to go along with it. But, I also got the feeling that Greg might have liked to know why at least. I wondered though if Xander even knew why. I certainly couldn't see any reason for it.

We hated each other.

I hated everything that Xander Bowen was.

Up until his recent girl ban, it was not uncommon for him to be seen hooking up with girls in the hallways. Which said nothing of all the girls he hooked up with at parties. There were rumours upon rumours of all the girls. Both coming from within the Bow camp

74

and from the girls themselves who decided they were suddenly Bows (what better way to become a full-fledged member of the Bow Squad than to hook up with their playboy leader?). Xander wasn't exactly your one and done type, but he didn't date and he certainly wasn't discerning about who he spent his time with.

And, that was just the very thick icing on top of a multitude of other things that made the cake that was King Douche unlikable. He had no time for people he deemed below him – which was anyone not in the Bow inner sanctum – unless he was using them for a hook up. He was rude and arrogant, expecting people to do what he wanted when he wanted. He was just... You just know those people who walk around like God's gift and you want to smack them in the face? Well, that was the King of the Bows, hands down.

The fact that he and Jason had been enemies for years was an unspoken rule. Everyone knew. It was practically one of the first things any new person in our year was told; JT and King Douche are enemies, you pick a side – no one was insignificant to the fight. It's how it was.

And, I'd been ruminating on this for the whole way through Home Group and wandering down the hallway so I ended up running into Xander. Literally. Again.

"We have to stop meeting like this," he drawled. He grinned down at me as I pulled my hands away from his chest.

"We could just stop meeting." Okay, so after the last twenty or so minutes of remembering why I hated him, I might have been a little hostile again.

"I thought we were over this," he said as he passed me the bottle of Coke almost apologetically and headed into the library.

I followed him without really knowing why.

"Over what?"

"This tantrum or whatever it is."

"It's not a tantrum. We hate each other. I'm just acting appropriately. Something you seem to have forgotten about."

"Ah yes, stereotyping – alive and well in high schools the world over," he said sarcastically.

"It's not stereotyping. We've been enemies for years."

"The *git and I* have been enemies for years."

"You hate me because I'm his…was his minion."

"No. You hate me because you were his minion."

I stopped and he kept walking into the stacks. "What?"

"You hate–"

"No, I heard you. What do you mean you don't hate me?"

"I didn't say that."

"Okay. What was the 'no' intimating, then?" I asked, hurrying to catch up as he dropped against the wall.

"Only that your statement was wrong."

"What do you think of me?"

"I think you want to get back at the git."

"Before this week."

"I think you should have already got back at the git."

"Before this week, King Douche," I ground out.

"Still the same answer. You should have before and you want to now."

"I don't–"

"I know you've been thinking about it."

I opened my mouth to refute it, but realised there was no point lying to him. "So what if I have? It's not illegal or immoral to have thoughts, it's just what we do with those thoughts that matters."

Xander nodded in condescending agreement. "Is it now? Well,

I put this to you. You want to make him jealous, make him see that he picked the wrong girl, you want him to know what it feels like."

I wriggled uncomfortably. How dare this arrogant butt-head see through me so well. It was his damned fault I was thinking it in the first place.

"You do. I can see it on your face."

"Okay," I practically exploded. "Okay. Say I do. What does it matter? I'm one of JT's girls," I said it sarcastically, but it wasn't completely incorrect, "who do I have to make him jealous–"

"Me." He was completely serious, all jokes aside.

I'd been ready to go on more of a tirade, it would have been a thing of true beauty and poise. I'd been ready to bemoan my lack of foresight in selecting a niche group of friends that made me unapproachable to the rest of the school – don't give me that, cliques are cliques no matter where you grow up. But at that, my brain just stopped.

"Close your mouth, Holly. A bloke could get the wrong idea."

I did indeed snap my mouth shut, but I was pretty sure I was still looking down at him like a complete idiot. "What?"

He gave me the sort of sinful smirk you'd expect might set you on fire, but it was wasted on me as I was still getting my head around the whole 'him' idea. I mean, I appreciated the smoulder somewhere very far in the recesses of my brain, but I wasn't getting to it anytime soon.

"Me," he repeated. "And put it this way, you'd actually be doing me a favour."

"How would *I* be doing *you* a favour?"

"You remember how I said I was avoiding girls?" he asked and I nodded dumbly. "Well, some of the Bows haven't quite got the message. I propose you use me to make your git–"

"Not my git," I breathed, on complete autopilot.

"–jealous and I'll use you to keep the wolves at bay," he continued like I hadn't spoken. "A mutual understanding, as it were."

I blinked. "Um…what?"

He rolled his eyes. "Fuck's sake! I'm suggesting we fake date, Holly. We tell people we're dating. I'm not harassed by the Bows and you can make that git of yours jealous."

"Not my git," I muttered again, still by autopilot as my brain whirred.

I didn't know what I hated more; that I liked the idea of it or that all jokes aside I was actually considering saying yes. So, instead of coming up with an answer, I brought logistics into it.

"How the hell is that going to work?" I asked. "Are you going to ignore all your friends, too? I can see the Bows taking the loss of their king so well," I snorted sarcastically.

The grin he gave me sent a shiver down my spine and not in an entirely unpleasant way. He held a hand out to me, totally unnecessarily suave. "No. I propose you join me."

I spluttered in an incredibly excellent way. "Join the Bows?"

He nodded. "Where I go, you go. And the rest of the school can fuck it."

"Rachel will go nuts…" I breathed, trying to think it through.

He shrugged, his hand still outstretched to me. "Rachel can do whatever she likes. The Bows will accept anything I tell them to–"

"Arrogant."

"But, true."

Well, I had to hand it to him, from everything I'd seen he wasn't wrong.

"What do you say, Holly? Wanna be my fake girlfriend?"

I glared at him, thoroughly unimpressed with his asking out skills. "That just makes it painfully obvious you've never dated before."

He grinned and a small part of me did think it might have maybe been quite charming. "Is that a yes?"

I ran it over in my head.

Could I fake date Xander? I mean, I sort of didn't hate arguing with him, so I could probably put up with him. I'd even had this weird…pull to him all that week… To the extent not all of our chats had been bickering. And if anything was going to make Jason jealous, fake dating King Douche would be the perfect way. I wasn't talking to my friends anyway – and Xander and Greg had been annoyingly persistent all week – so what did it matter if I suddenly started hanging out with the Bows? At least, I'd have somewhere other than the library to hang out at breaks; I didn't hate reading, but I didn't love it. And, if I was doing a favour for Xander, maybe I could use that to my advantage at a later date?

But, no. It was ridiculous. You didn't just fake date someone to make someone else jealous. It always went *so* well in the books and movies.

"No…" I said slowly.

Xander's smile stayed in place, but his eyes lost that humour. "Why don't you think about it? My offer isn't going anywhere."

I wanted to tell him that I wasn't going to think about it. It was just a no from me and it would never be anything else. But, who was I kidding? I was going to be thinking of very little else now.

"I need caffeine," I sighed.

"Your wish was my command," he answered as he indicated the bottle in my hand. "Sorry. That was the best I could do."

I nodded numbly and slid onto the floor next to him. Our

shoulders rested up against each other but we didn't study. We didn't even talk. I just sipped my Coke and tried not to think about fake dating Xander.

He didn't mention it the rest of the day. But, every time he looked at me, there was this humoured question in his eyes like he was daring me to admit my answer was never really a 'no'. That he knew I was *this close* to saying yes.

But, I couldn't. It was immature and stupid and it was Xander-freaking-Bowen for God's sake...

Chapter Seven

Saturday was the worst. At least I'd had homework to distract me for most of the week. And, Mark when he was being an unhelpful wiener. But, all that was done now so I tried to turn to my favourite movies to keep my mind off the sadness that crept in whenever thoughts of Nancy and Jason hit me.

But, all that did was make me remember all the times I'd watched these movies with them. The sleepovers we'd had, the secrets we'd shared, and the times we'd been so close.

While I tried not to let my self-imposed exile and epic-dick-behaviour weigh me down, I actually answered a couple of messages from Jess, Nigel, Amy and a couple of the others about what I was doing that night. I'd avoided them during lunch the day before by claiming Xander's idiocy needed my immediate attention. Jess had found that idea scandalous, but I'd assured her that Madame Renoir was to blame for that one – the fact I was one of the top students in French helped me get away with saying I'd been roped into tutoring duty.

I told my friends that I'd come down with something heinous – we blamed Xander for a while – so I wouldn't be able to make it that night to the various things people were up to. I chatted and gossiped with Jess and Amy in particular for a while about things

I'd missed out on during the week. I skimmed over the Jason and Nancy parts and hoped they didn't notice. Midway through my conversations, my fingers opened up my chat with Xander.

I found myself typing and I'd hit send before I knew what I was doing.

Holly Aberdeen:

I'm waiting for the perfect time to call you back.

So, okay, yes… I might have spent a lot of the week giving the Vengabus a break and listening to that song after he'd first mentioned it. It felt kind of poignant just then. I could relate it to how I felt about Jason (I'd love to find some place where we were okay again, where he and Nancy had hooked up and I hadn't acted like a spoilt brat) and also to how I was going to keep telling my heart we didn't feel about Xander (there was something oddly comforting and refreshing about him, and if I could find a time and place where I didn't feel weird exploring that then that would be great).

The bloop of my phone pulled me out of my musings.

Xander Bowen:

I'd have to have called you first :P

Holly Aberdeen:

I suppose you would.

I went through my movie list and tried to find something to watch. I flicked through the Horror section because I figured I'd find something there that would take my mind off my woes. Neither Jason nor Nancy had ever been Horror fans. So surely, that would be the best idea. I finally settled on *Mama*, which looked suitably scary.

A little bit later, my phone went off and it sounded far too loud in a moment of quiet on the movie. So, I jumped far more than necessary as my heart pounded like mad.

Xander Bowen:
You messaged first.

Xander Bowen:
You okay?

Holly Aberdeen:
Eh.

Xander Bowen:
The git being a git?

Holly Aberdeen:
He's not a git.

Xander Bowen:
Yes, he is.

Xander Bowen:
Huh. That is so much less fun over message...

Holly Aberdeen:
sigh I'll make it up to you Monday.

Xander Bowen:
:D I look forward to it.

Xander Bowen:
Anything I can do?

Holly Aberdeen:
What, no great innuendo?

Xander Bowen:
Thought you might stop talking to me if I did that.

Xander Bowen:
I can if it will make you feel better?

Holly Aberdeen:

Eh.

Holly Aberdeen:

What are you up to tonight?

Xander Bowen:

gasp are you asking me out, Holly?
:P

Holly Aberdeen:

I *was* pretending to take an interest in your life. But, now you've ruined it.

Xander Bowen:

Haha! Well, in the interest of your interest, a few of us are heading to Dan's soon.

Holly Aberdeen:

I assume you lot think that's fun.

Xander Bowen:

Angling for an invitation? ;)

Holly Aberdeen:

Uh, no. I'd rather do tequila suicides than go to a Bow party.

Xander Bowen:

Good little Holly Aberdeen knows what a tequila suicide is?!

Xander Bowen:

Also, if you ever do come to a 'Bow party' – seriously who calls it that? – we are doing tequila suicides!!

Holly Aberdeen:

Everyone calls it that.

Holly Aberdeen:

And, no, we're not.

Xander Bowen:

84

Yes, we are.

Xander Bowen:

Hate to love you and leave you, but I gotta
go get Greg. Wanker's whining.
I'll talk to you later?

Holly Aberdeen:

Maybe.

Xander Bowen:

Tease.

Holly Aberdeen:

Douche.

Xander Bowen:

:*

I ignored his kisses and went back to my movie. But, I was smiling again. There was something about his ability to annoy me that made me smile. It was ridiculous and I had no idea how someone I hated and found so annoying could make me smile with such regularity. But, I preferred that over the wallowing so I decided not to analyse it too much. I was just going to go with it. Besides, it was sort of fun to hate him to his face.

I let myself get totally immersed in my movies. And, I spent more time hiding behind a pillow and feeling like I was about to jump out of my skin than moping about Jason and Nancy. So, that was a plus at least.

Still when my phone went off again, it freaked the crap out of me and I picked it up while I busied myself with a sip of drink. Which was snorted out my nose as soon as I opened the picture that Xander had sent. It was dark, so I had to turn the brightness up on my screen. But, it was a picture of him and Greg doing one of those stupid duck face poses.

I wiped my chin and laughed as I replied.

Holly Aberdeen:

Is this pre-tequila suicides or post?

Xander Bowen:

I wouldn't dare tequila suicide without you!

Holly Aberdeen:

Oh no, please. Be my guest.

There was a short gap, then I got another picture of Xander kissing Greg's cheek while Greg made a hilariously sassy face.

I decided then and there that Greg was fun. He might have even been good people. But, given that he *was* Bow Inner Sanctum, I was going to delay judgment until I knew him better.

Holly Aberdeen:

What *are* you two doing?

Xander Bowen:

Thought we'd include you on the shenanigans.

Xander Bowen:

Greg says it's your turn.

Holly Aberdeen:

My turn for what?

Xander Bowen:

A picture.

I rolled my eyes but knew he'd just be even more annoying if I didn't. So, I opened my camera, freaked myself out by the image I got as it opened on front camera, struck a delightfully stupid pose with my tongue out and the peace sign, and sent it. I looked over it and knew I looked plain as; my hair was in a messy bun and I was in my pyjamas. It was a picture I'd never send anyone else. But, I didn't really care. I wasn't trying to impress anyone here.

A bit later, I got another reply from the boys.

Xander Bowen:

How do we know you just took that?

Xander Bowen:

Also, Greg says you look adorable.

Holly Aberdeen:

You doubt me?

Holly Aberdeen:

Oh, Greg does? Not you?

Xander Bowen:

Me? Course not. I definitely in no way think you look wonderful in that picture.

I thought it best to skip right over that comment, even if I had in some way elicited it.

Xander Bowen:

You might have a bunch of unflattering photos stored up.

If I didn't know better, I would have asked if Xander had ever met a teenage girl… Actually, any human being really.

Holly Aberdeen:

Why would I possibly store unflattering pictures?!

Xander Bowen:

For charming young men.

Holly Aberdeen:

You are neither charming. Nor am I trying to charm you.

Xander Bowen:

I'm terribly charming and you've already charmed me ;)

Xander Bowen:

You have yet to prove that was you just

then.

Holy Aberdeen:

No one's charming anyone.

Holly Aberdeen:

Doesn't the pic say in the info?

Xander Bowen:

No, it just says when you sent it.

We require proof!

Holly Aberdeen:

Lol, and how am I supposed to prove it?

There was no response for a while and I went back to my movie. Then, a video call request came through from Xander. I looked at my phone suspiciously like I was suddenly *in* some horror movie. I assumed butt-dial, but it kept ringing. So, I finally answered to hear music playing in the background.

"Hello…?"

A "HI!" and a "HOLLY!" got mingled as Xander and Greg shouted at me enthusiastically.

I laughed. "Hi."

"Give us a proper look, then," Xander said.

I moved the phone over my body and back up to my face, making a face similar to the one in the picture I'd sent. "See, just taken."

"A likely story!" Greg mused as the two boys' faces jostled for space on my screen.

"We'll accept it for now. What are you up to?" Xander asked.

"Watching movies."

"What movies?"

I turned my phone briefly so the camera was facing the paused screen on the TV. "*The Woman in Black.*"

"Is this another horror, Miss Aberdeen?" Xander chuckled and

I stuck my tongue out at him.

"I was going to watch *Silence of the Lambs*, but I thought I'd save it."

Xander grinned warmly and Greg looked at him as though trying to work out what that meant. Greg got this really weird combination of excited and knowing expression on his face. Until I heard someone call Greg's name in the background and he looked away. He patted Xander, waved at me absent-mindedly, and disappeared.

"Shouldn't you be mingling or something?" I asked Xander, popping a chip in my mouth and settling in more comfortably on the couch.

He shrugged. "Maybe."

"I could be watching my movie."

"Would you prefer that?"

I shrugged. "Maybe."

He gave me that grin again, "Maybe," and nodded as his eyes slid to something behind his phone. "Yeah. All right then, Holly."

"Hey! I can call you back now," I commented.

His eyes moved back to me. "That you can."

I opened my mouth to speak again, but Greg was suddenly back and the image on my screen went nuts for a moment.

"Dude, duty calls," Greg said. "Liv's not doing so well."

Xander looked behind him and nodded. "Yep. Be right there."

"Sweet." Greg pressed two fingers to his lips, then to Xander's phone camera. "Catchya later, Holl." And, he was gone again.

"Duty?" I asked Xander as he looked back to me.

Was that slight embarrassment on King Douche's face?

"Uh, it's nothing. I've just got to check on Liv."

"Don't tell me the King of the Bows actually looks after his subjects."

"Of course not. I'm heartless, shallow, arrogant King Douche, remember? You coming to the game tomorrow?"

I shrugged again, my heart giving this weird niggling feeling I was refusing to acknowledge. "Don't know yet."

He gave me a sweet smile. "Well, I will either see you tomorrow or on Monday. Enjoy your movies."

"Night, Xander."

He gave me a wink and disconnected the call.

I turned off my screen and dropped my phone on the couch next to me.

"Surely there isn't more to King Douche?" I muttered to myself as I picked up the remote and pressed play. "No. Don't be stupid, Holly. Like he said. Heartless, shallow, arrogant King Douche."

If that was true, why was my heart trying to smack me upside the head to get me to pay attention to it?

I just wished I'd spent more time pondering the enigma that might have been the King of the Bows instead of checking my phone half an hour later…

I ended up going to Mark and Xander's game – rugged up in whatever warm jumper I'd first found and not caring what I looked like – because I was pissed off and I refused to acknowledge my stupid little heart thought seeing Xander might make me feel better.

Nancy had posted up a multitude of pictures of her and Jason after that first fateful viewing the night before. They were tagged with things like #firstdate, #fiveyearsinthemaking, #BFFtoBF, #truelove and a whole bunch of other nauseating things. There was kissing and cute adorable couple spam that I couldn't help but stare at most of the night to the point that it was seared into my brain cells by the time I tried to go sleep.

So, sleep had been elusive for the *nth* night in a row and I'd finally slipped into unconsciousness while one of the *Resident Evil*s – I lost track of how far through them I got – played at something like four in the morning.

I'd woken up to a friend request from Greg, a headache, and an inexplicable urge to go to Mark and Xander's game.

I stood a little apart from the other friends and family members while I watched the first half of the game, huddled into myself and aggravating my headache by clenching my jaw. I made the stupid mistake of checking Facebook sometime during the game and saw Nancy had posted up a ridiculous motivational quote about knowing who your real friends are. She'd tagged Jason and captioned it, 'Can't believe all the love we've been getting ♥' like some couple ten years' older. And, I wasn't stupid enough to think it wasn't directed squarely at me and the lack of love I'd given either of them.

So, my mood soured further.

Honestly, what had she expected me to do?

I knew what I should have done. I should have bucked up and congratulated them. I should have put my feelings aside and been happy for the happiness of my two best friends. That would have been the decent, proper, nice thing to do. Why then had I been so caught up in the feeling of betrayal? I mean, Jason hadn't known how I felt about him– Well I hoped he hadn't and that was different, but I was sticking to that theory for now. So, he couldn't have actually betrayed me.

Nancy, though…

I couldn't stop thinking about what Mark had said Friday morning.

Had she only been coaching me the week before so I made a fool of myself? Had she been trying to get Jason away from me all this time? I should have given her the benefit of the doubt. Five years of best-friendship meant I should have given her the benefit of the doubt. But, there was this little niggling feeling in the back of my head that insisted there was some merit in Mark's words. Which made my heart hurt even more, and the poor little thing was already feeling battered and bruised enough.

And, that made me angrier.

I wanted payback.

It was immature and stupid and probably wrong of me. But, I didn't care anymore.

I wanted payback.

And, Xander's offer was looking mighty enticing...

"So, I'm stuck in stalker-land but you'll accept Greg's friend request the morning he sends it?" Xander sounded incredulous as he stepped up next to me like fate was hanging a huge lantern up for me and waving it in my face.

I shrugged as I watched Mark and the rest of the club keeping warm at half time while the coach tried to pep them. I really didn't feel like banter that morning, especially with my brain whirring and my heart nudging me insistently to take Xander up on his offer. I swear to God, if it could walk out of my body and hand him a flower it would do just that and be blushing like mad.

"What? No quip about stalker-land versus the friendzone?"

I shrugged again.

"I know, I know," he sighed ruefully as though I'd been helpful and answered. "That would require us being friends and we completely hate–"

"I'll fake date you," I blurted out.

Apparently, my heart had taken the wheel again and left my brain hogtied in the backseat while we all hurtled along at breakneck speeds into ever increasingly dangerous territory.

"What?" Xander asked.

I turned to see him looking at me with humour in his eyes.

"I'll fake date you," I repeated carefully, looking into his eyes so my meaning couldn't possibly be misinterpreted.

He looked me over carefully. Then, his name was yelled from someone in the team – could have been my brother, who knew. Xander frowned, but as though something concerned him. Finally, he nodded slowly.

"Okay. We'll talk after?"

I nodded. "Sure. Good luck."

He flashed me a smile that didn't quite reach his eyes and jogged off.

I stood on the sidelines for the rest of the game, trying to will my heart to stop beating so hard – *you're the one who agreed!* I reminded it – and forcing myself to breathe.

Unsurprisingly with Xander and Mark on the same team, they won.

Mark came over when they were done and looked at me suspiciously. "Do I need to ask why King Douche was talking to you at halftime?"

Guilt hit me and I refused to look at him. "Nope." I popped the 'p', my tell-tale bluff tell.

"Holly…" He gave me his best 'I'm the big brother, so tell me the truth' voice.

I sighed. "Madame Renoir asked me to help him with French,

okay? We were just talking about school."

Oh, my stomach rebelled against lying to my brother and my heart crossed its arms and glared at me in disgust. But, seriously, I was *not* telling Mark I'd just agreed to fake date the King of the Bows. That was not a conversation we were going to have. Ever. Like, not even death bed confession.

"Uh huh, and do you need to speak to him some more? Or, can we go?"

I jumped at the suspicion in his tone, but shook my head. "No. No. We can go."

Mark looked me over and I couldn't tell if he'd believed me and just wasn't pleased I was spending time with Xander, or if he was trying to work out what I might be hiding. "Okay. Let's go then."

I followed Mark to the car, pulling out my phone as I went.

Holly Aberdeen:

I've got to go. We'll talk later?

He wasn't slow in responding and I looked up to find him as Mark backed out of his car park. He was standing with a couple of the other guys, chatting amicably and giving them a fist bump. As I watched, he ran his hand through his hair and I had one of those moments where I could appreciate why girls fawned over him.

Xander Bowen:

If you're having cold feet...?

Holly Aberdeen:

No. I'm not. I just didn't think Mark needed to be involved.

And, I wasn't. It had been a rash decision to agree to his offer. But like all my rash decisions of the last week, I was going to see it through. Making Nancy and Jason think I was dating Xander would get back at the both of them.

Hos before bros?

That didn't seem to mean much to Nancy anymore, so I'd give her a piece of her own medicine. And, hopefully make Jason jealous at the same time.

Xander Bowen:

Are you hiding your boyfriend from your brother, Holly?

I could just picture the teasing condescension on his face and it should not have made me smile. It should have annoyed me like it had just last week. My heart should not have felt a slight pang of disappointment that I wasn't seeing it in real life.

Still, I couldn't go around encouraging him.

Holly Aberdeen:

FAKE boyfriend.

Holly Aberdeen:

And, you're proposal technique could use a little work.

Xander Bowen:

Naw, you wanna marry me? ♥

Holly Aberdeen:

God, no!

Holly Aberdeen:

I just meant that if you were ever going to actually ask a girl out, you probably want to make her think you're actually into it.

Xander Bowen:

Who says I'm not into you?

Holly Aberdeen:

Every sane person in the history of the world.

Xander Bowen:

That is just not true.

Holly Aberdeen:

*We've all seen the girls you hook up with,
King Douche, and they are not me.*

Xander Bowen:

Believe what you want, Holly.

Xander Bowen:

I'll see you tomorrow then, *girlfriend* ;)

Holly Aberdeen

*fake girlfriend.

Xander Bowen:

;) :*

Chapter Eight

"Good morning, Holly," Xander's voice boomed like a boxing announcer as he walked towards me.

"Good morning, Xander," I replied more evenly as I stuffed my last book in my bag and closed my locker.

I turned to face him and he leant towards me, making me press my back against the lockers.

"Did you hear the news?" he whispered and his tone made me smile despite myself.

"No. What news?" I asked.

"King Douche and JT's ex-minion are *dating*," he said scandalously, complete with eyebrow waggle and a small laughed escaped me.

"Fake dating," I reminded him.

He stepped towards me, his hand going to my waist. "Ah, but people don't know that."

"People don't even think we're dating."

"Not yet."

"Shouldn't you be post-gym right now?"

"I had better things to do this morning."

"Like what?"

His hand slid around my hip and over my arse as he gave me

one of Xander Bowen's patented smirks. My eyebrow rose even as my heart stuttered.

"That is a no from me," I told him.

His smirk made my heart flutter and I told it off. "Your vote's been noted, Simon."

I couldn't help but smile, even as I looked around the corridor warily. "Get your hand off my arse, Xander."

People were looking. People were looking at Xander Bowen backing Holly Aberdeen up against her locker with his hand on her arse while she smiled. Even as I felt a twinge of panic, I couldn't stop smiling at the look of mischief in his eyes.

At least, he slid his hand off my arse and back onto my hip.

"King Douche, people are staring," I hissed.

"How did you think this was going to go, Holly?" he asked, humour written all over his face. "People are going to have to know – and believe – we're dating if you expect to make the git jealous."

I stared at him, then registered he was giving me a highly expectant look.

"What?"

"You said you'd make it up to me…"

I tried very hard not to smile. "He's not–"

"Yes, he is," Xander said, then hung his head back and sighed dramatically. "That was much better. Thank you."

I huffed a laugh. "Okay. Moving on. As in to French, or we'll be late."

"You are such a party pooper." He sighed, stepping away from me. "But you can make it up to me."

"If you tell me it's by letting you touch my arse again, you'll get more than a no."

"Noted. No, you can make it up to me by holding my hand."

"Holding your hand?" I asked and he nodded. "Fine."

I offered him my hand and he took it before we walked in the direction of our French classroom.

"Holly," he whispered harshly as he leant towards me.

"What, Xander?" I replied in a similar harsh whisper.

"People are *staring*," he said with totally false concern.

I rolled my eyes. "I see that."

"Oh, git sighting!"

I looked further up the corridor and saw Jason was coming from the opposite direction. He was smiling as he was surrounded by people who were slowly peeling away to their classrooms as though loathe to leave his side. My hand slid out of Xander's automatically. Xander put his arm around my shoulder and leant his lips to my ear.

"It doesn't work if you chicken out."

"I am *not* chickening out."

"If you wanted to, it's okay. Just say the word and we're done. But, well…" He paused. "If not, I'm going to feel obliged to give him a bloody good show."

He was giving me an out. I could walk away from this with very little repercussions. Jason hadn't seen us yet and who cared what rumours ran around the school after his display at my locker…

"Okay. Get acting," I said before I really thought I'd come to any conclusion.

He broke into a disarmingly sincere smile. "Come on, then. Let me introduce the school to my new girlfriend," he said, giving my shoulder a squeeze.

I sighed, but I was resolved now. "Fake girlfriend."

He looked at me in a fondly exasperated manner. "It won't work if you tell people."

I rolled my eyes and he kissed my temple before dropping his nose to my ear.

"Laying it on a little thick, aren't you?" I hissed.

He ducked his head as we walked on. "Not at all. Laying it on thick would be me crushing you to those lockers and kissing you 'til your knees go weak."

I pretended butterflies didn't just explode out of my heart at that comment. Or, that my heart wasn't excitedly chasing them around. "Arrogant."

"But again, true."

I snorted and he gave me an almost adorable squeeze as he laughed. I put my arm around his waist.

People actually stopped and stared in the hallways as Xander Bowen and Holly Aberdeen walked past, the very definition of canoodling. There was no time to wonder if I'd made the wrong choice, we were doing it now and I was going to stick with it.

As we approached the French room, Jason's step faltered as he finally caught sight of us. Xander stopped us as casually as you please just outside the room and caressed my face gently. He ducked his lips to my ear.

"Don't look so scared," he chuckled, then kissed my cheek.

I nodded as he pulled away and looked into my eyes. Those pale browns of his searched my face for a moment, that mischief and humour still marking his expression. Something else crossed his face for a split second as he licked his lip, then he gave one nod, took my hand, and pulled me into the classroom.

I just caught sight of Jason's face and it was pale. It was really pale. Other than that, he looked far too shocked to know what to think. I ducked my head as I fell into the seat next to Xander.

"And, what do you think he'd do if I kissed you?" Xander's

voice was back in my ear.

"I don't know," I answered. "But, you might not like *my* reaction."

He laughed. "Oh, I don't know. I'm quite partial to a girl who'll kiss me back."

I whirled to face him. "You so certain of that are you?"

His eyes shone and he gave me a lop-sided smile. "I see the way you look at me," he said quietly so no one else could hear.

"With exasperation and a desire to maim?" I retorted just as quietly, and the other side of his mouth rose as well.

"How's denial treating you?" he asked and I was certain people would be thinking we were dating based solely on how close our heads were.

"Peachy," I replied.

"Okay. If we're going to convince people, you're going to have to know more about me–"

"What?"

"Well, we need to know things about each other–"

"I know plenty about you," I hissed, leaning even closer to him. "You're the bro-jock captain of the soccer team. You hook up with every Bow and Bow wannabe with tits and they might get seconds if they give you a blow job. You treat everyone around you as disposable and you've never even heard of being polite. You think throwing money at a problem will solve it, and if not a sexy wink will do it. You just assume every person alive wants a piece of you. And, you think you're so charming that it was a good idea to fake date a person who has hated you for years. I think that about sums you up, doesn't it?"

He looked at me carefully before he answered. "I was thinking some more positive attributes–"

"That's it? No defence?"

He shrugged. "What do you want me to say? That's what you know."

"So, it's all true?" I couldn't deny a part of me was hoping for a no; I was just starting to think there was something more to him than the rumour mill suggested after all…

"I didn't say that."

"Well, *do* you have anything you'd like to say?"

"Like what?" He pulled away slightly.

"I don't know! Anything."

He sighed and ran his hand through his hair before leaning closer to me. "Bro-jock captain of the soccer team I have no defence for. We both know that's true. As for hooking up with every Bow or Bow wannabe… Holly, that's the entire school – whether they're willing to admit it or not. Despite my best efforts, I just don't have the time for everyone. And, who doesn't like blow jobs?"

I suspected at least half the population across all genders. "Seriously?"

He shrugged again. "Look, I was thinking more along the lines of things we did and didn't like–"

"Well, we've established you like blow jobs."

A slight smile lit his lips but his eyes were serious. "I was thinking more like the fact your favourite drink is Mountain Dew because you think it's got just as much caffeine as Coke, tastes better and has a funky colour. Or, that you always smile at Madame Renoir's stupid jokes when you think no one's looking. Or, that you blush whenever someone compliments you. That you unabashedly love the Vengaboys even if they are fucking old-school. That you always hide the way you scrunch your face behind your hair when you're on the rag and the cramps get bad. Things that people…dating know about each other."

The first bell rang, but I barely noticed.

I just stared at him for a while. Talk about unabashed. King Douche had just cavalierly discussed my menstrual cycle without batting an eyelid. And that was just the tip of the frenzy on which my heart was leading my brain. How the hell did he know all that about me? I didn't know whether to launch a stalker alert or let my heart flutter around in little circles.

"What?" was apparently all I could manage.

The corner of his lip quirked. "I told you I notice some things."

I nodded and my lips suddenly felt very dry. "I see."

"Other than the scathing judgement of my finer qualities, have you got anything else for me?"

I blinked as I tried to think about what the hell I might have picked up on Xander over the years.

"You're left-handed, so your left foot is dominant. But the closer you get to goal, the better you do with your right. You like the red Powerade. For a complete arsehole, your friends are unwaveringly loyal so there must be more to you than meets the eye. And, I think I remember hearing something about you liking Linkin Park?"

"Not bad." He nodded as the second bell rang.

"I'll work on it."

"Peachy." He grinned as Madame Renoir called for quiet.

I smiled to myself as Xander sat back in his seat.

At Recess, Xander met me outside my Home Group with an

unnecessarily large smile on his face.

"Why do I feel like I'm not going to like where this is going?" I asked him.

"Come and meet the Bows," he said.

I shook my head. "Nope. I told you I would never sit with the Bows."

"That was before you were my girlfriend. People are already talking. May as well make that leap, Holly. Come on, I'll be there to catch you." He spread his arms out and I told my heart we weren't leaping into them.

Why did his smile have to be so adorably infectious?

I sighed. He was right. People were whispering and staring at us even now. If no one had just picked him up dropping the 'G' word, they'd soon come to the conclusion by themselves. May as well slam that next nail in my coffin.

"Okay. Fine!"

He grinned widely, wrapped his arm around me and led me out of the building.

He headed over to the patch of oval where the Bows traditionally hung out during breaks. I didn't need to see Rachel's indignant glare, because I felt it like a January sunburn. As we got closer, I did see it though and her lips were pursed like she had to physically restrain herself from saying something to Xander about my presence. Her eyes demanded an explanation.

"Xand, whatchya doin'?" she asked, putting on a good show of being conversational.

Xander's hand tightened against my shoulder almost protectively. "Right," he started in a very 'hear ye, hear ye' sort of voice and the majority of the Bows turned to listen to their king. "So we could only hide this for so long before I was unable to control myself, but Holly and I are dating."

To say there was a stunned silence might have been putting it mildly. Every Bow just stared at us in shock and I started to feel incredibly antsy and just a little bit like I needed to run away and bury my head under an avalanche. But, I could do this.

What would Nancy do? I asked myself, trying not to look like I'd rather be anywhere but there. I might not have been talking to her, but she certainly knew how to play to an audience.

Xander drew himself up – and me with him. "We're dating. She is my girlfriend. I am her boyfriend. I get it's a little out of the blue. Holly gets it's a little out of the blue. But, you're all going to have to suck it up and deal with it."

Miranda, a girl I knew well by sight but wasn't sure I'd ever really spoken to smiled at me, but she was about the only one. Rachel's scowl was one of epic proportions and I was surprised I wasn't struck down dead – Rachel Harris was obviously not quite as all-powerful as one had been led to believe. A few of the Bow girls eyed me warily like they were trying to work out what I had and they didn't (leverage and a lack of desire for Xander, for starters). And, the Bow guys seemed torn between making some kind of joke and following Rachel's lead. All but one; Daniel Viera eyed me about as pleasantly as Rachel. Although, Daniel Viera often looked like he had a rod shoved so far up his arse he could chew on it.

After what felt like an intense albeit silent showdown between the Bow King and Queen, Xander took my hand and went over to the picnic table that constituted the little sun of their galaxy. He sat down on the table, his feet on the seat, and drew me between his knees. He put his arms around me and laced his fingers over my stomach in a clear message to those watching.

Slowly, talk and shenanigans resumed. Although, Rachel and Daniel kept throwing me dirty looks. I didn't really pay attention to the talk and none of it was directed to me anyway; I was too busy trying to act natural and not be stiff as wood. After all, I was supposed to want Xander's arms around me. Talk ebbed and flowed for a while, the rumble of Xander talking or laughing vibrating against my back almost pleasantly.

"You smell amazing," came the warm whisper in my ear as the conversation kept flowing on around us. And warm here didn't just reflect the temperature of his breath on my cheek or what I felt as his nose dipped to my shoulder, but also the complete sincerity of the compliment.

Now look, I may not have been attracted to the lummox, but a girl's going to get goose bumps at something like that no matter who delivers it. And just between you and me, my heart may have skipped a little before it looked around in panic to see if anyone had witnessed its disgraceful display.

"Does that line ever work for you?" I asked, turning to half-face him.

His nose brushed mine and I felt far too close to those weirdly enigmatic cognac eyes and the smile I saw in them. "You'd have to tell me. I've never used it before."

My heart did another traitorous little skip and I hoped my cheeks hadn't gone fire engine red as I slid my eyes from his. "Of course you haven't," I answered sceptically, but somehow I believed his words more than my scepticism of his.

He chuckled and bumped his nose against mine to get me to look at him again. "You let me know if it's working, will you?"

I smiled and looked away from him, settling myself back against his body. "Sure. You can expect that with the emergency report that Hell's frozen over."

He snorted and tightened his hold on me for a second. "I look forward to it. Oh, hey. I have school practice tomorrow afternoon…"

"You do. It is known to happen on a Tuesday."

And no I didn't know his timetable, I just happened to know that all Saturday morning sports had practice on Tuesdays and Thursdays after school and that soccer was a Saturday morning sport.

"Your powers of observation astound me," he chuckled.

"Oh, sorry. Was there a point to that statement?"

"There was," he said, the smile still in his voice. "I thought that perhaps coming to practice would be a good *girlfriend* thing to do?"

"Did you now?"

I felt him nod. "I did. I was going to suggest my game on Saturday. But, I didn't really think we were at that stage of our relationship where I ask you to get up at the arse-crack of dawn to watch me run around."

I smiled. "How thoughtful."

The bell for the end of Recess sounded and he let go of me to stand up. I looked him over, wondering how much of his act was for show and how much was just him being the flirty guy he was.

"So?" he asked, taking my hand gently.

I looked down at our interlaced fingers. "So, I'll think about it."

He grinned. "Of course you will."

The Bows started heading towards their various classes and I spotted Nancy and Jason across the quad, hand in hand much like Xander and I now were. Jason was talking animatedly to Matt and Nigel while Nancy was laughing with Jess and Amy. None of them had seen me, but I had the exact same timetable as Jason and most of the same classes as Nancy – we'd set it up like that on purpose – so it was just a matter of time.

Suddenly, I was rethinking the wisdom of my plan as I froze to the spot; Jason was one thing, Nancy was another.

"You good?" Xander asked.

I looked up at him, hoping I didn't look as panicked as I felt.

He gave me a cocky smirk, but his eyes were a hell of a lot warmer than I would have expected them to be. "It's all good. You're stuck with me the rest of the day. I won't leave your side."

"If you have to pee?"

"I have a bladder of steel."

"Okay." I paused, trying to forget that piece of information. "And, if I have to pee?"

He shrugged. "Then I'll get to see how much nicer the girls loos are after all."

I snorted and looked down as he started leading me to English, with an added hand swing for good measure.

"Dude, have you – hey, Holl – done anything about that poetry crap?" Greg asked, appearing on my other side and talking to Xander over my head.

"Do I look like I did anything about that poetry crap?" Xander asked.

Greg shrugged, then looked at me like he'd forgotten I was there for a moment and just remembered, despite greeting me seconds before. "Hey, you've got a girlfriend now." He pointed at me and everything. "She's a girl. She likes poetry. Maybe she can help?"

I looked at him, flabbergasted. "Actually, she doesn't like poetry."

Greg threw his head back and sighed. "Ugh. I cannot afford another fail or Coach will bench me."

"Well, I'm dropping scary close to my own benching, man. 'Fraid I can't help," Xander answered.

I looked between them, still boggled that they were worried about study and wondering how far that extended – I knew the soccer coach was strict about grades, I'd had him for PE for three years and he was constantly on his players to keep up their averages or he'd bench them. And, Xander *had* been pretty attentive through Psych the other day…

"She said she didn't *like* poetry. That doesn't mean she doesn't grasp the concept…" I said slowly, knowing I'd regret it as soon as it was out of my mouth.

"Are you in the mood to help a couple of no hoper wankers, then?" Greg asked, giving me what I assumed he thought was an amiable, convincing smile.

I looked to Xander who had a question of his own in his eyes. Finally, I sighed. "Sure. Why not? First French. Then English. It's not like I had any other plans for my life."

Greg threw a companionable arm around me and chuckled enthusiastically. "Sweet! You officially sitting with us now?"

"Looks that way."

"Keep your hands off my girlfriend, man," Xander huffed a laugh.

And, that's when we came face to face with Nancy and Jason outside the classroom.

Nancy looked between Xander and me like I'd grown three heads or something. Jason meanwhile went somewhat paler than earlier and looked sucker-punched. He looked like I'd completely betrayed him and I had to say the feeling was rather mutual.

I supposed that was the last nail. There'd be no need for rumours now; Xander had just clarified for all necessary parties in this charade that I was in fact his girlfriend.

I felt Xander's arm go around me and he kissed my hair. "JT." I felt him nod against my hair.

Jason blinked, his dark blue eyes wide. "Bowen," he replied, sounding like he was on autopilot.

Nancy glared at all of us while she yanked Jason after her and into the room.

"Well, they just get more and more pleasant by the day, don't they," Greg said. "Good thing you're one of us now." He nudged me companionably as he headed for his desk.

Xander and I followed, his hand dropping to catch mine again.

I sat between Xander and Greg, actually feeling somewhat protected by the two big Bows. I knew exactly how Nancy would play this, so I just smiled at whatever Greg said and pretended I belonged there.

Chapter Nine

For a guy who had never had a girlfriend in his life, Xander did a damned good job at acting the part.

He was almost always holding my hand or had his arm around me. He kissed my cheek, looked at me like I was the centre of his universe, and brushed my hair off my face in a manner far too gentle for my liking. We sat together in every class, spent Recess and Lunch together, avoided Jason, Nancy, Rachel and Daniel together, and chatted most of the night on Messenger about absolute bollocks.

On Wednesday, home group marked our first separation at school since he'd made his announcement. We stopped outside the 12OB room and he smiled at me.

"What?" I asked.

He shook his head. "Nothing. I'll see you at Recess."

"If you're going to get all clingy on me, then I might have to break up with you," I warned him.

He huffed a laugh and his eyes roved the hallway. "You wouldn't do that. You like me too much."

"Oh, do I?" I giggled and his eyes found mine again.

He nodded and kissed my forehead absently. "I'll see you in a bit."

I shook my head and walked into the classroom, taking the random side chair I had for the rest of the week. Surprisingly, Miranda dropped into the seat next to me.

"Uh, hi…" I gave her an uncertain smile.

She gave me a wide smile. "Hi. How are you?"

"Uh. Yeah, good. You?"

She shrugged. "Fine. You coming to town with us on Friday night?"

I blinked. "I wasn't aware there was a town on Friday night…" I answered as two kids walked past us, muttering to each other.

Miranda giggled. "You two are the talk of the school."

"What?"

"You and Xand. People thought it was exciting enough that JT and Nancy got together? That was nothing compared to the talk going around about JT's right hand girl going out with Xander Bowen!"

I looked around and noticed that people were indeed staring at me even more obviously than they had the last two days. "Well, I'm sure they'll get over it."

She snorted. "It's like showdown of the century. Everyone's just waiting for the bust up."

"What bust up?"

She looked at me like I must have been an idiot, and to be fair I kinda sorta felt like one at that moment. "The one between JT and Xand. Everyone's convinced JT's going to try to win you back by fighting Xander."

I looked at her in utter disbelief. "They what?"

"Right, class. How are we?" Mr Burnett called as he walked in, carrying his typical stack of books.

"Morning, sir," we all chorused as Miranda gave me a knowing smile.

"Good. Roll. Holly?"

I raised my hand and then just sat, feeling the urge to fidget, as Mr Burnett called out the rest of the roll. There were whisperings around the room and panic shot through me as I wondered how much of it was about me. I knew it was ridiculous; not everything revolved around me, obviously.

After the roll had been called, we sat around and waited for the end of home group. Some kids went and talked to Mr Burnett about God knew what, while the rest of us chatted. Miranda started telling me all about what the Bows did on Fridays in town, and I did my best to concentrate while not focussing on the fact that apparently people thought Jason was going to fight Xander over me.

The thought was ridiculous.

Quite aside from the fact that Jason wouldn't fight anyone over me, he'd already had a fight with Xander in Year 10. Well, that was the last fight he'd had with Xander and Jason had lost. Badly. So, I really couldn't see anything that would be important enough for Jason to fight Xander over, let alone that thing being me.

The complete waffle in my brain was interrupted when I saw Xander leaning on the lockers across from our classroom – they had convenient windows all across the walls to the hallways with rows of lockers along the other side – and he winked at me.

Beside me, Miranda giggled and nudged me the way Nancy would have had any cute boy winked at me from outside the classroom. I was all at once touched by how nice she was being to me and saddened by the way my friendship with Nancy had gone sour. Mind you, there was a persistent voice in the back of my head that was warning me that Miranda's niceness could have easily been a ruse and she was just lulling me in a false sense of security before she and the other Bows murdered me in my unsuspecting sleep.

Then the bell for Recess rang and my worries were distracted.

"All right, I've kept you long enough. Get out and I'll see you lucky ones in class later," Mr Burnett called and there was the great scraping of chairs that signalled mass student movement.

"Well, hi," Xander said as Miranda and I made our way out of the classroom.

"Well, hi, yourself," I answered, feeling a lot more chipper at the sight of his comforting smile than I really ought to have.

He took my hand and Miranda and I followed him out to their table.

"So, I asked Holly if she was coming to town on Friday, Xand. And she told me she didn't know there was a town on Friday..." she said, a note of teasing to her accusation.

Xander's hand tightened in mine. "Ah, well. I didn't know if Holly would be ready for that, Rand."

Miranda scoffed. "She's ditched all her friends for you, the least you can do is act like she belongs with us."

Xander and I caught each other's eye and I watched as his softened.

It was interesting that Miranda saw it as me dropping my friends for him; it made me wonder what the rest of the school thought. Maybe if they all decided I'd dropped my friends for a grand romance instead of being a petty, jealous idiot that would make me look less like a bitch.

"We have a standing thing of heading into town after school on Fridays..." Xander started, "it'd be great if you came?"

Miranda snorted. "Sound less sure why not." She jostled me playfully. "Just give him some time. None of us guessed he'd ever

114

have a girlfriend, let alone someone not a Bow. He'll adjust eventually."

"How long exactly have you been together, anyway?" Rachel asked as we arrived at the group and Daniel stood next to her expectantly.

"About two weeks," Xander replied unhesitatingly and I freaked *the hell* out.

Rachel's eyes narrowed. "That explains your behaviour on Saturday. And, I suppose *she's* the real reason why you didn't come to Teagan's?"

Cue a significant relax. Whelp, at least my fake boyfriend hadn't been actual cheating on me at the same time my best friends had been hooking up. That was good to know.

I felt Xander shrug. "I had better things to do."

"You could have invited her."

"Technically, she was invited. But, we felt kind of awkward."

"And, are you going to make it official, or just parade her around the school?"

"Rach, what's your actual problem here?" Xander huffed.

Rachel crossed her arms, popped her hip, and looked between us. "I just don't know, Xand. I feel like someone's playing someone here and someone's going to get fucked."

"No one's playing anyone. You think I'm playing her? Like I have the energy to date someone just to play them? Fuck, it's like you don't even know me at all."

"Well… If *you're* not playing *her*…" Rachel frowned at me with all the power of a territorial mother.

"What's that supposed to mean?" Xander asked.

"I mean she's JT's." She shrugged. "Seems to me she's playing you, man."

"She wasn't and isn't JT's," Xander said so forcibly even I believed it for a second.

Rachel scoffed and looked me over like I didn't impress her. I didn't blame her, honestly; I didn't feel very impressive on my best days, let alone on the days I was pretending to date a guy I hated.

"Yeah, that's not what the looks she gives him say. And, it's mighty convenient she's suddenly not one of his after she finds out he's with Nancy."

Xander wrapped an arm around me like that was going to prove anything.

"Look, I didn't know about them and they didn't know about us," I said.

"Oh, so now you jump in to your defence?" Rachel said.

"I didn't realise you needed my input to rag on me," I quipped and Rachel's snide glare was less disinterested annoyance and more dangerously provoked.

"You watch it, Minion, or I'll send you back to JT with more than a broken heart."

"Rach!" Xander yelled.

"What? She's always been one of his and she always will be."

"We're not even friends anymore!" I cried.

"Yeah, why is that?" she asked, suspiciously.

"Loyalty's obviously *not* her thing," Daniel commented.

"The whole thing just blew up in our faces and I didn't know how I was supposed to face them knowing we'd both been keeping secrets," I answered, not really caring anymore what Nancy would do because I doubted she'd have been stupid enough to get herself into such a situation.

"So, now Xand has to be a secret?" Rachel sneered.

"Well, just look how well *you're* reacting…" I said pointedly,

116

raising my eyebrows.

She opened her mouth and I expected her to have some witty retort. Instead, she closed it, frowned at me, paused, then said, "I'll be watching you. One wrong move and I'm coming for you."

"Rachel, come on!" Xander huffed as she threw him a scowl and walked to the other side of the group. Daniel watched us for a moment longer and I was actually more afraid of him than I was of Rachel just then.

"Well, wasn't that fun?" Greg chirped and Xander glared at him.

The rest of my day wasn't much better.

Xander went off to Music while I had History, and Greg was sent along with me almost like a protective detail. Rachel and like ninety-eight percent of the Bows may have looked on me in suspicion, but Greg and Miranda seemed to accept that Xander and I were dating with no issues. But then, Greg had been issueless for the past week. He was quickly becoming definitely good people.

After History, Greg then walked me to English to meet up with Xander. After which the three of us went to lunch, the boys scrapping over something as insignificant as who was playing on whose team in PE after lunch. Weirdly, I thought it felt like the most normal thing in the world, especially when Xander threw me a cheeky grin from Greg's headlock like he was letting me in on the game.

Lunch was spent in Xander's arms in what was apparently becoming the usual. He talked over and around me, taking a few moments here and there to whisper something to me as I tried to fit in. I had to constantly remind myself that this was the guy I'd spent years hating. I'd hated everything about all the Bows, but especially their King. Sitting among them and blindly pretending I belonged, I saw they were just normal people like my group…my old group.

Miranda had the same Free and then Math with me after lunch. We sat in the Study Room and giggled like thirteen year olds most of the way through. I couldn't even remember what we'd talk about in hushed whispers, but I'd started to fall for the ruse that I could belong in the Bows. Sure most of them hated me, but they did nothing more than look at me suspiciously because they knew anything else would displease Xander.

Who had his Free last lesson, so I didn't see him before I jumped on the bus to head home. By the time I'd trudged through the door, I'd lost all sense of settled I'd told myself I'd had while hanging out with Xander and the Bows.

"Hey, little sist– Hey! You okay?" Mark asked as I plodded up the stairs.

"Eh," I replied with a shrug.

"That little bitch and his new girlfriend giving you trouble?"

I shook my head and kept walking.

"Is this one of those times I follow and make you talk to me, or not so much?"

"Eh." I shrugged again and he laughed. I heard his footsteps on the stairs, then he overtook me and was throwing himself onto my bed as I slouched into my room.

"Okay. Spill the beans, sister," he said, his hands lacing behind his head.

I threw my bag against the side of my desk and dropped into my desk chair. "You remember the Bows?"

Of course when Mark was at school, they were led by Rachel's older sister Dee. But, Xander had been making a name for himself for a while.

Mark shuddered. "Yes. Hard to forget when I have to see the great wankstain that is Xander Bowen at least three times a week. Why? What's he up to now?"

I opened my mouth to spill everything, but I just couldn't find the words. Instead, I tried to talk about my feelings without going into detail.

"He's being a regular douche as always." Which was sort of not really close to the truth at all.

"Okay, so what does any of this have to do with him?"

I sighed. "You ever do something *really* stupid?"

"Yes," he answered simply. "That's my job as the big brother. I do the stupid shit so you don't. Why? What did you do?"

I frowned at his accusatory tone. "I didn't kill anyone, for what it's worth."

"Why does it sound like that's the preferable option in this scenario?"

"I just haven't been able to talk to Nancy and Jason since last Monday…"

"And…?"

"And, I made friends with a Bow…"

Movement from the corner of my eye caught my attention as Mark bolted up right. "You what?"

I shrugged. "I…uh, made friends with a Bow. Miranda, nice chick. Anyway, we've been hanging out a bit and… I don't know. It feels fake, but I tell myself it's not. And other times it feels real and I have to remind myself it's not." I was pretty sure I was half-talking about Xander here.

"Uh, it probably feels fake because it is. Keep reminding yourself that," Mark replied like he'd just had to correct me that the sky looked blue.

I gave him my best scowl. "Gee, thanks."

He shrugged unapologetically. "What do you want me to say, Doll? She's a Bow and you're JT's–"

I stood up suddenly, annoyed. "I wish people would stop saying that!"

"Is that Rachel skank still the Queen Bitch?" He changed the subject only slightly.

I nodded.

"And, how does she feel about you suddenly hanging out with them?"

"She thinks I'm a spy."

Mark snorted. "Sweet. You should use that to your advantage."

"What?" I asked. "How?"

"Relay the information to JT on how to bring them down from the inside."

"This is high school, Marco. Not the Cold War."

He shrugged again. "Much of a muchness."

I gave him a conceding nod on that one; some days, high school did feel like a cold war, especially when you had groups like the Bows against Jason's group.

"Ha, even better! Try to date King Douche and break his poor little heart." He was laughing to himself until he looked at me. "What? Jesus, don't tell me you hooked up with him?"

I shook my head. "Uh, no. No, of course I didn't. I have taste."

Mark snorted again. "Yeah, 'course you do. I don't want to know. Right," he lay his hands on his knees and pushed himself to standing, "Mum wants a Skype date tonight. What's the homework front look like?"

I looked at my bag like it held all the answers. "Uh, get an early start on the next History assignment and some Math stuff I think."

"How's the stats study going?"

"Terribly, and we shall never speak of it again."

Mark laughed. "Burn it in a fire?"

"Burn it in a fire," I agreed.

"I'll get the acid for the ashes."

"Much appreciated, good sir. Now, kindly vacate my abode so I can try to wrangle Charlemagne into something worthy of a pass mark."

"You'll be fine, little sister. You got all the brains after all."

"Oh, is that why you're not a uni?"

We both knew he didn't have classes on Wednesdays.

He huffed a laugh and came over to ruffle my hair before kissing it. "You're a comedienne, you know."

"I'm brillo-pads, brother."

"Yeah, you are. I'll come check on you later. Study hard."

"Will do."

And that was Mark, more parent than our dad.

As he left, I felt a slight pang of guilt; I couldn't remember the last time I'd lied to my brother. Actually, no...scrap that, I'd lied the day before when I told him I hadn't eaten the last chocolate biscuit – not that he'd believed me. Oh, yeah, and the slight mistruth about what I was talking to Xander about the week before. But, I'd never lied to him about anything that felt big. Maybe fake dating your ex-best friend's nemesis wasn't all that big a deal in the grand scheme of things, but it certainly felt like it just then.

Chapter Ten

On Thursday morning, I woke up minutes before my alarm was set to go off as the heat of Xander's sinful smirk from the library the week before rudely hit me like an express bus up the Freeway. I sat bolt upright in bed and tried furiously blinking it out of my head. But, no luck.

Told you I'd get to it eventually.

It just took a little longer than usual.

I spent the whole day pondering it and what the hell Xander and I were doing.

Thursday was a day Xander and I only had our first double together. Miranda and Greg both asked me what was wrong in classes I had with them. But, they seemed happy to let me sit in contemplative silence after I'd smiled and told them I was just tired after not sleeping well.

Which wasn't entirely a lie.

I just couldn't believe what I'd got myself into. Everything in my head was telling me I was an idiot and to just get out before it was too late, back-peddle rapidly, make a slow exit from the room keeping your eye on the enemy. The enemy which, in this case, was Xander of course.

But, I couldn't stop myself waiting for his smile or looking forward to the way his hand fit in mine. I knew it was all for show, my head had no trouble remembering that Xander Bowen was *the* epitome of bad news. But, my heart could be found doing those stupid little skips and my lips turned up to match his smile whenever he flashed it my way.

I had to hand it to him, boy was a good actor.

His eyes were always warm and welcoming, they didn't wander and Greg had told me he'd refused the advances of three different girls point blank because of me – although I hadn't been named by name at the time – the week before. Which I thought was mighty suspicious considering we hadn't come to any sort of agreement until Sunday. Still, I sort of understood the madness in doing something to save face.

I was rearranging my locker after History before heading home – a last lesson Free meant I was free from school for the day – when I felt hands on my hips and a nose against my neck. I jumped, but the increasingly familiar scent that was Xander enveloped me. I still felt a little weird about it, but I remembered we were doing a thing here. Still, there was doing a thing and taking said thing to the extreme.

"What are you doing?" I asked him. "Don't you have class?"

I felt him nod as his arms wrapped around me, somewhat hampering my ability to repack my bag, but he seemed unbothered by that. "I do, but I wanted to catch you first. You heading home now?"

I lay my hand over his arm absently. "I was going to… Why does it sound like you're hoping for otherwise?"

"Well…" he started, and I could tell he wanted something, "I was thinking maybe we could get together tonight?"

"You do remember we're…" I looked around, turned to face

him, and lowered my voice, "only *fake dating*, right?"

He chuckled and it sent an unnecessary tingle running over my skin. "Yes, I do. I was actually hoping you might help me with the–"

"Xander!" I hissed as his hand slid down my back to rest on my arse. "Hands in new places, mister! Hands in new places."

Something shot through his eyes too fast for me to pick up, but he was smiling again momentarily. "Can't blame a guy for trying," he said as he held his hands up in defence.

"Can and will," I said, shaking my head and trying not to smile. "Can and will." I turned back to my locker. "Now, what did you want?"

"English study."

I nodded. "Ah. Okay, sure. Library?"

"I've been in there multiple times this year. I think that's plenty."

"Oh, but you got your first girlfriend out of it. Maybe it'll bring you luck," I teased and he sniggered.

"Yeah, sure. No. I was thinking mine or yours?"

I paused and turned a suspicious frown on him. "Preference?"

He shrugged. "Not really. I've got my car, so I can drive you home, we can study, then I can head home. Or, I can drive you home after? I'm easy."

"The whole school knows that's true."

Xander snorted.

"Mister Bowen! Don't you have somewhere to be?" Mr Burnett asked, appearing in the hallway.

Xander threw him a charming smile. "Sorry, sir. Just needed to ask Holly for her help with the poetry study."

Mr Burnett, like every other teacher at that damned school, fell for Xander's wiles. "Putting an effort into your study, Xander?"

Xander shrugged. "You know me, sir. Very dedicated."

Mr Burnett looked between us. "I was worried about the rumours, kids. But, maybe Holly will be a positive influence on you, hey?"

"She definitely has a *certain* effect on me, sir," he answered then breathed out heavily as I smacked him in the stomach.

Mr Burnett failed to hide his smile behind a mask of professional disapproval. "Get to class, Xander. I'll see you two tomorrow." And, he popped back into his classroom, calling for them to settle down.

"I've got to go. Meet me at my locker after school?"

"Don't you have practice tonight?" I asked.

He gave me a guilty as sin look.

"Oh, a clever ruse to get me to come to practice?" I gave a sarcastic laugh.

He started walking away from me backwards and gave an endearing shrug. "I'm nothing if not an optimist, babe."

I looked at him in amused incredulity. "Babe, now? Well, you're definitely something. I'll see you after school, yes!" I laughed as he did a little bow, spun, and jogged towards the gym.

So, instead of trudging to the bus stop, I trudged to the Study Room and slid into one of the many free desks, because who the hell stayed at school when they didn't have to? I'll tell you, about five or six super studious kids, me included now.

I sat through the last lesson, trying to make stats stick in my head. When the bell finally rang for the end of school, I didn't really bother hurrying to Xander's locker; we both knew where I was so he'd find me if he thought I was taking too long – a week of hanging out with the guy and I knew that much.

God, was that all? It felt like so much longer.

And, I wasn't sure if that was a good thing or a bad thing yet.

"Hey. You good, babe?"

I looked up and saw Xander closing his locker, an actual ounce of concern on his face.

"Is 'babe' going to be a thing now?" I asked.

He grinned, but he looked uncertain. "Should it not be?"

I shrugged. "I just don't know how I feel about 'babe'."

He dropped his bag and wrapped his arms around my waist, burying his nose in my neck. "How about darling?"

I giggled as my arms went around his shoulders. "What are we, fifty?"

"Sweetheart?"

"That'd be *from* the fifties."

"Honey?" He pulled back to look at me.

I wrinkled my nose in mock-disgust and he nudged it with his.

"I like it when you do that," he said softly.

My heart did that that thing where it hitched, then hid in case someone might have been watching. I cleared my throat and looked down. "Don't you need to get to practice, Mr Star Striker?"

"Like you know what a striker is," he scoffed teasingly.

"You're the forward responsible for getting the goals," I said as though talking to a particularly young child and I saw those light brown eyes widen in humoured surprise.

"Well, look at you being all fangirl."

I laughed. "It has nothing to do with you, thank you."

A smirk played at his lips. "That's right, your brother was senior captain before me, wasn't he? I hear he's captain of an under-21s club team now…?" he teased.

"He says like he is just so important that he never pays attention to his captain."

"Well, I am very good."

"Are you?"

I knew he was good. Even Mark admitted on numerous occasions that Xander was good. Much to Mark's displeasure, having Xander in the same team as him was only good for soccer.

"Not as good as your brother," Xander admitted.

"Oh my God, was that a compliment for someone else to your own detriment?" I gasped playfully.

He picked me up and swung me around so I giggled. "You take that to your grave, pookie."

I snorted completely in a completely undignified manner and burst into laughter.

Xander put me down and cocked his head to the side, his face deadpan. "Not pookie, then?"

I tried so hard to keep a straight face, but I just couldn't. "Come on, *babe*. Let's get you to practice."

He grinned cheekily, snatched up his bag and we headed for the secondary oval – because, of course stupid rugby got the main oval.

"I feel like you're not concentrating," I said, rolling onto my stomach and looking at him swinging in my desk chair. "Xander!"

"Huh?" he asked, looking up and I rolled my eyes at him.

"Where are you?"

A mischievous twinkle lit his eyes.

"Strike that. I don't want to know," I sighed and rolled back onto my back. "Okay. Banjo Patterson, remember?"

He said nothing and I sat up to face him. He was giving me the weirdest look.

"Did I flash you? My bad, but I *am* wearing stockings so really it can't have been all that exciting."

He blinked. "What? No…"

I looked at him for a moment. Something seemed to be going through his mind. And, I could tell mainly because there was that slight hint of exertion on his face that he got whenever he had to think about things more serious than his next hook up or soccer.

"What's up?" I asked.

He rolled the chair over to me, keeping his eyes glued to mine.

"Xander, I so don't have the energy for whatever crazy thing is going through your tiny, pea-shaped brain right now…" I sighed.

He stopped when the castors of the chair hit the base of my bed. There was a slight frown on his face as though he was debating something. He leant towards me, our noses bumping and I went cross-eyed to watch it.

"What?" I huffed.

Something flashed through his eyes, then his hand was on my cheek and he'd pressed his lips to mine. My brain froze and I jerked backwards, frowning at him in confusion.

He looked slightly confused himself.

"What was that?" I asked slowly.

That confusion deepened.

"Xander… Why did you kiss me? Fake dating remember?"

He bit his lip like whatever debate was going on in his head was seriously wigging him out. He ran a hand over his chin and sat back, breathing out heavily. Suddenly, the fact that he'd kissed me was irrelevant. Suddenly, I was more concerned that he hadn't liked kissing me.

Because, of course it made sense that I *wanted* King Douche to like kissing me.

He folded his arms. "Fake dating, yes. Believably fake dating?"

"Xander, where is this going?"

"Look, I have a reputation–"

"I am *not* sleeping with you!"

"I'm… " He huffed a breath. "We're not going there right now."

"Or, ever!"

"Not what I meant. Look, no one in the school is going to believe we're dating – regardless of what we say – if we never kiss or they don't see some kind of physical attraction going on. As much as I like you, that's just not me, Holly." He shrugged like he felt he should apologise, but he wasn't really sorry.

My heart skittered and my brain glossed over the fact he'd just said he liked me. "If this is some weak-arse attempt to hook up with me…"

He stood and ran a hand through his hair. "I'm not going to lie to you and say I don't want to, okay? You're just…" He turned to me for a moment and waved a hand at me.

"I'm just what?" I asked, suddenly panicked about exactly whatever I might have been.

"I'd never noticed, okay?" he asked.

"Never noticed what?"

"I mean, I'd sort of noticed. But, I'd never *really* noticed."

"Noticed what?" Seriously, I had to know what the hell was wrong with me.

"That you're… That you're gorgeous."

I frowned. "I'm not gorgeous…" I wasn't, it was just fact. I didn't think I was hideous or anything, but I knew I wasn't gorgeous.

He turned back to me sharply; the confusion was strong in this one. "What?"

I looked down at myself like I could actually see all of me. "I'm not gorgeous, Xander. I'm okay with that. I mean, I'd hate to be Nancy and have guys all over me all the time. One or two might be nice, but the constant flirting and–"

"That rank bitch has nothing on you."

"That's my best…was my best friend you're talking about there," I warned him.

He shrugged and ignored that fact. "That's not to say I'd never thought about you like that. But, that was before–"

"I am still not hooking up with you."

He shrugged again, almost like he was giving up the fight. "Fine. But, if people start questioning our relationship, it won't be my fault."

"Dude," I laughed, "if you want to kiss me, you can just admit it. But, trying to make something out of it…" I shook my head. "I would have thought resorting to tricks was beneath you."

"Firstly," he started, "it's not tricks. I'm serious. People are going to get suspicious, especially when we haven't changed our statuses on Facebook–"

"Because, it's not real if it's not on Facebook," I muttered to myself sarcastically.

"And, secondly," he stepped towards me, "of course I fucking want to kiss you," he grumbled as he took my hand, pulled me up, cupped my face with both hands and gave me the kind of kiss that was supposed to knock your socks off.

Except, I'm wearing stockings…

Still, I felt myself lean into him, my arms found their way around his neck as his went around my back and pulled me closer. My heart felt like it was doing a Jimmy Fallon victory dance and I told it to shut up.

Because, yes Xander was hot – to deny that would be like trying to maintain the Earth was flat in the twenty-first century – but I didn't like him. We were just using each other to mutual benefit.

As he kissed me with more enthusiasm than I thought I was worth or could elicit in anyone, I wondered if this is what lust felt like. And, I mean *proper* lust. Like the kind teen movies say teenage boys have that lead them to do stupid things and go through life with their smaller head in charge. The kind that throws all rationale and all sense out the window and literally says 'fuck it' – as in, go do that person now.

Then, my brain shut down and I just felt it, got completely caught up in the moment. His hands were warm on my body as he held me tightly, his lips were sure and – I had to admit – kind of demanding. But, I kind of liked it. Okay, I really liked it.

After… God I didn't even know how long, he finally pulled away from me, almost reluctantly, and stared at me like he'd never seen me before. We both breathed heavily and while I might not have seen it in real life often, I recognised eyes full of heated lust when I saw them. Because, yes, I watched as many rom-coms as I did horror movies.

"Fuck me, nice girls don't kiss like that," he said, leaning his forehead to mine.

"Cliché much?" I chuckled.

He smiled. "Clichés are clichés because they're clichéd," he said philosophically.

I smirked. "How many nice girls have you kissed, anyway?"

He huffed a breathless laugh and smiled. "Fair point."

We just stared at each other for a moment, until I forcibly reminded myself that I didn't like this guy. I cleared my throat, gave him my best intimidating awkward smile, and took a step back as I tucked a piece of hair behind my ear.

Thank God no one else is home.

"Well… That was…uh, that was certainly a kiss." I nodded in agreement with myself.

"Yeah, it was."

"So, if you felt the need to kiss me in front of people, then that could be a thing that could happen. I guess."

"Okay, then."

"But, you know, only as necessary." *Or, all the damned time!* an annoying voice in my head piped up.

"Of course, just enough to keep up appearances."

"Yeah. But, I mean, I think we'll be able to sell the attraction thing?"

Xander huffed another laugh. "Yeah, we're not going to have any trouble in that department."

"Good, okay. So, that's good then."

Oh my God, what was wrong with me? All I could think about was kissing him again. My skin tingled just thinking about it and I had to stop myself from taking another step towards him. This was ridiculous. I did not like him. I did not want him. It was just convenience. And yes, if he kissed me at school, then…

Then, I'd probably launch him into the lockers and give him a kiss to make *his* knees go weak.

"Good God," I muttered and turned around.

"What?" he asked.

"Uh, nothing. Um, so… Did that have anything to do with the lack of concentration? Or, is there anything else I can help with?"

"Well, you already said you weren't sleeping with me…"

I whirled around in shock, but his tone of regret was completely

132

overruled by the teasing grin on his face and I couldn't help but laugh.

"You're not as funny as you think you are."

"You said that about my charm too, and look where that got you."

I pointed a finger at him. "Kissing you for the sake of a charade does not mean I find you remotely charming."

He grinned widely, his eyebrows wiggling. "I still have eight days to make you realise you already think I'm charming."

I breathed out heavily. "Get a B on the poetry quiz and I'll reconsider where I stand on the charm factor."

I pointed to my desk chair and he dropped into it. I pushed him backwards with my foot and he laughed.

"Can't bear to be too close to me?" he teased.

"You just stay over there and concentrate," I said slightly breathlessly, and it was all the admission he was going to get.

Chapter Eleven

I was walking down the hallway toward the Study Room on Friday morning – because I'd decided to go to school rather than risk talking to Mark – when I saw Xander walking towards me. By the wicked smirk on his face, he had nothing pure on his mind.

Mind you, after his kiss the night before, my mind was thinking that the gutter looked like a mighty fine place to have a stroll for a while; none of this high road business for me, apparently, I was all for the low road.

Xander stopped me in the middle of the hallway and took my face in his hands, his eyes lighting up.

"If I kiss you, does that count as necessary or unnecessary?" he asked and my heart fluttered a little excited flamenco.

"Good morning to you, too," I answered, trying not to smile at him.

"Good morning." He gave me one of the most sincere grins I'd ever seen. "I mean, I just wondered if keeping up appearances now was a good idea, or…?"

My smile broke through unbidden. "You need to get to class."

"Maybe a kiss from my girlfriend will give me luck?"

Oh, I wanted to but I was not going to fall for him.

"What? Have you got the PE Olympics today or something?" I

asked.

"Maybe."

"Is Greg likely to beat you?"

"No."

"I'm going to put that in the unnecessary basket."

"And, if I'd said yes?"

"Still unnecessary."

He leant forward conspiratorially and it only made me want to kiss him more. "Well, how do I know which is which?"

"Let's go with the rule that, if you have to ask, it's unnecessary."

He nodded as he thought about that. "Okay, I can work with that. I'll see you at Recess."

I nodded, smiled, and walked past him. I was just starting to feel slightly disappointed he hadn't kissed me when suddenly he had my hand. He pulled me to him and kissed me. It was more than just a peck, but he pulled away before my brain shorted out and I felt the need to slam him against the wall. Even so, my breath came less easily than I would have liked. A million people could have been staring and I didn't care, because he was looking at me in a way that made me never want to look anywhere else.

Oh, that was dangerous.

"What was that?" I asked.

He smirked. "I decided I'd just never ask." And with that, he winked at me and sauntered down the hallway, meeting up with an unimpressed Daniel half-way.

I stood, stunned for a few moments, until I felt someone shove my arm and found Nancy glaring at me. With a condescension I didn't know I could possess, I looked her up and down.

"What?" I asked.

"So, what was that? 'Help me tell Jason how I feel, Nance, what do I say?' And you were dating *him* the whole time?"

I scoffed. "Says you. You were with Jason while you were goading me into it! What? You wanted to make me feel like a bigger idiot when he shut me down? You didn't even have the decency to tell me!"

"We were going to." There was something hard about her eyes, even as the rest of her face was looking appropriately apologetic and sincere.

"Oh yeah, when? When I got your wedding invitation?"

"I didn't know how to tell you, okay? It just happened. One minute we were laughing, then we were kissing. We only made it official after I talked to you on Sunday."

"This is so not making me feel better. I thought we were always honest about him."

"I didn't know how I felt about him until we kissed."

Mark's words flew around my head and I was sure I saw written on her face how clearly that statement was a lie.

But, I was going to try to be the bigger person. "I wouldn't have minded so much if you'd just given me a heads' up–"

"What would a heads' up have mattered? You were with the King of the Bows almost a week before." *Oh yeah, good point...* I'd need to remember that. "And I mean, King Douche? Holly, what were you thinking?"

I was certainly not thinking what I knew she was thinking; namely that she'd be quite happy to sleep with him and she was seriously wishing that she'd thought of doing it first.

"The heart wants what the heart wants, Nancy. You should know that better than anyone," I replied icily. "Besides, you've told me on numerous occasions that you'd do him, so how is dating him any worse?"

"Because a quick screw is nothing. Dating means you *like* the guy."

I shrugged. "So what if I do? He's funny and he's nice and he's sweet and he's got abs like you wouldn't believe." *Jesus, how much of that wasn't a lie?* "And, the Bows aren't actually all that bad."

Okay, so all but three hated me and one of them was only was lukewarm but putting on a good show of being my boyfriend. But, Nancy didn't need to know any of that.

"Sorry? You think you're a Bow now?" she scoffed and looked me over like dirty garbage. "Well, I guess you will be as soon as he's bored with you."

Oh, that riled me up. That got a fire going in my belly and made me want to rip her to pieces.

I mean, she wouldn't have been wrong if Xander and I were *actually* dating. But, for some reason, I still bristled against the implication he was just using me; using me on my terms was fine, any other terms and not so much.

My heart shook its fist at her.

"Do you know what, Nancy? You can go get fucked. You *and* Jason. If half a life-time of friendship wasn't enough for either of you to be honest with me, then I don't want or need you in my life. I knew how you'd feel about me dating Xander, and honestly I wasn't entirely sure it would stick because he *is* King Douche after all and Jason was my best friend. But, you two made the decision simple for me. It wasn't even a choice; you two dumped me before I even thought about it. So, I can have Xander and you two can have each other. You don't seem to need me anyway."

Nancy's eyes shone the way they did when she was trying not to cry when we watched a rom-com and the couple at the end finally get together because she knew we'd tease her. Except these weren't tears of happiness, these were tears of sadness and annoyance – if they were even real – and I felt my own welling.

"Well, I see how it is then. If half a lifetime of friendship wasn't worth *you* being honest with *us*, then we don't want you either."

"Fine."

"Fine."

We both made to storm away at the same time. Only problem was, we both had the double Free. So we walked awkwardly together, as far apart across the hallway as possible.

When I got to the classroom, Miranda was just arriving from the other direction. She threw a look between us and sympathy flickered across her face. She put an arm around me wordlessly and walked us into the classroom. I wasn't quite so oblivious to not notice the shade she threw Nancy or the glare she sent Jason's way either.

And, who would have thought; a Bow standing up for one of JT's minions?

It seems like maybe that cold day in Hell was heading our way after all.

Miranda was holding my hand as we walked out of last lesson Math and Xander frowned as he pushed himself off the lockers behind him like he was going to rain bloody thunder down on someone.

I'd put the altercation between me and Nancy aside for most of the day, but Math without the stoic presence of Xander beside me had seen Nancy act like a complete dick.

She'd talked to my ex-friends in a frightfully obvious stage-whisper about how I gave it up to Xander weeks ago and had been sadly begging him to date me ever since. The going story was that Xander had finally acquiesced if only to shut me up. According to Nancy, I was completely smitten with him, totally obsessed, and was probably a little mental. Jason did nothing through the whole thing other than look slightly pained and look at me almost apologetically.

But I mean, how sorry could he be if he didn't tell her to stop?

Heartbreak aside, I could definitely see now that sharing my fruit rollup with him on the third day of Reception had been a terrible plan. In fact, while I'd be busy thinking it had brought me over ten years of solid friendship and fun, what it had really done was break my heart into a thousand pieces and get them stomped all over.

Even the sight of Xander at the end of the day hadn't been enough to do much more for my heart than to have it wave its little white flag at him while it was face down in the dirt.

"What happened?" he asked, looking to Miranda for an explanation.

I was glad even he couldn't make this new betrayal better. But I was supposed to go to him for comfort, it's what couples did. So, I did. I just shook my head and walked straight into his arms, burying my face in his jumper. He hugged me unhesitatingly. And once in his arms, I told myself the effect of his deodorant and the weight of his arms around me was far less comforting that it actually was.

"Rand?" he asked.

"The little bitch is spreading rumours about our Doll."

I looked at her sharply.

"What?" Xander asked quickly to my reaction.

"Nothing. She just… Doll?"

Miranda smiled. "Holly. Dolly. Doll. Yeah?"

That was a seriously weird coincidence.

"Only my family calls me Doll…" I said slowly and watched as Miranda's eyes softened along with her smile.

"Well you're Xand's girlfriend, Doll. So, that makes us family now."

Oh my God. I wasn't sure I could take any more emotion at that point. But, at least this one was positive – so long as she wasn't still lulling me in that false sense of security. It still made my eyes water though.

Xander rubbed my back comfortingly. "Come on. We'll miss the bus if we wait too long." His tone was hard and, as I turned, I saw Jason down the hall watching us as Nigel jostled him.

On impulse, I leant up and kissed Xander hard and the boy wasn't shy about returning it ten-fold. I didn't even object when he touched my arse this time.

When I pulled away, he chuckled knowingly as his eyes flew behind me to Jason. But, he said nothing with Miranda so close. He merely took my hand and the three of us headed out, catching up with Greg as we went.

"Heya, Holly!" he cried excitedly and I noticed Jason's frown before I decided to stop worrying about him.

It was one thing for Jason to be dating Nancy – that I probably would have eventually come to terms with once the shock wore off and I'd stopped acting like an idiot – but he'd sided with her when he didn't stop her talking shit about me. So, I was done with him and I was done worrying about him. I was done with both of them. I'd show them I had something better and they were the ones missing out.

If the tables had been turned, Nancy certainly wouldn't have been shy in pretending she was having the time of her life. That girl could make the worst of all flus look enjoyable and fashionable.

"Whoa! What has our Holly looking so glum?" Greg asked, sounding legitimately concerned.

"JT's little bitch is spreading lies," Miranda spat and I was surprised at the vehemence in her tone.

"Settle, Rand," Greg chuckled, then was all business. "Right, how are we getting back at the skank?"

"Play nice, mate," Xander said quietly.

"Fuck that for a joke. If that mole–"

"Dude, she was Holly's best friend for years. Pump the breaks a little, yeah?" Xander said quietly over my head as though I wouldn't hear him then.

"Sorry, Holl," Greg mumbled, looking legitimately sorry.

I shrugged. "It's okay." And, it sort of was and wasn't at the same time; I appreciated him getting fired up on my account, but I was at odds about him talking like that about someone my heart had trouble letting go of. "Seems like a waste of friendship if you ask me, the way she's been acting."

"Well we're behind you, Doll," Miranda said.

"Doll? I like it!" Greg laughed, nodding at me like he really did just accept his king's rival's ex-best friend.

Xander took my hand, lacing his fingers with mine, and leant to my ear. "Is 'doll' better than 'babe'?"

"Pet names aren't required," I laughed.

He grinned, pressed a quick kiss to my lips and put his arm around me. I reached up and took the hand that was draped over my shoulder as we headed to the bus stop, blinking the slight rain out of my eyes.

"Ugh, you two are far too adorable," Greg gagged. "I get she's your first, man. But, I was looking forward to a burger this arvo! Don't ruin it for me, please."

Xander laughed. "Well if you can't eat it, I'll be happy to, man."

Greg shook his head with a laugh.

"What?" Rachel asked as we joined most of the other Bows at the bus stop.

"Greg's grossed out by Doll and Xander."

Rachel's eyebrows rose at the new nickname and her lips twitched, but she didn't mention it. "Trust the biggest man-whore to be hiding a mushy idiot," she said and I wondered if I was the only one who thought her teasing was a little less actual teasing; I could tell she was simultaneously supporting his decisions and warning him against them.

That was a new side to Queen Bitch Rachel than I'd ever seen before.

"Naw. You jealous, Rach?" Xander cooed, reaching over to ruffle her hair and she ducked out of the way, trying to hide a laugh behind a scowl.

"Dude! Don't be a dick," she chuckled.

I stood among the Bows, watching them chat and laugh and jostle, wondering how it was all so easy.

Five days ago, I hated these people.

Now, I wondered exactly why I'd hated them.

I couldn't say I liked any of them really, but each day I forgot a little more why I'd hated them. As far as I could remember, I just had. We knew they were all shallow, arrogant, rude, rich arseholes and we hated them. It was just the done thing by the kids who hung out with Jason to hate the Bows, and vice versa.

Rachel, Daniel, Sabrina – well, there were quite a few of them

– and almost everyone else largely didn't speak to me or spared me shifty glances, but I somehow didn't feel uncomfortable or bothered by it – their behaviour was really no different than it had been the week before. There was something I admired about that. And, I actually wasn't sure if it was because it meant they didn't just blindly follow everything Xander said or if it was because it meant they weren't as fickle and shallow as I'd always thought.

Greg was a little loud and boisterous at times, but he seemed to try to make me laugh, so I didn't hate hanging out with him. But, I still didn't know him well enough to like him. I knew enough to know he was good people. But you don't just like everyone who's good people, do you?

Miranda could have been as shallow as Rachel and just great at hiding it, but we joked and laughed and talked about things that girlfriends talk about, things I used to talk about with Nancy, even things I never felt comfortable talking to Nancy about. I was starting to like her, but there was this voice in the back of my head that told me she might have an ulterior motive just because she was a Bow.

And, Xander… God, where did I even start with him? The whole school knew he was a player and a cocky bastard, he was rude and condescending, and he liked none of the same things I did. But, he was also funny and sexy and there was something sweet about him, even if it was all in aid of maintaining a charade. After years of thinking he was an awful person, I couldn't quite bring myself to think well of him. But, I kind of liked being around him. I kind of liked the way he made me feel, whether that was real or even if it was fake.

It was amazing how well you could get by when you forced away all of the hang-ups you'd carried around for so long. And, I got by. Until my brain reminded me I was hanging around the Bows and I felt a moment of weirdness. But, it passed as Xander took my hand or ran his fingers over my cheek, as Miranda threw me a conspiratorial smile or talked about a cute boy with me, as Greg teased Xander with me or stood up for me against him, and I just didn't have time to remember I was living in whacko world for too long when I was with them.

I felt a tug and was pulled out of my musings with a humoured look from Xander.

"You good, Doll?"

I smirked and followed him onto the bus, which was filling to capacity quickly – apparently the only way to go to town on a Friday was by bus.

We shuffled on, packed tighter than sardines. The Maple Ridge Grammar kids filled the vehicle with rowdy chatter and laughter as they jostled each other.

I could never reach the hand holds easily, but we were packed in so tight someone was likely to break my fall anyway so I didn't bother so much. But, Xander obviously had other ideas about my safety. He grabbed hold of the top bar and wound an arm around me almost completely absent-mindedly as he talked with Greg and Daniel.

As Miranda and I were debating whether Kylie Jenner's ripped-butt jeans were something people should copy or not (let it be noted, Nancy would have said yes and would have thoroughly disapproved if I'd even hinted no, whereas Miranda had no qualms), I felt Xander's hand slide down so it was resting more on my arse than my back. I stopped in the middle of whatever I was saying to Miranda, my mouth open.

"What?" Miranda chuckled.

I wrinkled my nose and turned to look at Xander. He didn't turn to me, but I saw his smirk – he knew what he'd done...was doing... – and he gave my arse a slight squeeze. I frowned and gave him a slight elbow to the ribs. I felt him chuckle as he rearranged to pull my back against his front.

Thankfully, town wasn't too far from school – in fact, on a good day and when we weren't so lazy, you could walk there easily. We piled off the bus, Xander offering me his hand as I tried to judge the distance to the sidewalk so I didn't end up with my foot in a puddle.

I gave him a wry grin in thanks, took his hand and I half-hopped, was half-pulled off the bus. As I landed, he caught me round the middle and kissed me.

"Okay, yes. You are sickeningly sweet. Dude, get out of the way!" Greg said with a wink to me. He smacked Xander upside the head as he went passed.

Xander put his arm around my shoulders and we followed behind the rest of the raucous group, falling behind a little as the others trooped down Rundle Mall like we owned the place, still laughing and jostling each other. There was very little difference following behind the Bows or Jason's group, really. And, for a moment, I could pretend nothing had changed in my life, I could pretend that my friends were still my friends.

"You doing okay?" Xander asked softly after a while.

I looked at him, not sure if I was or not. "Should I not be?"

He shrugged and leant his cheek on my head for a moment. "Dunno. Just thought JT's minion might be feeling a little...conflicted about being out in town with the Bows."

I scuffed my foot along the pavement and his hand slid off my shoulder to catch my hand. "It's weird, but at the same time it's

145

not. You're not the people I'm used to, but I can pretend for a while that I've been with you forever."

I'd spent years fitting in; just because they were different people didn't mean the concept was any different.

He stopped me as the others disappeared into the Myer building. He looked down at me with that mischievous glint. "With me?"

I rolled my eyes. "Not with *you*, with you. With the Bows."

His arms went around my waist and I leant mine on the lapels of his blazer. "You can admit you like being with me."

"I'm not with you, Xander. Remember?" I said slowly, finding he wasn't the only one I was reminding.

He smiled and nudged my nose with his. "I remember. But, for all intents and purposes…"

He leant closer, but I pulled away as his lips headed for mine.

"What are you doing?" I chuckled, watching those cognac eyes carefully.

"Keeping up appearances, Doll."

"Xander, there's no one here to keep up appearances for…"

"Call it practise."

I put my hand to his chest. "Call it a complication."

"It's not a complication. Practise makes perfect."

I should not have found him adorable. I should not have liked the humour in his eyes or the way he looked at me. I should have found him annoying and pushy and stupid. So, I tried to hide my smile.

"Let's not make things harder than they need to be, huh?"

He pulled me closer and ducked his nose to my ear. "I don't think that's possible."

I laughed at the implication – shouldn't have, did – and pushed him away. "Of course. And, it's back to your cock again. Come on.

146

We're putting on an act for the people at school, let's not confuse ourselves what's going on."

My hand caught his and I pulled him towards the opening to the building.

"Nothing wrong with having a bit of fun with it," Xander said, persuasively.

I laughed, "I thought you were bored with girls?"

"You're not just some girl, Holly."

I was going to chastise him for his terrible flirting, but didn't have the chance. He'd pulled me back to him and was kissing me.

I couldn't decide what I wanted more; to keep kissing him or to never kiss him again.

He was nothing I wanted in a guy, but his touch made my heart sit up and pay attention and my skin tingle excitedly. It was crazy, but I couldn't deny that; he had an effect on me that was at once undesirable and addictive.

So, I kissed him a little while longer before we followed the others into the Myer building and down to the food court where Greg and I had a fry fight and Miranda and I half-heartedly argued about the best Bubble Tea flavour at Teaz.

Chapter Twelve

Xander walked towards me purposefully, a heat in his eyes that had no trouble making me pay attention straight away this time. I flushed and I was frozen to the spot.

He kissed me hard, one hand on my cheek and the other on my hip pulling me towards him. My stomach sort of slithered to the floor in a mindlessly giggly puddle, my brain shorted out, and my heart happily flopped down and made little angels in the lava that was burning pleasantly through me.

I grabbed the front of his shirt and ripped it open, buttons flying everywhere, and ran my hands down his smooth torso. Every muscle felt like perfection under my hands and his skin was blazing hot.

He picked me up effortlessly and my legs went around his waist like I planned to climb that man-mountain to the pinnacle of pleasure. He slammed me against the wall, his hand running down my leg and bringing it closer around him. His fingers slid under my shirt, igniting every place he touched. He skimmed past the sensitive flesh of my breast as he slid his hand around to my back and drew me closer, like he couldn't get enough.

I arched into him and–

And, real-world-Xander was totally talking to me.

I blinked, trying to pull myself out of the weird sudden daydream I'd found myself in. I wasn't quite as enamoured with the ostentatiousness of his house as I was with his half-naked body, apparently. But, that didn't mean that I didn't finally hear him through the fog of lust my brain was quite happy rolling around in while I was desperately trying to drag it out. It was like trying to drag Doug away from Vern's favourite poop spot.

"...led me to thinking we should go on a date," Xander was saying as he pulled the water out of the fridge.

Okay, I was definitely paying attention now. "A date?"

He nodded. "Yeah. A date."

"Xander, how many times do we have to go over this? Fake. Dating." I spoke slowly, wondering if he'd hit his head at his game that morning. "Fake dating does not require *real* dates."

He leant a hip against the bench and popped a grape into his mouth. "I didn't know you were an authority on fake dating now."

"Oh, I wrote the handbook. Didn't you know?"

He snorted. "I'll bet."

"I thought we were studying? Won't Greg be here soon?"

Xander shrugged. "For Greg, two o'clock means maybe three thirty."

I sighed. "And you couldn't have told me? I could have stayed home and done my own stuff."

"Exactly *because* you would have come later," he said with a cheeky little smile.

I rolled my eyes. "I have the next vocab test next week too you know."

"Which you could pass in your sleep. You're amazing at French."

"Because I study!"

"You study too hard. Haven't you been spending every night for the last two weeks studying? Every time I've messaged you, you've been studying. It's boring, doll."

I crossed my arms over my chest protectively, feeling somewhat defensive and just a little awkward. "Well, it takes my mind off the fact that I lost my two best friends and I'm pretending to date the biggest arsehole at school."

"Ha!" Xander cried and I looked up quickly, my eyebrow raised in question. "So, I beat the git at *something* at least."

I tried valiantly to hold back the smile his triumphant look elicited. "*That* is not an achievement to be proud of."

He shrugged. His whole demeanour was his usual level of nonchalance, except for his eyes…those were watching me carefully. "Beating him at anything is an achievement to be proud of. Although…" he walked over to me and put his hands on my hips, and I pretended that I couldn't look straight ahead and just stare at all that beauty, "being the first to kiss you was probably the sweetest of them all."

"First? Do you actually think you were unfortunate enough to be my first kiss, or that you anticipate Jason will want to kiss me one day?"

He smirked, but his eyes were hard. "Unfortunate's *not* the word I'd use. And, I thought that was the whole point of this little exercise? Make the git jealous so he'll realise he picked the wrong minion?"

I would have bristled at the moniker, but it had seemed to become more of an in-joke between me and…well not all the Bows – obviously – but more were less hostile to me by Friday than there'd been on Tuesday.

"Half the point," I reminded him. "Well, one-third the point. I thought I was helping you avoid the flirts *and* helping you get one over Jason?"

He nodded and his hands slid around to my back. "This is true."

"So really, you're getting more out of this than me."

"It could be seen that way I guess, yes," he said hesitatingly, like he wasn't sure if I was going somewhere he wanted with this.

"Why *do* you want to avoid the girls, Xander? Did they get boring?" I teased.

"Yes."

I blinked in surprise. "What?"

He sighed and pulled away from me as he ran a hand through his hair in a gesture I was starting to recognise as him feeling slightly uncomfortable. "I… Wow. Thinking about explaining it to you now sounds kind of shallow."

"That is nothing less than I'd expect from you, King Douche."

He threw a quick grin at me. "Okay, yeah. I got bored. The girls at school aren't challenging, there's no thrill of the chase, they don't make you work for it. It's just all shallow and meaningless and monotonous. I mean sure, it's *satisfying*. If you get my drift–"

I hadn't, but I did now. "Drift got." I grimaced.

"–but it's not exciting. I decided I'd had enough. I figured that my time was better spent on my soccer, maybe my grades so Coach doesn't bench me. And, you were the perfect beard for that."

"Not quite the slang you're looking for… But, I'd say those are sort of admirable goals you've got there."

"And, if I admit the goals came after the boredom?"

I snorted. "Then, I'd say that sounds like you."

"You know, I like that you don't tell me what you think I want to hear," he sniggered.

"I'm here to keep up appearances, Xander. Not to be

151

satisfying."

"You'd certainly be a challenge…" he said slowly, with a hint of flirtation.

I laughed and took a step back. "Well, I'd certainly make you work for it. Only, there won't be anything waiting for you at the end. So, don't get your hopes up."

"It's not my hopes I need to keep down." He winked and I cleared my throat like that was going to suddenly stop my cheeks flushing red.

"Just here to keep the wolves away, remember?"

He shrugged like it didn't bother him why I was there. Or maybe like we both knew I was there for another reason, but he wasn't going to correct me. Except I wasn't there for any other reason and I thought we both needed a reminder.

"Which brings me back to the date thing. Why do you think we should go on a date?"

"Seems like something a couple might do," he said as he pulled himself up onto the bench and I told myself I didn't avidly stare at the way his stomach muscles moved.

"Why don't you have a shirt on?" I blurted out.

He chuckled. "Like what you see?"

Yes. "No."

"There's no shame in admitting it," he said. *Yes, much shame. Epic proportions of shame.* "Here, I'll go first. I think you're hot."

I was pretty sure I blushed. "We've had this conversation. I'm not hot."

"Well, I don't know what kind of friends you had before you were a Bow–"

"Not actually a Bow…"

"–and I hate to shatter that fragile sense of self you have there,

152

but you are." He slid off the bench, came over to me and tilted my chin up to look at him. "Your eyes are a crazy amazing colour green. They remind me of a pitch in the middle of winter–"

"Hardly sexy," I muttered and he frowned like he wasn't going to put up with that attitude.

"Says you. The pitch in winter is my favourite place in the whole world." Well, we'll just skip over the way my heart clasped its little hands and swung around like an idiot... "Secondly, you have a crazy intelligently insulting wit. Your smile is beautiful and annoyingly infectious. Your body is something the stuff of a teenage boy's wet dream and it is seriously distracting. And, you're far too smart for your own damned good."

"I don't really feel like any of those are *actual* compliments..." I was confused; I mean I think it was sort of complimentary...? Maybe it had just been the delivery?

"Holly, why do you think I'm constantly touching you? Wanting to kiss you?"

"Keeping up appearances?" I asked, completely uncertain now.

He scoffed. "I can play a good game, Doll. But, I'm not *that* good. You're gorgeous, you're sexy, you're smart, you're funny. I can't keep my hands off you because I'm attracted to you. You're hot, Holly. I'm kind of disgusted that the people you called friends let you think otherwise."

"Well, I mean they didn't tell me I wasn't–"

"They should have been telling you that you were."

So, no. None of my friends had ever said I was attractive. I was occasionally told I looked better in something than usual, or that a top or new haircut looked nice on me. But, I couldn't remember a single time any of my friends had said I was pretty. I mean, it's not like looks are everything, I know that. But, when your friends call you beautiful, they're referring to more than just looks, aren't they? I mean, it's a package deal. Isn't it?

I didn't need to be held to society's view of beauty; I didn't need people to think I was supermodel sexy or anything. But now that Xander had mentioned it, I felt like it would be nice if someone thought I looked good just as me, that I was beautiful as much for my personality as for the shape of my body or my face, that I was pretty whether I was technically overweight or underweight or my acne was flaring up. Because weren't we all beautiful in our own way? And, didn't we have a right to be reminded when we forgot?

I realised, as we stood in his kitchen and I told my heart to stop staring at his naked abs, that not one of my friends – not even Nancy – had ever said anything of the sort. I think it had been something like two years since I stopped asking Nancy her opinion on my outfits because she always agreed when I asked if I looked…somehow not right.

I also realised that Xander seemed to be saying something similar to me right then. It occurred to me that the first person other than my blood relatives to ever assure me I wasn't unattractive was King Douche himself. And, that made me feel a whole lot of conflicting feelings.

"Why do you suddenly care?" I asked, wanting to stop thinking there was maybe more to the King of the Bows than rumour had you believe.

"Because self-doubt isn't sexy," he replied without missing a beat as though he firmly believed that self-confidence alone would make even the elephant man sexy.

"Then cue me being not sexy," I huffed.

He frowned. "Because I'm not likely to be dating a girl who doesn't believe in herself."

I frowned as well. "Arrogance *does* attract arrogance."

"Exactly." Gone was the sincere expression and back was that flippant tone and hardness in his eyes.

"Well, everyone can be surprised at how un-shallow you were in falling for me, then," I answered sarcastically.

He smiled at me, some sincerity through whatever was annoying him. "I think they already are."

I shifted awkwardly. "Should we get started, then?"

"On what, Doll? Me showing you just how hot I think you are by sliding you up onto this bench and worshipping you? Or on planning what will probably be the *most epic* first date in history?" He suddenly looked so genuinely excited that I almost agreed.

I opened and closed my mouth a few times as I tried to make the connection between my brain and my mouth work. My heart was tapping my brain incessantly, telling it to listen to Xander because either of those things sounded far better than what I'd had in mind.

"Uh…English study…" finally slipped out of my mouth about a hundred notches south of the witty, confident comeback my brain had planned.

He shrugged as though he didn't care, but his eyes held a flame my stupid little heart was quite happy to let set it on fire, and the smirk on his face was smouldering. *How the hell did he just change between moods like that?*

"If we start before Greg gets here, then we'll just have to do that study twice…" he said as though mulling it over.

Was it getting difficult to breathe in there? I think it was getting difficult to breathe in there. But, I had to admit, it wasn't uncomfortable in the slightest. "Okay, well, I… I don't need…worshipping…" *Want, though…?* "And, I am *not* going on

155

a date with you. So…"

"So, that only leaves talking," he sighed dramatically.

He took my hand and I was still reeling from the dip my mind was taking in the gutter at his words. As he pulled me along, I didn't much care if he was taking me up to his room to do whatever Xander Bowen, King Douche did when he worshipped you. It was only until I felt myself not moving anymore that I realised I actually was in his room.

"Kitchen bench not good enough for you?" I heard myself quip rather intelligibly and wittily, taking an absent-minded look around his room.

Honestly, his room was a little bit of a letdown. I'd expected grandeur and…well, I don't know. Something that didn't look like Mark's room, only about two or three times the size – spatial awareness had never been my forte. There were less trophies than I expected Mister I-Win-Everything to have. His bed was bigger than mine, so maybe a king? *Fitting.* He had a normal student desk, a large TV facing the end of his bed, there were a couple of pieces of clothes dropped around the place, stacks of magazines, some books that I was fairly sure were only textbooks, and…actually a large bookcase on the same wall as the door behind me covered in books.

He laughed. "You watch your mouth, Doll. Or I might forget my gentlemanly side and throw you on that bed."

My heart skittered and would probably have beaten him to his bed had I not kept a decent grip on it. "I wasn't aware you had a gentlemanly side. If this is you being a gentleman, I'd *love* to see you not being a gentleman."

I'd still been looking around his room so I hadn't seen him coming. I only realised when he'd pushed me against the wall behind me, his hand beside my head. "I'd love it if that was serious." He looked me over, his eyes full of heat.

I felt myself smirk despite everything in me telling me to diffuse the situation. "Oh, I was serious. I would love to see that, Xander. I can only imagine what you're like with all those other girls."

He looked conflicted and I was well aware that I shouldn't be trying to provoke him. I just wasn't sure yet if I wanted him to throw me on the bed or argue with me. Because let's face it, a nicely timed argument might remind me why I didn't like this guy. I'd forget all about wanting to kiss him and touch him and throw away all my morals.

"You're not those other girls, Holly," he said quietly and with a sincere tremor to his voice that I didn't want to understand. He pushed himself away as he cleared his throat. "How are you with games? Nothing like a bit of killing to soothe the sexual tension." His tone was aiming for flippant, but I could tell he was feeling that sexual tension just as keenly as I was.

"I wouldn't know. I haven't played–"

"Well, my first job as boyfriend–"

"Fake boyfriend."

"–is to teach you how to kill things." He picked up some controllers and dropped to the bottom of his bed, patting the spot next to him. "I solemnly swear to keep my hands to myself unless told otherwise." He spared me a wink and I conceded with a smile as I walked over to him. "Don't worry if you're not very good to start with, there's a learning curve."

He passed me a controller and spent a few minutes going over the play functions. I nodded, taking it all in as best I could and trying to remember it. It was a lot easier than I expected. So about half an hour later Xander was sitting staring at the leader board where I was sitting higher than him.

He blinked in disbelief.

"Don't worry if you're not very good to start with…" I said, trying and failing to keep a straight face.

"You think you're so good?" Xander broke into a grin and pushed me over playfully.

"I think the leader board thinks I'm so good," I chortled, smiling up at him.

"You couldn't even let me win out of the goodness of your heart?"

I was still laughing. "I had no idea what I was doing! I'm pretty sure I was just mashing the keypad."

He shook his head, our noses almost brushing. "Seriously? Doll, that's even worse!"

"If it makes you feel better, I might have played something similar with my brother. But, it was on the Playstation…"

"Oh, something similar?" He beamed.

I winced. "Only vaguely similar… I mash the keypad with him, too."

"Do you beat him?"

I wrinkled my nose. "Sometimes."

"Spare a guy his dignity," he laughed.

"I'm not sure you had any to begin with," I snorted.

He cried out only mockingly indignant and tickled me. Both of us were laughing hard until our eyes met.

Slowly, our laughter died on our lips and suddenly the situation was terribly serious and rather tense. It was a good kind of tense, a skin tingling and a heart fluttering in anticipation kind of tense, but it was still tense. I shouldn't have let us get that kind of tense. But now I was here, I had zero motivation to slam us into reverse.

How about that he's a playboy wanker? my brain tried to remind me and my heart just wandered around with its fingers in its ears.

"Holly…" he breathed, leaning towards me slowly.

"Otherwise…" I said, equally breathlessly and not sure if I regretted it immediately or whether I just hated it felt like it took him so long to respond.

Heat flashed through his eyes, but he lowered himself down slowly as though giving me plenty of out time. On one hand I appreciated it, on the other…

I reached up and pulled his face the rest of the way to mine. I felt him smile against my lips for the briefest moment, then his tongue was in my mouth and I was just kind of focussed on that warm, brain-melt he gave me.

I felt his hand on my side, then it trailed over my hip, down the outside of my leg. When he changed direction, his hand slid up the inside of my leg. He moved it slowly, exploring. I kissed him harder and slid my fingers into his hair. As his hand reached my hip again, his fingers ran over the inside of it and his thumb just skimmed between my legs, sending a shockwave of tingles through me–

Then the doorbell rang and he paused.

He pulled away and leant his forehead to mine, his eyes still closed.

"Thanks, man," he muttered to himself as he brushed his nose against mine, then pushed away to standing with a deep breath.

I lay for a second, my brain rushing through all the potential situations that could have played out had that doorbell not rung.

"I'll be back in a tick."

I sat up at his tone. It was something like regret, mixed with

159

annoyance, but also resignation. He gave me a short smile as he grabbed a t-shirt, his eyes still full of that heat, and headed out to let Greg in while my heart totally didn't traipse down What If Lane and seriously regretted that t-shirt.

Chapter Thirteen

Greg gave me a knowing smile as he paused in the doorway to leave after a few hours of actually surprisingly successful poetry study. There'd been a bunch of jokes and laughing and Greg teasing Xander with me, but the boys both seemed more confident for the test than before we'd started.

"Yes, I'm taking her out. Happy?" Xander sighed.

Greg shot me a wink as though riling Xander up was doing me a favour. "Nah, man. Don't on my account. Just would have thought the two of you would've jumped at the chance to go out like a normal couple now everyone knows."

"We made plans, man." Xander was giving him very serious 'get out' vibes and I could barely supress a smile.

Greg looked like he wasn't believing a word Xander said. "Do these plans involve more than going to get a burger, going to a party, and/or driving around?"

"Yes," Xander huffed.

"Because nothing you've ever been involved in – that could even remotely be classified as a date – included anything else."

"I'm taking her to a movie."

"What movie?" Greg folded his arms over his chest.

"The new Guardians," Xander said, unhesitatingly.

"And, Holly wants to see the new Guardians?" Greg raised his eyebrows at me like he very much doubted this. But, I could cover well enough.

"Actually, I'm a big fan." Although if this meant I'd have to go to the movie with Xander, I was going to rip him a new one. If I did, I'd take him to *Alien: Covenant* when it was out as payback.

"Really? Comic books?" Greg asked, dubiously.

"Judgey much?" Xander huffed.

Greg shrugged. "I've just never heard her talk about it. Who's your favourite?"

"Well I'm a Vibe girl, and – total cliché, I know – I quite like Ironman."

"Crossing universes?" he said as though he was a little in awe of my audacity.

"I believe in equal love."

He smirked. "If you're such a big fan, what are their real names?"

"Really, dude?" Xander asked.

I shrugged. "Cisco Ramone's or Tony Stark's?"

Greg's eyes widened slightly. "How do you feel about cars?"

I smiled, pretty sure I knew where he was going with that. "Haven't seen Fate of the Furious yet and I'm looking forward to it, but I haven't got my hopes up it'll be any good. But I mean, the driving scenes are what you watch it for though, right?"

"Saw?"

"I actually think the story progression and character motivation is quite interesting. And I think it's a complete misconception that they get gorier as they go."

Greg smiled slowly. "Damn, man. She's a keeper."

"Yeah," Xander huffed awkwardly. "I've noticed."

My chest tingled at the weird hint of sincerity in that comment.

"Whelp," Greg said, rubbing his hands together. "I look forward the traditional evidence on Monday. You two have—"

"Wait. What traditional evidence?" I asked quickly.

Greg grinned. "Xand's infamous hicky," he said as Xander answered, "Don't worry about it."

I wasn't sure if Greg was being serious or not. It didn't help that he and Xander were sharing a wry smile.

"Sorry, the what now?" I blurted.

Xander snorted, no doubt knowing exactly what I'd think about him giving me a hicky. "Ruin the moment, why don't you?" He looked at Greg.

"Dude! I am quite frankly surprised we haven't seen one yet. Either you're losing your touch or…" Greg petered off, his eyes going wide.

The guy looked like he'd discovered some huge secret. Maybe he'd realised we were bullshitting our way through this. Shit, he knew! I looked at Xander, who didn't look terribly concerned. But, then Xander never really looked concerned about anything. In fact, I'd never—

No, not the point.

"Or what, Greg?" I asked slowly.

Greg was smiling; he definitely thought he'd figured out a secret. My heart pounded and it wasn't the kind I'd become used to around Xander. Not that it was supposed to around Xander… And really, it didn't.

"Or Xand really likes you…" he said like that was supposed to mean something to me.

It obviously meant something to Xander the way the boys both looked at each other. I thought Greg would be teasing and

163

condescending, but he looked genuinely happy and I saw a message I didn't understand on his face. Xander did seem to understand it, though. But whether he was happy about it or not, I couldn't tell.

"Well, I mean… We *are* dating…" I said lamely.

Greg threw me a smirk. "You certainly are. I just never thought I'd see the day when Xand liked and respected a girl enough to wait around for her. Power to you, Doll. Glad someone's keeping him honest."

He held his fist out and I bumped it uncertainly with mine.

"Okay!" Xander cried, grabbing the winking Greg and pushing him out of the house. "I think that's quite enough of that. You two can have your moment on Monday when she tells you all about our date."

"Bye, Doll!" Greg said as Xander closed the door on him. "Rand and I want all the details Monday!" he yelled through the door.

When Xander turned back to me, my glare was waiting for him.

"What?" he asked with a shrug and a barely supressed smile.

"Really? Now we're going to need to go on a proper date," I accused.

He gave me a lop-sided smirk. "Yes, we are."

"You could at least pretend not to be so happy about it."

"Would it help if I took my shirt off again?" He pouted.

Yes. "No." I hoped I was frowning as much as I was intending to be.

Xander's lip quirked into that lop-sided smirk again. "You sure?" he cajoled.

I forced my face to remain annoyed, but I was pretty sure I wasn't fooling anyone. "Very sure."

He shrugged, complete with hands in the air. "All right then. Your loss."

"I assure you, I'm not complaining."

He leant towards me and I was hit with whatever enticing body spray he used. "Your lips say no, but your eyes say yes."

He was just so... *Argh!*

He looked good, he smelled good, there was an annoyingly appealing twinkle in his eyes, and that hint of mischievous laughter playing at his lips did wonders for his charm factor. And, the boy knew it. He knew it and he knew how to work it.

But, it wasn't going to work on me. I surely had more willpower than that.

"Why do you have to be so..." I huffed.

"So what? Charming? Are you ready to concede, Doll?" He waggled his eyebrows at me and even that was somehow charismatic.

Almost. I tried to harden my glare. "No. Not charming. So... Ugh! What time is this movie, then?" I figured I'd give him one victory to take his mind off securing another.

He gave me that split-second grin that lit up his face before whipping his phone out. I watched his fingers play over the screen nimbly as he talked. "Eager for the trademark Xander hicky?" he chuckled.

Something weird twisted inside me and I wasn't lying when I answered, "No. I can't say I'm looking forward to being treated like a thousand girls before me."

He froze. The only thing that moved was his eyes to look up at me. He blinked heavily like he was surprised by something, or he'd just found out this whole time that everyone else saw in black and white. He lowered his phone slowly and looked at me properly.

"Doll…"

I shook my head. "Just pick a time, Xander."

I pulled my own phone out to do… Well, whatever it was I did on my phone to pass the time these days. But before I even had it unlocked, Xander was taking my hands in one of his and tilting my chin up to look at him.

"There haven't been a thousand girls, Holly…" he said softly. "And, as for the hickies…"

I shook my head and pulled away from him. "I don't really want to know."

"Holly…" he sighed. When I looked back at him, he was running his hand through his hair. "Do you know why JT and I are enemies?"

I blinked as I realised I didn't actually know the reason. I couldn't remember what had started it. "No."

"Yeah," he huffed, "me either. I just know we are. I hate the way he walks around thinking he's better than anyone. I hate the way he has no time for anyone he can't use. I hate the way he threw Tara away like–"

"That never happened!" I said vehemently. "And, none of that is true!"

Xander looked at me with a little scepticism in his eyes. There was no argument about how he knew Jason was all that and more. There was no indignation or puffed up bluster. He just looked at me like he was waiting for the lightbulb to go off.

"What?" I asked.

He gave me an adorable little shrug. "Nothing. Just, here I was thinking that the git had treated Tara like absolute shit and…"

"He didn't. Not like people say." I breathed out quickly. "He could have done better, true. But, it certainly wasn't that bad and it

166

wasn't all his fault."

Xander nodded. "Well if that story's not entirely true, it makes you wonder what other rumours flying around our school aren't entirely true either…"

I frowned. "Everyone *knows* you're a player, Xander. You make out with random girls in the hallway, over half the girls at our school have a story about you, and people see you at parties. *I've* seen you at parties."

He just nodded aggravatingly calmly. "Okay. Fair call. I'm the womanising arsehole we all know and love."

I didn't like where the conversation was leading my brain. "Did you find out what time the movie was on?"

He sighed like he was steeling himself. "If you could do absolutely anything in the world, what would be your ideal first date?"

I looked at him sharply. "I beg your pardon?"

"Personally, I'd want to talk. I'd want to do something together. Not sit in a darkened movie theatre, the only thing differentiating us from everyone else being that you might hold my hand."

"And what would the guy who's never been on a date before do while he's passing up the opportunity to cop a feel in the back row?" I asked.

One side of his mouth quirked because he knew I was teasing him. "I don't know. I'd hoped my girlfriend might have some pointers?"

"Fake girlfriend."

"Sure."

I breathed in as I thought. "I don't know. Maybe…bowling?" I hedged, saying the first thing that popped into my head.

"You bowl a lot on first dates?"

"I've never bowled on any date, actually," I corrected him.

"A first for both of us then."

I couldn't help but smile at him. His blatant, cocky confidence had this infectious nature to it. I couldn't help but be temporarily conned into believing that he was actually as amazing as he thought he was, that I could be that amazing with him, that we could be that amazing together.

"You good to go in that?" he asked, pointing to my jeans and jumper.

I nodded. "If you'll deign to be seen with me like this."

He gave me a smile of such force that it nearly blew me away. "I'd be seen with you in your daggiest PJs, Doll, and be proud to call you mine."

Well then. My heart totally didn't just sit down and eagerly await his next dashing compliment with a gigantic smile on its face. But, I think I played it cool enough.

"Oh really? You think you're worth my daggiest PJs?" I asked. "You're worth my absolute comfiest, safest, personal, me-time clothing?"

He cocked his head to the side. "Not yet," was all he said with a slight tilt to his lips.

Okay. Heart? You just scoot on back here now please...

I was going to have to wrestle the damn thing away from him if he kept saying things like that. My brain was about to beat the little thing around the head with a rolled up magazine and haul it back where it belonged – namely, locked up safe from falling for Xander's (un)charming personality. Because I was not an idiot.

I cleared my throat. "When did you want to go?"

He looked at his phone. "Well, what if we go now? We can pop past Nordburger for dinner and still make it to the movie later?"

"Sure. Why not?" I replied, thinking at least I wouldn't have to come up with an excuse for Greg as to why we hadn't gone to the movie after all.

"Sweet. Let me change my shirt and we can go."

"You need to change?"

He gasped sarcastically. "Only change twice today? Doll, I have a reputation to maintain!" he said as he grinned.

I watched him jog up the stairs and breathed out, all humour at his joke unfelt. Butterflies took up residence in my chest and I had to force myself to breathe normally. I had the sudden mad urge to run away. Far away. I didn't care where as long as the King of the Bows wasn't there. But, I was stronger than that.

I could do a date with King Douche. It wasn't a big deal. It wasn't going to be any different than hanging out at school… Only there was no one to keep up appearances for. What did you do on a non-date that you could then tell people about as though it was a date? Would Xander really hold my hand? Would he expect me to kiss him? And, what about this hicky thing? I was not at all interested in that…

Okay, a tiny part of me was interested in that… But, I chastised it terribly.

Two weeks ago I could have called or messaged Nancy and talked through my nerves or excitement or dread or whatever the feeling in the pit of my stomach was. I probably could have talked to Jason at a pinch. But, I had no one now.

I'd shut myself away from my old group – none of them would want to hear about my misgivings for my first proper date with King Douche. And, the Bows were all ridiculously loyal to Xander – I couldn't imagine even Greg or Miranda being on my side if I told them I was nervous. They'd just regale me with all Xander's good points (not that he had any) and probably joke about hickies.

"Okay. Shall we go?" Xander asked as he jogged back down the stairs, pulling a jacket over his shirt.

I nodded. "Yeah. Sure," I breathed.

He took my chin in his thumb and forefinger and looked at me closely. "You okay?"

I nodded again. "Totally fine. Let's bowl."

The look on his face suggested he didn't quite believe me, but he nodded once. "Okay. Mind if I drive?"

"You worried the girl is a terrible driver?"

He grinned. "Not at all. I just have this chivalrous streak that makes me feel like driving you for our first date is more romantic."

"Nothing about tonight needs to be romantic, Xander."

His grin fell a little, but he covered well. "Let it not be said that King Douche doesn't do a first date properly. Now. Your chariot awaits, my lady."

I mumbled to myself, but let him take my hand and walk me outside to his car.

His car – not his parents' car that he drove like most kids our age, but his own car – was a Beamer, of course. Yep, BMW. What kind, I didn't know. But, I knew it would have been expensive. Then again, I was pretty sure his dad had a Ferrari and their house sure made it look like they weren't hard up for money.

Xander let me sit in my own head as we drove to Kingpin Bowling. The carpark was expectedly full for a Saturday evening, but Xander managed to catch someone leaving. He met me at the back of the car, took my hand and we went inside. He dealt with all the paying and lane and shoe stuff while I looked around in the hopes that no one we knew was there as well; it was Adelaide after all.

As we walked to our lane, I got a little bit more with the program. Xander was smiling at me warmly and he was exuding that infectious charm again.

"If you're as freakishly good at this as you are at mashing the keypad, I might break up with you," he teasingly warned me.

"Bollocks!" I scoffed. "You're far too enamoured with me."

He grabbed me around the waist from behind and buried his nose in my neck. "Well, that's true," he said as we crab-walked the final few steps to our lane's bench.

I remain adamant that my heart didn't almost fall for it, but I did giggle.

"Okay, enough. There's no one here to con, King Douche."

He chuckled roughly and let me go. "You know," he started as he sat down and started changing his shoes, "I don't even remember the last time I went bowling."

My heart tripped over its untied laces and my stomach plummeted. "Jason, Nancy and I used to bowl all the time."

He slid across the bench so his hip bumped mine, his hand across the back behind me. "Watch out, Doll. We're about to make some amazing memories that'll wash all your pain away."

I looked at him sceptically.

"Okay, not *all* your pain maybe. But, I'm going to do my best to make you forget it at least for a little while." He kissed my nose and jumped up before I could react. I busied myself with my laces. "Now, how do you like your balls?"

My eyes snapped up to him and I found him wearing that cocky smirk. He threw me a wink.

"I always find bigger's better. But, I worry about your piddly little arms…" He gave me that stupid teasing pout.

I stood up. "There is nothing wrong with having piddly little arms. Better than your… How much do you actually have to work out for those muscles?"

Oh, he got cheeky now. He took two steps towards me and swung me into his arms. "You let me lift you and I probably won't have to go to the gym at all."

I tried to supress my giggle. "You calling me fat?"

He ran his nose up my neck. "I'm not calling you anything. If I was, I'd say you were perfect just as you are."

Calm down, heart. "You're not using me as gym equipment."

"I promise you won't notice." He span me so my legs were straddling his waist and I decided that it was probably sort of a requirement he touch my arse at that point. "Little holding you against a wall, little carrying you upstairs." He winked again. "It won't matter if your knees go weak."

I had this very strange flutter in my chest that I pushed away with gusto. But, I gave him a smile as I wrapped my arms around his neck; the whole body flirtatious thing I could allow for a moment, but nothing else was going to be involved here.

"You think you kiss *that* well, do you?"

Those cognac eyes fairly shone and I didn't hate being that close to see them. "Oh, I know I do."

I let towards him. But instead of kissing me, he dropped me gently to the ground and turned to the rows of balls.

"Come on then, Doll. You never did tell me your size."

"Uh, six. I think."

He frowned at me. "Six? That's a little light isn't it?"

I shrugged. "I don't know. It's just what I usually use."

He nodded. "All right."

He picked up a couple of balls for each of us and put them on our machine. While I finished tying up my shoes, he keyed our names in. When I looked up again, I found he'd labelled us 'Doll' and 'KingD'.

I raised my eyebrow at him and he gave me that split-second grin. "You're up, Doll."

I picked up my ball and took my place. I threw and watched as the ball meandered down the lane. I hit the pins just right of centre and it took down five of them.

"Oo, nice," Xander said.

I picked up my second ball and threw it again. Naturally, I missed entirely and it went slipping down the right gutter.

"Ah, shit. Well, I doubt I'll do any better," Xander commented as we changed places.

After a few rounds, it was painfully obvious that Xander had been completely bullshitting or at the very least doing a terrible job of making me feel better; he got a strike or spare basically every bowl. I meanwhile wasn't doing very well.

"Doll, can I offer some advice?" he asked as I picked up my ball.

"What, King Douche?"

"Do you want to try the eight?" He spoke slowly, like that was going to be less insulting or something.

I sighed as I looked at the pins then him. "Do you think it will help?"

"I'm not really well-versed in *all* balls, Doll." He winked again. "But, I figure a little bit more weight might get you a bit more…oomph?"

I waved my head around as I thought about it. Finally, I decided why the hell not. "Okay."

He grinned and jumped up. "How's this?" He picked one up and showed it to me.

173

I returned his smile. "Fine. Thank you."

He held it out for me. As I took it, he pulled it towards him, pulling me with it.

"Xand–"

He pressed his lips to mine quickly then jumped away with an impish smile. "Off you go then."

I wrinkled my nose at him in a terribly unbelievable display of annoyance and turned to take my shot. I let go of the ball and watched it roll down almost the middle of the lane. When the hideously fluoro orange ball hit the pins, the lot of them crashed to the ground for my first strike ever!

I threw my arms in the air as I heard Xander cheering. I span and we shared a huge smile.

"You did it!" he yelled, looking the most proud and excited I think I'd actually ever seen anyone but maybe Mark be of me.

"I did it!" I yelled back.

He opened his arms and I ran into them in excitement. Hang this idea of not giving him the wrong idea or getting too close or whatever it was that made my brain tell my heart it was an awful idea. I was happy and I wanted to share it with him.

I threw my arms around his neck as he picked me up and span me around, both of us laughing. He held me tight and I did likewise as he let my feet hit the ground again. I pulled away far enough to look at him. His eyes were warm.

"Thank you," I said.

"You're welcome. It *is* a boyfriend's job to make his girl's life better."

The romantic in me beamed at the same time as the modern woman in me frowned. "I don't think that's how it works."

"Why not? A partner's supposed to be there to lift you up," he

174

did just that for a second with a smile, "when you're down, help you reach your goals, walk through life beside you. They're a best friend, a confidant, someone you can count on."

Well, I guess I couldn't be mad about that. "That would be sweet. If we were actually dating."

"*If* we were actually dating." He got that infectiously charming look in his eyes and I looked down to hide my smile. "All right. My turn!" he said and I couldn't decide if he was forcing the joviality or not.

But, the rest of the night went well. We laughed and we talked and paid each other out; Xander was an excellent performer who spent as much time teasing himself as I did. Like all our previous Messenger conversations, he was surprisingly easy to talk to and the conversation flowed easily and naturally. We had burgers for dinner, where he did a marvellous walrus impression with his chips. And, we got to into the cinema just before the ads were finishing with a great giggling and awkward shuffling over people to get to our seats.

I even let him hold my hand.

Chapter Fourteen

I looked up from my phone when I heard Kate's high-pitched giggle as she said Xander's name. She was leaning up against him, her hand on his chest, and looking up at him as she batted her eyelashes. I knew flirting when I saw it, not that I was terribly good at it myself. I watched with some disinterest as he pushed her away with his charming smile. But, it seems she wasn't giving in that easily.

"Do you share him? Or just know you can't keep him honest?" Nancy appeared beside me and I jumped a little.

"What?" I asked.

She kicked her head to Xander. "Is there a limit on how many other sluts your *boyfriend* gets to hook up with a week? Or do you play it by ear?"

I frowned at her, wondering where the hell my best friend had gone. I wondered if maybe she *had* liked Jason this whole time. I just didn't know why she had to be acting like this and dragging him down with her.

Then, the actual implication of her words hit me and I realised a sight like Xander being hit on was supposed to make me annoyed because we were desperately in love, or some shit. And I won't deny that a part of me had felt a little jealous about it, but I'd just momentarily forgotten that my automatic response was supposed to be one of outrage and indignation, not amusement and indifference.

I deepened my frown at Nancy, then walked over to Xander and Kate. I couldn't have told you what I'd been planning to do. But when I got there, I walked straight in front of Kate, slammed Xander against the lockers and kissed the hell out of him.

Keeping up appearances or not, I may have thrown a little more into it than I'd meant to and his response was dangerously close to making my knees go weak. By the time we pulled apart, we only had eyes for each other. Except, I couldn't look too hard into his because there was something in there that something in me was about to respond to but couldn't, not if I was walking away at the end of this with my dignity intact.

"What was that for?" he asked, slightly out of breath.

"Oh, you didn't like it?" I asked flippantly, pushing off him and I saw Kate must have walked off.

But, he grabbed my hand and pulled me back to him. "Oh, I liked it far too much," he said, running his finger down my cheek. "It just seemed a little PDA for you."

"I just thought you could use a reminder as to who you were dating."

He leant to my ear. "Fake dating."

I shrugged and threw his usual reply back at him, "Sure."

"You keep kissing me like that and I might forget we're fake dating, Doll."

"Xander Bowen doesn't know how to real date." I pushed away from him again and winked at him. My heart had this weird feeling in it, but I kept my smile in place.

He grinned at me charmingly, my heart forgetting its previous mood and doing little skips. "I dunno. Saturday seemed like a pretty good date to me."

I scoffed. "Says the guy who's been on… Count them, one date."

He smirked, lighting up his eyes. "Well, you'll just have to take me on more."

"Maybe I will."

His smile grew for a second, then he pressed a quick kiss to my lips as he took my hand and we headed out for recess. I looked back for a moment and saw Nancy staring after me. She had the weirdest look on her face; I could have sworn she was plotting my most grisly murder, but she also looked like a five year old who'd lost their parents at the zoo.

"Ignore her, Doll. She and the git can suck it."

"She probably does," was out of my mouth before I could remind myself what a filter was.

Xander snorted and his hand tightened on mine. "Is that me having a bad influence or are there sides to you I haven't met yet?" he asked.

I nudged him with my shoulder. "You'll have to wait and find out."

"Oh, I look forward to it. But, I put my money on it being the second one." He gasped dramatically. "Don't tell me, Little Miss Prim-and-Proper has a dirty side!"

I felt my cheeks warm. "No. Of course not."

He tugged me towards him and I looked up at him. He breathed in heavily. "You do!" he said with a smile like all his Christmasses had come at once.

"I do not." I tried not to smile from awkwardness.

"Oh, you do!" He wrapped his arms around my waist and

dipped his lips to my ear. "And, exactly what does it take to bring out this dirty side?" he practically purred in my ear.

Goose bumps chased themselves across my skin and I swear my stupid little heart went chasing right on after them. *You.* "That would require me having one."

Xander's hand left my back and slid downwards. I frowned at him expectantly as I watched him try not to smile. Honestly, a part of me didn't really care that he was touching my arse. It was the implication I couldn't let stand; the touching of arses or anything else remotely more than lips would send him the wrong message. It would send *me* the wrong message. We weren't really dating; ergo there was to be no...funny business. The previous Saturday was to be the only exception.

Xander didn't move his hand this time and I didn't do anything to make him. "Did you lock it up because the git was a prude? Or was it Nancy?" he asked, a challenge in his eyes.

I pressed my lips together to stop my smile before I answered. "Neither. Just because you're dirty enough to make Lucifer blush doesn't mean the rest of us are."

Xander was damn close to that infectious charm. "You're getting comfortable with me, Doll."

Yes. "I'm doing nothing of the sort."

"You are. You're–"

"Right, let's see it then," Greg chuckled as he bounded over to us.

I glared at him, and it wasn't because he'd interrupted our conversation. "Sorry, mate. Nothing to see," I answered as I pulled my collar away to show my mark-free neck.

Greg's excitement faded, only to be replaced a moment later with that knowing smile. "Well, then. I'm expecting to be best man." He winked as he pointed between us as though it was decided.

I tried hard to keep a straight face as Xander sighed, "Mate, it's not–" and Greg's face fell again.

"The hell it isn't," Greg said with a knowing look in my direction. I had the weirdest feeling that Greg was disappointed with Xander because he thought Xander was treating me badly by not admitting there was more here.

"And, if I'm just a prude?" I asked.

Xander snorted and I glared at him, knowing he was still thinking about my apparent dirty side.

"Oi! Don't be rude to our Doll," Greg said and grabbed him in a head lock.

The boys tussled for a moment and then Xander actually accidentally got a flailing fist to the side of Greg's head as Greg paused with his mouth open and a handful of Xander's school shirt in his fist.

"Shit!" Xander cried. "You right, mate?"

"Me? I'm fine. But, that?" he pointed to Xander's neck.

"But, what?" Xander asked with enough of his usual cavalier nonchalance.

"What the fuck!" Greg chuckled as Xander looked at me like I was the root of all his problems.

Xander shrugged out of Greg's grip and pulled his collar back over the hicky on his neck. "Seems our Doll could teach me a thing or two." His usual nonchalance here slipped a little.

He was less pleased by the situation than had been the plan and I didn't blame him.

So yeah, Xander and I had thought it would have been funny if I gave him a hicky since Greg had seemed so excited about the whole thing. What had started out as a joke as I'd straddled him in his car – can you see where hindsight might have been helpful here? – had quickly escalated into a very real make out session which had only ended when my phone went off, sounding very loud in the small, quiet space. All I could say was thank God Mark liked to check in when he hadn't heard from me for a while, otherwise my whole theory of 'don't cross lines' would have been well out the window.

It had become too real, too quickly and I don't think either of us could really deal with the reminder as well as we might have liked. Well, I wasn't really dealing with it and it made me see him not really dealing with it either, whether he was or not.

My body's memory of the weekend was the only reason I could think that I'd fairly crushed him against his locker and a part of me really wished I hadn't. Too many kisses led to hearts forgetting what was going on; I could feel it, and I knew I couldn't let it happen.

"Well, fuck me," Greg breathed, bringing me back to the present situation.

"Rather not," I heard myself quip and then I grimaced.

Xander wrapped his arm around my shoulders as though everything was fine. "Oh yeah, Doll's got a dirty side we've only just warmed up," he said in answer to Greg's look of shock.

We all started back over to the Bows.

"Oh, I'm looking forward to this," Greg chuckled.

"There is nothing to look forward to," I emphasised.

"I beg to differ," Xander whispered in my ear before kissing my temple and I almost felt like everything was okay for a moment.

"Oh! Tell us about the big date!" Miranda said, jumping over to us in excitement as she saw us.

My gaze was drawn to Rachel's scowl like I had it on radar. Damn, but I knew I'd have to wait for that cold day in Hell before even a tiny drip of water melted off that cold exterior. Daniel standing sentry-like at her shoulder wasn't helping either.

"Yes, we're so excited. We just couldn't wait a minute longer," Rachel drawled with more sarcasm than I thought any one person could ever own. She could certainly give Deadpool a run for his chimichungas.

Xander gave me a slight squeeze. "Rach, can I talk to you?"

Rachel looked at Xander and nodded. He let go of me, grabbed Rachel's arm and dragged her away while Miranda took hold of my arm excitedly.

"Come on, come on! I want to hear the goss!" she squealed.

"Uh, we went bowling…" I started, my eyes on Xander.

As I told Miranda and Greg about the date, my eyes kept sliding to Xander and Rachel. They were obviously fighting. But, it was the sort of fighting only people really close do. The sort of fighting where you can say anything and you know your relationship with the other person can't be ruined. Eventually, Xander pulled her into a hug and she hugged him back fiercely.

I wasn't sure if I was supposed to be jealous or hope I wasn't ruining whatever they had. On one hand, maybe Rachel felt for Xander what I felt for Jason and was just really good at hiding it. Like hook-up-with-every-single-guy-available-(or-not)-except-him good at it. On the other, maybe they were just really good friends. I didn't know what to think; the evidence could go either way.

Unsurprisingly, Rachel wasn't in a hurry to soften her attitude to me anytime soon. And, I couldn't blame her. In fact, I was glad for it. Anything to help me remember none of it was real.

Because Xander and I were becoming far too good at keeping up appearances and I kept forgetting to worry about the consequences of getting too physical.

The fact was, his kissing aside, I really did enjoy spending time with him. He was nothing like I'd thought he was. He was actually quite nice, he made me laugh, he was smarter than I'd expected, and he was always attentive. It was weird, seeing there be more to someone that I'd thought was so black and white.

But, all the Bows were like that.

Like my old group, they had in-jokes, they recollected stories, they teased each other, and there were specific dynamics that I was finally beginning to pick up on. Like how it was obvious that Britt and Max kind of liked each other but neither of them had realised it yet even though every Bow was just waiting for them to. Like the way that Greg was the goofball jock everyone thought he was, but he was seriously there for anyone if you needed him. Like the way that Daniel and Xander butted heads like some kind of betas fighting for alpha, but still grinned at each other when they shared a joke. Like the way that Rachel was always overseeing the whole group as though she was some prison warden making sure no one stepped out of line. If someone got nasty, she was there to kick them in the arse and make them play nice. But, in a good way.

Jason, Nancy, me and the others always used to talk about how the Bows just sat there talking about sex and makeup and how much money they had and how much they'd thrown up that day to lose weight. But, there was none of that. Well okay, there was a little about sex and makeup, but not to the extent that I'd have expected. It was the normal amount – whatever that was.

To some degree, when I looked at it disturbingly closely, the Bows were actually nothing like my old group.

Just like I'd been told, the Bows stuck together, they looked out for each other; it made Jason's group look like they hated each other. Sure the Inner Sanctum was a little clique-ier, but it was only because they were legitimately closer. I watched Rachel, Xander, Miranda, Greg, Daniel, Tara, Teagan, and Sabrina interact and I could see how important they were to each other.

"Where have you gone?" Xander asked, his nose nudging my ear as Daniel said something to Greg.

I hugged his arms to me and half-turned to him. "Nowhere. I'm good."

"You sure?"

I nodded and leant back into him. "Totally sure."

"Okay." He kissed my hair and went back to whatever he, Greg and Daniel had been talking about.

I was standing with them while they waited to start their soccer practice. As usual, Daniel didn't look at me, he didn't direct any conversation towards me, he acted as though I wasn't even there; Xander may as well have just been hugging himself. I felt a small twinge of discomfort about that given I'd never really encountered being disliked by someone I spent a good deal of time around.

I mean, I'd always known that not everyone liked me – that was just life and I'd not liked most of the people who didn't like me. The Bows were a perfect example of a whole lot of people who didn't like me and I hadn't liked in return. And not everyone was hostile in their dislike of me; some of us could be perfectly civil with each other even if we didn't like each other – because that was called being polite and a decent human. But three weeks ago, I could have walked away from the hostile people, I could have avoided them.

That was a little difficult now that I was fake dating their king. It was also a little difficult given – other than their dislike of me – I couldn't really remember why I'd hated them.

"All right, guys!" Coach called. "Let's get to it, yeah? Maybe we can all go home before we freeze our bollocks off."

"Female company notwithstanding," Greg called out and Coach nodded at me.

"Female company notwithstanding, aye," he replied.

Xander laughed along with the others as he gave me one more squeeze before he let go of me and followed Greg and Daniel onto the pitch. I dropped down onto the bleachers to watch them warming up. The metal of the bleachers was cold under my arse, but that was winter for you.

I watched as the boys almost lazily kicked the ball between each other as a warm up until I heard a familiar voice call out to me.

"I'm here. Sorry, I'm here!"

I looked over and saw Miranda hurrying over with a wave. I returned it and went back to watching the boys as she dropped beside me with a breath.

"Sorry, I was talking to Dan. Then I remembered I was supposed to see Mr Burnett."

"Talking to Dan?" I asked without thinking, my tone insinuating.

"Yeah... Why?" she asked.

I realised I had completely overstepped my bounds and that wasn't okay. I shrugged. "No, nothing. What were you talking about?"

Miranda sighed, but she was smiling. "Yeah. I know. I

shouldn't."

I pretended not to have any idea what she was talking about. "Shouldn't what?"

Miranda laughed and nudged me gently. "I know you're not that stupid, Doll."

I shook my head. "I don't know what you're talking about."

"Sure you don't. Come on. We're friends. Tell me what you really think."

I shook my head again. "I'm not a Bow, Rand. I don't have an opinion."

She snorted. "Bullshit. You're as much a Bow as I am. And, you're my friend. As much as I'd rather not admit I might have poor taste in guys, it is up to my friends to tell me."

I smiled as I looked down for a moment. "You don't think I'm a little biased? Ex-minion and all?"

She nudged me again and I nudged her back. "Maybe I could do with a little bias? Some outsider-cum-insider perspective?"

I clicked my tongue as I looked at Daniel. "I actually don't know," I said honestly. "The fact he hates me aside, I don't know if I think he's such an arsehole anymore. But, I guess I don't know that I've seen anything that will make him a good boyfriend...?" I shrugged again, not really sure what I was rambling about.

"Hm. Fair enough," she mused and we fell into a contemplative silence.

I'd been entirely honest with her. Ignoring the fact that Daniel hated me with more gusto than I'd ever hated Xander, I was starting to think there was more to him than the rumours swirling around the school.

It was almost ironic that Miranda had said I was as much Bow as her given, until a few days ago, I'd believed the same as the

186

whole school that she was just another wannabe fringe Bow. We'd all firmly believed she was just hanging on for dear life to the walls of the Inner Sanctum like some unwanted parasite. God, could we have been further from the truth!

I could see now why we'd thought that; Miranda was shy around everyone but Xander, Greg, Rachel and now for some reason me. The Bows were constantly trying to include her, but she always seemed a little anxious about it. I hadn't worked out why that was yet, but I could already see that the rumours about Miranda were bullshit.

And, from the little I'd seen of Daniel, I wondered if some of them were too. He was totally the cold, distant guy the rumours said, but I wondered how much more there was to him.

Even now as I watched their soccer practice, Daniel was laughing at something Xander and Greg had done. His face was open and carefree, none of the usual closed off arrogance we usually saw him wear around the school. In fact, with his friends, I rarely saw that closed off arrogance in anything more than jest. Unless he was looking at me.

I still wasn't convinced he was boyfriend material or all that nice, especially not for someone as sweet as Miranda. But, I also realised I was in no position to judge him. I didn't know him well enough.

I almost laughed at that thought.

A month ago I wouldn't have hesitated to judge him. I would have told Miranda all the things I knew to be true about him; he was mean and shallow, he went through girls almost as fast as Xander and was colder than Rachel. But, sitting with her and realising she knew him better than I ever would, I knew I had no valid opinion to give her.

"Is it a shame he's so attractive?" she sighed, pulling me from my thoughts.

I smiled. "If you'd asked me a few weeks ago, I'd have said he wasn't attractive."

"Why?" She gaped at me like I was some foreign breed.

I laughed. "Because we all thought he was some rich, snooty, arrogant arsehole. And, I just didn't find that attractive."

Miranda gave me a small smile. "And the rich, arrogant arsehole look's grown on you, has it?"

I elbowed her lightly. "Xander is definitely a rich, arrogant arsehole."

She giggled. "Is that not *the* defining feature of a Bow?" she teased.

I looked at her in some surprise. "Well, I suppose."

She grinned. "We know what people think of us, Doll. But, if we let everything people said about us get to us? What kind of life is that?"

One I live, I acknowledged to myself as I realised I thought I'd gone through life not worrying, but actually worrying quite a lot what other people thought of me.

"So, that's a no on Dan, then?" she mused.

I huffed a laugh. "For now, maybe."

"Yeah, probably for the best," she said happily as she took hold of my elbow and we watched the boys practise.

Chapter Fifteen

As I walked into school on Thursday morning, something seemed a little off. I couldn't put my finger on it until Recess and by then the evidence was piling up.

People were either smiling at me or glaring at me.

Some of the smilers were people who'd never looked at me once. Some of the glarers were people I'd considered friends. Or at least friendly acquaintances.

The reason for such a reception was made obvious while I was in my locker.

"Well, *I* heard JT only hooked up with Nancy because he found out about Holly and Xander," someone said and I nearly dropped my Psych textbook on my foot. It crashed into the locker under mine as I tried to catch it, but hopefully no one noticed.

Another person scoffed. "I heard it was totally the other way around."

"It can't have been," the first girl said, "Holly and Xander got together like a month ago."

"That's what they say."

"Well I'm behind Holly and Xander, they're much better together than JT and Nancy."

"I'll reserve judgement until I see who lasts longer."

I snuck a look around my locker door and saw two girls I thought were in Year Ten.

"Well," the first girl said, "I've seen Nancy since she hooked up with JT and she's become a total bitch. I don't know why he's still with her."

"Meanwhile, Holly looks like a deer caught in headlights every time Xander touches her. Do you think they've slept together?"

The first girl shrugged. "I heard JT and Nancy were pretty close when someone walked in on them."

The second girl scrunched her nose up. "Well, I'd rather sleep with Xander over JT any day. Even if he got bored with me."

"He's not getting bored with Holly. You have to have seen the way he looks at her. If they break up, it's because of her."

"JT will be thrilled."

They shut their lockers as they laughed, then walked away.

I stared into my locker for a moment, not quite sure what to think. I mean, it sounded an awful lot like the school was…what? Betting on us versus them? I knew for a fact those two girls were Bow wannabes, so I wasn't surprised they sounded like they were on Xander's side. But, I was surprised when that meant being on my side by default…

"What am I talking about? Side?" I muttered to myself as I pulled my books out with slightly more zeal than necessary.

I felt a hand on my arse and there was a voice in my ear. "There you are. You get out early?"

Sure, that voice was warm and there was something annoyingly pleasant about it. But, this was Xander we were talking about. The guy who did get bored, who had confided to me that part of why we were doing this was because of his boredom. I kept somehow conveniently forgetting that. We were fake dating, that was all. I couldn't let myself forget because I wasn't stupid enough to think there was anything about me that changed that.

Friends we could do, and I felt like we might have actually found ourselves there. But, this was fake dating. It was keeping up appearances. There was nothing more to it than friendly flirting masquerading as puppy love.

"Hands in new places, Xander," I grumbled as I slammed my locker shut.

At least he did remove his hand quick smart. "Whoa. You okay?"

"Sure. Why wouldn't I be?" I asked as I pulled my bag over my shoulder and slumped away.

"Uh well, I haven't seen a tantrum for a while, doll," he answered as he followed. "You under-caffeinated? Hormonal?"

I rounded on him and I watched his eyes go wide. "Hormonal? Why is that guys' first assumption? A girl's a little short and you just assume we're hormonal?"

He held his hands up in defence. "Okay. I'm sorry. You're right. I shouldn't make assumptions." He paused and leant towards me between his hands. "Are you hormonal, though? Because I'm okay with that. I mean, I get that it legit messes everything up. You've just got to tell me when to be sensitive."

"Firstly, if that's your theory, how about you try just being sensitive all the time—"

He wrapped me in his arms and ducked his nose to my ear. "Because you're fun to tease and I know you enjoy it." Well, he wasn't wrong. For the most part. "But, I get if you don't when you're on the rag—"

"We're not breakable just because we're bleeding, Xander!" I huffed, but I didn't pull away because he was making me feel a

191

little bit better.

"Oh, I know. I've spent something like five years trying to work out how to make Rach feel better when it hits. And, believe me, that's not been easy! And, I know you're not all the same. But, I do understand a little of it. Well, I try at least. You've just got to tell me what you need."

I sighed and relaxed against him. "I'm not on my…period. But, thanks."

"Okay, caffeine then?"

I shook my head against him.

"What's up?"

"Nothing. I just… I'm fine now."

He tipped my chin to make me look at him. "Holly. Talk to me."

I huffed. "Some girls were talking about us and I… I remembered what we were doing here, okay?"

Those cognac eyes softened. "People are always talking about us, doll."

I nodded. He wasn't wrong about that either.

"What were they saying now?"

"Oh you know, they were basically betting whether you and I will last longer or Jason and Nancy."

Surprise crossed his features, then he got that cocky smirk that was almost charming. "Well, it'll be us. Duh."

"Well, duh," I agreed half-heartedly. "It's easy to stick out something fake."

"Holly, what's the matter?"

How about the fact that you're a total enigma and I have to remind myself I don't like you? How about the fact that no matter what we're doing here, none of it's real? How about the fact that it's just keeping up appearances no matter how real it feels?

192

"It's just weird to think that people are putting Jason and me on different sides." And, it was true; I had been thinking that too. "I mean, the whole not talking to him thing is made easier by the fact that he's not standing up for me at all with Nancy. But…"

"It's just become unavoidably real that you and the git are on opposite sides of the warzone."

I looked up at him sharply. How the hell did he manage to seem to know what I was thinking all the time?

"Something like that."

He nodded, his face as serious and tender as it ever got. "I'm here, Holly. Anything you want. Anything you need. If it gets too much…?"

He left it lingering, but I knew what he meant and I didn't want that. I could think we were friends now, but how would we still be friends if we broke up? I'd alienated myself from my old group and without the few Bows I had now, I'd have no one. It was selfish and probably no more advisable than fake dating Xander in the first place, but I didn't want anything to change. I was too afraid of what I'd wouldn't have if anything changed.

I shook my head. "No. I'm fine. It's just… Taking some getting used to."

He gave me a supportive smile. "You don't have to do it alone."

I had that feeling again of us being that great together, but I didn't push it away this time. I let myself believe that whatever friendship we had could survive whatever was coming without mixing up any romantic notions.

"Thanks, Xander."

He gave me a cocky surprised face. "Oh, you thought I meant me? Oh, no. I just figured, you know, Rand or Greg would be more than happy to…" He petered off laughing as I whacked him.

"You're not as funny as you think you are."

"I so am, though."

I shook my head and leant up to kiss him. "You're not," I told him before I pulled away.

His hand went to my back to keep my face near his. We looked each other over and I was frozen by what I saw in his eyes. But, I didn't know why.

"What?" I asked.

"That's the first time you've kissed me."

I rolled my eyes as I pulled away a little. "I've kissed you a lot, Xander."

A smirk twitched at the corner of his lips. "It's the first time *you've* kissed *me*."

I frowned as I realised what he meant. "No. It can't be."

"It can and it is."

"I'm sure I've kissed you before."

He shook his head slowly and I knew he was enjoying this. "You haven't. I would have remembered."

"I so have."

He was still shaking his head slowly, that smile in his eyes. "No. Not like that you haven't."

I didn't think he needed to be taking whatever he was from this. "That? That was just keeping up appearances, Xander."

He obviously didn't believe me. "You like me."

The tell-tale flush in my cheeks didn't help me deny it. "No. I hate you. Remember?"

He was fighting the smirk. "Of course you do."

I pressed one more kiss to his lips in all the admission he was going to get that I might not have hated him anymore and pulled away. He chuckled, but didn't say anything about it as he put his arm around my shoulder and we headed for the Bows' picnic table.

People did a very poor job of pretending they weren't eyeing us off as we walked through the school. And, I couldn't help but wonder what they were thinking, what they were saying. Were they trying to judge how long Xander and I were going to last just by looking at us? Did anyone guess it was fake and would use that against us? Was it just those two Bow wannabes and it wasn't actually the whole school at all?

Xander gave my shoulder a squeeze as though he knew I was stressing and I relaxed. I leant against him for a moment as a silent thank you and I had the feeling he'd got the message.

Recess passed as I tried to gauge the reactions of the rest of the Bows. I tried to turn it off, but I couldn't help wondering how many of the Bows were siding with Xander and me against Jason and Nancy.

Kids walked closer to the Bows, their eyes on me and Xander, whispering to each other.

Had they been doing this the whole time and I'd just not noticed? Or was this something new? Did it have anything to do with the expected bust up Miranda had mentioned?

"What are you doing on Sunday, Doll?"

I blinked and had the perfect excuse to stop my brain overthinking everything as I looked at Liv, who I was sure had never called me anything before, let alone my new nickname.

"Uh, I am…" I paused, thinking. "Nothing. I'm not… No plans," I answered.

I felt Xander's hand tighten on my stomach for a moment as he laughed with Daniel and Greg about whatever it was those boys constantly found to laugh about. He pulled away and I lost track of whatever shenanigans they got up to as I focussed on Liv.

"Why?" I asked.

Liv looked at Miranda with an excited smile. "We thought it would be awesome to have some girl time?"

I looked at Miranda with a question.

She nodded. "We thought we could go into town, do some shopping – window of course, because Mum will kill me if I put anything more on her card this month."

I awkwardly joined their laughter like I had any idea what they were talking about. "No. 'Course. Um, yeah that sounds great. What time and where do you want me?"

There was mass squealing and I was hugged from both sides by two very excitable Bows.

"Awesome!" Liv and Miranda cried, then finally pulled away from me.

I slid my eyes to Xander. He was wearing a knowing smirk, but his eyes were softer. He gave me a wink and a nod and turned to punch Daniel on the arm. I decided it was still not worth my sanity trying to figure out most of what motivated him.

"Um, okay…" Miranda mused. "How about Mall's Balls at eleven?"

"Oh, yes! Get some shopping in and then some lunch!" Liv said, her eyes making me think she was legitimately excited about me joining them.

I nodded. "Sure. Sounds awesome."

I smiled as best I could while I was telling my nervous little heart to calm the farm. Friends invited friends to go places; it was normal. So, I wasn't really a Bow? I was (fake) dating Xander and they were accepting me. Maybe.

God, I didn't know if the idea they'd never accept me was more terrifying or the idea they might. But, if they hadn't liked me before, there was nothing I could do that would make them like me less, surely?

I smiled and nodded and did my best to join in on the ensuing 'where shall we go' and 'what do we need' conversation; Miranda it seemed wanted a new outfit for the upcoming giant Bows' mid-year party and Liv was running out of places to find her favourite lipgloss that she was worried the company had stopped making.

"What about you, Doll?" Liv asked and I gaped.

"I don't know. I think I'm good. But, I like looking as much as the next person," I chuckled.

"What are you wearing to the party?"

I opened and closed my mouth a few times. *Was I going to still be fake dating your king to be at the party?* "No idea. I'm sure I can rustle up something decent–"

"Make overs!" the girls squealed as they shared a look.

"Make overs?" I asked uncertainly.

Any make over I'd been involved in with Nancy had basically just been her telling me that I was as good as I was going to get while we gushed about how amazing she looked.

Liv waved a dismissive hand at me. "I know. I know. You're gorgeous. But, who doesn't like make overs?"

Uh, me. Although, Liv looked totally genuine, so I nodded. "Okay. Make overs."

There was more squealing and I was enveloped in another hug as I looked to Xander for some assistance and the bell rang.

Xander just winked at me and I sighed as I resigned myself to the hug.

Liv let go of me and Miranda looped her arm with mine as she started leading me to the study room for our Free. I looked back at Xander in panic. But, he only gave me that infuriatingly infectious smirk and blew me a kiss.

I let Miranda and Liv natter about the shopping trip and every one's make overs as we wandered through the hallways. We paused at the door as we said goodbye to Liv and I noticed Tara had joined us.

"You still good for shopping on Sunday?" Liv asked her.

Tara nodded. "Yep, totally. I need a new pair of nice flats. My last lot are caked in dried sand after the New Year's party."

"Excellent!" Miranda smiled. "We'll catch you guys later!"

"See ya," Liv said and headed for whatever class she had.

Miranda started into the classroom, but I felt a hand on my elbow.

"Uh, Holly?"

I turned and found Tara hovering. I blinked and kicked some politeness into myself; I wasn't getting through all this by acting like a dick. I forced a smile. "Uh, hey."

She gave me a small awkward smile. "Hey."

"Uh, what's up?"

She breathed out heavily. "Xander asked me about the whole JT thing…"

I felt my cheeks go red. "He did what? Oh my God. That's not… I mean… Okay?" Was I supposed to apologise for something? Had Jason told me the wrong side of the story?

"I just wanted to say I'm sorry for saying those things about you."

I felt even more mortified as I imagined Xander telling her to apologise to me. "No. Please… You don't have to. Xander shouldn't have–"

She shook her head. "He didn't. You know he doesn't actually order us about, right?" she laughed and I joined in awkwardly.

"I am starting to realise that yes."

"Good. He just asked about it and – I don't know – getting to know you lately, I realised that maybe I...overreacted?"

I blinked again, still somewhat confused. "Oh. Uh. Thanks?"

She gave me a full smile. "I was with Rach and Dan about you, convinced you were going to hurt Xand. But, I see you with him. Sure, you look freaked out a lot. But, I've never seen anyone look at him the way you do."

"How do I look at him?" I asked quietly, not sure I wanted to know the answer.

"Like you see him. He's not just King of the Bows to you. He's just Xander."

"Well to be fair, I hate the King of the Bows," I gave an awkward laugh and I was so pleased when it seemed like Tara understood the joke I'd intended.

"Exactly." She grinned. "Anyway, I just wanted to say my piece. I'll catch you later. Yeah, Doll?"

I wasn't sure if my heart felt kicked or overexcitedly hugged. "Yeah, for sure."

She smiled and it was nothing but friendly. "See ya." She gave me a wave and headed off.

I stood there, sort of surprised that it felt a whole lot like I was winning over the Bows, one by one.

Chapter Sixteen

I jogged up to the imposing front door of Xander's place and rang the bell, no idea what he had in store. I'd been told 'come comfy', whatever that meant. Hopefully jeans and a hoody were considered comfy by the dictionary of Xander.

When he opened the door, his phone was to his ear and he gave me a mouthed 'hey' as he waved me in.

"…yeah, that's fine," he was saying as he rolled his eyes, but he wasn't looking at me. "No, I'll check in with her tomorrow." He paused as he closed the door behind me. "Yeah, sure. No. Have a good time." He paused again and scrubbed his hand over his chin. "Yes, Mum… Okay… Sure, love you, too." He didn't really sound convincing.

He pulled his phone away from his head and pressed his screen. He stared at it for a second before he looked up at me.

"Hey," I said with a small smile.

He gave a huge sigh and his responding smile didn't reach his eyes. "Hey. Sorry about that. Mum and Dad just… Got in."

I nodded. "Oh. They're away?"

He huffed as he ran his hand through his hair. "Yeah. They do that."

My eyes took in his tense shoulders, the annoyance in his eyes he was trying to hide, and the way his usual lazy smile was seriously forced.

"Often?" I wondered if that was why I'd never seen them around. Not that I'd spent an inordinate amount of time at his house.

He turned and headed for the kitchen. "You could say that."

I didn't know if I should press or not. On one hand, he sounded the same as usual; cocky, relaxed, devil-may-care. Had I just been on the phone to him, then I would have believed it. But, I couldn't shake the look I'd seen on his face.

"They like to travel. And, Dad makes sure he has to travel for work. A lot," Xander said as he pulled the fridge open.

"Oh…" What was I supposed to say to that?

Xander shrugged, the muscles bunching under his t-shirt as he stared into the fridge. I watched his hand tighten on the door. "It's all good. What almost-eighteen year old wouldn't want the freedom of the house to themselves like ninety per cent of the time? No parental supervision. Do what I want, when I want. It's great."

I couldn't help looking around the huge house, not that I could see most of it from where I was what with the lack of x-ray vision and all. If Xander had this place to himself most of the time, how lonely would that be? What did he do all by himself? Maybe that was why he was out with the Bows so often? Maybe that was one reason he played soccer outside school? He'd be around more people and not have to be in the palatial place all alone.

"Yeah, I bet." I tried to sound upbeat and supportive.

He shot me a look over his shoulder and I couldn't tell if he was joining me in some joke that I felt like I'd made but missed, or if he was annoyed by something. I hoped it wasn't me.

"You wouldn't want this whole place to yourself?" he asked,

wryly.

I took a chance and my answer was completely serious. "Not all the time, no."

"Why not?" he asked, pulling a bottle of Mountain Dew out of the fridge.

I pulled myself onto the barstool and we locked eyes across the counter. "Well, it's a big place. I think I'd get lonely."

"Are you suggesting King Douche is lonely?" he teased.

I looked him over. No. I found it hard to imagine the King of the Bows ever being lonely. He was surrounded by people constantly. If anything, I'd have thought he'd like the peace and quiet at home compared to the constant barrage of attention he got at school and parties. But, the look in his eyes suggested Xander got lonely and I knew I'd be lonely.

I also felt like we were getting far more serious than either of us wanted. "I wouldn't dare suggest King Douche is anything other than the arrogant, laid-back guy we all know and love."

The corner of his lip tipped up and he turned to get a couple of glasses out of the cupboard behind him. "Well, of course. I'm far too shallow to have depths."

When he turned back, he certainly looked it. Gone was the hard, haunted, uncertain look in his eyes. He looked the same as he always did; lazy arrogant smirk and those crinkles around his eyes that never failed to make you want to smile.

"How else would I get away with sleeping with so many girls?" His eyes went harder again and he leant towards me.

"Well, naturally." I looked around. "Although, I'm surprised you bring them back here. Don't you worry they'll never leave?"

He shrugged, that smirk playing at his lips. "I don't tell them my parents are away. You'd be surprised how fast they leave when they think my dad's about to walk in."

I wasn't sure how serious he was being now. We seemed to have strayed into territory where we were having two conversations, and I was barely able to keep up with either. I wanted to ask him how many girls there had actually been, but I also didn't really want to know the answer. Instead, I looked down at my hands on the counter.

"And yet you tell me."

"Well, the reason's obvious, isn't it?" he asked and I looked back up at him in question. "Obviously, I want you to stay."

My face heated in a combination of awkwardness and happiness and I looked down again, having no idea how to respond to that, while my heart twirled in little circles. "So, what were your plans for tonight?"

"Well. As much fun as I had improving your bowling technique, I thought we could stay in and get to know each other."

"Stay in and get to know each other?" I clarified, thinking that was hardly teenage behaviour.

He nodded as he poured the drinks. "Yep. I was going to make us dinner, I have our double feature on stand-by, and I thought we could talk. Last I recall, I'm doing much better on the couple's quiz."

I frowned in confusion.

"I apparently know more about you than you know about me?"

"Oh." I nodded. "Right. Sure."

He huffed a small laugh. "So, I thought I'd get a start on dinner and you can ask me anything."

He turned away and started pulling things from cupboards and the fridge.

"Anything?" I asked.

He nodded and made a noise of agreement.

"Wow. So much freedom. I wouldn't know where to start."

He laughed, but it was rough. "Yes, you do. I know exactly what you want to ask me."

"Really? And, what's the answer?"

"The simple answer is not as many as you think."

I blinked and took a sip of my drink so I didn't blurt out anything embarrassing. I set the glass down again and cleared my throat. "How did you know–?"

He spun back to me and leant his elbows on the counter. "Doll, it was written all over your face just now."

My face had gone warm, but I kept my eyes on his. "And, the not simple answer?" I breathed.

He gave me a crooked smile. "I've hooked up with my fair share, but I haven't slept with nearly as many girls as the rumours suggest." He turned to the stove and turned it on.

Not knowing how I wanted to answer that, I tried to keep the tone light. "And that rumour that you slept with Daniel?"

"Ah. Well, a gentleman doesn't like to kiss and tell." He threw me a wink over his shoulder and I couldn't hold back my smile.

"Does this particular gentleman make a habit of sleeping with Daniel?"

"Would that be a problem?" he asked, completely cavalier as he chopped something and dumped it in a frying pan.

I blinked. "No. Of course not. I guess I'd just like to know if I'm competing against half the population or the whole thing."

"Would it matter?"

I realised that, no it didn't matter at all. I really only wanted to know because I had a perverse interest in his sexuality. But, why was that? It seemed like it was all over the media; who was dating who, who came out, who didn't, what the public's reaction was, over and over again it was reinforced we were supposed to care. But, his question made me realise that I thought it was no more interesting to me than anyone else's love life – I was interested because I was nosey and I liked the idea that people were happy, but that was as far as I was bothered. I mean, I wasn't going to change my immediate reaction overnight, but I was going to try harder to be less interested in what other people got up to in the privacy of their own lives no matter who they chose to do it with.

"Doll?" Xander asked and I looked up to find him watching me carefully. "I was joking… About me and Dan. I love the dude like a brother, but I just don't think we'd be compatible. Romantically. We're both…dominant… You know?"

I flushed harder. "Lovely image, that." Because what I needed when I already had to stop myself fantasising over Xander was to imagine him in compromising situations.

He flashed me that split-second smile and went back to whatever he was doing.

"You know, that wasn't really a number…?" I started.

"Were you after a number?"

I shrugged to myself. "I don't know."

"Do you know how many guy's you've hooked up with?"

"Yes."

"Really?" he asked sceptically and I was both glad I couldn't see his face and wished I could see it.

"Yes. But, when there's been about three it's easier to remember the number."

He scoffed and I saw him nod. "Fair point. About three, though? That's a little vague, doll."

"Well, what base do you count as a hook up? Or, does just the meeting of lips count?"

He turned back to me in the middle of sucking something off his thumb and I had a moment. "I can think of a number of hook-ups where there was no meeting of lips. At least, my lips didn't touch anything." He gave me that wink, but something seemed different about it, like he didn't believe in it or something.

"Yeah, I remember how much you like blow jobs," I muttered with a nod. "Okay. So considering a hook-up is anything remotely sexual, how many girls?"

He looked me over with that smouldering expression and I felt like I needed a fan or something. "I'd say something like fifteen different hook-ups. I had sex with…five of those."

My mouth dropped open. "Five?"

He shrugged and it was almost self-conscious. "Yeah. Five."

"That's all?"

He looked at me, stunned. "What do you mean, that's all?" he asked, a disbelieving smile crossing his face. "Is that not enough?"

"Well, I'd heard something like fifty. So, I mean, five's kind of a letdown. Don't you think?"

He stared at me like he didn't know if I was real or not for a moment. Then, he burst out laughing.

"What?" I asked, his laughter making me smile.

He waved a hand at me. "You've got to be the first person who's been disappointed in my number of conquests."

"Well, look. I was expecting double digits, Xand. Five's a little underwhelming after that."

He shook his head, wearing that adorable smile, and went back to dinner. "Uh huh, sure. Next question."

"Okay, favourite drink. I know you don't really like Mountain Dew."

He chuckled and goose bumps spread across my skin. "I don't hate it. But, how do you really hate something that looks like radioactive waste? I mean, what isn't cool about that? Besides, I thought you knew this already?"

"So, I was right with the red Powerade?"

He nodded, his back to me. "You were. Blue is hands-down amazing, but it needs to stay super chilled and nothing stays super chilled enough in summer. So, I got used to red."

"Okay, and what about Linkin Park? You call Vengaboys old school?"

He huffed. "Yeah, okay. But, at least they're still releasing music—"

"When did they last release something?"

"This year. *One More Light*. And, you can hardly talk. When did the Vengaboys make anything new?"

"2014. It was a Christmas album."

"Wishing you a very Venga Christmas?" he sniggered.

"No. But, that might have got them number one," I replied with a smile.

"How did you even hear about them?"

I thought for a moment. "I think I heard them on Mix and gave them a good old Shazam?"

He snorted. "Yeah, I'll bet. What do you like about them, anyway?"

I smiled, just thinking about it. "It's impossible to listen to one of their songs and not smile. No matter what kind of mood I'm in, it always makes me happy. What about you?"

"Eh." He shrugged. "I guess they're catchy. That one about wanting him in her room? I can get behind that."

I giggled. "Linkin Park."

"Ah." He paused. "I don't know. Their music...speaks to me. I get it."

It was one of times we were teetering on real, on serious, on some part of Xander I wasn't sure that I was ready to admit existed beyond the shallow visage of his reputation. I was torn between delving deeper, seeing if there really was more, or pulling away. In the end, he decided it for me as he put the dish in the oven and turned with a flourish.

"Right. That needs something like a half hour, maybe an hour." He waved his hands. "It's all very colour by numbers."

"Colour by numbers?" I clarified.

He nodded. "Yeah. You know. You've got to let it guide you."

I frowned as I thought about that. "I guess I can see where you're coming from. But, I don't think that's a thing."

"Huh," he huffed. "Weird. Why not? Makes total sense." I decided not to correct him. "Anyway, I propose–"

"Little early, don't you think?"

He smirked. "Cute. What say we fight it out in the virtual arena, then movie while we eat?"

I nodded. "I can get behind that."

He came around the side of the counter and held his hand out for me. I took it and he surprised me when he led me across the entryway and into a huge living room.

"Did you leave your socks out or something?" I asked him.

He turned to me with a smile. "I didn't think I could be trusted to control myself. Whole house to ourselves. All night. My room. I'm a gentleman, Holly, but my restraint only goes so far."

I laughed, knowing he was only joking. "Somehow, I doubt your restraint will be schooled by a change in venue."

"And risk making a mess in Mother's good room?" he gasped

208

sarcastically, but I got the feeling he'd heard a lot to that effect in complete seriousness during his life.

I smirked and shook my head. "You're of course assuming that I have complete control over my restraint," I laughed.

He pulled me to him. "Oh, is dirty Holly coming out to play?" he teased.

I frowned at him, or at least I tried. "There is no dirty Holly, remember?"

He tightened his hands around my waist and I slid mine up his chest. "I remember you're in denial," he huffed a laugh.

"I am not in denial."

"You will be when I finally beat you."

I laughed as Xander pulled away slowly and turned the TV on. I dropped onto the couch as he got everything started, then took the controller he passed me.

"What's your poison?"

"Mario Kart!" I said happily and he smirked at me.

"You think you can beat me on Rainbow Road again?" he asked sceptically.

I nodded. "Totally."

He shook his head. "That was a complete fluke."

It had been. The one time we'd played. But, I wasn't about to tell him that.

"Rematch, King Douche. Let's do this."

His eyes widened and he was trying not to smile. "You're on, Doll."

So, we loaded Rainbow Road and we went into combat. For the first lap, I kept to the middle of the front half of the pack, just managing to avoid falling off the road. Xander though was less lucky. Or, he was just less good. He spent so much time waiting for Lakitu and his cloud to fish him out and put him back on the track that we all lapped him quickly. Lap two saw Xander's swearing and muttering crank up a notch and keeping myself on the road was becoming a little more difficult because I kept laughing.

Of course, he noticed and I was sure he was trying to put me off by making me laugh harder, which just made us both fall off. By the time I finally got to lap three, I was number eleven and even six Bullet Bills weren't getting Xander through his lap two in time. I also had tears running down my face and Xander was spending more time trying to use my controller than his own.

Somehow, I got across the finish line. Our heads were close to each other and we were laughing like crazy. I dropped my head to his chest because I felt like I was about to fall over from laughing so hard.

"Okay, I concede," Xander panted, "you are the almighty Rainbow Road Warrior."

I snorted. "If I ever need to go fishing, I'll call you and Lakitu."

He tipped my face up to look at him and there was that shine in his eyes, that infectiously (not) charming smile, that look that conned my little heart into thinking we could be amazing together. As we looked at each other, our laughter merely became a shared warm smile and I had to tell my heart to stand down from the expectant beat it was suddenly marching around quite happily to.

It was dangerous, I knew. But then, I liked the way Xander made me feel. It wasn't just my heart, it was my brain too. I liked the way we could chat and laugh and do stupid things together. I liked how comfortable I felt with him even if I was trying to remember that I wasn't supposed to. I liked the way he seemed to like me for me, that he appreciated me as I was, not who I felt like

I was supposed to be.

Maybe we could cross some lines, sometimes, and my heart would be okay? So, while I told my heart not to look, I reached up and kissed him softly. As we drew away from each other, the humour in his eyes had become wary; like he was trying to work out what I wanted so he didn't overstep any bounds.

"Holly…" he breathed.

I looked into his eyes and replied, "Nothing wrong with having a bit of fun with it."

He flashed me the split-second grin that my heart liked more than it should and kissed me. My arms went around his neck despite the weird angle. There were elbows and knees and contortion that I sort of ignored in favour of enjoying his kiss.

Somewhere along the way, we'd lain down and he was lying half over me as we made out like it was going out of fashion – as Mum's beau would say. I didn't know how long we were at it. But, a steady beeping from the kitchen pulled Xander from me with a confused frown on his face.

He broke into a grin as he looked at me and jumped up. "I think that's the smoke alarm," he sniggered, then ran off.

I followed after him, obviously more worried than him.

But, dinner wasn't ruined. The cheese on top was just a little black and could easily be avoided.

Chapter Seventeen

I wasn't sure how much longer I was going to be able to keep this up.

A girl could only pretend that people didn't hate her for so long. And, the number seemed to be growing, not shrinking.

Despite the fact that things had seemed strained with my old friends and we didn't talk in person, I'd still been talking to them a little online. But, we were swiftly running out of things to talk about, especially when I was completely out of the loop on the group chat. I tried catching up on it on Monday night, but realised that forty-eight percent of what was talked about related to things that had happened in person. Which wasn't surprising really.

But, it did make me realise that I didn't really have any substance with them. And I was starting to think I never did.

I tried to think about the things we used to talk about; I was sure we'd talked about books and movies, bemoaning what was leaving Netflix, we'd talked about sport or news, or even assignments. But, trying to keep up with the group chat since I'd left, there was none of that. It was all gossip about the whole damned school; gossip about what stupidly embarrassing thing the nerdy Drama geeks got up to, or who Daniel or Rachel had last hooked up with and that Xander must have been hooking up with people behind my back, which stoner had got the most recent detention, who'd fought in the quad, what people were saying about me and Xander and Jason and Nancy.

I stared at the group chat on Tuesday afternoon, for some reason thinking I'd be able to get involved this time. But, it was all the same. And, I wondered if I was that shallow. Had I made up all that stuff about books and movies and assignments? Could I go back through the conversation and find that all it had ever been was rumour and gossip and rehashing our day?

And it was, as I was staring at the screen, that I was kicked out of the chat. It was suddenly unavailable to me. I blinked and my already unsure heart staggered to a stop and stared disbelieving at the phone with me. It tapped the screen, just to make sure we weren't imagining things.

Nope. I'd been kicked. Not just kicked. Blocked. I'd been blocked from the damned chat I'd started like three years earlier.

I wasn't sure if my heart was going to sit in the corner and cry or go on a Godzilla-sized rampage. Both options seemed pretty good just then.

So, of course, my afternoon got better.

"We ready to go?" said the not entirely unpleasant voice in my ear as his hand found its way to my arse.

But, I was not in the mood for keeping up appearances. I pulled away from him a little more violently than was probably necessary. "What have we said about hands!" I hissed angrily.

Xander's face fell from that uplifting smirk to confusion. And, given what had happened on Saturday, I didn't blame him. It hadn't got any more physical than the standard before dinner, but I hadn't been staying on my side of the line the way I should have. And, I only had myself to blame for my behaviour. Both then and now.

"Doll, everything okay?" he asked and my heart got even more unsettled at the tone of confused despair in his voice; because the last thing I needed was to hurt his feelings.

"Fine. Don't you need to get to practice?" I snapped.

I made to leave but he caught my hand and pulled me back to him. "Holly, talk to me. What happened?"

I sighed, telling myself he didn't need to get involved in all my grumps. "It doesn't matter. It's fine." I looked over him in his sport uniform. "You'll be late."

"So, I'll be late." He shrugged, trying to look in my eyes.

Score one for the short chick.

He put his finger under my chin and I finally let him tilt my chin up, but I made it clear I was annoyed with him. He smirked, knowing I was being stubborn as much for stubborn's sake as I was actually mad at him.

"Don't make me call you pookie…"

I had to bit my lip, but even then I couldn't help my reaction to him; he made all the bad things seem less bad. With him, I could take a deep breath and put everything into perspective again.

I'd walked out on my friends and I'd started (fake) dating Jason's rival, did I really expect that everything would be the same with them? Especially with Nancy parading around the school telling everyone how deranged and obsessive I was about Xander. Not that I'd heard any of it in person since Maths a couple of weeks earlier, but the rumours had spread like wildfire. You could see it in the way the kids looked at Xander and me like they were trying to see how placating he was really being.

It also added more fuel to the steadily burning fires of the debate as to who was going to last longer, to the discussions of who was the better couple, and the anger coming out of the Bow Inner

Sanctum.

My girl's day on Sunday had actually gone well.

Okay, if well here meant that they dragged me from shop to shop while everyone but Miranda seemed unsure about how friendly they were supposed to be with me, then it went gangbusters. Tara and Liv alternately seemed to forget I was there and pay too much attention to me. Britt had been there as well and stoically ignored me while Miranda stayed pretty much by my side the whole day as though she was worried I was going to wander off and get lost.

There'd been a running into Daniel and Greg moment where I was worried Daniel was going to drag me off my by hair and berate me for something horrible. But, he'd just raked his gaze over me like I may as well not have existed and then the boys were shooed off and we went back to our day. Tara got her flats. Miranda got her outfit. And, Liv got a good stockpile of her lipgloss.

And, what did I get? I managed to avoid everything but what I was told was a really cute outfit. It wasn't a bad outfit, I guessed. It was this little maroon lace tight, short t-shirt and flared black skirt. Let's just say it could have been so much worse.

"Holly?" I heard Xander say and I quit reminiscing and looked at him. "Are you sure you're okay? You seem completely out of it."

I nodded. "Fine. I just... No. I'm fine."

He took a deep breath and looked at me a little exasperatedly. "Okay, let's go."

I closed my locker, gave him my hand and followed him. But, we didn't head to the oval. "Xander?"

"Mmm?" he answered as he pulled me along and I suddenly wondered if there was a shortcut in the school I'd never known

215

about before...*that magically went in the wrong direction...?*

"Where are we going?"

He finally tucked us away in a side courtyard. He dropped down onto the bench and patted the seat beside him. "Sit down."

I looked at in in confusion. "You have practice."

"Come on."

"Xander, you can't skip practice."

"I'm not skipping. I'm going to be late. Remember?"

"Xander–" I started quite forcefully but he interrupted me as he leant his elbows on his knees and glared at me.

"Babe, I play or practice at least five days a week. I can take a few minutes out to prioritise my girlfriend when she's upset." He sat back again. "Now, are you going to sit or make me stand up with you?"

"You getting too old to stand up?" I stalled and he smirked.

"There's a lot of things I'll do for you. But wasting my prime years on unnecessary standing is not one of them."

I snorted. "Prime years?"

He nodded sagely. "Yep. I will never again know such good times as these. It's all downhill from here."

I sat beside him with a laugh. "Well. The things I have to look forward to, huh?"

"Oh no. You won't hit your prime 'til you're like thirty."

I looked at him. "What? Why?"

He winked at me and the corner of his mouth wouldn't stay down no matter how much he looked like he was trying to make it.

I nodded, fighting a smile of my own. "Yeah, I rescind that question."

"Okay, my turn then. What's up?"

"Why do you think anything's up?" I asked, fiddling with my

bag strap.

"Okay. It's that sort of day? No worries." He ran his hand over his chin before putting it on the back of the bench behind me. "So, Mum and Dad decided not to come home last night. Something about a party in Morocco they couldn't possibly miss for some couple they'd only just met. She finished off with the traditional 'you know how it is, darling,' and I responded with the usual 'of course I do', then she told me they loved me, reminded me to check in with my aunt and hung up."

My heart jiggled in what I couldn't decide was excitement or nervousness. We were back to that semi-serious tone and I wasn't sure if I wanted to investigate it more or not. I hadn't been brave enough to look into why I felt a little uncomfortable about the whole potential of Xander's serious side. I didn't know if it was our history, or I was never going to be free of caring what people thought of me, or any other number of reasons I didn't even want to contemplate.

"Where's the world that doesn't care…" I muttered.

"What?" Xander asked.

I shook my head and looked at him. "I don't know."

He smiled softly, almost uncertainly. There was nothing of the cocky arrogance about him, but this hesitant demeanour didn't do anything less for his charm-factor than the smirk that conned you into all sorts of trouble.

"Well, I'd call you back, but that seems a shameful waste of data just now. Besides, I look far better in person."

I huffed a laugh and looked at my lap.

I heard Xander breathe out deeply.

"I've seen my parents probably something like a total of seventy-two hours in the last six months. That doesn't include the time I was asleep or at soccer or anywhere but at home. So, some of that's on me. But, they've been in the city," he breathed out again, "I think the equivalent of two weeks in that time? At the very most."

He sounded so…lost, so uncomfortable.

My heart and I snuck a look at him from the corner of my eye. My heart peered around my ribcage, wondering if it was allowed to go to him. I decided that maybe, just this once, I'd let it.

"I'm sorry, Xand."

He shrugged. "It is what it is. I have soccer and the Bows and you–"

"But, you're lonely."

He looked at me askance and his smirk only just reached his eyes. "King Douche is never lonely."

"Maybe not. But, it seems Xander is."

He looked away and nodded. "Maybe."

I felt like this was one of those quid pro quo moments. If only because it was a return of the trust he'd shown me because there was a mountain more his tone and his eyes were saying about his feelings than the words alone.

"The group kicked me from the chat," I said quickly before I lost the nerve to open up to him.

He twitched like he was trying not to react in a certain way, I just wasn't sure what it was. "They what?"

"I know it's a stupid thing to get weird about. And, in the grand scheme, who cares. I just–"

"Holly, it's not stupid." Xander turned to me and cupped my cheek. "Okay? It's not stupid." He pressed a kiss to my forehead and looked at me seriously. "I'm not going to pretend I care about them beyond what they mean to you – you're far too intelligent for that to be anything but insulting. But, I get it. I can't imagine what it would be like if I lost the Bows. Okay? Everything else aside, I don't know what I'd do without Greg and Dan. Life would suck without Rand, Tara, Teag, Sabrina." He scoffed. "And, no Rach? Fuck, I wouldn't be strong enough to deal with it the way you have."

"What? Deciding to fake date your ex-best friend's nemesis?"

"I was thinking more along the lines of still being able to smile and not sit at home and eat ice cream by the tub."

I lifted up his t-shirt and looked at his abs. "I somehow don't see you sitting at home and just scarfing tubs of ice cream."

He grinned. "Trust me, I pay for it dearly after."

"I don't believe you."

"Fine. You, me and at least six tubs of ice cream."

"Four litre?" I panicked.

"One."

I nodded. That I could do. "It's a date."

His smile was warm as he wrapped me up.

"The stupidest thing is, I miss Jason," I told him, safely unable to look at him with my face pressed into his shoulder. "But, then on the other hand I sort of don't because he hasn't once stood up for me with Nancy. And then I remember something we used to do together, something we'd laughed at and I just miss him so much."

I felt him stiffen, but then he just hugged me harder. "That I find less easy to sympathise with, but I'm trying." And, he really sounded like he meant it.

I smiled despite everything because I was pretty sure, if the roles were reversed, that Jason wouldn't even try. "I guess it's like Rachel–"

Xander barked a loud laugh as he pulled away and shoved his

fist to his mouth. He shook his head as he shook with silent laughter and waved a 'hang on' hand at me. I frowned, unable to not smile in the face of his laughter, but completely confused.

"Sorry," he panted as he tried to take deep breaths. "Sorry. But, I just… No. Wow. Okay. So, me and Rachel? Not a thing that will ever happen. I mean, Hell could freeze over and it's still a hard pass on that one." His eyes focussed on me for a moment and he sobered. "But, the concept of betrayal isn't beyond me. Babe, what can I do?"

I shook my head. "I don't know. I guess I'll get over it?"

He rubbed the back of his head and looked totally out of his element. "Have you talked to him?"

"About what?"

He shrugged. "Anything. Everything."

"No. I had words with Nancy. But, Jason… No."

"Would it help?"

"I don't know." I honestly didn't know if I wanted to hear what he had to say or just keep on keeping on.

"Would talking *about* him help?" he said slowly, like he was already regretting asking.

"What do you mean?"

He shrugged. "I don't know. But, I hear that talking about people sometimes helps you move on or something. I don't know, I've never done therapy or anything but–"

"I have," just blurted its way out of my mouth. Neither Jason or Nancy knew I'd been to therapy, I always felt they'd judge me for it regardless of how they actually would have reacted.

There was silence for a moment and I refused to look at him. "Did," he cleared his throat adorably awkwardly, "you want to talk about that?"

220

I looked up at him with a smile, appreciating the effort. "There's not a lot to talk about. When my parents got divorced, they sent Mark and me to a psychologist for a few months to 'help with the changes' they said. I was ten and learning about putting things into perspective and accepting change, teaching myself to not focus on the wrong things instead of the right things, to analyse myself to be wary for signs of depression or anxiety. I still don't know if I'm doing it right." I gave an awkward huff of a laugh. "In hindsight, Mark and I don't think he was a very good psych."

Xander cleared his throat again and I felt him shift in his seat. "Any…signs?"

I shook my head. "I don't think so. I mean, I can't say I think all of my split-second decisions of the last couple of weeks were my finest moments. And, the Bows can be a little stressful. But, we're all good on the signs front."

"Stressful?"

"It's okay. I guess it's better than not having anyone, you know. Better to belong among hostility than not at all."

"Doll…"

"That *was* meant a little tongue-in-cheek, Xand."

"But only a little?"

I shrugged. "Yeah. I mean, you're a pretty good distraction, but I can only pretend for so long that any of your friends like me."

"That's not true. I'm pretty sure Greg and Miranda are about to stage a coup." It was a testament to the fact we might have been having a moment that he didn't comment on how good a distraction he was; I could only imagine the effort it took him.

I smiled. "I appreciate that. But, they're loyal to you. They all are. They're good friends." I scoffed and looked up at the leaves swaying above us. "Who would have thought I'd ever say anything nice about the Bows?"

"Dan's a total arsehat," Xander commented like that might make me feel better.

I laughed. "Still a good friend to you though."

"Is there anything I can do?"

I shook my head again. "No. Thanks, though. It's just nice to have a wallow sometimes, you know? Just kind of sit and be sad and annoyed, then the moment passes and you don't have to hang onto it."

"You know. We can…"

I looked at him in question.

"I'm here, Holly." He was so sincere and my heart looked at me for permission I was happy to give before it scooted on over to him. "Anything. I'm here. I'll wallow with you whenever you want, if you'd like. I'm always on Team Holly, no matter what anyone else thinks."

"You don't have to do that."

"What else is a boyfriend for?"

"Fake boyfriend."

The seriousness didn't leave Xander's eyes as his teeth caught his bottom lip and he nodded once. Something about the action had my heart slapping my brain upside the head, but I couldn't have told you why that was.

Chapter Eighteen

Xander's head leant on mine and he smiled. "You so do, I see it in your eyes."

I tried so hard not to smile that my cheeks were already hurting. "I do not." But, it came out more of a laugh.

He nodded. "You so do."

"I don't think you're charming."

"Why not? I'm totally charming!"

I leant one hand on his chest while I cupped his jaw. "No. That would be cocky and arrogant and maybe a little attractive."

He snorted. "Maybe a little attractive?" he repeated, mock-indignantly.

I nodded. "Those things don't amount to charm."

Xander opened his mouth but we were interrupted when someone yelled "Holly and Xander!" excitedly as they walked passed us like they were cheering for us.

Xander and I both looked up. But, I assumed the person had gone since there wasn't anyone close enough to us it could have been.

As my eyes scanned the hallway, I saw a guy younger than us further down the hallway. He was shaking his head at me in disgust. I was pretty sure I recognised him as the guy who always won the chess games. Then, I was completely astounded as a girl I knew to be a Bow-wannabe came up next to him and glared at Xander.

Xander's hand tightened against my back, but it felt more surprise than comfort.

"They are getting *really* serious about this," Xander said softly.

"I thought you loved gossip," I said looking at him.

"I'm usually amused by gossip," he answered as his eyes kept scanning the corridor. "And quite often indifferent. Not the same."

"Oh, and this isn't amusing?" I teased and he looked at me with a smile.

"You a comedienne now?"

I nodded. "Unlike some people, I'm very charming."

"Yeah, well that's not wrong," he said begrudgingly and wrapped his arm around my shoulders.

I laughed as I leant into him and we headed down the corridor. As we went, I saw Jason weirdly on his own for once. The conversation with Xander the day before played over in my head and I made another one of those split-second decisions. I patted Xander's chest.

"Give me a minute, yeah?" I said to him absently.

"Yeah, 'course. I'll see you out there?"

"Yep."

I felt him kiss my head and then he was gone. I shook myself out and walked towards Jason, telling my heart that the kids in the corridor weren't staring at me in morbid interest and refusing to look because my brain knew they were.

"Jason?" I touched his arm gently and he jumped.

He turned and looked at me like I was a mirage he was expecting to disappear again. "Yeah." He nodded.

I looked down for a second. "Um. Hi."

"Hi."

I did a great impression of awkward Xander and cleared my throat. "How are you?"

He looked at me and then around the corridor like he wasn't sure if it was a trick question. "Fine. You?"

I nodded. "Fine."

We stood in seriously sizzling awkwardness for too many stressful heartbeats. But, it was nothing like the sizzle with Xander, this was all the wrong kind of discomfort. I couldn't look at him so I stared at a patch on the bottom locker next to his leg.

"Did you want something?" Jason finally snapped and I looked up.

His blue eyes were hard, the skin around his mouth taught like his jaw was clenched. I couldn't see any sign of the boy I'd grown up with. There was no sign of the boy who'd re-enacted Disney movies with me in the living room over and over until our parents went mental. There was no sign of the boy I learnt to rollerblade with, the boy who pretended he wasn't any good at it so I thought I was better at something for once. Gone was the boy I'd called almost every night before bed for years and just talked. Gone was the boy I shared ice cream with, the boy I told most of my secrets to.

The guy in front of me hated me.

I wondered if this was the guy Xander saw when he looked at Jason. The guy that Xander had never liked. Was this the person the Bows saw? What sort of person had they seen in me when I'd stood next to him? If it was anything like the guy in front of me now, I wasn't surprised most of them still hated me. I was surprised more didn't still.

"Yes? No?"

I blinked. "I just… I don't know. I thought we could—"

"Could what? Talk? You're dating King Douche. What's left to say?" He slammed his locker.

"I don't know. How about an explanation? How about an apology? How about you explain why you didn't tell me about you and Nancy?"

"Nancy said…" He paused and my heart dropped to the floor, expecting the worst. "Nancy said we'd tell you together. You weren't supposed to find out like that. Nancy said we should act natural until we had a chance to tell you together. She said—"

"Nancy said? Nancy said? Since when don't you think for yourself?" I asked.

This wasn't the Jason I knew. This wasn't the guy who blazed the trail, who made the rules and the decisions. This wasn't the guy who walked around with a confidence to rival Xander's and a smile for everyone.

He shrugged. "Since I trusted her to know how you'd react."

I blinked. "Why? Why would she possibly have known better than you?"

Jason gave a weird grimace-frown and wouldn't look at me. "We'd talked about it… A lot. She said you'd be…"

His nose wrinkled like he wasn't sure if he should keep talking and my heart shuffled back into a corner in fear. What the hell had they talked about? He knew. He had to know. She must have told him. *He'd known this whole time?* And he'd not once ever done or said anything about it. God, that was worse than him just never seeing me.

"Nance said you'd need some…time with it. I didn't expect it would send you into the arms of the King of the Bows."

I swallowed. The least I could do here was try to save face, keep

226

up appearances. Maybe if I focussed on that, I could ignore the panic trying to grip me that told me Jason had known all this time how I felt about him and… What? Just hadn't cared?

"We were together before that," I said, but my voice sounded choked.

Jason frowned. "Before that?"

I nodded. "About a week before." When were we supposed to have got together? I don't think we'd covered this. I was going to have to ask Xander for a day or a date or something more substantial that round-about numbers.

"You were already dating King Douche?"

I nodded. "He's…not like we thought he was."

Jason gave me a superior snide look. "And you were stupid enough to fall for it?"

I bristled. "There wasn't any stupidity involved. Thanks for that great vote of confidence. I thought you were supposed to be my best friend?"

"And, I thought you were mine. But, best friends don't go fucking my rivals."

My throat hitched. "No one's *fucked* anyone," I spat and I watched the surprise on his face. "Oh, did you actually believe that story your girlfriend's spreading?" I sounded calm enough, but my heart was giving that Godzilla tantrum a go because I could see in his eyes that he'd believed everything that Nancy had said. I looked around quickly – noting that every person in the corridor was conspicuously staring at us – and stepped closer to him. "Xander asked me out, I'll have you know." Not really a lie. "I resisted for you," it wasn't *quite* a lie, "for as long as I could. But, I like him. I really like him, Jason." That was less a lie than was advisable. "But, I haven't had sex with him and there aren't any plans to change that

221

any time soon." That one was definitely not a lie.

Jason swallowed and I saw him looking for bullshit. Other than Mark, Jason had been the only person I'd thought could read me like a book, especially if I tried lying to him. Which had made the fact that he'd never noticed I'd liked him –when even apparently Xander had – all that much weirder.

"I was going to deny my heart for you, Jason Isaac Thomas. But, I didn't feel quite so bad about it after I realised you'd lied to me."

"I lied to you? At least I dated within the group. What I did was acceptable."

"Acceptable?" I asked; so ten years boiled down to meaning less than stupid high school clichés and rules and regulations, did it?

"You're the one who crossed the social lines and broke everything!" Talk about breaking; his voice broke on the last word.

I blinked. "Broke everything?" I scoffed. "I would have gotten over my moment of crazy, but you're the one who just sits there while Nancy rags on me constantly! You're the one who's believed every lie out of her mouth."

"Oh, I thought you *really liked him*?" Jason sneered and I'd given up looking for any sign my best friend was still in there.

It seemed like no matter what my intention had been in coming to talk to him, there was no resolving this. Any idea of finding my way back to Jason one day in any capacity was slipping further and further out of reach. Which made me feel less bad about what I said to him next.

"I do. But, I would have had less incentive to hang around a bunch of people who hate me if you'd been a better friend!"

"A better friend? That's rich. You know I hate him. You know

I've hated him since I met him."

"Yeah, and why is that, Jason?"

"You know why!"

"I don't think anyone does!" I snapped and it was the truth; it seemed no one could remember why Xander and Jason hated each other beyond it being a fact.

"Because he's a smarmy arsehole. He just turned up and expected everyone to bow to him and his money and his smile. So, he's a decent soccer player? Whatever. He's always been rude and arrogant and a total wanker. But, what did my feelings matter? You had to have what you wanted. You always have to have what you want."

Oh, that was so far from what I'd wanted. And, I couldn't remember the last time we'd done anything I wanted over what he'd wanted.

"You have no idea what you're talking about. If you and Nancy talked so much about it, you'd know that's not true. What happened to the guy the school worshipped, huh? What happened to the guy Mark passed his mantle onto? Where's the Jason I knew?"

"Maybe you never knew me."

I scoffed, "Yeah, because you knew the real Holly."

It had just come out. But, as soon as I'd said it, I wondered how true it was. I wondered if maybe Jason and I had never really known each other after all. Had we just been the person we thought the other wanted us to be? The person we knew wouldn't get unfriended or teased? Not that I had time to dwell on that as he scoffed right back.

"I'm the only one who does know you. You think that wanker *knows* you? There's only one part of you he wants to know and shame on you for giving it to him."

Did he actually still believe I'd slept with Xander?

I blinked hard, hoping the tears weren't going to fall. "You know what, Jason? I hope you and Nancy are very happy together. I can see I chose the right guy for me in the end."

My hand went to my nose in some weird half-arsed attempt to keep the tears back as I turned and hurried away from him. But, I was stopped when someone grabbed my arm. I was about to yell at Jason, but it was Daniel's face I saw glaring down at me.

"I knew it was only a matter of time before you went crawling back to him," he said, anger and contempt deep in his eyes. I'd never noticed there was a light brown fleck in the green, but I was plenty close to see it now.

I sniffed. "I wasn't crawling back to anyone," I answered, pulling my arm from his hand.

"Do you give the idJit daily reports? Or, are they only weekly?"

The tears were only going to be held back for a little longer and my brain was currently the only one trying to keep those floodgates closed; my heart had pulled out a row boat to ride out the inevitable storm in the most dramatic way possible.

"It's the first time I've spoken to him in weeks," I answered.

"Monthly then? Well, I guess you didn't want to be too obvious."

I breathed in deeply, about to lose my tenuous hold on many things; keeping my fist out of Daniel's face was one of them. But, my fist in Daniel's face wasn't going to go well, especially when the way back to Jason was getting more difficult to see. So, I did a really un-Holly thing; I was completely honest regardless of the consequences. I gave up trying to fit in, to placate someone else, and I just told Daniel exactly what was going through my head.

"Daniel, I get it. Okay? I get this macho act you've got going.

Protect Xander at all costs. I get it. I'm all for it. You have no idea how all for it I am. But, right now? Your timing sucks, man. I'm literally about to have a break down and it's not going to be pretty. So, you want to go at it? We can go at it. All free shots, I'll let you say whatever you want. I'll even yell back if it'll make you feel better. But, right now I'mma need to just bawl my eyes out over the fact that my best friend isn't the guy I thought he was. I need to just be completely emotional about the fact that I chose Xander and, while that was the right choice, it's not an easy one. You can hang around and wait until I'm done. Or, you can yell at me later. Preference?" My voice had started to waver dangerously, my throat had that hot pressure in it and my eyes prickled. I sniffed and looked at Daniel seriously.

"Uh…" He frowned as he looked me over. "Later is…fine."

"Okay. I'll find you when I'm done." I nodded and made for the nearest bathroom.

And, once there, I locked myself in a stall and I just let myself cry. I couldn't remember if I'd cried before then or not. I couldn't remember if I'd dealt with anything before that or not. I tried to use my perspective. I tried to identify what I was feeling and put it in context, to work out what I needed to do to get through this. There was only one thing one my mind.

Xander.

Xander would know what stupid thing to say to make me feel better.

Somehow, the King of the Bows could cheer me up without any effort when I couldn't remember the last time Jason had actively done the same. That realisation alone had me feeling like I was mourning something I'd never had in the first place. And that made me feel like an idiot.

231

I felt the tears slow and wiped my nose. I sat for a few breaths, hoping my eyes hadn't gone totally puffy but also sort of not caring if they had. Finally, I pulled myself together and up, rinsed my face, shook myself out and headed out for the Bows' table.

When I got there, I found Daniel talking to Xander. They both happened to look over and see me coming towards them. I stopped in front of them and let out a deep breath. Xander would know how to make me feel better, but I owed Daniel a conversation first.

"You okay?" Xander asked me and I nodded to him distractedly.

"We doing this or what?" I asked Daniel.

He looked at Xander like he wasn't sure anymore, but he nodded.

"Xander, can you excuse us a minute?" I asked, not taking my eyes from Daniel.

"Uh…should I be worried?" Xander said slowly.

"Not at all." I kicked my head sideways and didn't wait for Daniel to follow me.

"Okay, say it." I stopped a little way away, looking forward to getting a second confrontation over. I was almost feeling like I could confront Rachel after this, but I was going leash my heart on that one until further notice.

"Say what?" Daniel replied.

"Whatever is it you need to say. How you hate me. How I'm no good. How I'm just a spy for JT. Whatever it is you feel you need to tell me, tell me. Whatever piece of your mind you need to give me, give it." I even crooked my fingers at him, cheesy old Kung Fu movie style.

"Are you…okay?" he asked, stilted like it cost him an effort.

I almost though I saw a chink in the armour, that maybe there

232

was a way to win his trust one day. I reminded myself how I'd feel if the tables were turned and didn't blame him. That gave me the courage to plough on.

"This isn't about my feelings, Daniel. It's about yours."

He stretched his neck. "Fine. You're not good enough for him, you know."

I nodded. "Noted."

"You can think he's fallen for you, but he'll wake up one day and realise you're just using him."

"And, what am I using him for?" I asked, feeling this odd sense of clarity and calm, like my heart and my brain weren't quite connected at the moment, like my heart was running off adrenalin and felt like it could take on the Hulk single-handedly.

Daniel blinked like whatever he'd been expecting this to be…this wasn't it. "The idJit might not have noticed you, but Xand will see through you soon." You've got to hand it to him, he rallied well.

"I don't know what you think is going to happen–"

"I'd say the same thing to you. You think JT's going to suddenly turn around and notice you now? You've been invisible to him for years. Although how is fucking beyond anyone. Your crush on him was the most obvious thing in fucking history. You think you can use Xand to get back at him for choosing the slag? You hurt him and I will hurt you, you understand me?"

I nodded. "I understand you. Although, my crush on Jason was obviously not the most obvious thing in history since, as you say, I was invisible to him for years. It might be beyond your brain, Daniel. But, it's not impossible for someone to stop liking one person and fall for another. In fact, it's kind of normal. Especially at our age. You think anyone our age is getting married and

233

growing old together?"

"So, Xander's a passing fancy then."

I groaned; why did people do this? "No. I don't know how long we have. But, I'm not stupid enough to think we'll still be together in twenty years."

"And if he is?"

My heart paused in its distractions to look at him. "What?"

"If Xand's decided you're the one and you come in and tell me he's not? What am I meant to do with that? Do I hurt him now or pick up the pieces you inevitably leave behind?"

My eyes slid to Xander. "I'm not…" I breathed, not sure what I wasn't. "I don't want to hurt him."

"Yeah, you might want to think about that while you've decided you're not in it for the long haul and while you're sneaking around with JT."

"I'm not–"

"I don't care, Holly. You need to decide. Because Xand's not the kind of guy who's not one hundred percent sure before he does something. You wonder why you're his first girlfriend? I hope to God he's seen something in you I haven't, because the alternative is fucking heartbreaking."

He made to walk away and I stopped him. "Daniel… I do really like him…"

Daniel stared into my eyes and that frown didn't change. "Yeah. You like him now. But, how long until you've decided it's enough? Ten years? Fifteen? Less than one? I get not planning to be together forever, Holly. We're seventeen. But, just expecting to not be? How the hell does that work? Why bother?"

I swallowed. "It's just how it is."

"With who?" he asked, throwing his arms in the air. "Who gets to dictate how long your relationship lasts? Last I checked it was the people in the relationship. None of us are going to tell him he shouldn't be with you no matter how much we want to. Something about you makes him happy and we're not ruining that. But, I don't care what decree Rachel passed down. If I think you're going to hurt him, then I'm stepping in."

I shook my head. "I'm not going to hurt him." I couldn't tell him how much I wanted that to be true.

"It's simple loyalty, Holly. I get you're not used to it. But, it's a nifty concept."

With that, he turned on his heel and stalked off. I stood there for a moment, not sure what to think or to feel.

I had the school seemingly slowly taking sides, but I knew the Bows were going to stand behind Xander. There was no Xander and Holly in their minds. It didn't matter that everyone else was cheering for the both of us. To the Bows, it was Nancy and Jason in one corner, Xander in the other, and me in the middle with one foot in either corner. I didn't know how I could show them I was in Xander's corner. But, I knew I was going to have to do something.

Although, when I saw Jason later that day and saw a slight dusky patch forming on his cheek that looked eerily like a bruise forming and a corresponding mark on Daniel's fist, I wondered if maybe the real me – no holds barred – was the only thing that would prove my loyalty, the only thing that would prove I was in Xander's corner after all.

I'd done everything to fit in with Jason and my old group, done everything I could to be that person who wouldn't get teased or shunned. Well, look what had happened to that girl. It was time for me to stop simpering. Time for me to stop tiptoeing. Time for me to stop just being Xander's unsure (fake) girlfriend out of her depth. It was time I acted like I wanted to belong, like a Bow. Time for me to just lay my heart out there and hope to God someone other than Xander could like me for me.

Chapter Nineteen

"I'm winning the bet," Xander chuckled in my ear, his arms around my stomach as we walked awkwardly across the quad.

I scoffed. "You are not."

"I am. Do I have until midnight or half three?"

"For what?" I asked.

"To win."

"Point's moot, I will *not* think you're charming by half three or by midnight."

He squeezed me and laughed. "We'll see about–"

"Bowen!" the very recognisable voice of Jason shouted across the quad from behind us.

"Oh, have I been a *bad* boy?" Xander asked me teasingly and I snorted.

"Probably, but I doubt he knows about it."

Xander chuckled. "True. Unless, he's–"

"Bowen!" Jason yelled again, closer this time.

I turned in Xander's arms.

"Oh, git sounds pissed!" Xander smiled.

I smiled back. "It's you, of course he... Oh..." I'd peered around Xander and saw the utter fury on Jason's face as he walked towards us. "Oh, yeah, he's pissed. I've never seen him so piss–

Jason!" I yelped as Jason pulled Xander around and punched him in the face.

That caused interest from the students in the quad and they started gathering around, presumably expecting this fight that I'd been hearing about since this whole mess started.

Xander took a step back and frowned. "You right, Thomas?"

Jason pointed at Xander. "You think you're good enough for her?"

Xander wiped the blood from his lip, smirking. "You think *you* are?"

"I know what you want from her and she deserves better," Jason said, pointing at Xander.

Well, wasn't this an interesting turn of events?

Xander still smirked, but his eyes were hard as they flashed to me. "What she deserves is a best mate who isn't going to break her heart by lying to her. And like it's any of your business, but there does happen to be one girl I can't get into bed at this school and that girl happens to be my girlfriend. Which is more than fine by me."

The crowd was still growing and muttering could now be heard at that last statement; yes, King of the Bows freely admitting as though he didn't care that he'd failed in a conquest was going to be the talk of the school.

"Why would you waste your time on her, then?" Jason seemed genuinely confused by this prospect.

Xander looked at Jason like he'd just asked why grass was purple and Xander couldn't for the life of him work out what was wrong with Jason to think such a thing.

"Uh firstly, arsehole, I'm not wasting my time on her," Xander answered, stepping forward and I actually believed he meant everything he was saying. "Unlike you, I appreciate spending time with Holly for Holly, not what I think she'll do for me. *If* we have sex, that's on her terms." Sounded like a slightly pointed message to me, but I was a little distracted. "And secondly, where do you get off treating her like shit then trying to dictate *any* part of her life?"

Jason punched Xander again, and Xander just let him. Xander shook himself out and stretched his jaw, but made no move to hit Jason back. I wondered why; I mean, Xander could easily take Jason out.

"I suggest you walk away, Thomas..." Xander said slowly, his voice low.

Jason looked both terrified and resolute. "It's you who should walk away from her, arsehole."

"Well personally, I think that should be Holly's choice." He stretched his jaw out some more. "She chose me, Thomas, and I am *just* selfish enough to stay with her until she tells me she doesn't want me. Why don't you run along back to your girlfriend? I can't imagine she's going to be very impressed to hear you're fighting for another girl."

"I'm not fighting for her!" Jason said indignantly, and I suddenly realised he couldn't even say my name. Even two days earlier, he'd never said my name.

Xander chuckled mirthlessly. "Yeah? Well I will fight for Holly, arsehole, so step the fuck off." A tingle ran through me as my heart twirled around and I bloody well believed that statement.

"Seems to me that you're damaging your reputation with all this, Bowen," Jason sneered.

"Oh yeah? And how do you figure that?"

"Girls'll think you've gone soft. Whatever game you're playing with her? Whenever you get bored, things won't be the same after. Your reputation won't be the same after."

The crowd was watching avidly; I could feel the anticipation coming from them like a palpable living thing. They were waiting for the huge bust up, they were waiting for typical Jason-hating Xander Bowen to stop using his words and start using his fists. I got a feeling they'd get what they wanted soon enough.

"Fuck my reputation. I'm not playing any game with Holly, Thomas. And maybe I have gone soft, but at least *my* girlfriend is a gorgeous, smart, funny, beautiful girl who's kind to everyone around her, and not some raging hag happy to step on anyone to get ahead."

Oh my. My immediate reaction was to feel conflicted about Xander ragging on Nancy and I was sad and angry that Jason had picked a fight with my (albeit fake) boyfriend, but I realised that they probably deserved it at that point. And, it had to be said that my heart wouldn't stop jumping about in excitement over the fact Xander was standing up for me in front of who knew how many kids with nothing but honesty radiating off him. Xander's reputation had just taken a serious nose dive and, weirdly, he couldn't have looked more fine with that.

Jason twitched and Xander's pretend joviality fell.

"You hit me one more time and I *will* swing back, Thomas. We all remember what happened last time." Xander's voice was as cold as his eyes as he rolled his shoulders.

Jason looked like he was going to think twice about it, but obviously his smart brain wasn't in charge. He lunged for Xander, who was ready for him this time. The two boys fought and I wished I could say that I felt bad for Jason. But honestly, if he was going to use me as some bullshit excuse to fight Xander while avoiding

240

looking at me and acting like anyone wanting to be with me was a mystery, he deserved everything that was coming to him.

Jason got one more good crack to Xander, who stumbled back a little.

"If you hurt her!" Jason snarled and I was done with this stupid display of whose dick was bigger.

I stepped forward. "I am more than capable of looking after myself, Jason. No thanks to you."

"Doll…" Xander said, concern in his tone.

Jason's eyes flew to him, narrowing. "I thought only Mark got to call you 'Doll'?"

"People who *love* me get to call me 'Doll'," I shot back without thinking.

"If he told you he loves you and you believe him, you're a bigger idiot than I thought you were." Jason's eyes were full of hate and anger, and I was willing to bet mine didn't look much more pleasant.

A fist shot out and smacked him in the face. It took a moment for the pain to kick in for me to realise it was my fist.

Oh. My. God. That hurt like a bitch!

"Ow…" I breathed and felt arms go around me. I would have known they were Xander's even without the educated guess by how well I fit between them; I drew far too much comfort from just knowing he was with me, but I really didn't have the mental capacity to do more than appreciate it just then.

"I didn't realise it was necessary to let the whole school know something that only needed to be between us," Xander spat at Jason and I could feel how tense he was; my guess was he was super pissed at that point. Whether it was because he blamed Jason for the staccato throbbing in my fingers or for me telling the whole

241

school he was in love with me, I didn't know.

"Yeah, because the King of the Bows fell in love with her," Jason sneered and I was highly offended that he made that sound like anyone falling in love with me was unfathomable. Was it ridiculous that anyone could fall in love with me? Had Jason not noticed me all that time because I wasn't that kind of girl?

Xander's arms held me tightly. "Just because you didn't see what you could have had until she'd moved on, doesn't mean she's unlovable, you fucker."

"What?" Jason scoffed. "The man-whore King Douche seriously thinks he's fallen in love?"

I would have wondered where the Jason I knew had gone, but my hand hurt so. Damn. Bad. And really, I was finding it hard to feel anything but the pulse beating steadily enough for me to dance out a samba to it just then.

"So, what if I have? I don't see how it's any business of yours." Xander leant his head to mine. "You okay?" he whispered, nuzzling my check with his nose, and I nodded against him. Even through the pain, I told myself that wasn't just warmth and sincerity and something eerily akin to that love that was being thrown around; he was only keeping up appearances. "Want me to hit him some more?"

I gave a weird half-laugh, half-sob and shook my head.

"You sure? I'd do anything you asked, Doll."

I nodded, tears welling as I gave up trying to tell my heart Xander was just putting on an excellent show. "I'm good, thanks."

"Bowen! Thomas! And…Holly…?" we heard the voice of the soccer coach.

"Hey, Coach," Xander said casually, his arms still tightly around me like they could protect me from the world.

"I want to say I know better, but it looks like you lot have been fighting." Coach paused. "Bowen?"

"Ah, well… Yes. Basically, yes."

"Who started it?"

Xander sighed as though he was thinking. "You know... I don't rightly know, sir?"

"Thomas?"

Nothing audible from Jason.

"Holly?"

"I'm fine, Coach," I squeaked, realising too late I'd answered a question he hadn't asked out loud.

Coach sighed as well. "Bowen, if you don't give me anything, I'm going to have to send you all home."

"Oh, that would be a shame, Coach," Xander said, barely hiding the sarcasm from his voice. I knew how pissed off he was based on that fact alone.

"And I might bench you next game…"

Xander's hand tightened on me momentarily, then loosened again. "I don't know what to tell you, Coach." I felt him shrug. Guilt hit me, but we all knew we'd fare worse if we started trying to explain anything.

"Right, that's it. The three of you pack your things and get gone. I don't want to see you back 'til next term. Bowen, we'll discuss any potential benching next practice."

"Come on, Doll," Xander whispered to me softly, kept his arm around me and led me away. "I'll give you a ride home, yeah?"

"Oh my God. I *cannot* face my dad right now." The idea filled my veins with ice.

Xander huffed a laugh and kissed my head. "My place is empty." I heard the unsaid 'as usual'. "Shall we go hang there for

243

a bit?"

I nodded.

We collected our bags and he bundled me safely into his car, looking far too deeply into my eyes for my usual level of comfort. But, at that moment I was going to allow it. I needed it. And weirdly, I felt like maybe he did, too.

He got in the car and neither of us said anything as he pulled out of the carpark.

I was a tumult of emotion.

On one hand, my heart was moping about all the things Jason had implied, the fact he'd been barely able to look at me, and hadn't said my name once. After a life-time's worth of friendship, that was all it came down to? It was incomprehensible that anyone could fall in love with me and, if they did, Jason thought they were wasting their time? I just... God, that hurt worse than my hand.

But then, on the other, my heart couldn't stop fluttering in excited nervousness. I mean, Xander had said a hell of a lot of things he hadn't needed to; even to keep up appearances he hadn't needed to say that much. And, he'd sounded like he meant them. No amount of chastising on the part of my brain or pain thanks to Jason could stop my heart obsessing over that. No amount of distracting excitement on the part of my heart could stop my brain wondering how long until it started to admit it wondered if we weren't just keeping up appearances after all.

I watched the roads and buildings pass by until Xander took my hand. It wasn't the first time I'd tensed at his touch – but it had been a while – and it wasn't all because of the ache I was still feeling. His touch was gentle, like he well remembered I'd just thrown my first punch with that hand and it had landed on my ex-best friend's face.

"It's okay," I said as I still stared out the window, my voice a little rougher than I'd intended it to sound. "There's no one to impress here."

"Holly, I…" he started, sounding about as sincerely awkward as I'd ever heard him.

But, he didn't continue and finally he let go on my hand.

When he pulled into his driveway, he was at my door sooner than I'd organised myself to get out. He opened the door for me and I gave him a short smile.

We continued not saying anything until we were in his kitchen and I pulled myself up onto the bar stool.

"What are you doing?" I asked half-heartedly as he rummaged behind me.

He arrived in front of me with a bag of frozen peas and held his hand out. "Here, let me."

I gave him my sore hand and he ran his fingers gently over my knuckles. The motion stung a little, but even though I flinched I wouldn't pull away.

"Not bad for your first hit," he said softly, the smile on his face hesitant like he was trying to bring one out in me.

"Who says it was my first?"

Xander broke into what looked like one of his unbidden grins. "The way you were *obviously* not expecting it to hurt so much."

I gave a small smile and looked down. "Yeah, okay."

He laid the packet of peas on my hand, his other hand holding mine steady at the bottom of the pile.

"Are you okay?" he asked and I looked up to find an oddly vulnerable look on his face.

"I feel like I should be asking you that question."

He shrugged. "It was hardly my first time."

I scoffed. "I don't think you have anything left to do for the first time."

His gaze flickered between my eyes uncertainly. "There's at least one thing, but I'm not sure it hasn't happened while I wasn't looking…" he whispered.

I looked down again and cleared my throat; there was quite probably only one thing to which that sentence alluded and my brain wanted nothing to do with it. My heart? Well, that little guy was sneaking a shy peek around my ribcage with far too much hope.

"Why didn't you just hit him back the first time?" I asked. "You could have avoided all…that…"

"All what, babe?" he asked gently.

I swallowed. "Oh you know, the bruising and stuff…" I replied, totally not referring to the bruising and stuff. I wouldn't have batted an eyelid at Xander whaling on Jason if I'd known I could avoid hearing all that.

He tilted my chin up to face him and those gorgeous cognac eyes pinned me. "He had no right to say any of that, Holly," he said forcefully. "You are not unlovable. Being with you is not a waste of time. And *I* will always fight for you."

"I'm sorry I basically told the whole school you were in love with me…"

He smiled and ran the back of his fingers down my cheek before cupping it. "It's okay–"

I shook my head and looked at the peas. "It's not okay, Xander. I mean, there's keeping up appearances and then there's–"

"Holly, nothing I said to that git was a lie…"

I huffed a laugh, but I hadn't really heard him. "He was right. Your reputation is going to tank. I've just made it all that much harder for you. Girls will expect more from you. I was supposed to make things easier for you, not worse. I'm sorry, Xander."

He tilted my head up to look at him and I found his eyes alight with humour and a smile playing at his lips. "Holly…"

"Thank you," I heard myself saying.

Confusion tinged whatever he found humorous. "For what?"

I shrugged. "Sticking up for me? Fighting for me?" I narrowed my eyes as I looked him over, thinking. "Why *didn't* you hit him the first time?"

Xander busied himself with checking my hand. "Because as much as I hate the git, he was your best friend. I know what he means to you."

My heart felt like it had slammed itself against my ribs in its excitement to get to him and the poor thing was feeling a little stunned. "What?"

Xander shrugged, still not looking at me. "Look I know JT and I have a past, but you and he have a past too. And, I guess I just thought your past with him was more important at the time."

I bit my lip so I didn't laugh out loud. "I won't tell anyone, I promise."

"Won't tell them what?" he asked.

"That Xander Bowen, King Douche of all things Bow, is actually capable of thinking of the feelings of someone other than himself and his dick."

Xander looked up at me quickly, a slight cocky smirk at his lips. "Ah, now. That's not strictly true…"

"Really? Why is that?"

"Well Doll, because there is only one other person on this planet whose feelings I'm capable of thinking about and, half the time, my cock's in on that anyway."

I looked down to hide my smile because we both knew that statement wasn't strictly true either; he cared about all the Bows. "You're insane."

There was a pause and when he spoke his voice was somewhat more serious. "Why did the git think only your brother was allowed to call you 'doll'?"

I sighed. "I don't really know. Jason called me 'doll'…once, I think? I remember being really surprised at him and he never did it again. I never knew why. Maybe he thought I didn't like it?"

"You let me call you 'doll'…"

I huffed a small laugh and watched my hand as I stretched it out; it didn't hurt quite so much anymore and it was feeling less hot. "I let you do a lot of things I wouldn't let anyone else, Xander."

"Really, like what?" he asked playfully.

"Well for starters, I let you tease me mercifully. I let you bring out some seriously dubious tendencies in me and…" I stopped.

"And, what?"

I looked up at him slowly. There was something about that afternoon that made me feel more for him than I thought I should, and I didn't even try to remind myself we were only fake dating. It wasn't like I'd forgotten, but more that I couldn't convince myself that absolutely everything we were doing was fake.

He had legitimately stood up for me and, no matter how much he said he didn't care he'd ruined his reputation, I knew he'd be feeling something about it. The guy was well known for his lack of attachment and he'd just all-but confirmed to half the school that he'd fallen in love with me – I was supposed to be keeping the wolves away, not making them think he was a changed man after all this. And, there was something about that level of commitment to my honour that made me want to do some seriously inadvisable

248

things with him just then.

I tried to work out why my brain was telling my overly excitable heart that it was a terrible idea. I was getting the feeling that even if our dating was fake, whatever friendship we seemed to have found didn't have to go anywhere. And, I *was* attracted to him. I was even starting to think that maybe I actually liked him.

"I let you make me think you're a better man than Jason will ever be," I said slowly, remembering what I'd said to him the day all this had begun.

His humour turned to surprise, then his eyes softened. "No one thinks I'm a good guy, Holly."

I shook my head. "I don't think you're a bad guy."

"I'm shallow. I'm arrogant. I'm rude–"

"You're kind. You're sweet. You're funny. You're loyal to your friends."

"I put on a good show, doll." I didn't think he sounded like he was even convincing himself there and I wondered why he seemed to be trying so hard to convince me.

"You've already shown me more loyalty in less than four weeks than I think Jason has since the third day of reception."

He cleared his throat like he was embarrassed or something and looked down at my hand, running his fingers over the bruising gently. "What else do you let me do?"

"This…" I said as I took his face in my hands and kissed him before my head talked me out of it. Because I did want to, even if part of me knew it was setting myself up for a world of pain.

He responded instantly, putting his arm around me and bringing us closer together. I melted against him as I wrapped my arms around his neck. And I didn't worry that I was giving him the wrong message. I didn't worry that I was giving me the wrong message. I just let myself like the guy for a little while.

Later that night, when I was home again, I watched the clock avidly. At 11:59, I accepted Xander's friend request. Because there was no way even my brain could keep telling me I didn't find him charming.

I got a message from him less than a minute later.

Xander Bowen:
Does that mean I won, then?

      Holly Aberdeen:
      Yeah. You won.

Xander Bowen:
Cool.

      Holly Aberdeen:
      What? No gloating?

Xander Bowen:
Nah. I didn't want to ruin it.
I smiled to myself as I replied.

      Holly Aberdeen:
      Night, Xander.

Xander Bowen:
Night, babe.

Chapter Twenty

Xander Bowen:
What are you doing now?

Holly Aberdeen:
I have literally just landed!!
How are you already being so annoying?

Xander Bowen:
Greg's taking a dump and I'm bored.

Holly Aberdeen:
Ew. There is such a thing as over sharing.

I opened up a conversation with Greg as I made my way out of the airport.

Holly Aberdeen:
Xander's sharing the news on your BMs.

Greg Hook:
Why does that not surprise me?

Xander's face bubble lit up.

Xander Bowen:
Did you dob on me?

Holly Aberdeen:
What? Are you five? Who dobs anymore?

Xander Bowen:
You apparently.

I laughed as I shook my head.

Holly Aberdeen:

I have to go find my mum. I'll talk to you later.

Xander Bowen:

You'll probably talk to Greg first.

Holly Aberdeen:

I promise I won't talk to Greg first

So, of course, Greg's face bubble lit up.

Greg Hook:

Why aren't you talking to me now?

I grumbled and opened Xander's chat.

Holly Aberdeen:

I think that also counts as dobbing.

Then, I went back to Greg's.

Holly Aberdeen:

Is he being as annoying in real life?

Greg Smells Bad:

Worse.

Greg Smells Bad:

When are you coming home?

Holly Dolly Oxen-free:

What's happened to your name?

Holly Dolly Oxen-free:

Woah! What's happened to mine?

Greg Smells Bad:

Who do you think happened to them?

King D'Awesome:

You know me. Personal boundaries aren't my thing :D

Excellent, Xander had somehow got into Greg and my chat. I

didn't know why I was surprised.

Holly Dolly Oxen-free:

How do you know we weren't having
personal private conversations behind
your back?

Greg Smells Bad:

I imagine that's what he was hoping for.

Holly Dolly Oxen-free:

How did you even get here?

King D'Awesome:

Sneak infiltrations. And this way, I can join
in. See:

Damn, that Xander. He's such a butt!

Rabble rabble.

See? I'm excellent at it :D

I heard my name and looked up as I saw Mum waving to me from further down the pick-up zone. I turned off my screen and, shoved my phone in my pocket and weaved my way through the crowds too Mum and her car.

"There you are, beautiful girl!" she cooed as she wrapped me up in her arms, heedless of the duffel over my shoulder.

"Hey, Mum," I mumbled into *her* shoulder as she almost crushed me. "Where's the beau?"

Mum pulled away and waved a hand as she walked to the car. She pulled open the boot and smiled. "He had to work. But, he'll be home for dinner. So, we'll have a girl's afternoon!"

I felt my phone buzzing in my pocket as I dropped my bag into the boot and gave her as warm a smile as I had. We got into the car and she navigated her way out of the airport and towards her house while I tried to think of plausible answers to whatever crazy questions she might think up.

In Mum's mind, girl's afternoon meant only one thing; ask Holly all the awkward questions and don't take no or silence for an answer.

She thankfully didn't start until we were back at her place with a fortifying cup of coffee.

"So, tell me about this boy?" Mum said, her hands wrapped around her mug as she stared at me from under her fringe.

I hid my surprise behind a frown; why would mum know about any boys? "What boy?"

She rolled her eyes at my attempted deflection. "This Zach or whatever."

My frown deepened with some idea of who she meant. "How do you know about any Zach's or whatever?" I asked.

"Mark was…" she waved her hand like she was looking for the word, "worried. He called."

"He dobbed?" Then, I sighed at myself, "I've spent too much time talking to Xander," I muttered.

"Ha! That's it. Xander." I don't know what accent she was trying on, but she rolled all sorts of letters there. "Very sexy name."

"Ew. No." I grimaced and pointed at her. "None of that." Although, she wasn't wrong.

She grinned. "And not just study it seems. So… You like him? He likes you? What's going on there?" She waggled her eyebrows and I frowned.

"Just study."

Mum scoffed. "Not just study."

I rolled my eyes and weirdly found the truth coming out. "Okay, fine. Fake dating."

"Fake dating?"

"Yes. Fake dating."

"Is that a thing that actually happens?"

I felt the sudden urge to strangle my brother for telling Mum anything about anything. "Apparently," I huffed. "Mark doesn't know that part, though."

"Oh, something Mark doesn't know!" Mum was in full-on gossip mode.

I glared at her. "Just… It just happened. But, it's not real."

"Okay. And, how did it just happen? Did it have anything to do with…? Mark mentioned…something…but, I don't really remember." She waved her hand aimlessly.

Trust Mum to have remembered there was a boy but not why or even that there was absence of another boy.

I cleared my throat. "Jason and Nancy got together. I…reacted… Ergo, Xander and I are fake dating."

Mum frowned like she was trying to connect more dots than there actually were. "I assume that makes sense in your teenage brain?"

Well, it had at the time. "I guess."

"And, why are we fake dating? Why not real dating?"

I sat up quickly and rearranged, and I knew she noticed. "Because Xander doesn't do…real dating—"

"He doesn't? Or, you don't?"

I glared at her and pretended she hadn't interrupted. "Besides, we're young. We're just supposed to have fun. You said so yourself." I waved it off like everything was good.

She didn't say anything and I looked at her more closely. I didn't have a lot of reference, but I was almost sure that that was what a proper, with-it mum was supposed to look at you like.

"Oh, Doll…" she said slowly.

"What?" I asked nonchalantly like my heart wasn't totally

invested in the hope she was going to give me some actual motherly advice.

"Your dad and I didn't work out. But, that doesn't mean that you and Xander aren't meant for the long-haul. Kids your age are supposed to believe in forever and hope and the power of love to beat all obstacles."

"Well, obviously I didn't get the memo," I grumbled. My heart was still super keen for this Mum-advice thing, but my brain didn't want to hear it anymore.

"Holly, the beau and I might not make it. Despite having some more life experience under our belts and having a little more concept of forever, any number of things can happen. Sometimes you just fall out of love. No amount of planning or growing up or preparation can stop that…"

I shifted in my seat. My brain was starting to get on the bandwagon, but this side of Mum was different and new and I wasn't sure how to deal with it. She'd always been the fun mum, the games and jokes and shallow conversation mum. I knew she loved me, don't get me wrong. But, serious heart-to-hearts had never been her thing. They'd always been Mark's thing.

"But, I mean… Statistically–"

"Statistics?" Mum scoffed. "Doll, where are you getting this?"

"From that psych you sent Mark and me to. He said that statistically, people who meet in their teens will never make it, it's just a fact of life."

Mum grumbled some very unfavourable words. "I have wished so many times over the years we didn't send you to him. The only solace I had was that Mark was too busy being a teenage boy to listen much and I hoped you'd be too much of a teenage girl one day to remember."

"Nice gender stereotyping there, Mum."

She huffed. "You know what I mean. Seriously, I can't open my mouth these days without the wrong thing coming out. No matter how benign my intentions, I end up insulting someone."

I shrugged. "World we live in, I guess."

Mum rubbed her eyes. "I get it. I do. Things need to change for the better. I just wish it was easier to retrain forty years of instinctive thoughts and reactions."

"Yeah, well. We'll get there one day. At least you know you're trying to do better."

"Doesn't help the people I inadvertently insult."

I nodded. "Suppose not, no."

"It's a bit like Jason and Nancy, I guess…"

I frowned at her weird segue. "How?"

"Well, no matter how much they didn't intend to hurt you, they did," she said slowly.

I scoffed. "Yeah, I'm not sure about that anymore."

Mum squealed in excitement and I looked at her in concern. "What?"

She sighed and looked at me, but she looked at me with pride. "Dolly, you've always had a tendency to over-analyse the way your behaviour affected other people. Your father and I are to blame for that. You saw how our behaviour affected each other and you strove to make sure your behaviour didn't hurt anyone else. But, baby, it was about time you turned some of that introspection out."

"What do you mean?"

"Well, people can do shitty things to us and it isn't because we've done anything to deserve it."

I looked down at my cup. "I know."

"I know you know. But, when it came to Nancy and Jason, I've

257

never seen you realise that before."

I shifted uncomfortably. "I mean, I guess I… Sometimes I didn't…" I sighed because she was right. Even if she hadn't seen it first-hand a lot, she was still right. I'd made excuses for their shitty behaviour without even realising it until now. "Okay, I maybe let them treat me a little shittily."

"A little?" Mum scoffed. "How about that time you wanted to do the talent show and you ended up watching as they did the number together and you got credit as the *costume designer*?"

I leant forward as I glared at her. "Just how much do you and Mark talk behind my back, Mum?"

She looked very self-satisfied. "Enough that I know more than you think, Doll."

I huffed and was just about to try out that Godzilla tantrum my heart seemed so invested in lately. Then, Mum spoke and threw me totally off-guard.

"How did you think it would work with Jason?"

I blinked at her. "What?"

"Well, you won't real-date Xander," again with the weird rolling of letters there, "but you were all ready to storm in and tell Jason how you felt?"

"Now you conveniently remember?"

She shrugged coyly. "I don't forget everything forever."

God knew I loved this woman, but ugh.

Although, her question resonated in me in a way that I hadn't been prepared for. It was a good question. I wasn't sure I knew the answer to it.

"I don't know," I grumbled. "Jason does dating? I didn't think he'd be able to hurt me? I trusted Nancy when she said I should tell him, assuming she knew something I didn't? I don't know, Mum."

258

"Why did you think he couldn't hurt you?"

I looked at her and didn't want to answer that question. The answer was pressing up against the edge of my mind, but I didn't really want to acknowledge it. "I don't know."

She nodded. "And, can I ask why you think Xander will be able to hurt you?"

I looked at her, annoyed. She was supposed to ask bothersome questions, but they weren't supposed to be intrusive and make me take a look at myself. I was supposed to tell her there was no beau of my own and then listen to her prattle about how we needed someone sometimes and how a good partner was good for us. Actually, as I thought about that, I was starting to see dangerous parallels between her and Xander. But, tangent.

"Because he sleeps around, he drops girls like they burned him, and he's shallow and insincere. He makes for an amusing friend, but a boyfriend he is not."

"Well, he certainly sounds like a teenage boy," she quipped.

I barely heard her though, because my heart was busy asking my brain how much of that I still believed. It wasn't even just rumour anymore. It was actions, it was words straight from him. I knew him now. I took a deep breath before it felt like I was going to suffocate. Even I heard my breath hitch, so I'm not surprised Mum did too.

"Doll?"

I held a finger up and frowned as I thought about it. "Okay. I'm not sure, but maybe the real reason I'm worried he could hurt me is because maybe he's not actually like that at all, but maybe he still couldn't like me the way I might maybe like him?"

"That's a lot of maybes, Dolly."

I nodded. "Yeah."

259

We sat in silence for a moment as I panicked over what I was supposed to do with that information. I knew I didn't hate him anymore. Honestly, I'd known that first week I didn't actually hate him. But, the idea I liked him? And, maybe I *like* liked him? That gave my heart a nervous twitch I'd never felt before.

"Thank you, Holly," Mum said softly.

I looked up at her in surprise. "What? What for?"

I saw her eyes were glassy, but she was smiling. "For opening up to me. I know I haven't been the world's best mum, but I've always wanted to be there for you. Thank you for trusting me."

I felt my face flush and my heart clasped its hands in front of it and gave a shy smile. "I've told you things."

"Not like that."

I looked up at her and smiled. "I'm learning a little bit more about opening up to people other than Mark."

She nodded and a smile played at her eyes. "I see that."

"It's not as bad as I thought it would be."

"I'm glad."

"I blame that Zach or whatever guy."

Mum snorted and we both laughed. "Then maybe he really isn't so bad after all?"

"Maybe not."

"But, not boyfriend material?"

I looked back at my now-empty cup. "That trust is still a little hard to have."

"Do you know what he wants?"

"Not really."

"Could you ask him?"

I was about to shake my head, but figured a little more honesty for one day wouldn't hurt. "I'm afraid if I do, he'll tell me the only

260

thing I don't want to hear."

"I get it. Why make a problem where there isn't one?"

"Exactly."

"And, what if he wants the same thing?"

I thought back to Daniel's words the other day. I wondered if, no matter what we had, I'd already written us off, or if I could go into this with all that belief in forever and hope and love and wait to see what happened. That was the part that scared me the most; that it would become real and it would break and that would hurt more than it not being real in the first place.

"What if it doesn't work out?" I asked her.

"Dolly, your plane could go down on the way home. A meteor could hit the house. You could be diagnosed with cancer. We don't know when our ending will be, but we can chose to make the most of what time we have. Your dad and I had some really good years, baby. And I don't regret any part of it, except maybe not walking away earlier and saving us all some heartache. Maybe you two won't work out, but think of what you might have if you just take that chance. You could be happy."

"I'm happy now. What Xander and I have now is good.

"Okay. But, what if you could have something amazing?"

I took a deep breath, trying not to remember that infectious smile of Xander's that made me think that exact thing. "I'm trying. I don't know how to let go of that…worry."

"All it takes is a little faith, doll. A little faith and a little loyalty."

There was that damned word again. I was starting to wonder if I'd ever really known proper loyalty outside my family. And, even then, the concept was touch and go.

Mum reminding me about the talent show from a few years ago

was dredging up other memories and I was seeing them differently now.

The time I wanted to go to Mark's first amateur soccer game, but Nancy kept dragging me around the shops saying that her crisis was super important and we'd be done soon. The time I'd waited for weeks to not watch the last Harry Potter movie without both of them and then I'd found out they'd watched it without me because I was visiting Mum. The time Jason had wanted to go to The Beachouse because his crush was going even though I had a massive headache, so we went and I ended up puking and he didn't even get the girl.

Maybe I was looking unfavourably on those memories because we'd had a falling out. Maybe I'd been spending too much time around Xander. But, maybe I'd also let them walk all over me a little bit without really stopping to notice it. Maybe the two people I'd thought were my best friends in the whole world hadn't been as blindly loyal to me as I'd been to them?

"Okay, I think I've been serious Mum for long enough. I was supposed to be helping, not making it worse. So, I vote more coffee and a movie!"

I smiled, knowing her well. "One of yours?"

She shook her head. "No, Doll, one of yours. I dare you to scare the pants off me."

I grinned at her. "Are you sure you're ready for this?"

She nodded. "Yes."

So, while she made coffee, I found a movie.

And, that kick-started an actually really great few days together.

The beau came home in time to cook us dinner – by no coincidence, his actual name was also Beau. And, having started that little-bit-closer connection to Mum made hanging out with

262

Beau easier too. We laughed and joked and ate way too much. Mum and I had a few more heart-to-hearts. I even shared some of my annoyance with Xander's constant messaging and didn't deny it when Mum teasingly told me I liked it. We hadn't become the best mother-daughter team in the world in a few short days, but I got on the plane on Wednesday feeling a whole lot better about everything.

Until I saw who was waiting for me when Mark pulled up to the house after collecting me from the airport. Xander sat on our front steps with Doug.

"What the hell is he doing here?" Mark muttered.

My heart went into hiding and I felt butterflies in my stomach. "Dunno."

Mark continued grumbling to himself as he grabbed my duffel out of the boot and marched straight passed Xander into the house. I was slightly slower in making my way over to him as he stood up.

"Hey," I said slowly.

"Hey." He grinned down at me and something about amazing wandered through my brain.

"Oh. Here." Xander lifted his hand and I saw a wilted daisy in it, a smile on his face that suggested he was very proud of himself. "Welcome home."

"Uh, thanks," I replied, trying not to smile as I took the flower from him. We just looked at each other for a while (but, my brain kept a tight leash on my heart) until I had to break it. "So, did you want to come in?"

Xander was practically vibrating with pent up energy. "Oh, I can't. Gotta get my shit and get to practice. I just wanted to make sure you didn't die in a fiery plane crash!"

"What is up with you and Mum and plane crashes?" I wondered.

"She and Zach know these things, Doll," he answered like he was an expert on the matter as he tapped the side of his nose and winked.

And, yeah, I might have spent most of the last week calling him Zach after I told him Mum thought that was his name for a while. Needless to say, Greg thought it was hilarious. I was with Greg on that one.

I nodded. "Sure they do. Right, so I'll talk to you later?"

He smiled warmly. "Sure. Maybe we can hang out tomorrow?"

I shook my head. "Maybe."

"Tease."

"Douche."

He blew me a kiss and waltzed off down the path with a laugh.

"French, huh?" Mark asked as I closed the front door behind me and Doug.

I jumped and looked at him. "French. Yeah."

Mark looked me over and I *think* I got away with lying to him again.

Chapter Twenty-One

Miranda was rifling in my wardrobe when Mark popped his head into my room, obviously just back from his game – which meant I could expect a message from Xander any minute, no doubt.

"We should have bought shoes," she called and Mark frowned in that direction. Miranda emerged, blowing hair off her face. "I should have asked about... Oh, hi," she said as she saw Mark.

"There is a Bow in your room, Doll," Mark said as though it was an infestation I wasn't aware of and he wasn't sure what to do with.

I pressed my lips together to stop myself from laughing at the shocked and intrigued way he was staring at Miranda. I swear, I would have said he'd never seen a member of the female species before the way he was looking at her.

Miranda rallied like a damn pro as she waved at him, her cheeks only flushing a little. "Miranda. Definite Bow. Yep." I had to say, I did love the unapologetic pride she had in who she was and the way she could just get over what people thought about her; I really wanted to be more like her.

"Uh, Mark." He nodded.

"I remember." Miranda's face got a slight touch more pink about it.

"Okay, introductions have been made. What can we do you for?" I asked my brother.

He shook his head and looked at me. Then he frowned. "That new?"

I looked down at the outfit the girls had talked me into buying on our girls' day. We didn't have to leave for a little while, but Miranda and I were doing a pre-party fashion show just to make sure I was going to wear the best thing.

"Yeah. Like it?"

Mark's face went an adorable mix of awkward and exasperated. "You look…" He wrinkled his nose. "Okay. You look nice."

"But?" I sniggered.

"You just don't look very…you."

I looked down again. "In a bad way or a good way?"

Mark shrugged. "Neither. Just… It's different."

I nodded. "Okay." We all stood in a bit of an awkward silence for a moment, then I asked him, "Did you want something?"

He blinked. "Yeah. Did you want me to drop you off tonight?"

I looked to Miranda. She looked like she was trying and failing to keep her eyes off Mark. I tried very hard not to smile when I looked back to Mark and saw the feeling was apparently mutual. I just couldn't tell what either of them were thinking – I could have found my brother dating my new friend or he thought she was going to murder us in our unsuspecting sleep.

"Thanks. That'd be good, yeah."

Mark nodded, gave Miranda a small smile and headed out. Miranda looked back to me and we both burst into laughter. Only, I didn't really know what we were laughing about. I just knew I liked laughing with Miranda.

"Okay, so shoes?" I asked her, as I tried to get my breath back.

266

Miranda jumped like she'd only just remembered the whole point of her coming over early and nodded. "Right. Shoes. I mean, you're lucky Xand's tall. So, we can pick anything. How are you with heels?"

"Terrible."

Miranda shot me a grin as she disappeared into my wardrobe again. I was quite happy to just let her pick whatever she thought was going to work, as I'd told her the day before when she'd hinted she'd quite like to get ready together. I wasn't really expecting the huge bag of makeup and hair styling things that had arrived on the doorstep with her, though. But, she hadn't expected to use any of it on me, so I was feeling more comfortable with it.

"How terrible is terrible?"

I snorted. "Uh, they'll be off within maybe a half hour?"

"Is that all heels, or are wedges good?"

"Do I have wedges?" I asked, thinking it wasn't a good sign if I had stuff in there I'd forgotten about.

Miranda pulled a pair out; they were chunky black bootie sort of things that had to have been an old pair of Mum's. She held them up with raised eyebrows. The longer I didn't say anything, the more energetically teasing her eyebrows got, until I finally laughed and nodded.

"Okay, okay, I'll try them."

I pushed myself off the bed and took them from her and realised that I wasn't sure I'd ever had this sort of relaxed hang out with Nancy. I couldn't remember a single time I felt completely comfortable just trying on a bunch of clothes and dancing around my room like an idiot with another human being in there with me. I'd been quite happy to watch Nancy do exactly this, but Miranda actively encouraged me to get up and dance with her. And, she even got excited about the Vengabus. I didn't feel any weirdness or like I should just sit down again because I wasn't doing it quite right, and I didn't actually care if I wasn't doing it right because Miranda didn't seem to care either.

It was the weirdest sensation and I finally let myself believe that Miranda wasn't just lulling me into a false sense of security. She'd actually become a proper friend who I felt like I could trust with anything. Well, almost anything; I wasn't exactly about to tell her that I was only fake dating her king but maybe might quite like him.

We spent the next hour and half singing and dancing and laughing so hard that Mark actually thought there was something wrong with us. But, he still drove us to the party, keeping his mouth shut even though I saw him look at us in the rear-view mirror in concern a couple of times as we giggled.

We pulled up to the house and I heard Mark sigh, but it sounded more like he was reminiscing than anything else. Miranda hopped out and I leant into the front seat and smiled at my brother.

"Memories?" I teased.

Mark snorted. "Less than is probably ideal. Dan Walker always threw the best parties."

"Yeah, well seems his little sister learnt a thing or two."

"Sabrina, was it?"

I nodded. "Yep."

Before the Bows were the Bows, their group's Supreme Leader had been Rachel's older sister Dee, who'd been good friends with Sabrina's older brother, Dan. There were a ton of Walker kids and the responsibility to host The Winter Party was passed down the line almost reverently – there had been a mock-ceremony last time and everything. When Maple Ridge was out of Walkers, I felt a little sorry for the party scene.

"Right, pep talk. Behave, don't drink too much, don't do anything I'd do, and certainly nothing I wouldn't do–"

"Yeah, all right Mr Stark," I sniggered.

He threw me a smile. "I'm serious, Doll. You might have done a bunch of Bow parties before, but you were never a Bow bef–"

"Hey, whoa! Not a Bow!"

He nodded. "Okay. Amendment. You weren't hanging out with Bows before. You think our lot can party hard…?"

"Marco, it's not like I haven't seen them in action. I'll be sensible, 'kay?"

He nodded again. "Okay."

"Besides 'our lot' got a lot softer after your year left."

Which was true. In Mark's time, Jason's group (Mark's at the time) had been able to give Dee Harris' group a run for their unnecessary riches. Now? No way in hell. The Bows would wipe the floor with the… *Daniel had called them idJits, hadn't he?*

Mark snorted. "I'll bet. How are you getting home?"

I shrugged. "Dunno. I think I've got a ride." I wasn't going to tell him that Xander had mentioned getting me home. "But, I'll text you?"

"Sounds good. I'll be around."

"Cool." I leant through the seats to kiss his cheek and shuffled over to the door.

Just before I got out, he spoke again. "Doll?"

"Yeah?" I asked, half out of the car.

"That Miranda chick seems okay."

I grinned. "You say that because you think she's cute."

I saw his smile before he turned away. "The two things can be unrelated, Dolly."

I flushed warm, knowing he would have hated admitting anything nice about a Bow.

I got out of the car and saw Miranda was waiting for me with a questioning smile. I answered it as I waved to Mark.

"Did he have terribly scathing things to say about me?" she joked with a smile.

"Quite the opposite actually."

"Really?"

"Really," I answered as I let her take my elbow. The interest she'd had obviously didn't extend far enough to ask me what sort of things.

"Okay, you ready to make your grand entrance?"

I nodded. "Go on then."

Our 'grand entrance' was a lot more low-key than Miranda had seemed to expect it to be, but I was quite happy with that.

As usual for The Bow Party of the Year, the place was packed, the music was loud, the lights were low, and it was hot despite the chill in the air outside. This year the theme was 90s, so people were dressed accordingly and I'd heard Sabrina talking for weeks about the playlist for it; I didn't recognise the current song, but I liked it.

"Is Xand here yet?" Miranda asked, her lips close to my ear to be heard over the noise.

I had a very surreal moment where I realised *I* was the one who was expected to know best what the King of the Bows was up to. It was made even weirder as I saw some of my old friends huddled across the room –*idJits*, I tried out the term again.

The fact that the Bows and the idJits were at the same party – let alone a Bow party – was a matter of course, despite the ingrained hate there. Parties at Maple Ridge were one of those things that basically had an open invitation and you just ignored

270

the people you hated if you decided to go. Jason, Nancy and I had still boycotted them sometimes under principal just because we could. In hindsight, I doubted the Bows even noticed.

Nigel turned and saw me. My automatic reaction was to smile at him as I used to. But his eyes slid to Miranda, still attached to my arm and now waving enthusiastically at someone, and he glared.

I cleared my throat and looked at whoever Miranda was waving at and all my discomfort was gone as I saw Xander sort of dance-walking over to us as he mouthed along to the song – something about no scrubs? I laughed as Miranda let me go to let Xander wrap me up and hug me tightly. He dipped his nose to my neck and told myself I didn't get goose bumps.

"Hey," he said, pulling away to look at me, then grinning at Miranda.

"Hey," I answered. "You started on those tequila suicides already?"

He broke into that split-second grin that made my heart flutter happily. "Without you? Never, Doll."

I shook my head at him, but didn't get a chance to respond as Daniel had jumped on his back with a shout.

"Duuude! Anna's dancing on the fucking table!" he yelled and Xander grinned.

"Dan, on the other hand…" Xander winked at me.

"What, man?" Daniel asked, sliding off Xander's back and eyeballing me.

"Tequila suicides," Xander explained and Daniel threw his arms in the air.

"YES!"

He grabbed Miranda's hand and tugged her after him. I watched them, smiling at Daniel's enthusiasm and wondering how much more he needed to drink that night. As I was still watching them, I felt Xander's hand on my waist as he stepped closer to me and I looked back to him as I registered the song had changed to something slower. He started swaying us gently as he stared at me

"What?" I asked.

"You're taller."

I smiled as I looked down. "Yeah. Rand insisted I try them."

"You taking orders from a Bow now?" he teased.

"No. I happened to agree with her."

His fingers trailed along the space of naked skin between my top and skirt, making goose bumps flare to life across my skin and my stomach flutter.

"And, this?"

I looked up at him and cocked my head in question. "You don't like it?"

He shook his head with a small smile. "Oh, I like it. You look amazing." He dropped his forehead to mine as our hips swayed together. "But, I'm quite fond of those pyjama pants of yours, too."

I laughed. "Those pyjama pants aren't exactly party clothes."

Xander shrugged as his hand splayed on my back and we drew closer together. "Who cares if you're comfortable?"

I smiled. "I'm not uncomfortable like this."

He nodded. "Good. I'd hate to think you dressed up for me."

I looked down at him in his oversize flannel shirt and the bright yellow shirt tied around his waist with the baggy white t-shirt and even baggier jeans. "Well, at least it's obvious you didn't dress up for me."

"Is it?" he asked and I looked up at him quickly.

"Did you?"

He gave me that nonchalant shrug. "If I did, is it working?"

I lay my head on his shoulder as I giggled and wrapped my arms behind his neck. "Yeah, Xand, it's working."

"Sweet."

He kissed my temple and I looked up at him with a smile. I reached up and kissed him. His arms tightened around me and mine seemed to think it was a pretty decent idea to reciprocate.

When the song changed to something a little more upbeat and I finally I recognised it, I looked at him with my mouth open in mock-surprise.

"What?" he asked.

"It's your song," I told him.

He looked at me in confusion until the words 'Mr Vain', where he laughed roughly. "That it is, babe."

He took my hand and spun me around, making me laugh. He pulled my back to his front as we danced together and I didn't care if people were looking, I didn't care about keeping up appearances, I didn't care about anything else except us in that moment. And us in that moment had a very real tinge of amazing about it.

"You want a drink?" he asked me when the song was finished.

I spun back to face him. "We are not doing tequila suicides," I warned him.

"Not tonight, no."

I blinked. "I seriously thought that argument would be longer."

He grinned. "Nah, I'm Sober Salvador tonight." I frowned at him in confusion. "Our designated driver?"

"You call your designated driver Sober Salvador?" I giggled and he wrapped me up tighter, knowing I was teasing him.

"Yes, thank you. Brings a touch of class to it, don't you think."

"Well, we both know you need all the class you can get."

"Oi!" he chuckled, lifting my feet off the floor for a moment. "I'm proper classy."

"Yeah, no." I paused and looked at his head. "You should have a sombrero."

"What?"

"For Sober Salvador."

He shook his head with a wry grin. "Do you think a sombrero would suit me?"

"It can't hurt, surely," I teased.

He laughed as he took my hand and led me through the crowd. I hadn't paid close attention to anything much beside him, but I did a double-take as light flashed over something. And no, I wasn't wrong. I froze and Xander looked back at me.

"What?" he called over the music. "You okay?"

All I could do was nod as I pointed at the thing on Anna's skirt as she was apparently still dancing on the table – Daniel on the other side of the table was completely thrilled.

"Xander, what is that?" I yelled back and he came back to look at it.

"What's what?" he said in my ear.

I grabbed it and pointed it towards him. Anna ignored me as she kept dancing and I ignored the fact I half hand my hand up her skirt as I barely kept a hold on it. I pointed at the button with my other hand.

"Team Bowdeen?" I asked him and I saw him smirk.

"That's not half bad."

"Xander!" I snapped.

He shrugged, looking at me in that totally innocent way he had. "What?" I glared harder and his smile almost broke through. "It's brilliant."

"Did you know about this?"

He shook his head and tugged me away from Anna's tabletop shenanigans. He pulled me through the kitchen to the quieter laundry. "No, I didn't. But, it's okay."

"Xander, they made freaking buttons. Buttons! Who the hell even made buttons? Where the hell did they–"

He stopped me with a kiss and I leant into him. Just as I was forgetting my own name, he pulled away with a smile.

"You good?"

I nodded, a little breathless. "Buttons, though?"

He laughed. "Just let them do their thing, babe. Come on, let 'Team Bowdeen' show them how it's done."

He gave me one more kiss and led me back out to the party. He barely left my side all night unless I had to pee. We danced with the Bows, watched Miranda and Daniel go head to head with shots – Miranda won – and avoided glares from the people I'd come to know as idJits.

Jason and Nancy made a good show of dancing close together very suggestively and, based on the looks Nancy threw me, I was supposed to feel something about that. But, I had to say I didn't because I was actually having a really good time at a party, and a Bow party nonetheless. No matter how many glares or passive-aggressive bumps I got from my old friends, a Bow was there to make me smile as we sang along with the songs we knew and danced like no one was watching.

As the night went on, I saw more and more 'Team Bowdeen' buttons on people and I started seeing the hilarity in them; they were just a harmless bit of fun and I wasn't going to worry about who had organised it or why it had happened.

I even danced with Daniel at one point while Xander had an eye

275

on Sabrina and Tara who'd decided to join Anna on the table again. And actually, I'd noticed a whole bunch of times when Xander was looking out for people, and not just Bows: as we went down the stairs at one point, he helped a girl who almost fell when she was jostled in the crowd; he smoothly started a conversation when a girl had backed a guy up against the wall and didn't seem to notice he was panicked; he took drinks off Daniel and Miranda every now and then; he just generally kept a watchful eye over the whole party much like Rachel would do for the Bows.

"He's a good guy," Daniel's voice was loud in my ear even with the music blaring.

I looked at him and nodded. "I know."

He looked me over. "Just don't fuck it up, yeah?"

I gave him a small smile. "Is that almost a blessing, Dan?"

He fought his own smile. "The two of you are good together. I hate to admit it, but you are. I just don't want to see him hurt."

"Are you going to remember this tomorrow?"

He grinned and I could see why people fell over him. "Only tomorrow will tell."

I laughed, suspecting that was code for 'not likely'. "All right. Well, I'll tell you something then, Daniel. I really like Xander. But, I'm scared he doesn't like me the same way."

Daniel looked at me like that was the stupidest thing he'd ever heard. "Look, I was surprised at his big announcement – we all know Xand's reputation. But, Doll, I've never seen him happier than when he's with you."

My heart felt like it had been given a beautiful balloon and it was going to float away. But, happiness didn't equate to romance. I was pretty sure I'd been happier with him, too, but that still didn't mean we were suited for long-term or that Xander liked me the same way – it was becoming difficult to deny – I liked him.

I thought again to what Mum had asked; what had I really expected to happen when I'd been ready to tell Jason how I felt? Had I expected we were going to date? Had I thought that it was doomed before it began and was going to go through with it anyway – believe in that hope and love stuff and just enjoy it as long as I had it? Had I not worried because the idea it might end wasn't as scary then as it was now?

I couldn't remember if I'd had a plan or not.

I looked at Xander, who had his hands in the air as a few of them jumped along to the song whenever it told them to. He had one of those huge smiles on his face.

But even if I did like him, how did I get over that fear it would end? How did I let myself believe he liked me the same way?

He caught my eye and I smiled at him.

There wasn't anything more to think about and I was going to stop overthinking it. Mum had been right; I needed to stop overthinking things and just live.

Xander made his way over to Daniel and me, looking like he was reading far more into us dancing together than he needed to. Which is not to say he thought Daniel was trying to cut in on his turf, he just looked like he thought Daniel and I were becoming friends. I wasn't so sure drunken given semi-permission meant we were going to be friends any time soon.

"Can I cut in?" he asked Daniel, who nodded.

"By all means, man."

Daniel left us to it and Xander hugged me close with one arm as he titled my face up with his other hand. He wore that infectious smirk that totally conned me and I let my heart feel whatever it wanted. I met his lips halfway and held him tightly.

I felt his hands slide over my arse and smiled against him. "Xander?"

"Yeah?" he asked, mock-innocently.

I shook my head with a laugh. "All right, just this once," I said against his lips and kissed him again.

Chapter Twenty-Two

My phone dinged and I looked over at it. The little notification light was pulsing green and the screen was still blank. I licked my fingers semi-clean, wiped them on my jumper much to Vern's displeasure and picked it up to find a message from Xander.

KingDoosh:
What are you up to?

He'd decided to change our names in our chat and I hadn't really wanted to change them back.

Dollface:
Wallowing. What are you up to?

KingDoosh:
Wallowing?!

KingDoosh:
Why wallowing?!

KingDoosh:
You okay?

Dollface:
I've fallen to the communists.

KingDoosh:
Well, they do have some convincing arguments...

Dollface:

I didn't take you for a fan.

KingDoosh:
Of what?
KingDoosh:
What does it mean?

Dollface:
IT Crowd.
I'd guess my first assumption was right then.
Dollface:
I'm suffering the wrath-filled tantrum of the raging hormonal beast below.

I watched the little 'someone is typing' and the pulsing dots for a little while as I scratched Vern's ears, which pricked as we heard Doug barking outside. The longer it took for him to reply, the less I was sure if he'd got it or if he hadn't.

KingDoosh:
Ah.
KingDoosh:
Anything I can do?

Dollface:
Thanks. But, no thanks.
Dollface:
It's not pretty. The only thing that will help is trashy rom-coms, blankies, and junk food.

He didn't reply straight away, so I went back to my movie. It was about half an hour before I realised my phone hadn't gone off again. I checked my phone again, but there was still nothing from Xander. I frowned, but shrugged; Xander was known to get distracted in the middle of a conversation, and I didn't know what he was up to that night. Besides, whether we were or weren't still faking, I didn't expect him to have any interest in period-Holly. I wasn't terribly interested in period-Holly, to be honest; she was sore and angry.

I picked another movie – yet another screening of *A Cinderella Story* – and rearranged my wounded womb under the warmth of the cat. God, it felt like Alien was going to come ripping out of there and I was so not amused.

"Holly!" I heard Mark yell up the stairs and heard Doug barking again.

"What?" I yelled back as I paused the movie to hear him better and he screamed my name again. "What?" I screeched back louder, wincing at the pain that elicited in my lower stomach, and Vern jumped off my lap with an annoyed mewl.

Seriously, why did evolution think it was a good idea to make it painful to speak as punishment for not getting pregnant? Rude.

"There's something here for you."

And yes, I did check the time because I'd suddenly forgotten it was about nine o'clock on a Thursday night and I wondered who the hell would be delivering me anything now – late night shopping notwithstanding.

"No one, you loon," I muttered as I pulled myself off the couch with a grimace and wandered towards the stairs.

"Holly!" Mark yelled.

"I'm coming!" I screamed as I dropped down the last few steps and turned to the front door. "Uh…?"

Mark glared at me questioningly as he pointed at Xander in the doorway. Mark might not have like that Xander was at our front door, but Doug was giving him a good sniff.

"Hey," Xander said with a nod.

"Were you expecting company?" Mark asked.

"What the hell are you all yelling about?" Dad asked coming out of the living room and Doug went running to him with his tongue lolling about.

"Holly's got a visitor," Mark replied sullenly.

Dad looked between us all: me in my daggiest, comfiest clothes and wrapped in a blanket; Mark incredibly unimpressed; Xander at the door with some shopping bags.

"Aren't you on Mark's soccer team?" Dad asked Xander.

He nodded. "Yeah. I go to school with Holly."

Dad smiled. "Cool. You kids have fun."

And, he wandered back into the living room again as Doug trotted after him. I gaped after them.

"Where's the parental control, buddy?" I called, feeling like it applied to Doug as much as my dad.

"Oh, uh… Be sensible?" I heard Dad call uncertainly and I muttered something very uncomplimentary under my breath.

"Doll. Explanation here?" Mark said.

I turned back to the slightly more pressing concern. "Ah, right. Well, Xander is…"

"Merely delivering period relief," Xander finished as he held up the bags.

I flushed like all the blood in my body wasn't trying to make a break for freedom down south. Mark's questioning glare told me he was even less impressed that King Douche was at our door delivering a care package.

"What do you know about period relief?" Mark asked him, crossing his arms.

"Uh, about five years of doing the same for Rachel Harris," Xander replied as though Mark would know that meant something.

I guessed it did mean something to Mark given he paled. "Shit, your Queen Bitch on her period is not something I'd want to be involved with."

"Can we all just stop saying period?" I snapped.

"What?" Xander and Mark said at the same time.

I held my hands up. "It's just weird. Aren't boys supposed to be weirded out by this stuff? I mean, *I'm* weirded out by this stuff."

They both shrugged in comical unison. I huffed and started wandering back up the stairs to the waiting Vern as he rubbed against the bannister at the top.

"Uh, Doll? Is he coming in, or what?" Mark asked.

"I don't care, Marco. He can do what he wants."

I heard them talking to each other for a bit as I headed for the TV room upstairs and eased myself onto the couch. I was just curling myself up into the vertical foetal position when Xander bounded up the stairs.

"I can do what I want?" he quipped and I glared at him through my blanket. His eyes widened and he nodded. "Okay. Moody?"

I nodded and burrowed into my blanket. "You were right, then."

He looked amused. "About what?"

"Hormonal thing," I answered grumpily, wishing he hadn't been right.

"Why is that bad?"

I shook my head.

"What?" he asked.

"Talk hurts."

He nodded and came over to the couch. "Can I sit?"

I nodded and rolled over a little to make room for him. He dropped next to me, putting down the bags – which Vern automatically stuck his head into – and I rolled back over to lean

283

against him. He wrapped an arm around me and rubbed my lower back. Oh. My. God. It felt amazing. I swear I was about to start purring.

"What can I do?"

"Remote," I said.

He leant forward as best he could without disturbing me and grabbed it. "What now?"

I held my arm up and mimicked pressing a button. "Play!"

He chuckled and pressed the button. The movie flared to life again and he just kept rubbing the spot on my back that seemed to magically make all the pain lessen to the dullest ripping sensation. It was even better than a hot bath, a heat pack, and six hot chocolates all rolled into one.

"How did you do that?" I asked.

He took a moment to respond and I had a sneaking suspicion he'd been totally engrossed in the movie. "Huh?"

I smirked at him, but didn't mention it. "That massage thing. Did you know that was going to work? Or, was that just a complete fluke?"

He grinned, looking thoroughly pleased with himself. "I worked out a couple of years ago that it helps Rach. I didn't know it was going to work for you, obviously, but I figured it was worth a shot."

I leant my head back against him and snuggled in. "Yeah, well count that as something Rachel and I actually have in common."

He laughed and I felt myself smile. "You've both got me, too."

"Yeah, she's not as happy about that as you seem."

I felt him shrug. "Rachel's protective."

"I've noticed."

"It's not a bad thing." Xander sounded completely defensive.

I lay what I hoped was a reassuring hand on his chest. "I know. It's a good thing."

Xander shifted a little like he was uncomfortable. "She'll get over it. Eventually. I mean, she can't hate you forever."

I wondered how much it actually affected him. How much was this fake dating thing actually affecting something real in his life? I might not have had any reason to like Rachel, but I did stop to think about how my actions were affecting them. And, I'd heard Mum when she'd suggested not everything was about my actions alone – I got it, I so got it. But, I was pretty sure this was one of those times that it was my actions that could make or break something.

I pushed off Xander for a moment and looked at him. He turned to look at me with a question in his eyes.

I tucked my hair behind my ear and stared at his chest. "Is everything okay with her? Rachel, I mean."

"Why would you ask that?" he said slowly the way Mum and Dad had answered when Mark asked them if they were getting a divorce after we'd heard them yelling at each other and they'd pretended everything was fine.

I shrugged and pulled my blanket tighter around me. "Things seem…tense between you two. I get Rachel and I aren't friends… But, I don't want to come between you."

Xander tilted my chin up to face him and I saw him wearing a small smile. "Babe, nothing comes between me and what's important to me."

"Nothing?" I asked, coyly.

There was that split-second flash of a smile, but his eyes were sad. "Okay, my parents aren't exactly something I can do anything about. But, I fight for what matters, Holly. Surely you've worked

285

that much out by now?"

I nodded and found it difficult to look into his eyes. "I'm getting there."

"Good." I heard the smile in his voice. "So yeah, Rachel and I are a little bumpy at the moment. But, she's not going anywhere. She's too damned stubborn. And, I've got no intention of changing you and me…unless you do?"

I looked up at him quickly and blinked. Did he want to end this? "Change us?"

Those cognac eyes were watching me carefully. "If you wanted to…change things, then we can."

"Things are okay with Rachel?"

He nodded. "They're fine. You're not coming between her and me, and she won't come between you and me."

"And, you don't want to fake break up?" I asked.

He looked completely taken aback. "Break up?"

"Yeah. I mean, if you're regretting this whole fake dating thing or…whatever, then I don't want to be putting you out."

"Regretting it?" he asked, his eyes still wide like he didn't know what language I was speaking.

"A conversation usually involves more than just one person repeating the other," I told him.

"Repeating?" he said blankly, then smiled and we laughed, but something about him seemed off. He pulled me in close for a hug. "I'm not regretting anything, Doll."

The strength of the relief that washed through me was completely tinged by the raging hormonal beast below, I knew that. I knew that had we had this conversation at any other time of the month that I'd be happy, just not this ridiculously happy. My heart felt like it had expanded three times its usual size and was spinning around on the side of some mountain range in the sunlight singing. But, I let myself just enjoy the way he made me feel.

"So, no need to change anything."

He gave me a gentle squeeze. "Sure."

I looked up at him as my heart froze in its elated skipping, wondering what was up with that tone. "You can be honest with me, Xander." I took a deep breath, ready to hear that something I was now willing to admit I didn't wanted to hear. "This only works if we're both into it."

He looked me over as though he was trying to find the right words. "I'm pretty sure we're both into it."

"Pretty sure?"

There was that hint of a smirk at his eyes. "Well, I can only speak for myself and I am most definitely into this. I'm all for a lack of breaking up of any sort."

I smiled, my heart frolicking in the waves of relief. "Okay. So, we're good."

He wrapped his arm around my shoulders and kissed my head. "Yeah, babe. We're good."

My heart had gone back to skipping, but my brain was trying to take a second look at Xander because something didn't seem quite right. It was like he had that mask on again, like he was stuck between being the guy I knew from the rumours and the guy who didn't seem like that at all. I wasn't sure why that might be, but I leant up and kissed him quickly and the sincere smile that that elicited on his face finally reached his eyes.

"I'm not sure how advisable that is with your brother in the house," Xander mock-whispered in my ear. "Unless you're about to tell him we're dating?"

I scoffed. "Yeah, no. I'm not sure either of us would like his reaction."

"So, should we maybe put a little distance between us then? Room for the holy spirit or whatever?"

I snorted as I sat up to look at him. "What *have* you been watching?"

He shrugged adorably. "I don't remember. But, I thought it sounded kinda funky."

"Kinda funky?"

"Yeah. Opposite of anything I'd want, obviously. But, you know, it conjures a very specific picture."

I nodded. "Yeah. That it does."

We just sort of got distracted looking at each other for a while. My skin tingled and my heart jumped up and down in nervous excitement. I felt like something was about to happen. I had no idea what might be about to happen, but I was looking forward to it. There was such softness in Xander's eyes, and that tiny little lift at the corner of his mouth, that I willingly walked straight into the con for a moment. I was totally willing to believe we could be amazing.

"How are you feeling?" he asked finally, running his hand down my cheek softly.

"Feeling?"

"You need chocolate? More pain killers? Hot water bottle?"

I gave him an appreciative smile. "I don't have a hot water bottle."

The grin that spread across his face had my heart melting into a little puddle of swoon. "Well, you're lucky I planned ahead."

He gently extricated himself from under me and leant forward. He reached into one of the bags and pulled something out of it, a look of half-triumph and half-hesitation on his face.

"It's the best I could do on short notice," he said.

"That's not the first time you've said that," I replied as I stared at the hot water bottle with the owl cover.

"Well, I guess my flaw is I'm not a patient guy. I wanted to help now, so I got something that maybe wasn't perfect. But, I figured in this circumstance it was better than nothing."

"Just that one flaw?" I asked, sliding my eyes to him and pretending my heart wasn't melting for a totally different reason.

He returned my smirk. "Yeah, all right. One of many. Should I have waited until I found a frog?"

I shook my head. "No. It's great, thank you." I snuck a look at the bags on the floor that Vern had left in peace. "Just what else do you have in your bag of tricks?"

There was that self-satisfied, split-second grin. He pulled one of the bags towards him and started pulling things out.

"A snuggly friend," he said as he passed me the beautiful stuffed unicorn.

"Am I not a little old for stuffed toys?" I teased.

His mouth dropped open in mock-disgust, although I trusted his words were serious. "No one is *ever* too old for stuffed toys, babe. What are you? Some kind of heathen?"

I grinned as I hugged the toy to me. "No, of course not."

He nodded. "Right. So, chocolate – a must, obviously."

"Obviously." I took another look at the packet and saw exactly what they were. "Chocolate-covered snakes?"

He threw me a seriously smouldering smile. "They're your favourite."

"They are." How did he know that?

"Mountain Dew because why not."

"Of course."

"And, last but not least." He pulled a jumper out of the bag that

289

was going to be far too big for me.

I looked at it. "Did you think you were going to get cold?"

There was actually a very small flush creeping up his cheek and he licked his lip. He cleared his throat and waggled his head. "Uh, actually… I know I should really stop comparing you to Rachel, but she's really my only point of reference for this stuff… And, well, there's something she seems to like about wearing either her brother's jumper or mine when she's on her period. So, uh, I kinda thought it might help?" He shrugged, as self-conscious as I'd ever seen him. "I don't know. I just thought it was worth having as a back-up. You know?"

He finally looked at me and that laughter that was threatening to erupt dissipated at the vulnerability on his face. Xander-freaking-Bowen, King Douche of all things Bow, was legitimately just doing whatever he could think of to make me feel better. My heart felt all fuzzy – but in a good way – and I smiled at him.

"That was really thoughtful, thanks."

He shrugged, still looking adorably awkward. "You don't have to…" He twitched like he was trying to shake off that awkwardness and cleared his throat again. "It's all good."

I took the jumper from him gently and shucked my blanket. "Anything's worth a go."

He helped me pull it on and he snuck a quick kiss as I got it over my head. We smiled at each other and I couldn't help thinking of my conversation with Mum again. But, we'd just had the conversation about not changing anything; he'd just said he was happy as things were. And, it wasn't like I wasn't happy as they were…

Unless Xander had been hinting he wanted to change things the other way? That he wanted to make it real? I froze for a second, wondering if I'd missed my chance to find out what he wanted. Because I didn't think I had the courage to bring it up again. The idea of just asking him sent a ripple of panic through me. What if he hadn't meant that and he didn't like me *like that*?

"It suits you," he chuckled, pulling it down so it wasn't bunching up.

I looked up at him and smiled, putting my worries on the backburner for now.

"Thanks."

As I snuggled into his jumper – which smelled like he'd only just taken it off – I told myself whatever we were or weren't, I was happy with him. I could worry about working out what I was going to do about that later.

"Any good?" he asked as I re-settled against him.

"Yeah, it's not too bad," I replied, seriously down-playing just how much better it made me feel.

He laughed and I was sure he could tell. "Good."

Xander hung out with me for a while, watching my rom-coms and rubbing my back now and then when the cramps got bad. Mark seemed to avoid coming upstairs almost like he didn't want to risk seeing anything he didn't want to know about. I wasn't sure if or how I was going to try to explain this to him later, but Mark had always waited for me to broach topics so I felt confident in my ability to come up with something before it came up.

After Xander left that night and I climbed into bed with my new hot water bottle, I left his jumper on. I fell asleep easily, despite the pain in my womb, feeling like Xander was still there with me and comforting me.

Chapter Twenty-Three

"It'll be fine," Xander said as I pulled into the carpark and he brushed my hair back.

"It will, Doll," Miranda agreed, leaning forward from the back seat.

"You're one of us now," Greg added.

I threw Xander a glance – we both knew that we were having a different conversation than Miranda and Greg.

There was something about that night that was stressing me out. It was by far not the first time I'd been out with the Bows since Xander and I had started 'dating', but it felt like it. Maybe it was because it felt like Rachel got more suspicious with each new Bow who seemed to take to me. Maybe it was because, now more were talking to me, it felt like there was more room for messing it up – I was still going with the theory that I should just be myself, but I just couldn't stop worrying they'd never trust me.

Whatever the reason, I hadn't even needed to voice my hesitation; apparently Xander, Miranda and Greg could just tell. No one had ever just been able to tell before, even Jason with his seeing-right-through-me hadn't been able to tell. I didn't know if I'd hidden it better before or if I'd just been with people who didn't care about seeing it.

Or, maybe Jason had never actually been able to see right through me after all.

I stopped thinking about that right there because the last thing I needed was to get even more weird and emotional than I was already about to get.

"Doll?" Miranda asked and I nodded.

"Yeah, no. I'm fine. Why would I not be fine?"

"Because Rachel can be a dick?" Greg hedged and Xander threw him a pointed look. Greg shrugged. "What? Dude, we love her. But, you know it's true."

"She cares, Greg," I said softly and Xander gave my knee a squeeze. "There's nothing wrong with that."

"She could ease up on you, Doll."

I looked at Xander, trying to send him a message, trying to tell him I got it and it didn't *really* bother me. To be honest, Daniel had been worse and even that wasn't what bothered me. Why didn't it bother me? Well, I guess I just liked that Xander had some really great friends. I totally preferred the ones who were on his side *and* seemed to accept me, but I got what we looked like – to Rachel and Daniel particularly – so I could hardly be put out that his friends were suspicious. I wanted them to trust me and like me, but I understood why they didn't after all the years of animosity between us.

I got out of the car as the others kept arguing about whether Rachel should or shouldn't be a dick to me. I almost smiled as Miranda and Greg seemed to be arguing from all sides while Xander was just trying to get them to drop it. When they'd all finally got themselves out, I locked the doors and shoved my hands in my pockets as I headed for Grill'd.

"Doll?" Xander said as he jogged after me.

"Yeah?" I asked as I took his hand.

"You sure you're fine?"

"You asking constantly is only making me not fine. I'm good, just a little nervous for some reason. I could have said no."

He put his arm around me and I tucked my arm around his waist. "Okay, I'll stop asking. What did you tell Mark we were doing tonight?"

"I told him I was heading out with Rand and some of the girls."

Xander snorted. "Anyone would think you're hiding your boyfriend from your brother, babe."

"Fake boyfriend, *babe*," I replied, although my heart whacked my brain with that rolled up magazine.

He laughed and he squeezed me closer, then I felt his step falter.

"What?" I asked

He laughed harder.

"What?"

"I think I just saw another of those buttons."

I looked around, but didn't see anything. "Really?"

He shrugged. "Who knows?"

"Where did they get them anyway?"

"Dunno–"

He was cut off as Greg bounced into him with a, "Okay, I want *all* the burgers!"

We all laughed.

"Then, you shall have all the burgers," Xander jokingly decreed as we walked up the steps to Grill'd and saw the others already waiting for us.

My smile fell at the frowns Rachel, Daniel and Sabrina threw me, but I managed to shake it off as they just decided to ignore me and talk to their friends while we took a seat and others started filing up to order.

Miranda and I got pulled into conversation with Liv, Tara and Britt about whether hot guys made comic book movies worth it as Xander and Greg started talking to Daniel about how badly they thought Xander would be penalised for his fight with Jason. I was heavily on the side that comic book movies were worth it no matter who was in them, and none of the girls minded even if they remained unsure.

As the food came out, our conversation moved onto if we needed to go into town again before school went back

"What do you need this time?" I asked with a wry smile and the girls all returned it.

"Nothing," Tara conceded. "I just thought it might be nice to hang out."

"We can fashion show like those movie montages, that's always fun," Britt said.

"Oh yeah!" Liv cried excitedly. "I am so down for that. We can try on all the hideous things."

Miranda laughed, "We'll need a whole day just for half of those."

"Yeah, true. How about we stick with a style?"

"I vote fluoro," Miranda said.

"Seconded," Liv agreed.

"Me too. Doll?" Britt asked.

I laughed. "I'll be honest, I actually don't *hate* fluoro." I winced as I waited for their reaction.

But, they only gasped in mock-horror.

"Really?" Britt leant forward as though she needed to find out my secrets so she could try them herself.

I nodded. "Really. I'm not sure it suits me. But, I'm not opposed to it as a concept."

Miranda shook her head with a smile. "Takes all sorts, huh? Well, what would you suggest then, Miss Fluoro?" But it was said in a way that I was in on the joke, not that it was at my expense.

"No. Fluoro's good."

"Sweet. How about we–?"

"Woah!" Greg's voice was loud enough it drowned out half the table. "Was that a...? How do you even pronounce that?" Greg pointed at some kids walking past us.

"What?" I asked, looking around as I shoved another chip in my mouth.

"Looked like...Thomigan?" Greg said uncertainly, peering at something, and I had a feeling I knew what he was talking about.

"Thomigan?" I clarified. "I guess so. Thomas and Milligan?"

"Bowdeen's well better," Tara said matter-of-fact.

"Well, that's because Xander and Doll are well better," Liv said.

"Oh, so you're on our team then?" Xander teased as he looked around the table and I pretended not to see glare that Rachel, Daniel and Sabrina shared.

The girls laughed.

"Of course," Britt answered. "Unlike those two idJits, you two are an actual proper couple."

I nearly choked on my drink and Xander nudged me with a smile.

"Why are they idJits anyway?" I asked, looking around.

"I ask myself that every day," Greg sighed dramatically. "I just don't know how people could be such arsehats."

"No," I laughed. "I mean, why do you call them that?"

"Id-Jits. JT. It just seems to work," Xander said with a shrug.

"Like Xander's King of the Bows, your JT is King of the idJits," Rachel sneered.

"Jason's not *my* anything," I answered, staring her down.

"Does *she* even go to our school?" Greg asked, pointing at another girl sitting at a table a few away from us.

"She doesn't even go here!" Tara laughed as we all turned to look at the random girl; she was wearing a 'Team Bowdeen' button.

"I don't think so…?" Xander said slowly.

"Didn't you hook up with her?" Daniel asked and the two boys did a stare-off to rival the one Rachel and I had just done.

"Yeah, I don't think so, mate," Xander replied as though it was a warning.

"You sure?" Daniel pressed, leaning towards Xander. "Wasn't she at that party a few months ago?"

"I think I'd remember."

"Oh, yeah. I was thinking of her sister." Daniel winked at Xander, then looked at me.

Xander threw a chip at Daniel with a chuckle. "Fuck off, mate. Just because you missed out on her."

Daniel smirked and Xander joined him. I had no idea what the exchange was supposed to have meant, but it seemed everything was all good again.

"Who came up with Thomigan? That just sounds whack," Greg mused.

I felt Xander shrug. "Who knows? I don't even know where the damn things are coming from." He looked up for a second. "If anyone finds out, can you grab me a couple?"

"Of the Thomigan ones?" Tara asked and Xander smirked.

"Them, too."

"Why the hell do you want theirs?" Rachel snapped.

Xander leant over the table towards her. "For the love of irony, Rach."

I could see she was stuck between being annoyed by me and amused by him. Finally she gave him a smile and shook her head. "You're the whack one."

"I commend them for Bowdeen though," Xander continued on as he grinned around a chip at her. "It sounds great."

"Maybe you should change your name then?" Daniel teased him, though it sounded somewhat scathing to me.

"Yeah, we'll get on that when we get married," Xander said with a wry grin and everyone looked at him in surprise.

"Yes!" Greg yelled. "I already called best man!"

"That's Rachel's job, surely," Miranda asked and I swear Rachel's glare almost struck her down dead.

"Xand's not going to need a best man. That's a fucking terrible idea," she said, her tone cold enough to send unpleasant goose bumps chasing across my skin.

All the laughter at the table stopped and I wished I could just melt into non-existence.

"Rach, give me a break. It was a joke," Xander said quietly.

"You don't joke about marrying the minion, Xander," she said.

Xander dropped his burger and pointed at her. "Your attitude is starting to shit me off, Rachel."

"Your attitude's been shitting me off for weeks. You know she was talking to him the other day? What do you think they were talking about? It seems he's finally noticed her now. How much longer do you think she'll be yours?"

Oh, my cheeks flushed and I refused to look away from my lap so I had no idea what anyone else looked like or if they, like me,

298

were pretending we weren't there. I could feel Xander tense beside me.

"Of course I knew she was talking to him. I'm the one who told her to talk to him!"

"You want to push her into his arms?"

I had a feeling I wasn't supposed to butt in here and I wasn't sure I'd be able to defend myself without making things worse anyway. So, for better or worse, I kept my mouth shut.

"I'm pretty sure that's Holly's decision, Rach. She wants him, what am I going to do, huh?" Xander asked.

"You're going to fucking mope and I'm going to have to pick up the pieces is what."

"What's your point, Rach?"

Rachel stood up quickly, her hands landing heavily on the table. "My point is that the minion is going to go running back to him as soon as she gets the chance. You think you're anything but something to make him jealous? She's playing you Xander and you're too fucking whipped to notice."

Now Xander stood up to face her. "Then don't hang around, Rachel. It's not that hard. When Holly's with the git you can tell me you told me so and let me wallow on my own."

I wanted to say something here about how I wasn't going back to Jason, no matter what happened. But, I didn't know how to voice that just then.

"You know I won't do that," Rachel answered.

"Why not? You need my permission? Go ahead, Rachel. Walk away."

"Don't you pull that on me, you arsehole. You know I'm not going anywhere. When she finally breaks your heart, you know I'll pick up every damned piece no matter how long it takes."

I finally looked up at her and I saw she meant it; Rachel was worse than a territorial mother, she wasn't just some mother hen, she'd fight tooth and nail to protect Xander's heart and, as awkward as I felt about the fact they were arguing over me, all I had for her was respect. I could only see it from her perspective, and I wouldn't have trusted her either had the tables been turned.

"Don't you dare fuck it up, Minion," she snarled at me and shoved away from the table.

"Rachel!" Xander yelled as he briefly touched the back of my head then headed after her.

"Gosh. Mummy and Daddy fighting again," Greg sighed sarcastically.

"Shut up," Daniel muttered, giving me one hell of a death glare, then he got up and followed them, Sabrina following close behind.

I should have felt more shaken. I should have felt more uncomfortable. And, I did feel uncomfortable. But, I didn't feel uncomfortable for me. I felt uncomfortable for Xander. Even after we'd talked about it the other day, I still worried about the way he seemed stuck between Rachel and me. Nothing seemed worth that, not whatever friendships I'd found with Xander, Miranda, Greg or whatever might have grown with a couple of the others given time.

Miranda nudged me companionably and put an arm around me. "Don't worry about them. Mum and Dad fight, it's what they do. They'll make up and everything will be fine."

"Mum and Dad?" I asked.

Tara gave me a wry smile. "It's what we call them when they go at it like that. It happens over much less than you."

"I should go…" I shrugged out of Miranda's arm and stood up.

"Doll, don't worry about it. Rachel's just worried about him. She'd be like that with any of us. Hell, she was like that with the

Tara and JT thing, you just didn't see it," Greg said, still stuffing himself with chips.

Tara gave him a look to shut up, then gave me a smile that I knew was an apology. It was unnecessary, but I appreciated it anyway.

"You know Darcy?" Liv asked and I looked at her, confused.

"Who?"

"You know, Mr Darcy. Pride and Prejudice?"

"Oh, uh. Yeah, I saw that once."

"Yeah, well Rach is our very own Darcy. She'll go to any length to protect her friends. She just doesn't go about it the right way."

I looked up, but couldn't see Xander or Rachel so didn't know where they'd gone. I sighed. "I know she means well. I get it. If it was one of you and Jason, I'd…"

I didn't know what I'd do anymore. When there was that thing between him and Tara, I'd been exactly like Rachel… Just not to Jason's face. And, Nancy had probably just thought it was jealousy talking. In a way, it had been. But back then, what was now the Bows and the…idJits – I was still getting used to that – were less distinct in our year level; it had just been Xander versus Jason and the social lines had been more blurred.

Now, I'd seen a side to Jason I wouldn't defend, a side of him that I thought didn't deserve my loyalty. Not if he wasn't going to stand up for me once – and picking a fight with Xander totally didn't count.

"You'd what, Doll?" Miranda asked.

"I would have been the same once," I said.

Miranda tugged on my arm. "Come on, sit back down. Don't worry about them."

"Yeah, you've got us. It just takes them a little longer to get over hang ups," Tara said with a nod.

I gave them all a smile. "I totally ruined your night out."

Liv snorted. "No. If our night was ruined, it would have been Rachel's temper that did it. Honestly though, Doll, when we say this is normal for them… It's normal. Like every week or two. Frankly, it's not a good night out if they're not yelling at each other."

"Yeah, I think the longest they went was like a month," Tara said. "We actually thought they'd stopped loving each other. We were all ready to pick sides in the divorce."

"It was a stressful time," Greg finished and I smiled at them all.

"You don't all have to be so nice to JT's ex-minion," I told them.

Miranda put her arm around me again. "Doll, our King's never smiled as much as he has in the last few weeks and you've been nothing but nice to us when we've let you–"

"She's right, though. You're nothing like the stuck up bitch I thought you were," Greg interrupted and Tara threw a chip at him.

"You don't tell people things like that, dickweed," Tara snapped and I laughed.

"It's fine. I get it."

By the time Rachel, Xander, Daniel and Sabrina came back to the table – Xander's arm around Rachel's shoulders, so I hoped everything was okay – the rest of us were back to laughing again and talking about the sort of nonsensical things that you talk about. Greg was doing a fantastic example of his 'sweet' dance moves and Xander and Daniel joined him, much to the amusement of the other Grill'd customers who obviously realised that our group was prone to theatrics.

The rest of dinner went well enough. Rachel, Daniel and

Sabrina ignored me and otherwise acted normal. Especially when Greg and Xander broke out into a rendition of Britney Spears' 'One More Time', complete with standing on the bench seats as they sang at each other.

"God, they spent too long helping with that playlist," Sabrina muttered with a smile to Liv.

It wasn't until a little later that we were walking to Cold Rock that Xander held me back from the rest of the group as they jostled and yelled at each other companionably.

"You okay?" he asked.

"You have to stop asking me that." I smiled at him.

"I'm sorry about her. I told her–"

I put my finger over his lips. "Xand, I need to earn her trust. I'm not above doing that, I just don't know how. It's not ridiculous. I mean, she could be a little more civil about it, yeah. But, she's fighting for the same thing as me so I just have to work out how to prove that to her."

Xander was smirking at me knowingly.

"What?" I asked.

"Fake dating."

I blinked. "What?"

"There's keeping up appearances, babe, then there's trying to win over the Queen Bitch of the Bows." He wiggled his eyebrows at me and I couldn't help my smile.

"So? Just because we're fake dating, that means I can't want to show her I'm on your side?"

"Oh, you're on my side?" he teased.

"I thought it was 'Team Bowdeen'? Where else would I be?"

He shrugged and looked behind me. "Don't know. I guess I just figured if it was *all* fake, then you wouldn't be on a side?"

"What are you suggesting Xander?" I asked him.

"Nothing. Nothing at all." That hint of humour played across his face.

"Xander?" I pressed.

He gave me that infectious smile that made me believe we could be amazing. "What? I can't like that you want to win over my best friend?"

"I thought that's what girlfriends are supposed to do?" I said teasingly.

"Oh, real girlfriends, yeah," he replied, just as teasingly.

"What about friends?" I asked, really not sure what he wanted and too afraid to ask.

He looked at me. "What *about* friends?"

"Where do they stand on the winning your best friend over?"

"Depends what this friend's intentions were."

We looked at each other seriously, both seemingly looking for something. My heart felt like it had one foot in either side of the ring, only it wasn't Jason in the other corner; honestly, it hadn't been Jason in the other corner for a long time. I didn't know who or what was in the other corner, but my heart wanted to take another step towards Xander. And, between my brain and me, we let it. But, my heart was hesitant this time, like it wasn't sure how it felt.

"What if she just wants to show you that loyalty she's heard so much about?" I hedged.

A frown crossed his face for a second. "The conversation you had with Dan the other week?"

"What about it?"

"You guys have a talk about loyalty?"

I shrugged. "Might have."

Xander swore under his breath and I laughed. He looked at me in confusion.

"You know, one thing I've learnt in pretending I'm a Bow is that the one person I thought was the most shallow guy I'd ever had the misfortune of meeting had better friends than I've ever had." I held a hand up because I knew he was going to get comforting on me. "That is not me looking for sympathy, Xander. I'm being serious. Just like I was serious when I said you standing up for me with Jason the other week was showing me more loyalty than he'd ever shown me. Wherever this goes, however it ends, you've opened my eyes to the fact that I was a complete arsehole before.

"I blindly followed Jason when he'd done nothing to deserve it. I thought he was wonderful and funny and smart and amazing. And, for what? For the fact that Mark had left him in charge of a bunch of people the Bows now call idJits?" I shook my head. "I'd like to think I can be a better person now I've realised how damned judgemental I was. It's not going to happen overnight, but I've got faith."

"Holly, I've always thought you were amazing," he said, taking my cheeks in his hands and looking into my eyes. I felt my heart take one more step and there was less hesitation this time. My brain and I half-heartedly cautioned it without knowing how he felt, but it stoically had its fingers in its ears again.

"Xander…" I breathed.

"I don't know how or when this is going to end either, but you have to know that. You have to at least know that I've always thought the world of you."

I smiled at him and reached up to kiss him.

Just as he wrapped his arms around me, Rachel was yelling at us, "Come on, you two! You can canoodle when we have ice cream in our hands!"

305

I pulled away from Xander as he laughed. "She's thawing," he assured me.

"Slower than the damned ice caps."

He snorted as he put an arm around my shoulder and we headed down the street. "She'll get there, babe. Just wait. She'll see what I see."

"What you see?" I scoffed.

"Yeah."

"When?"

"When I look at us."

"And, what's that?"

"Something amazing," he whispered in my ear as he squeezed me and my heart almost went running the rest of the way to him whether he could really like me like that or not.

Chapter Twenty-Four

Everyone was going insane.

More people were wearing buttons by the time we were back to school. Seriously, I had no idea where they were getting them from; *no one* seemed to know where they were getting them from. Madness aside, I really wanted to know how I could make my own – I'd like something really random I could put on my bag all old-school.

Anyway… I'd spent all day roaming the school and watching fights break out between friends and enemies and people previously totally indifferent to each other about which couple was better than the other and who was going to last longer. It was utterly ridiculous and none of it helped the fact that I could no longer deny I'd fallen for Xander.

Like actual, proper, I-did-really-like-him-after-all fallen for him.

But, who does a girl talk to about falling for her (supposed-to-be-fake) boyfriend?

I felt like the most clichéd romance heroine in history.

But, who was I supposed to go to for advice?

Miranda thought I was already in love with Xander. Nancy was acting like a raging bitch and on the other side of the battlelines.

Jason was so not the friend I'd spent ten years thinking he was. Mum had gone overseas with the beau so I didn't want to make her feel obliged to have a conversation I wasn't sure how to have and I thought we might have already had. I already couldn't handle just imagining the hurt response from Greg. And Rachel would probably punch me in the face, which I kind of felt like I deserved at this point.

That only left Mark…

"So…" I started as I hovered in his doorway on Monday evening.

"What?" Mark asked and I knew he wasn't looking forward to what I had to say. I can't say I was super thrilled about it either.

"We talk about everything right? I mean, no matter what the problem is, I can come to you about it…?"

He pushed away from his desk and looked at me. "Of course. Why? What's the matter?"

I sighed. This was the conversation I'd been avoiding for five weeks (not that I was counting). "So, you know how Jason and Nancy started dating and I made friends with a Bow?"

"Yeah…" he said slowly, clearly still not thrilled about where he thought this might be heading.

"Well, funny story… King Douche and I got to talking and…" I took a deep breath.

"And what, Doll?" Mark asked quickly.

"We decided it would be a good idea to – okay, don't hate me – it would be a good idea if we," I paused, "fake dated," I finished really quickly as though he might not hear me but it totally counted as me telling him.

"Fake dating?" Mark asked in that slow tone that I knew meant he was trying to work out what to actually say.

308

I closed my eyes as though that was going to give me the confidence to tell him the whole story. It came out like complete word vomit. "Yeah. So, apparently he wanted off the menu for a while but the girls didn't seem to get the memo. Then, he puts the idea in my head that hooking up with someone else would make Jason jealous. So, I start think about that– Well, I can't stop thinking about it, more like. But I figure I'm too mature for stupid games. So, I initially say no when he says we can solve each other's problems. But, then Nancy gets under my skin and he's not such a douche and I say yes. And, we hang out and he's funny and..." I took another deep breath and opened my eyes. "I think I fell for him."

"You what?"

"I think I fell for him."

"So you fell for a guy while you were trying to make the love of your life jealous?" he asked sceptically.

I winced, wishing he hadn't put it like that so I didn't feel stupider than I already did. "Uh, yeah."

"So, all that time 'studying'..." he sighed. "God. I wish I hadn't expected this..." he muttered.

"Expected it?"

Mark ran a hand through his hair. "Yeah. You're not exactly subtle, Dolly. I was just seriously hoping I was wrong and you weren't lying to me about it."

That hit home and my heart crumpled at the thought I'd disappointed him. "I'm sorry, Marco..."

He waved away my apology and I knew that meant he forgave me, even if he thought I'd been a complete idiot. "Just... Tell me what happened. How did you possibly fall for King Douche?" I knew Mark wasn't pleased – he knew Xander well enough from years at school and club soccer to know his reputation well – but I also knew he was going to hear me out.

"He's not... He's not what I spent all those years thinking he was–"

"You mean he's seduced you into idiocy?" He interrupted, then paused. "Wait, when he was here in the holidays?"

I sighed heavily. "No one's seduced anyone into anything. I know the rumours say he's a douche, a player, *so* not the boyfriend type. And that's all he was before. But, I have to ask myself if that was a mask or if he's changed. Because then, yeah, he wallows with me when I've got my period, we laugh and talk, he stands up for me against Rachel and Jason–"

"Hang on. In what world does that make sense?"

Where's the world that doesn't care... ran through my head.

"No. Not together. Rachel's been an utter bitch about me. But, Jason started a fight and we got sent home and–"

"Whoa!" Mark cried and stood up. "Back up. Go from the beginning."

So, I did. And I left nothing out.

By the end of it all, Mark looked like he seriously regretted his life choices. "Okay," he sighed, pinching the bridge of his nose. "Okay. So, you've been fake dating all this time. And now you think you've actually fallen for him?"

I nodded. "I know he's attractive. Everyone knows he's attractive. But, there's more to him. Or at least, I think I see more in him. And, I can't."

"You can't what?"

"I can't see more in him?" I didn't know why that was a question.

Mark looked about as confused as I felt. "Because he is or isn't

310

a douche?"

"Both?"

"Doll, he's…" Mark grunted in annoyance as he almost turned away from me.

"Go on. Say it." I knew what he wanted to say and, well he'd heard me out, it was only fair I heard him out.

He grimaced as though he knew I wouldn't like what I heard. "He sleeps around, Dolly. He used to hook up with any number of girls at the soccer parties. He's vulgar, he's arrogant, he's a self-entitled wanker. And, that's just what I see of him three times a week…" He sighed. "I know he's got this unfailing ability to make you think you're special–" He paused at my semi-sarcastic frown. "Not that you're not special… Just… Damnit," he muttered as he whirled around for a second.

When he turned back to face me, he ran his hand over his mouth before he continued. "I don't want to see him hurt you the way I've seen him hurt a whole bunch of girls before."

"Pot, meet kettle," I said to him.

"It's different, Doll."

"How, Marco?"

"I'm not the one my little sister's fallen for." He stopped and frowned. "Why aren't you taking this worse?"

I shrugged and dropped onto his bed, tucking my legs under me to sit cross-legged. "You know he's only slept with five girls?"

Mark blinked. "No. Last count was… Shit. I reckon he was on at least fifteen before I left and that was – what? – almost two years ago."

I shook my head. "Five." I even held my hand up in case Mark had forgotten what five looked like.

"Five?"

I nodded. "Five. And he thinks five is a big number, just for the record."

I couldn't tell if Mark believed what I was saying or not. "And, what did you say?"

"I told him it was a little underwhelming after the last count which – by the way – is closer to fifty now."

"Holy fuck!" Mark breathed and I knew I heard awe in his voice. "Fifty?"

I nodded.

"But, he says it's five?"

I nodded again.

"And, you believe him?"

I shrugged. "I think so. I can call him out on his bullshit, Marco. But, I don't think he lies to me about the important stuff."

Mark dropped onto his chair backwards and scooted it towards me. He leant his arms on the back and looked at me carefully. "Doll, he could still be playing you."

I took a deep breath. "I know. But, I... I think there's more to him. Or, less..." I frowned, trying to work out exactly what I meant. "Less than the rumours? More to his personality..." I shrugged. "Either way."

Mark shook his head. "I'm going to need to think about this, Dolly. I just... I don't know what to think about this." He checked his watch. "Look, why don't you come to practice with me? Let me see you two together and I'll let you know."

"Let me know what?"

"Well, I assume you want to know if he really likes you or not before you decide if you need to stress about falling for him?"

I shrugged. "Maybe?" I had no idea what I wanted. I just knew I couldn't do it all on my own anymore.

Dating Xander had been a serious crossing of social lines and there were plenty of people who were already not happy with how things were. Falling for him meant there was definitely no going back.

I didn't think I wanted to go back anymore – or had anything to go back to – but neither did I want to lose what I had now if I'd read Xander wrong, if he was just *really* good at keeping up appearances. I couldn't imagine being cast adrift, completely alone with no one. It was weak and shallow, but it was true.

"Okay. Just answer me one thing. And, let's keep in mind that a yes or no is more than enough. Have you slept with him?"

"No."

We looked at each other and I knew he was looking for bullshit. Finally he nodded.

"Okay. Good."

"When are you leaving?"

"Five minutes ago, preferably."

He packed up his stuff and I followed him down to the car. I was torn trying to work out if I should give Xander a head's up that he was supposed to act naturally with me, but also without worrying about repercussions from my big brother. I could think of very few ways of telling Xander anything that wouldn't make him either back off or overdo it.

In the end, I didn't tell Xander anything. Mark pulled into the car park and I got out of the car, my eyes already scanning for Xander.

"I'm going to go get changed. If your boyfriend's in there, I'll send him out," Mark said dryly.

"Right. Sure." I nodded and wandered over to the bleachers that surrounded their oval.

I climbed up a couple of rows and sat down, blowing on my hands to keep them warm. The Saints' pitch wasn't well known for its lighting, but the boys made do.

"Hey, what's up?" I heard Xander's voice after a while.

I stood up as I looked towards him and smiled. "Hey."

"I didn't know you were coming."

"Neither did I."

He smiled and held his arms out. I rested mine on his shoulders and let him bunny hop me off the bleachers. I didn't take my hands from him and he looked down at me half in humour and half in suspicion.

"If your brother murders me, it's not my fault," he said.

I grinned. "Understood."

When I still didn't let go of him, he frowned. "I'm serious, Doll. I might be a decent player, but Cap's not going to care if he sees us like this."

"What if it didn't matter?"

His frown became surprise. "What if what didn't matter?"

"Mark."

"I'll pull your favourite line now. There's no one to impress here." He smiled but it didn't quite reach his eyes.

As I reached up to him, I replied, "So?"

His eyes softened before he flashed me that split-second grin and I leant up to kiss him.

"Bowen! Less kissing, more jogging!" a voice yelled and we turned to see the club coach with his arms crossed. Mark was behind him, watching us carefully.

"Right, that's me out." Xander pressed one last quick kiss to my forehead, then gave me a wink as he started jogging backwards before he turned and joined the rest of the team.

314

I watched them with their fitness and their drills –not swimming this Monday – my eyes drifting between Mark and Xander.

When the coach called a break, I noticed that Mark kept his distance. But, Xander came over with humour in his eyes.

"So, am I to assume your brother knows about us?" he asked me, one of those unbidden smiles playing at his mouth.

I opened my mouth and closed it again. "I don't know what you mean."

Xander looked behind me and nodded slowly. "Well, I mean that he just asked me about you in a less than friendly capacity…?" As his eyes slid back to me, his eyebrow rose in question.

I swallowed. "You and Mark have never really been friends…" I offered weakly.

Xander sucked his teeth, the corner of his lip tipping up. "True. But, I think he was referring to you and me not just being friends?"

God's sake, Marco! I cursed as I looked up. "Couldn't tell you why he did that." And, look, I wasn't lying; I didn't know why a guy who knew it was supposed to be fake but that I wasn't sure anymore how fake it was had decided to just come out and ask Xander what was happening.

"Couldn't you, now?" Xander asked, climbing the bleachers to look me in the eye.

"No." I watched him for a second. "Out of curiosity–"

"The truth," he answered with that weird ability to read my mind.

I blinked. "The truth?"

He nodded. "Yep."

"And, what's the truth?"

"Ah, now. That's between me and your brother."

"I'd think I was allowed to know how you felt about me,

Xander," I replied indignantly.

"Do you not already know?"

I breathed in and my heart dropped down to listen enraptured. "Should I?"

He put his finger under my chin so I wouldn't look away and gave me that smile that made it impossible to even want to look anywhere else. "I told him I think you're amazing. That I love everything about you, from the fact that you unapologetically don't let me get away with anything to the fact that you make me smile even when you're calling me King Douche. I told him I loved hanging out with you in whatever mood you were in. I love that we can insult each other but be having a serious conversation at the same time. I love that we don't really like the same stuff, but we can share that stuff with each other. I love that you beat me effortlessly at most games despite the fact you have no idea what you're doing. And, I love that I can tell you things I can't even tell Rachel and I know you won't look at me with anything less than that adorable contempt in your eyes." He was smiling so I knew he wasn't being entirely serious about the contempt, but still.

"Xand, I don't–"

He nodded. "I know, Holly."

I gave him a smile and told my heart to sit back down. I felt like it had started jumping around so excitedly it was about to fall off the bleachers.

"Right, I gotta get back to it. We'll talk later?" he asked and I nodded.

He gave me that full smile and jogged off.

On the way home, Mark begrudgingly said, "He likes you. Proper likes you. Whether he's in love with you or not, I dunno. But, you can move onto phase two of the freaking out about falling for him now."

My heart paused in its little victory dance as it wondered what the hell we were going to do with that information. Somehow, getting the verdict from Mark made it real. Made it maybe like what we were doing had already become real when I wasn't looking.

But, we didn't have a world that didn't care. We had a world that cared too much.

Could I really have fallen for him? Could he really have fallen for me?

Maybe it was just keeping up appearances, after all.

Maybe we were just friends and I'd just forgotten that's all it was.

Or, I had to stop freaking out because it really was more. I just had no idea how to find the courage to have that conversation with Xander on the off chance that even Mark was wrong.

I staggered out of the way as a girl stormed out of a classroom in front of me the next day.

"You don't know what you're talking about," she yelled and I saw another girl walk out of the same classroom and glare at Xander and me.

"See?" the second girl asked as she pointed at us. She was wearing a 'Team Bowdeen' button and the first girl was wearing a 'Team Thomigan' button. "They are much more believable and at least they're not spreading horrible rumours around the school." She stopped and looked at me. "You're not spreading horrible rumours around the school, are you?"

"Uh… About what?" I asked her.

"About JT and Nancy."

I blinked. "Am I supposed to be?"

"See?" second girl asked the first again. "Holly's still nice!"

Xander grabbed my hand a pulled me away from them with a chuckle.

"You seem more amused this term."

He shrugged. "It's more amusing this term."

"Why?"

"It's hilariously dramatic," he snorted.

"You don't care at all?"

"Babe, if I cared about everything people said about me, do you know where I'd be?"

I shook my head. "No. Where would you be?"

"I wouldn't have you."

I frowned at him. "I doubt that very much."

"I'm serious. Do you remember the things you said to me the day you ran into my arms crying?"

"That's not quite how–"

"Had I let myself care about any of those words, we wouldn't be here now."

"You're not at all concerned that Year Eights we don't even know are fighting over our relationship?" I asked him, looking back to where the two girls had now been joined by another girl and guy.

"It's high school, Doll. Ridiculous bullshit happens. Does it change anything for you?"

I looked back at them for a moment, not sure if it did or not.

"Holly?"

I turned to him. "This isn't what I expected to happen."

His eyes softened. "A lot of things have happened lately that I never expected to happen, but I can only control my actions. Do you think anything we do will make them stop gossiping about us? Stop them arguing?"

"Nancy's going to love this," I muttered.

"So, what?" Xander said forcefully. "I'm in this one hundred percent, Holly. More than. The team they're supporting isn't just something they made up, they got it from somewhere and do you know where that somewhere was?"

I shook my head.

"They got it from us, babe. They got it from seeing us together. You think we're just that good at keeping up appearances? Or, you think maybe there's a reason half the school is fighting for us?"

I swallowed hard and my heart felt like it had been dropped on its head. "What?" I heard myself scoff.

Xander opened his mouth, closed it, and sighed. "Just…" He pulled me close and rested his cheek on my head. "We make a good team, Holly."

And the next few days didn't get any better. More buttons appeared and more fights broke out. Even more telling than the fights were the silences, the obvious chill between two people when I walked past them. People were actually having stand-offs in the corridor, arguments, people cheered or booed as Xander and I or Jason and Nancy went past.

As I'd predicted, Nancy loved the attention. She flounced past her supporters and threw serious shade to the 'Team Bowdeen' kids – seriously, it was ridiculous, but what else was I supposed to call them?

And Jason? He walked along with Nancy like he was some trophy boyfriend. He avoided looking at me and saw through his

319

smile as Nancy fuelled any and every rumour about me through the school.

Of course, the more Nancy loved it, the more Rachel hated it. She and Xander fought. A lot. But, she never left his side, she was seen glaring at anyone with a 'Team Thomigan' button to the point I saw a couple of kids actually take them off and throw them away in front of her in legitimate fear. And I would never dare say anything to anyone, but I was pretty sure Rachel looked very self-satisfied by the action.

Xander took it all in his stride, smiling at people who yelled complimentary things to him or told him they were on our team. He did nothing to dispel rumours or settle people down, he just walked around the school with that cool, calm confidence of his. There was more of the old Xander in him, the one I'd believed he was before I'd run into him in the boys' locker room.

But, I just wasn't sure if this was just a different kind of keeping up appearances; if it was that mask I got the feeling he wore or if it was proof Xander had always been the guy I'd thought he was and not really the guy I'd fallen for after all.

Chapter Twenty-Five

By lunch on Thursday, things had unsurprisingly not quieted down. I wasn't sure if it was getting worse or it I was only just finding out about it all. I'd been trying the whole 'ignore it and it will go away' thing, but it didn't seem to be going away.

I stared at my phone and was sure it was a mistake.

*You have been added to the group **Team Bowdeen**.*

It didn't look like a mistake.

A whole bunch of notifications came through from the new group and I hesitated; did I want to know what was going on in there? No... No, I didn't. I exited Facebook and put my phone in my pocket just as I heard Mr Burnett's voice calling me.

I turned and saw him hanging out of his classroom.

"Got a minute?" he asked, looking at me pointedly so I knew I didn't really have a choice in the matter.

I nodded and hurried through the kids in the corridor. He closed the door behind us and sat on the corner of his desk as he indicated I take a seat, too.

"So, Holly... Some interesting things going on at the moment."

I cleared my throat and wasn't sure how to play this. "Uh, in what way?" I asked.

He gave me a look that told me he knew I was being a bit of a dick and he'd really rather I wasn't.

I tried again. "I don't really know, to be honest. It all just kind of happened."

Mr Burnett's face softened and he nodded. "Okay. Good first step. The buttons, though?"

I shrugged. "I don't know. I honestly don't know where they're coming from."

He nodded again. "And, the rumours?"

"Uh, which ones specifically?"

His eyes widened. "How many *are* there?"

I scratched the back of my head. "You know, Mr Burnett, I'm not sure you want to know."

He breathed out heavily. "I'll be honest, Holly. When I started teaching, I didn't think it was going to be a walk in the park. But, I can't say I expected to see a whole school choosing sides over who was dating who."

"If it helps, I didn't really expect it to happen either."

"It's starting to cause problems, Holly."

I nodded. "I've noticed."

"Three Year Elevens had a fight this morning in the Art Room. Paint as well as words were thrown. It wasn't pretty."

I gave him an apologetic smile. "I don't know what I can do about it, to be honest. Xander and I have been trying to ignore it. I figured even if we tried to get people to stop, then they'd just keep going."

"That's sensible. Which leaves it up to the staff to try to calm it down. Any suggestions?"

I grimaced. "No…?"

He nodded. "Okay. Well, I guess, just keep ignoring them then and hopefully something else comes along to take everyone's minds off it."

I stood up. "I'm sorry, Mr Burnett…"

"For what, Holly?"

I shrugged. *For a lot of things.* "For everything that's happened."

He waved a hand at me. "You aren't to blame for other people's actions… Nancy, on the other hand…?" His eyebrows rose and I stifled a smile.

"Should you really be saying things like that to a student?"

He sighed. "No, probably not. But, I'd be less surprised to find out she'd orchestrated the whole thing. Don't listen to the rumours, Holly. Trust me, no one who really knows you would believe you capable of any of those things."

I blinked and tried to hide my surprise; what exactly *had* he heard? "No, of course not. Thanks, Mr Burnett."

He nodded once. "I'll see you tomorrow for home group."

"Uh, yeah sure," I replied as I headed out, wondering what other rumours Nancy had been spreading.

There'd been the ones about me sleeping with Xander and then becoming obsessed with him, I'd heard one or two about me sleeping with Daniel, there had even been a fairly persistent one about me sleeping with Daniel and Xander at the same time. But, I'd – on the whole – tried not to listen to what other people were saying.

Xander had been right, we could only control our actions, not other people's. I had to take a leaf out of the Bow playbook and not care what people thought about me. It wasn't going to be easy; I'd spent almost eighteen years trying to live up to other people's expectations of me and I wasn't sure what my expectations for me were anymore. But, I was going to have to work that out and just

323

be myself.

As I walked through the corridor, I had to wonder why people cared so much about what other people got up to. It seemed so useless to be so invested in the relationships of four people you barely knew. But, there were signs of it everywhere; aside from the buttons, posters had started appearing in support of either couple.

I was wondering more and more where that world that didn't care was and how the hell I could meet Xander there.

Everything that had happened with Xander in the last few weeks was tinged with other people's opinions of it, everything we'd said or done had been designed to make people think a certain thing. We'd been keeping up appearances, and spectacularly by the reactions of the people around us. Only, I couldn't pinpoint exactly when the fiction had ended and reality had started. My heart had been entangled in the half-truths and lies.

Like the song, the future was so unclear. I didn't know how to go forward or backwards anymore. I liked Xander and I wanted to believe he liked me. There was just that fear holding me back from finding out once and for all; fear that he couldn't really like me the same way, fear that we were doomed to end like my parents, and fear that even if he did like me and it worked out that talking about it might change us somehow.

I wanted to find that world that didn't care and work it out. I wanted to go back and see how it could have played out just the two of us, something real, both in it one hundred percent from the start. I wanted to know what Xander and I looked like without all the bullshit and other people watching our every move.

So, it was on that happy note that I bumped into Rachel. As usual, she was glaring down a fury, but my heart honestly just waved its little white flag at her and wished it could just ask her to confirm that my fears about Xander were unfounded, that he was real with me.

"Uh, hi," I said slowly since it seemed like she wanted to talk to me.

"I was just given this." She opened her hand and there was a button in it that read 'Holly for Queen' with a bow underneath it. No guesses needed to work out what that one meant.

I opened my mouth, then closed it. Because what the hell could I say in defence of that? Sure, I'd had nothing to do with it, but what did that matter to Rachel?

"Has Xander seen them?" she asked.

"I… I don't know," I stammered. "It's the first time I've seen it." Her glare hardened and I garbled quickly. "I don't want to be Queen, Rachel. It's your spot and I'd never dream of taking it from you."

Okay, I was wrong. Now, her glare hardened.

"I don't care about 'spots'," she spat. "I care about Xander and what he's going to think when he sees this. You think I'm worried you're going to take some irrelevant status that was *awarded* to me by a bunch of people who don't even know me or my friends? No one gets to tell my friends who I am to them, Minion. You understand? Only they get to choose and, as far as I'm aware, no one's opinion has changed."

I nodded quickly, not really sure where she was going with this.

"You're the people who call us King and Queen. You're the people who decided I was some popular arsehole. It doesn't matter to me what relationship you have with Xander because I know where we stand and I know we have each other's back. We've had each other's backs for longer than you pined over JT. So, you think you can come between us?"

325

I shook my head. "No. I don't want that. No one wants that."

She looked me over and I knew she didn't believe me.

"Look, Rachel... I understand why you're worried. Like I told Daniel–"

"You've talked to Dan?"

I nodded. "Yeah, he and I got this bit over with last term."

She frowned. "This bit?" she repeated.

"The dramatic confrontation. Whatever you want to call it. Look, I don't know how to show you I'm in Xander's corner, but I'll spend every day we're together doing just that if I have to."

"You *will* have to," she sneered.

"Okay. Then, I will. That whole loyalty thing you accused me of knowing nothing about? I get it now. I mean, I really get it. I get I was a judgemental dillweed and there is no excuse for that. But, I've seen it, Rachel. I've seen Xander's changed–"

She scoffed and I stopped. "Changed?" she asked, looking me over. "Xander hasn't changed, you idiot. He's always been the guy you've finally noticed. You think it's easy to walk around a place where people think *one* thing about you? Xand's perfected that damn mask." So, I was right about that, then. "He hasn't changed, he just obviously saw something in you that told him he could take that mask off around you. What you need to do now is not mess it up. I wasn't being facetious when I said I'd send you back to JT with more than a broken heart if you hurt him. So, don't you dare let me down, Minion."

I shook my head. "No. Of course not. The last thing I want is to hurt him."

"Then don't," she said before she walked away.

I finally let out a breath I didn't know I was holding in and looked around the hallway. It was far too much to hope that no one had noticed the King of the Bows' Queen and girlfriend going at it, as evidenced by the whisperings and staring.

"We are way passed out of hand now," I muttered to myself and I headed out to find Xander.

I got to school just in time for home group on Friday, so I missed seeing Xander until Recess. And this time, when I saw him, I definitely felt more than just amused indifference

A girl not in our year was leaning up against him at his locker and he was looking at her with humour. I felt Miranda grab my arm and pull me towards her as someone ran into my shoulder from behind. I looked at the offending someone and saw Nancy walk past with a self-satisfied smirk on her face.

"Doll," Miranda said, "I'm sure it's not what it looks like."

I nodded. "No. Sure it's not." But, my heart wasn't feeling quite so sure.

As we got closer, I heard the girl's words. "Oh, but you enjoyed it last time…"

Xander chuckled. "That was last time, Jess. Now, I'm spoken for."

"Are you sure? She doesn't have to know." She ran her finger down his chest and his eyes fell on me. He stopped her hand just as it reached his stomach, then pulled his eyes from me.

"Jess," his voice was more warning than joking now. "Not going to happen."

She pouted in a way I assumed guys were supposed to think was attractive. "Not with that attitude, it won't." She winked at him.

I cleared my throat and this Jess jumped as they both looked at me. Xander looked like he was trying to press himself into his locker to get away from Jess, who looked like she was trying to go with him.

"Oh. Hiya Holly," she said with as fake a smile as I'd ever seen.

"Do I know you?" I asked her, looking her over with as many cares as Rachel usually gave me.

Jess' smile only widened. "Your *boyfriend* does."

"Well, bully for him. Maybe when your legs can support the weight of your ego, you can stop using him as a leaning post and I can have a word with him," I said, feeling like a total arsehole. But, I had a feeling Jess wasn't fawning all over Xander of her own volition if that 'Team Thomigan' button on her skirt had anything to do with it, and that pissed me off.

"Doll…" Xander started, looking panicked and I shook my head at him once.

Jess stood up straight and smoothed her shirt in such a way I was sure Xander was supposed to be paying attention to her not insignificant cleavage. She batted her eyes at him, licked her lips, slid her gaze to his crotch and gave him that weird pouty smile.

"I'll see you later, Xander," she said, throwing enough insinuation into that one sentence she deserved an Oscar.

"Bye, Jess," Xander said, his eyes on me.

She flounced away, swinging her hips completely unnecessarily because the only ones looking were Miranda and me.

"Doll, it wasn't–"

"I'll give you a guys a minute…" Miranda said. She gave me a pat on the arm, scowled at Xander, who looked at her in questioning surprise, and headed outside.

"Doll–"

"Xand, it's fine."

He gaped like a fish out of water for a few seconds. "Wait, what?" he finally managed to ask.

"Keeping up appearances, remember?" I said, not knowing why I was feeling so cold towards him.

After Nancy had pushed past me and given me that look, I wouldn't have put it past her to have put Jess up to flirting with Xander. What she hoped to achieve, I didn't know. Maybe she wanted to cause a rift? Maybe she thought I'd break up with him if I believed he was cheating on me?

Then again, maybe there was some bet going around that Jess had hoped to win by breaking Xander and me up, and Nancy didn't even have anything to do with it. I had no idea about everything that went on at that school behind my back and I quite frankly didn't want to know. Teenagers could be arseholes; I knew that from first-hand experience as one and being surrounded by them.

"Holly…?" Xander started.

I sighed and tried to put on a happier face. "What?"

"Jess and I… That was a while ago. Well-before you."

I nodded. "It doesn't bother me what…" I looked around and realised that people were looking at us. I leant towards him, "what you get up to, Xander. Last I checked, we had a specific understanding of what this was. You want to see where that offer leads? That's up to you. But, don't expect this to work if you screw around."

I made to walk outside but he gripped my wrist and held me firm. His eyes were hard as he looked into mine. "The only offer I'm interested in is if it leads to you. I'm not really sure how much more obvious I can make that, Holly."

My heart fluttered but my brain whacked it upside the head as that fear that his words were all for show flooded me after what I'd just seen. "Don't go saying anything you'll regret, Xander. You don't owe me anything."

"Holly." He tightened his grip on my wrist to stop me leaving. I could have if I'd really wanted, he wasn't holding that tight, but I waited to see what he had to say. "I know I don't owe you anything. You're not an obligation or a regret or whatever it is you seem to think I see you as right now. I told you last week I was more than one hundred percent in this and nothing's changed. Unless it's changed for you?"

But, what exactly was 'this'? Was it the way I felt about him or was it keeping up appearances as friends?

"What do you want from me, Xander," I asked.

"I don't want you to be the one feeling obligated."

"Even if I did want to end this, I wouldn't know how," I hissed, thinking now was really not the time to start this conversation.

"So, you don't want to end it?"

I sighed. "Look around you, can you see what we've done here? It's damned madness."

"So? We'll get through it together."

"Will we?"

"What about that friendship thing you were talking about? Or are we only friends when it's convenient? What happened to that whole loyalty thing?"

"It goes both ways!"

He nodded. "I know. But, what did you want me to do? Make a scene?"

"Well, we couldn't have that," I said, sarcasm-heavy.

"Babe, what's the real problem here? Are you jealous? Did someone say something? Is there something I'm missing? Talk to me. I'm here for you."

I lay my head on his chest.

Yes, I'd felt jealous seeing Jess and him like that. Yes, people were saying a whole bunch of things. I just didn't think the school hallway was an appropriate or private enough place to talk about changing things in either direction.

He wrapped his arms around me. "What's up?"

"I don't know," I told him.

I felt him nod. "Okay. Anything I can do?"

I shook my head against him. "No. Thanks, though."

"Always, Doll. We're 'Team Bowdeen', it's you and me against the world."

I pulled away to look at him and found him with that damn charming smile.

"Okay, you and me against the gits," he conceded.

I felt myself smile at that. "Okay, Xander. It's you and me against the gits."

I pressed a quick kiss to his lips and we went outside to meet up with our friends.

Chapter Twenty-Six

The next week, I still hadn't found the courage to talk to Xander and he hadn't brought it up again.

Nancy was walking around the school like she was a queen in her own right, talking to kids about how strong her relationship with Jason was and how she'd heard that Xander and I were having problems. I'd avoided most of her gossip for a while, but it was hard to miss this when she was sitting behind me in class. Funnily enough, she tended to only do it within earshot when Xander wasn't in the same class.

Miranda and Greg were stoic supporters, telling me not to worry about it and to ignore it. I was pretty sure Greg told Xander everything Nancy said after each lesson he missed, but Xander never mentioned it outright.

I wondered how weird it was that the Bows – notoriously the most gossipy, shallow, conniving group in the whole school – were the ones avoiding salacious rumour when my old group – idJits was seeming more apt by the day – were spreading it around like it was going out of fashion. But, then I just realised that everything I'd seen in the last few weeks made it look like that's how it had always been; the idJits spread the rumours and the Bows were the ones who just let it go while the rest of the school got on the bandwagon.

More girls flirted with Xander and not all of them were wearing 'Team Thomigan' buttons. One even went so far as to kiss him and I had seriously strong feelings about it despite how quickly he pushed her away.

There was absolutely nothing fake about the jealousy I felt as my heart got ready to Godzilla tantrum the crap out of her. But, I refrained from any kind of violence, physical or verbal. Instead, I just turned and walked away.

"Doll!" I heard Miranda call and then the distinct sound of Xander swearing.

"Leave it, mate. Give her a minute," I heard Greg say as I pushed my way into the girls' bathrooms and took a deep breath.

"Doll," Miranda shoved her way in and I heard Greg and Xander squabbling outside the door.

"I'm fine, Rand." Although, it really wasn't.

"He didn't want to–"

"Fuck that!" Xander snapped at Greg as he fell through the door.

"Xander! You can't be in here," Miranda said in a harsh whisper, then looked around to see if anyone else was in there.

Xander looked around. "Huh. The girls' loos really aren't that much nicer than ours after all."

"Xander, get out." I pointed behind him.

"Babe, let me explain."

"I don't need an explanation, Xander. I need a second to relax."

"You don't understand. She just came onto me–"

"I know!" I snapped, running my hand over my hair. "Xander, I know. But, I still need a second, okay?"

Miranda started pushing him out of the room. "Come on, big guy. You can let her yell at you later."

I gave her a small smile.

"We'll meet you outside then, yeah?" Xander said in a small voice as he let Miranda push him outside.

He wouldn't let the door close until I'd nodded and I hated how much worry there was etched on his face.

When they were gone, I took another deep breath.

I totally believed she'd just come onto him. She was only the sixth girl in the last few days. But, that didn't mean I'd enjoyed seeing it. It didn't mean I enjoyed the reminder of everything I'd thought of him before all of this. So, he might not have been as much of a player as I'd thought; he'd still done pretty well for himself and I was past denying I wanted him to just be mine. I also didn't enjoy the reminder that he could have any girl he wanted, so what was he doing with me?

I think it was safe to say I'd officially accepted I had to talk to Xander about how I felt. Now, I just had to work how I was going to do that and where I'd find the courage to maybe hear something I didn't want to. As I tried to work that out, I took one more deep breath and pushed my way out of the bathroom.

Okay, just 'hey Xand, let's be real'? I asked myself as I headed for the main doors of the building. *'As in, let's make this happen'? Or, maybe he'll bring it up again? Come on heart, you're usually vocal enough. What's your input on–?*

"Oh, so you didn't take both at once?" I heard Nancy's voice and looked around.

She was sneering at Sabrina, who was glaring back at her. Jess and Kate stood behind Nancy while Tara and Teagan stood with Sabrina.

"Funny, I'd heard that about you," Sabrina answered.

Nancy gave this ridiculously fake laugh. "I've only slept with one guy, so couldn't have been me." She shrugged like she was innocent.

"Oh, that's weird. I'd heard you were a total slag."

"Oh, no. I think you're confused. It's Bows that are the sluts. Didn't you hook up with Max when he was going out with Britt? I guess it's never too early to start your future career. How well *does* Mistress pay?"

I was definitely confused now; Max and Britt hadn't gone out, all the Bows were just waiting for it.

"Better than plain old whore," Sabrina shot back.

"Well, you'd know."

"Do you not have any fresh material?" I spat at Nancy and they all turned to look at me. "Seriously, do you not have any other insult than that someone had a threesome? That's boring, Nance. I mean, the stories I could tell about you. Only slept with one guy?" I shook my finger at her. "Lies are bad for the soul, Nancy Milligan. You really going to stand there and slut-shame Sabrina? How about you stop giving a damn about what other people get up to, huh? She wants to have a threesome, that's none of your damned business!"

"She's actually had a threesome?" Nancy asked, her mouth dropping open as she looked at Sabrina.

"Next time you want to spread a rumour, Nancy, it's probably better you at least pretend to believe in it. It's not your business who someone sleeps with. It's no one's business but theirs. So back off and leave Sabrina be."

"You're sounding mighty defensive there, Holly. Something you want to share with the class?" Nancy sneered.

"Yes, Nance. I had the *craziest* sex of my life last weekend when I let Daniel and Xander tag team me. Then, they decided to

335

stop taking turns," I said sarcastically, knowing it was the stupidest thing to say as soon as it was out of my mouth; it didn't matter that every person listening would have known I was being sarcastic, Nancy could say that I'd admitted it now.

And, by the triumphant look on her face, she knew it.

"Just go and worry about your own sex life, Nancy, and stop caring about other people's. Trust me, your sordid interest does *not* go both ways. No one could care less what you and Jason are *not* getting up to."

A cheer went up from the onlookers as Nancy flushed bright red. She huffed in annoyance and turned to push her way through the crowd. Sabrina looked at me in shock.

"Sorry about her. She's a bit of a dick these days," I said awkwardly.

Sabrina shook her head. "You didn't have to do that."

"I know. But, Bows stick up for each other. No matter what."

Sabrina looked like she didn't know whether to smile or frown and I even more seriously rethought calling myself a Bow than I had as soon as it was out of my mouth.

"Thanks, Doll."

I ignored my heart as it waved its victory pennants at winning over Sabrina Walker of all people and just smiled at her. "Anytime."

When we got out to the Bows, Xander was just staring at me in concern. But, that just turned to confusion when Sabrina took my hand and gave it a squeeze before she went over to Rachel. Who, of course, was totally thrilled by the exchange I'm sure.

But, it didn't take long for Sabrina to tell people that I'd stood up for her. At least, I assumed that's what she told them based on the new way they were looking at me. Even the Bows who already called me Doll were looking at me differently, like I'd earned the nickname now or something and not just because I was their King's girlfriend.

I hadn't expected things to get better. But, I guess I hadn't expected that they'd get worse either. Rumours were flying around the school and people were fighting more than before. Punches were thrown in the hallways, people yelled at each other, things were being hurled around the place; it was chaos.

Girls were still flinging themselves on Xander, more literally than figuratively. It got to a point where Greg and Daniel were actually acting as bodyguards to keep girls off him. Xander, naturally, seemed fairly unfazed by it all unless they got to close, and I saw them get too close. As long as Greg and Daniel did their jobs, Xander laughed and smiled and didn't exactly send the adoring masses the right message in my mind. I got the whole concept of not causing too much of a scene or being a total dick, but my heart did watch him and wonder how much he was enjoying the attention.

It wasn't helped when I walked past some girls on Wednesday and heard them talking about it.

"She hasn't dumped him yet."

"Well, maybe someone has to do more than just kiss him?"

"How are we supposed to do that?"

"I don't know. It's Nancy's plan, ask her."

I felt sucker punched. It was one thing to spread rumours and just be a general dick, but to actually send people to flirt with my boyfriend so I'd break up with him?

I'd wondered, but I had to admit that had been hurt-Holly talking. Rational-Holly hadn't actually believed that someone would actually do that. Were we stuck in some ridiculous fantasy land? Who actually does that?

Who actually fake dates a guy they hate, then falls for him while she's trying to make her best friend jealous?

I was getting really sick of my brain…

So basically, things weren't going wonderfully.

I couldn't seem to find a time to talk to Xander about everything. At school, he was inundated with girls or he was cracking jokes about Jason and Nancy with 'Team Bowdeen' kids. Out of school, I was too scared he'd tell me the only thing I didn't want to hear – no matter how much I told myself it was stupid – so I pretended everything was okay.

My brain was all in on this now; we liked him and we needed to do something about it. It was my heart who was holding back now, like the contradictory little bugger it was. Seemed like the damned thing was fine to frolic after whoever it wanted as long as there was a safety net. But, my brain wasn't interested in being a safety net anymore, it was interested in being amazing. It just had no idea how to admit that to Xander.

I was starting to feel like I'd come full circle and it made me really look at how this all started.

So, I was neck-deep in my own mind when I ran into that chess prodigy guy in the library.

Micah! His name's Micah.

"Sorry, Micah," I muttered and went to move on.

"What?"

I looked at him and suddenly wondered if he wasn't Micah after all. *Shit.* "Sorry," I repeated, hoping we could move past the me getting his name wrong thing.

"No. You said my name."

"Was I not supposed to?" I asked him.

"I didn't know you knew my name."

I gave him a small smile. "You're Micah. You're the guy who's aces at chess." I shrugged, hoping to any and all deities that I was right.

His mouth dropped open as he looked at me. "You know who I am?"

"Am I not meant to?" Were there more parts to this school than I was aware of?

He nodded. "You're really not meant to."

"Sorry...?" I tried.

He shook his head. "No," he breathed. "Don't be sorry. You know who I am."

I nodded. "Yeah. I do." I caught a picture on his diary. "Hey, I recognise that poster."

He looked down and back up at me. "You've seen *Vampyr*?"

"Not yet, but it's on my To Watch list. It's the Camilla one, right?"

He smiled. "Yeah. 1932. It's really good."

"You like the older stuff?"

He nodded again. "Usually, original is always better. What they did to *Prom* Night?" He shuddered. "But, the new *IT* looks really good. I've got high hopes."

I grinned. "You're a horror buff?"

His eyes lit up the way Mark's did when he talked about soccer. "Nothing's better than that edge of your seat tension!"

I laughed. "Yeah, I totally get that."

"What's your favourite?" he asked.

I thought. "Uh. At the moment, it's a toss-up between *Alien* and *The Babadook*."

"Ripley's amazing!"

"She's total kickarse." I grinned.

The bell rang and he looked around quickly. "See ya, Holly," he said with a wide smile.

"Bye, Micah."

He hurried off to class and I did likewise. But, when I saw him later that day, he was wearing a 'Team Bowdeen' button and he gave me an enthusiastic wave that I didn't hesitate to return. Not bad for a guy who was glaring at me the term before.

But, that was about the only minor win among the chaotic nonsense that went on just because I'd started dating Xander. So, it wasn't surprising when the principal called an assembly on Thursday to 'discuss the recent behaviour'.

I settled myself on the seat between Xander and Miranda as people muttered and chattered around us.

"Okay, everyone. Let's have some quiet please," Mrs Danvers called from the podium and silence fell over the room. "We need to talk about this teams business. It's getting completely out of hand. All buttons supporting one team or another are herewith banned from school property. Your teachers will be taking them off you when you get back to class. The disrespect and ridiculous behaviour we've seen this term has been astounding, students. I don't know who started it and I don't need to know. But, it stops today. Our school is supposed to be a safe place where you can learn and grow and spend time with your friends. It is not a warzone to play out a morbid obsession with two of our senior couples.

"What Holly and Xander, and Jason and Nancy do is their own business. I will not tolerate people calling each other names and spreading malicious lies. I don't know why you think this is acceptable behaviour. I had hoped that it would all settle down and it was a phase that would pass. I see now that it's not going to do so on its own. So, consider this a formal warning to you all. Respect your fellow students and keep your noses out of things that have nothing to do with you. Please." She paused and sighed. "Okay, that's enough lecturing. Get back to class."

There was the shuffling of mass movement, but I still managed to overhear some more highly pleasant things about me.

"Apparently, she's happy to share." I heard the hissed whisper from behind us.

Someone else snorted. "That is so sad. Can you imagine being that into a guy that you'd just let him sleep around?"

"Hello? It *is* the King of the Bows. Wouldn't you share him?"

"You're assuming I haven't already."

They both giggled and I thankfully didn't hear anymore.

My cheeks had totally heated by now and I felt Miranda take my hand.

"Don't listen to them. You know he's not sleeping around."

I nodded as I looked to Xander, telling myself I did know that. He'd been talking to Daniel and was busy laughing, so I assumed he hadn't heard what they'd said. Still, I slipped away while he was distracted and Greg finally caught up to me on the way to History.

"Doll, you okay?"

I nodded. *Not really.* "Yeah. Fine."

He nodded, but I couldn't tell if he believed me or not. "You sure? You know we're all here for you…"

"No. Holly's real," a voice said and I looked around to see Farrah, who was in Micah's year and talking to a couple of friends. "And, she's really nice."

Farrah caught me looking and she smiled at me. The girl who'd glared at me only a few weeks earlier was smiling at me. My smile back was nothing but sincere.

I nodded to Greg again, this time feeling it a little more. "I think I'll be okay, mate. Thanks."

He grinned at me in that cutely goofy way he had as we walked into the classroom and sat down.

And, did the principal's decree stop the madness?

Ha. What do you think this is? A happy ending?

Chapter Twenty-Seven

"Jason!" I yelled as Xander dodged Jason's flailing arm.

But, did they listen? No, of course not. I winced as Xander landed a punch on Jason's cheek. Not that Jason didn't then get another hit to Xander that also made me wince.

"Xander! Enough!" I tried again. "Xander, please!" I screamed as Greg lay a hand on my arm.

But, no pleading on my part was going to make either of them stop and my heart glared at the both of them as it pretended it wasn't hurt by that. Especially by Xander. Where was the guy who hadn't hit Jason because of what he meant to me?

I threw my arms up and huffed in annoyance. "I give up," I grumbled.

"Doll, it's not about you this time," Greg said.

"Is that supposed to make me feel better?" I asked, shooting him a glare.

He shrugged apologetically. "Their whole school lives has been boiling down to this point. One of them needs to emerge victorious."

"Why? What are they even fighting for?"

Greg shrugged. "Only they know. Honour? Top spot? Maybe it *is* about you?"

I rolled my eyes. "No one's fighting for me." Not when Jason had never really ever and Xander had no need to. "Why can't they just yell at each other? Why do they need to hit each other?"

"We're boys, Doll. We don't know how to use our words."

I frowned at him, despite the sarcasm in his tone. "That's bullshit and you know it."

His shrug was of the brush-off variety this time. "Yeah. But, sometimes words aren't enough. Sometimes it's the guy with the least bruises who wins."

That was also total bollocks.

"This is high school, Greg!" I snapped. "It's not Thunder Road. It's not the freaking Hunger Games. It's not..." I huffed. "I'm too annoyed to come up with anymore references. But, it's not a damned fight club–"

"Nice one."

"Shut up," I muttered.

I looked around the gathered crowd, just waiting for a teacher or the principal or–

And, there was Coach's whistle.

"Bowen! Thomas! Let's break this up!" he yelled at them, his voice carrying.

But, even that wasn't enough to make the boys stop this time.

Coach looked over at us and saw Greg.

"Hook, a hand please?" He looked around and must have seen Daniel. "You too, Viera."

Daniel and Greg hurried in and grabbed Xander's arms as Coach tried to get hold of Jason. But, Jason got one more shot off at Xander's stomach while Greg and Daniel were holding his arms behind his back. The crowd gasped in excitement.

"You watch yourself, Thomas," Xander snarled as he broke free

344

from his friends and swung at Jason again.

Jason ducked and slammed his fist into the side of Xander's head as the crowd of kids almost all gasped in horror. My heart almost leapt out of my mouth as I saw Xander fall and he didn't seem to be getting back up again. Not by himself anyway.

Coach finally had Jason pinned and there was an audible sigh of disappointment that rippled over the gathered students. Daniel and Greg managed to get some response from Xander and help him up. Xander shook his head as though trying to clear it.

"I'm fine," he growled at them. "Let me guess?" Xander said as he turned to Coach. "I'm benched?"

"You're benched, you've got detention next Friday, and I'm going to have to call your parents, Bowen."

Xander glared at him, but only nodded before he threw off Greg's and Daniel's hands, grabbed up his bag and walked over to me.

But, I shook my head and walked away. I was so not dealing with this now. Greg had been right, it hadn't been about me. I didn't know if it had ever really been about me or I was just some pawn the two of them used in their ridiculous power struggle. I didn't even know what I would have preferred it to be.

In much the same way I'd thought I'd liked Jason without really knowing him, had Xander done the same with me? Had he only liked whatever person he'd made me into in his head? I didn't really want to think about it. My heart wallowed in it and my brain was the one wandering around with its fingers in its ears at this point. But as usual, my heart was leading the way while my brain tried in vain to get it to listen to reason.

"Holly!" Xander called, but I kept walking.

Of course, him and his long legs caught up to me easily.

"Holly, what's wrong?"

"Nothing's wrong, King Douche." This time, I wasn't sure it was an endearment. "I just have to get home."

"Let me drive you."

"I'm fine taking the bus," I snapped.

He grabbed my elbow only long enough to let him get in front of me. "What's going on?"

"I don't know, Xander. You tell me."

"Let me drive you home and we can talk."

"I don't really feel like talking."

"Okay, let me drive you home and we won't talk?"

Why did that tone tug on my damn heartstrings? I tried reminding it we weren't talking to him at the moment, but that thing didn't care. "Fine," I grumbled as I swerved to head for the carpark.

He didn't try to talk to me the whole way home. But, he didn't hesitate to jump out of the car and follow me up the front path. I looked over and saw Mark's car wasn't in the driveway, and I knew Dad would still be at work, so I could be thankful for small mercies I guessed.

"Doll..." he started, but I ignored him as I tried to get my key in the door.

I finally got the damn thing unlocked and open.

"Holly... At least, tell me I can call you later?"

I rounded on him. "No. Okay. No. I'll see you on Monday."

"Holly, what did I do?"

My heart stomped its tiny little feet in a terrible attempt at a Godzilla tantrum and I glared at him. "Nothing."

"Holly–"

"That's it, Xander. Okay? The whole school has gone bat shit

346

bananas because we decided to fake date. But, I guess I can deal because you're different. Except then maybe you're not and I don't know what's going on anymore."

"What do you mean different?" he asked.

"Different. Not King Douche of all things Bow. Just Xander Bowen. But, I can't tell anymore. For weeks, it was just Xander but now there's so much Douche in you."

"Holly, what are you saying?"

"I'm saying I don't know what we're doing anymore and I don't know why we're doing it."

"I can't answer that either, but I can tell you what I'd like us to be doing–"

"If this has anything to do with sex, you're getting another bruise and it won't be anywhere Jason's hit you so far," I warned him.

"It's got nothing to do with sex. What do you think I am?"

"I don't know!" I answered sarcastically. "You seem pretty Douchey to me at the moment."

"Damn it, Holly!" he snapped. "This isn't what I want. I don't want to be fighting with you."

"What do you want, Xander?"

"I want it to be real, Holly. I want us to be real. I've been trying to work out how to actually finish the conversation with you for weeks. Every time I think we might be about to, you pull away, and I don't want to ruin anything by pushing it."

"You should have trusted your instincts," I told him, my brain trying to tell me not to listen to my fearful heart.

It was doing that thing where it slapped my heart upside the head and was desperately trying to get my attention. But, I was resolved to ignore it. Before my brain had a chance to hogtie my heart in the back seat, he thankfully spoke.

"Why? Because I'm the King of the Bows?" he asked, his voice heavy with sarcasm. "People expect me to be one thing, Holly. So, there's very little point in me acting any differently around them. But, I thought you were different. I thought I could be myself with you and you'd see me. Sometimes, I think you do. And others, you only see the actions that support your idea of me. But, that guy isn't me, Holly. I'm not the guy the rumours say I am." He paused and grinned ruefully but it didn't reach his eyes. "Well, that's not all I am."

I knew that. I did. When I wasn't acting like a dick because he'd been fighting Jason and I wasn't scared he didn't mean it, I knew that. It had taken me two months, but I did see him. And I wanted to believe I was different. I wanted to believe that what we'd found was something real. But, how did I shut up that niggling fear in my heart?

"I do see you Xander. Or, at least, I see who you want me to see—"

"That is me, Holly! Outside what you so affectionately call the Inner Sanctum, no one sees this side of me. Fuck, even Rachel doesn't know how bad it gets with my parents."

"Great, another reason for her to hate me," I muttered.

Xander caught my hands in his. "She only hates you because you have the power to hurt me," he said softly.

I looked up at him, so badly wanting it to be true. And, I had to admit, everything on his face was telling me it was true. But, fear gripped my heart.

"When did this stop being fake?" he whispered as he dropped his forehead to mine and I couldn't answer. "Because I'm not sure it ever was."

My throat caught. "Xander–"

"Be honest with me," he said. "Other than what we told people, how was it fake?"

I sighed. "We started all this when we hated each other, for one thing."

"No, you hated me."

I leant my head on his chest. "We didn't know each other."

"Isn't that the whole thing with dating? You're drawn to someone, so you ask to spend more time with them and you get to know if they're right for you or not?"

"And, am I right for you?"

"You were right for me before I asked you to fake date me."

"Xander, this is about more than just getting one over on Jason–"

"It has *always* been about more than just getting one over on that git. Why do you deny it?"

I looked up at him, into those enigmatic cognac eyes, and told myself to buck the hell up. I'd told myself this whole time that King Douche didn't do relationships, that he didn't do dating, that he was just in it for the joke. But, I could almost believe it was just Xander standing in front of me now.

"Look at what we've done," I said softly. "What we've lost. What you could still lose. Are you saying I'm worth losing Rachel?"

"You lost your best friends out of it."

I gave him a sad smile. "Some friends they turned out to be. The Bows have been better friends to me than the idJits ever were. And, we both know that means a lot. The problem with you, King Douche," He smiled back at me at the name that was definitely endearment this time, "is that you're too loyal for your own damned good. But, you can't throw Rachel away for me. I'm not worth it."

Xander cupped my cheek. "Don't say that. You're worth everything I am."

"I'm not. I decided it was a great idea to fake date my best friend's enemy, a guy I professed to hate, who I then just–" I stopped and looked up at him.

"What is so wrong with admitting you fell for me?" he asked and I could tell that he was trying to keep the hurt from his voice, it was obvious in his eyes though.

I took another deep breath. It was now or never. "The idea that you might not really feel the same. The idea that this might really end and I'd have lost something amazing."

The hurt slowly dissipated as he took in what I'd said.

"What?" The corner of his lip twitched as he smiled softly as though he was holding back a full-blown smirk and there was a touch of exasperation in his eyes. "That I might not feel the same?"

"Yes. That it might all just be words. That you got conned by your own con. That if we finished that conversation then it would be over because you didn't feel the same way after all."

"The same way?"

I could see we were going nowhere fast while he was trying to not ruin the moment with jokes. I grabbed his arm and dragged him inside, closing the door behind us.

"Yes, Xander. The same way. The same way I feel about you."

"How *do* you feel about me?"

It was one of those times I wished I found him annoying. But instead, I had to fight a smile. I could have teased him, I could have drawn it out like every other conversation, but I just wanted it sorted one way or the other.

"I like you, Xander. Like, I *really* like you. I have to wonder if it was ever fake, too. Because while I thought I was trying to make Jason jealous, I don't know that it was ever really about that. I completely fell for you and it scares the hell out of me."

A slight frown crossed his face and I didn't blame him. "Why?"

I sighed. "Because I have this ingrained sense we're doomed. My parents met in high school and it was great for a few years, then it wasn't. They grew apart. The psych told me it was inevitable and it's just followed me around."

That frown got a little deeper. "And yet, you and the git…?"

I nodded. "I know. I was apparently not worried. Which makes me think…" I paused, a whole bunch of thoughts flooding me that brought all that fear right back.

"What, Holly?"

I opened and closed my mouth again as I tried to get my brain and my heart on board. But, it was a no go. One thought flashed bright in my mind and I couldn't shake it.

"Holly?"

I took a deep breath as I looked up at him. "I wasn't worried about Jason. I didn't have that feeling of impending doom… What if that's just because we're not meant to be?"

He stepped back. "What?"

"Well, what if it's a sign? We're not meant to be, so I can't shake this feeling we're doomed. I feel like we're doomed because we are."

"That is the stupidest thing I've ever heard," Xander said, totally emotionless.

"What if you're just not right for me? Or, I'm not right for you? We just got caught up in keeping up appearances and fell for our own bullshit."

Xander ran his hand over his jaw and I couldn't read him. There was nothing there. He wasn't the cocky King Douche and he wasn't even the Xander I'd thought I'd seen lately. "You what?"

I scoffed. "Holly Aberdeen and the King of the Bows? How did I really think that was going to work? We're not right for each other. We just forgot what it was."

Xander's face went from emotionless to hard. "Are you lying to yourself now, or just me?" he asked.

I flung my arms up wildly. "No one's lying to anyone, Xander. We just don't belong togeth—"

I came to a crashing halt as Xander threw open the front door and stormed out. I watched in total bewilderment as he climbed into his car and drove off.

Chapter Twenty-Eight

On Monday, the same as he'd been most of the weekend, he was cavalier King Douche keeping up appearances for the Bows. As far as I could tell, no one was going to have noticed anything had changed between us. And honestly, I didn't have the balls to talk to him about it. But, I could see through whatever mask he'd put on and I saw he was hurting. Although, Rachel wasn't glaring at me any more than usual so I had to hope she hadn't noticed.

I was minding my own business until I ran into Nancy on the way out to lunch.

"You right?" I asked her. "Spreading any more rumours today?"

She shrugged coyly. "Really, I didn't actually *need* to bother after I had Jason convinced you had sex with King Douche."

I rolled my eyes. "Very original, Nancy. I'll bet you were very proud of that."

"I was proud at how quickly he believed it once I told him you said that was why you missed Teagan's party."

Nancy sneered at me and I looked around the corridor. Thankfully, there wasn't a crowd yet, but there was going to be soon. I could see they were already thinking about it.

"You did what?" I asked her. "When?"

"Oh, I told him all about the conversation we'd had the day after."

Apparently not the actual conversation. "Why?"

Her smile was pure evil. "How else was I going to get his mind off you?"

I blinked. "What?"

"He almost didn't believe me. All I heard was 'Holly, this' and 'Holly, that'. He couldn't believe you were actually with King Douche. So, I had to convince him. I had to convince him just how much you were *with* King Douche, though it pained me to break his heart so. But, I knew you wouldn't have had the balls to actually sleep with him. Such a virginal little prude."

I was pleased I felt no more pain at her betrayal or losing her friendship. I was just annoyed with her and the fact I'd fallen for whatever act she'd seemingly played me with for five years.

"So, what was it Nancy? You just had to have him? Why couldn't you have just told me you liked him?"

"The amount you whined about him? How would that have gone?"

"Oh, I don't know. How about 'hey Holly, you know how we said we'd be honest about Jason? Yeah, I like him, too'. It's not so hard Nancy!"

"If I'd told you, what would you have done? We'd already kissed anyway, so–"

"So you still decided to encourage me to tell him I liked him! That is way worse. You could have just told me you guys kissed and you felt something. Or, Nancy... Or! Is it just because you liked him the whole time and you were lying to me?"

Nancy gave me that pure evil smirk. "You always were so gullible, Holly. I could tell you anything and you'd believe it. And

Jason was never any better."

"What the hell happened to you?" I asked her, feeling my throat burn.

So, Jason maybe might have been slightly manipulated into treating me the way he had? It still didn't excuse him for not using his own damned brain.

"What do you mean?" Nancy asked, flippantly. There was nothing but scathing condescension in her eyes, nothing but hate and a serious desire to hurt.

"What happened to my best friend?"

"Nothing. You're the one who changed." She raised her voice so the growing crowd wouldn't possibly miss her words. "You went deranged for the King of the Bows of all people. I don't even recognise you anymore. Have you been eating enough? Or, does he like them weak and frail?"

What kind of insult even was that?

"Step the fuck off, Milligan!"

The whole quad went silent and I turned to see Rachel throwing her glare of fury on Nancy for once. I must have been dreaming. I was pretty sure I was dreaming. My heart slapped my brain and I managed to gain back some function as I saw the crowd part for Rachel to stalk towards Nancy.

"Ragging on Holly stops now, you troll," Rachel snarled and Nancy's face became a mask of ugly condescension.

"You need your King's Queen to fight your battles for you?" she asked me.

"Bows look out for each other, bitch. Something you seem to know nothing about."

People were muttering now and I was pretty sure they were finding Rachel Harris sticking up for Holly Aberdeen more scandalous than the time Xander admitted I wouldn't sleep with him. No one would have missed that there was zero love, let alone like, between us.

"I suppose Xander's cast-offs do need to stick together."

Rachel stepped towards her and Nancy did a good job of trying to hide her intimidation. "You want to watch what you say about our Doll, you raging hag. The whole school knows how much you coveted our precious King, there's no point denying it. What? Did you make a pass at him and he shut you down?" Rachel looked Nancy up and down slowly. "He always has had taste."

"I wouldn't touch him if you paid me."

"The feeling's mutual, don't worry."

"Well, that's the only thing we have in common. Until Holly betrays *him* too."

My heart lurched, but I didn't stop to wonder why just then.

"You're going to want to stop now, Milligan," Rachel warned. "Lest I say something I regret."

Nancy sneered at her. "Wouldn't that require you having emotions?"

"How does it feel to come second with both of them?" Rachel snapped and Nancy went white.

"I don't come second."

Rachel scoffed. "No. I suppose not. You knew you had no chance with Xander, so you didn't even have the balls to try. And you never really let it be a fair fight, did you? You knew you couldn't compete if they both knew the truth so you lied to them. You manipulated two people who trusted you."

"You don't know what you're talking about," Nancy said, her voice quavering.

I didn't even know what Rachel was talking about.

"I'm the Queen Bitch of all things Bow, I know everything that goes on in this school, remember?" She leant close to Nancy and I wasn't sure who else heard her next words, "I am what this school made me and I will use it to ruin you if you open your mouth one. More. Damned. Time."

I saw Nancy visibly gulp before she turned away and hurried off. Jess looked between Rachel and me with plain shock and awe on her face, then hurried after Nancy. There was a slow clap making its way around the crowd and I let out a shaky breath.

"You okay?" Rachel asked me.

She was still glaring and I wasn't sure if it was because she was still pissed with Nancy or if she was just showing her usual level of appreciation for my existence.

I nodded. "Yeah. Thanks."

Rachel shrugged it off. "It's just how it is, Bows against idJits." I was pretty sure she was being at least semi-sarcastic.

I nodded again somewhat pathetically as she stalked away. I made my way to my locker, then went to the library instead of meeting up with the Bows. But, Xander found me a few minutes later, hiding in Architecture again.

"I just spoke to Rachel," he said stiltedly.

I nodded. "I'll bet."

"You okay?"

"Sure."

"Did you want to talk about it?"

I shook my head. "Not really."

"Okay, I'll... I'm here if you need anything, you just have to say."

I paused before I said, "Will you sit with me?"

He huffed a really relieved breath and dropped down beside me.

I shuffled over a little and he lifted his arm to let me snuggle into him. When he lowered it again, he held me tightly and rested his cheek on my head.

I'd spent all weekend in his jumper, like a total addict, while I tried to work out my feelings; I didn't want to believe that Xander and I were wrong for each other, but what other reason would have me so worried about it ending? One second my heart was telling me to leap off any and all surfaces and see how far that belief in love and hope and forever would take us. Then the next, it was hiding in fear that we'd just plummet into pain. It seemed my brain had given up even trying to have a say.

I was really hoping we wouldn't have to talk about any of it again. Ever would have been my preference. But, I knew that wasn't going to work. I just wanted to put it off as long as possible.

Thankfully, Xander didn't say anything. He just held me, rubbing my arm or kissing my temple now and then comfortingly. I had to admit there was something I liked far too much about it. But then, there was something about Xander I seemed to like far too much, too. Even if we were wrong for each other.

The next day, I was too busy staring at a highly inconsolable Nancy as Jess awkwardly patted her shoulder that I didn't see Jason before I'd run into him.

We both blinked, cleared our throats, and took a hurried step back.

"Sorry," he started.

I shook my head. "These things happen." I started walking away.

"No. I meant I'm sorry about everything."

I stopped and my heart was the first one brave (or stupid) enough to look at him. "Pardon?"

"I'm sorry about everything. I… I didn't handle any of this well."

"Shouldn't you be less worried about apologising to King Douche's girlfriend and more worried that yours is crying?" I asked, nodding in Nancy's direction.

Jason opened his mouth, closed it, and nodded. "Yeah. We're not… I…" He sighed. "I broke up with her."

I blinked in total surprise. "You did what?"

He shrugged and shuffled his feet awkwardly. "I just got the feeling like I didn't know her anymore."

"Yeah, there's a bit of that going around," I muttered.

"I got you were being a dick, but I didn't think that warranted the way she was acting and the things she said about you."

I nodded, deciding I wasn't going to nit-pick about who was a dick first. Although, I guessed Jason didn't know that Nancy had been a dick first. I was so over everything that I really didn't think he needed his eyes opened to just how much of a dick his girlfriend was. He'd wanted her? That had been his choice to make. Not sticking up for me? Well, that was maybe not entirely his fault.

"It's fine. What else is high school for if not finding yourself, making poor decisions and spreading a million unjustified rumours?" I asked sarcastically.

I was starting to see that pretty much every rumour I'd ever heard about anyone was unjustified bullshit. All the scandalous ones anyway. Okay, when I say starting to see, I was like one hundred percent sure. Well, maybe ninety percent. Either way, I was done judging people based on rumours; my new philosophy was that if I didn't know you, I wasn't qualified to have an opinion about you.

Jason gave me a ghost of a smile, but there was more apology in it than anything else. "I don't know what happened to make her act that way. I thought maybe something else had happened between you two–"

"It did," I interrupted, thinking now was as good a time as any to bare my heart for him. *Not literally, get up.* "Aside from years of conversation, she spent the whole of that Sunday helping me to work up the courage to tell you how I really felt."

Jason had been watching me the way people do when they think they know sort of what you're going to say. But, at that, his whole face changed and I could see it was the last thing he was expecting.

"How you really felt?" he asked slowly.

I nodded, thinking that maybe unearthing one of Nancy's lies wouldn't be more trouble than it was worth. "Yep. Nancy spent the whole day helping me to decide how best to tell you I'd always loved you. I was about to do just that when I saw you kissing her at her locker."

He was staring at me like I'd told him I'd been a dragon this whole time and everyone but him had been able to see the real me. My heart, in a moment of delirium I'm sure, tried breathing fire. Unsurprisingly, it didn't work.

"What?" he breathed. Then he chuckled. "No. You never…?"

I sighed. I had a feeling of detachment from it all now, at least when it came to Jason. Whether he'd known and ignored it or never known, I wondered now if I'd never really been in love with Jason and that it was Nancy's betrayal that had stung in the whole saga of them getting together. Jason had really only hurt me by not sticking up for me when it seemed such an easy thing for King

360

Douche to do.

"Oh, no. I did. Well," I amended, "I thought I did. I was convinced that I was madly in love with you, that I would always be madly in love with you. I was going to tell you that Monday morning after Nancy and I had practised what I was going to say all the previous day."

"But, Nancy and I were already together by–"

"I know. I know that now."

"But, Nancy said…"

I huffed in annoyance. "I am super sick of hearing about 'Nancy said', Jason. Seriously, what did she do to you that made you lose everything that made you…you?"

He looked at me in sharper focus. "She said you didn't like me."

Now, it was my turn to be shocked and confused. "What?"

"For years, she told me you didn't like me. Not like that. Not like I liked you. I thought if anyone would know it would be her. I tried not to annoy her with it, but she seemed to just be able to see it and she told me she asked you again and how you felt hadn't changed. I…" He scoffed. "I liked you for so long, Holly. I got to a point I assumed you knew and you were just pretending you didn't so it made things easier. So, I hid it because I didn't want you to feel weird about it."

My heart had fallen on its arse at this point in complete shock, all thoughts of moving away to become a dragon and rescue princesses forgotten. My brain was frozen and had zero thoughts. None. It was empty. My surprise had just sent any and all thoughts packing.

But, that was fine because Jason kept talking. "So, when we were at Teagan's party and somehow we ended up kissing…?" He shrugged. "I just kind of felt it was the right thing to do to ask her

361

out?"

Of course he had. Because he was, deep down, the Jason I'd known forever. Mostly.

"It's not like you got her pregnant," I joked without thinking, then grimaced; the Holly he knew would probably never had said something like that. That sort of remark was entirely Xander's fault.

Jason looked me over with a small smile, but it was sad. "He's been good for you."

I frowned. "What?"

"King Douche. You look… I don't really know how to explain it. But, you seem more…confident. I see you laugh more. I guess he was the right guy for you after all?"

I swallowed hard. "Jason, I…" I sighed, knowing I had to be honest. "I thought I was in love with you. But, I wasn't. I'm not going to go all teen rom-com on you and say something ridiculous like Xander's shown me what real love is. But, as much as the Bows hate me, I get to just be myself around them, around Xander. I was about as low in their opinion as it was possible to get so I stopped trying to impress them. But, it didn't matter. They started to like me anyway." Something knocked into the back of my stunned heart, but I didn't quite understand it yet.

"You weren't yourself around us?"

It was my turn for apologetic smiles now. "I thought I was. I thought I fit in perfectly. I thought I was happy… And, I guess I wasn't unhappy. But, it wasn't until I didn't feel like it was worth trying to impress anyone – that I knew they couldn't think any less of me – that I realised there were parts of myself I…didn't advertise. And, weirdly enough, the Bows actually accepted me anyway. Most of them."

"Holly, I'm sorry."

I shrugged. "It's not your fault I was a shallow idiot. Well, I'm probably still a shallow idiot in many ways, but I'm trying to work on that."

"You think I'm a shallow idiot?"

"I think Nancy's a shallow idiot and I'd like to think we didn't know any better." I shrugged again. "I don't know. We're teenagers, aren't we supposed to be shallow idiots?"

He gave me a sad smile. "Yeah, I guess."

The bell rang and I pointed behind me completely wankily. "I should go."

He nodded. "Yeah. Me too, I guess."

We then realised that we had the exact same classes all day and huffed a laugh.

"I guess we could…?" I said.

"I mean we're going the same way…?"

We walked along and I wasn't sure if it felt normal or not.

"So, King Douche is…?"

Oh, I was *not* talking to Jason about Xander. "Yeah, I don't think we're there, Jason. I don't know if we'll ever be there."

He nodded. "No, yeah. I get that."

We stopped inside the door and hovered awkwardly.

"Maybe one day, though," I said quickly before I ducked my head and dropped into the seat next to Greg.

"Tell me you didn't just walk in with the git?" he begged me.

"Can't do that, mate."

"Why did you just walk in with the git?"

"We were talking."

"I noticed. What about?"

"About the fact Nancy and Jason broke up, Greg," I said.

"So, you and Xand won?"

"Yeah. We won," I answered, hoping he'd just shut up.

He didn't say anything for so long that I though he was going to drop it. But, finally he asked, "Why does that not sound like a good thing, Doll?"

"Xander and I are good." Well, not so much. "But…" I sighed. "Look, Jason just told me that he liked me. Okay? It just took me off-guard."

"Well, duh."

"What?" I looked at him sharply.

Greg shrugged. "Everyone knew you were his best girl, Doll. We just didn't know why he never did anything about it when you clearly felt the same."

It was all starting to make sense now; Greg last term, Rachel the day before, Jason's behaviour. "Because Nancy was busy telling us the opposite," I said softly.

"Ah…" He stopped and frowned a little. "This doesn't…change anything, does it?"

"What do you mean?"

"You and Xand. You're not…going back to the git are you?"

I huffed a humourless laugh. "I'm not going back to the git, Greg. Even if I knew how to be his friend right now, I don't think he'd do very well with the whole me and Xander thing. Not for a long time."

"So, you did pick Xand, then."

It wasn't a question, but I looked at him with a question.

"It was always on the back of our minds, Doll. We were always going to worry that you were just trying to make the git jealous."

I smiled to myself as that something bumped against my heart again. "I really did pick Xander."

Greg gave me that adorably goofy smile. "Plus, the dark side has cookies." He paused and looked at me. "Can you bake? I tried once and it didn't go well. But, I do like cookies. We could just buy them, I suppose? What do you think? Is homemade better?"

I didn't have a chance to answer as Miss Potts got the lesson started while I tried not to burst out laughing and something was incessantly trying to get my attention. I just had to work out what it was.

Chapter Twenty-Nine

I'd thought the school had gone insane before? It was nothing on what they were like with a winner.

All the kids who'd paraded around with a 'Team Thomigan' button were laughed at and teased for being idiots regardless of the fact that the threat of detention hung over the whole school. Those that didn't maintain they were always 'Team Bowdeen', at least. Mr Burnett had had a few choice words to say to me about the whole thing and Xander was… Well, Xander was being King Douche about it all.

He was parading the corridors like the king he was, waving at people's congratulations, encouraging them and letting them cheer for us. It was everything like the King of the Bows of old and nothing like I'd come to think of as Xander. I was completely confused about when he was and wasn't wearing that mask, and I was getting mighty sick of the way people were still at each other.

So, when I bumped into Rachel and she said something like, "Happy you won?" I snapped.

"No, I'm not happy we won. This is complete and utter madness."

She looked me over with barely concealed disgust. It seemed even coming to my defence the other day didn't qualify us for any sort of friendship. "I'm sure it will all die down when you dump him."

"I'm not going to dump him," was out of my mouth before I'd thought about it, but I didn't sound very happy about it.

Her eyebrow rose as she looked me over. "Wow. The passion you have for him is astounding. I'm surprised the two of you manage to keep your hands off each other."

I rolled my eyes. "I couldn't dump him anyway," I muttered to myself.

"Has he always been an obligation to you? I have to wonder why you were ever with him."

I scoffed humourlessly. "Well, I wasn't, was I? Not really."

"What?" she asked. "So, you never grasped that whole loyalty thing after all?"

"No. Not like... It was all fake!" I hissed at her, losing all hold I had on anything. "Okay? We were never really dating. I'm sure that's incredibly pleasing to you–"

"What?" she repeated.

I sighed, wishing I was still that person who worried over every single thing she did when it came to other people. If I was still her, then maybe I wouldn't have blurted out my biggest secret to the last person who should have known.

"None of it was real, Rachel. We were just keeping up appearances."

"Keeping up appearances?"

I nodded. "Yes. Pretending. Not. Real."

"You thought you were pretending?" she scoffed.

Was she going deaf? "Yes. That is usually what not real means."

"Uh huh." Rachel's slight disinterest disappeared as she glared

367

at me. "Let me tell you something, Holly. You may have thought you were pretending, but I have never heard such bullshit, even out of Nancy-fucking-Milligan's mouth. I'd never seen you as real as you have been since this whole thing started. You used to walk around this school completely fake and snotty and simpering and annoying. Now, you're real. I believe your smile, I believe the words that come out of your mouth even if I don't like them, and I believe you when I see you with Xander."

"Did you not hear me? It was fake. We were just keeping up appearances. He was supposed to be helping me make Jason jealous and I was supposed to keep the wolves at bay while he got one over on the git."

Rachel's glare didn't let up. "I hated you."

That had not been what I was expecting her to come back with. "Uh…thanks?"

"I hated the way you trailed after JT, looking at him with those puppy dog eyes and just hoping he'd notice you. I hated the way you pretended to have time for people when it suited you, but never when it was inconvenient. I actually could never really put my finger on it exactly – it was more of a feeling – but I hated you–"

"Hate to interrupt the epic tirade, but is there a point to this?"

Rachel sighed. "The point is, it didn't matter that I hated you because Xander was completely smitten. The idiot always has been."

I blinked. "He what?"

She nodded. "He's always had this weird thing about you. Even though he and JT were *mortal* enemies and you were simpering all over the git, Xand just couldn't help himself. I'd see him smiling as he watched you laugh, frowning when you looked like you were upset. So, you knew he was using you, but I assume by the look on your face that you didn't know he'd been waiting for the first opportunity to get you away from the idJit?"

I shook my head and Rachel gave me the first friendly smile I'd ever seen on her face. It was only small, but it was there.

"He's always liked you. I don't know why and I don't know how. And, he'd almost given up on you looking at him as anything but the King of the Bows. He'd waited so long to see you look at him differently, I thought he'd seen it when it wasn't there. I refused to even look so I couldn't see if you were. I was convinced you were going to hurt him."

"But, you…? You argued with him about me, but you never told him to break up with me?"

She shook her head. "No," she said like that would have been unforgivable. "It wasn't my place to ruin his relationship. I told him what I thought and, when he asked me if I wanted him to dump you, I told him not if he was happy. I told him I hoped I was wrong. I told him that every part of me distrusted you. He told me he was happy. He told me I was wrong. He told me I just had to see. And, then I realised I didn't actually know you well enough to really judge."

God, didn't that seem to have been the lesson of the last few months?

"And now?" I asked.

"Now, I see it."

"You see it?"

"I see it. I see what he wanted me to see."

"What did he want you to see?" I asked, hoping she was not going to come back with the words I thought she was.

"That the two of you are amazing together."

"Oh, God. Anything but that," I muttered.

369

"What?" she spat.

I shook my head. "It's a thing."

"What thing?"

"A thing. Xander has this…this way of looking at me sometimes and I let myself forget that it was all fake, I'd let him con me into believing we could…" I took a deep breath. "That he was amazing. That I could be amazing with him. That we could be amazing together."

"And, that's a problem?"

"How long will it last, huh? How long until we finally both realise that it's not going to work? That the King of the Bows and JT's minion aren't compatible?"

"Really? This is the reason Xander's not yelled at me all week? You two are fighting because you think it won't work?"

I blinked as I looked at her. "I guess…?"

She rolled her eyes. "Look, I have no advice for you on whether it's going to work or not. I'm not the relationship type. The whole thing just sounds too hard. But, anything can happen, Holly. You both want each other, but it's sure as hell not going to last if you don't take steps to let it."

That something from the day before smacked up against my heart again and my brain smirked rather self-satisfied as I thought I was finally getting it.

"Are you really going to be an idJit about this?" Rachel pressed.

"About what?"

"You don't fear losing something you don't want, Doll."

And there was the lightbulb moment. The thing that had been trying to get me to acknowledge it was bright as day and I got it.

I hadn't been worried about Jason and me ending – or him saying no, or whatever could have happened – because I hadn't

370

actually liked him enough for it to really bother me. But, Xander? The thought of losing Xander was terrifying. And, I'd finally realised that it was exactly because of how much I liked him.

"I want Xander…" I said to myself.

"You want him? Go get him, then."

"Go get him?"

She nodded. "I told you not to hurt him. And, you did. So, you're going to fix it."

"Because it's *my* job?" popped out and I rolled my eyes at myself.

"Yes. You break it, you fix it. As much as we both know he's more than capable of fucking up, I know it's almost impossible that he screwed this up. He waited for you longer than even he knows it, there wasn't a chance in hell he'd ruin his chance."

"So, I should…"

"You should fix it before I fix your face."

I opened my mouth and frowned. "I want to say you're joking there…?"

"It depends on what your next move is."

"Let me just get this straight… The Queen of the Bows giving me permission to date her King?" I asked.

I was gratified when I saw a genuine smile cross her face, and this one even reached her eyes. "I'm quite happy to pass the mantle onto the queen of his choice." Then, she got serious again. "So long as she doesn't mess it up."

I nodded and tried not to grin. "Did we just become friends?"

I could see she was supressing a grin of her own as she looked behind me. "Yeah, I wouldn't go that far, Minion. Yet."

Chapter Thirty

I tapped the microphone unnecessarily. The feedback hissed and I winced. Now I was here, I wasn't sure how far I was going to go with this. But, something had to be done.

I'd spent the last few days being awkward with Xander, as I tried to work out how to fix it, and watching the school fight. One answer stared me in the face. It was probably a little dramatic, but I needed to get a message out there, to everyone. So, there I was on Friday morning during my free in the Principal's Secretary's office and I'd convinced her to let me use the PA system.

"Hey. Uh, Holly Aberdeen, great crosser of social lines, here." I cleared my throat. "I've been thinking lately about social lines. A lot. Like probably too much. I've been thinking about how we sit in the comfort of our clique, with the people we call friends, and we judge everyone else. Hell, we judge those people we call friends. It's like each of our little groups is some kind of ancient kingdom with its rulers, and regulations that we're expected to follow if we don't want to be banished.

"I never thought this was ridiculous. I was one of JT's minions and I was happy with the unspoken rules that governed my life because I thought I agreed with them. I knew we hated King Douche and the Bows. I knew what we thought about the Drama kids. I knew who was acceptable to talk to and who wasn't. And, I didn't bat an eyelid because I believed in the system. I believed that every reason we had for thinking about people in a certain way was justified."

I leant back in the seat for a moment and Miss Michaels nodded at me encouragingly. God, this was harder than I'd expected. I sighed and sat forward again.

"Then, something happened and I realised that everything I'd thought was bullshit. Utter. Bullshit. I'd sat in the comfort of my clique and judged people based on nothing but rumour. Rumour I probably inadvertently had a part to play in spreading, true. But, what did I actually know about any of them? I spread the hate because I was so wrapped up in my own little world that I didn't stop to think about anyone except how they related to me.

"So yeah, I did the unthinkable. I crossed a social line. I left JT for the King of the Bows and I had no choice but to get to know the people I'd spent years hating. But, the heart does crazy things to a person. At first, I just pretended I belonged. I told myself it was no different to hanging out with my old group, just no one talked to me and no one liked me. Then Greg and Miranda came along." I felt myself smile. "And they accepted me because they thought I made Xander happy.

"I'll tell you, it took much longer to win anyone else over. But, as I was busy trying to forget I belonged anywhere but in the midst of the Bows, I saw them in a whole new light. And you know what, Maple Ridge? The Bows aren't just your standard rich, shallow, bitchy popular kids. They're no different to anyone else or any other group. When it comes down to it, we're all the same."

I sighed again. "People aren't two-dimensional! They don't fit into the neat little boxes we give them. And yet, the whole place went crazy because JT's minion started dating King Douche. We divided the place into who shipped Jason and Nancy or who shipped me and Xander. Friends went to war against friends. For no other reason than what you thought of as someone else's scandal. And for what?" I took a deep breath, not sure I was ready for this after all.

"I'll tell you what for–"

There was a banging on the window and I looked up to see Xander outside in his PE uniform, his face pure panic, his fist against the glass. "Holly? Don't do it! You don't have to do it!" came his muffled shout.

I shook my head at him sadly. "It has to end," I said, the microphone still on. "I'll tell you what for, Maple Ridge. For a lie. Because I spent years madly in love with my best friend and I didn't believe he could ever love me back, especially not when he had his tongue down our mutual best friend's throat. So, in an act of complete immaturity, I agreed to Xander Bowen's proposal – we fake date. The plan was simple, I hope to make Jason jealous and Xander gets one up on him while getting girls off him for a while.

"And look, I'm not proud of the choices that led me here. I alienated myself from the people I thought were my friends and I lost my heart more times than I care to admit. But, I wouldn't change it for the world because it opened my eyes." I looked up again and my eyes locked with Xander's. I knew he was pleading with me to stop, but I couldn't. Not yet.

"I saw the bubble I lived in and I tried to break free. Xander and I might never have been real, but I realised what I'd had with JT wasn't either. I was one bad rom-com away from worshipping the ground Jason walked on that I didn't notice that he never really saw me for me because I wasn't myself around him. Who did see me for me? Who could I not hide from? The guy we all thought was the biggest womanising piece of shit in this whole place."

Even through the obvious distress on his face, the corner of Xander's lip quirked a little in response to my assessment of him. I gave him a small smile and look down.

"Xander Bowen might be King of the Bows, but he's certainly no douche. He knew how hard it was for me to be around people who didn't like me and he made it as easy as possible. He and Rachel clashed more times than I can count over the fact she was convinced I was going to hurt him. As much as that was awkward for me, I could only dream of having someone in my life who fought to protect me that way.

"And, these were the people I hated. I can't say the Bows aren't shallow. We're all shallow. They don't act any differently with people not in their clique than the rest of us do, yet we judged them and gossiped about them while we secretly wished to be one of them. Why? Because the need to belong is strong. The need to belong is so strong that I refused to ask myself why I was just happy to pretend I belonged with the Bows until well after I did.

"I learnt quickly that I belonged with the Bows in a way I never belonged with JT and most of them probably still hate me. Because I was my complete and utter self. They couldn't like me any less, right? When I stopped trying to impress people, I found they liked me better, they trusted me more.

"So, I'm done with hate. I'm done with lies." I found Xander's eyes again and knew this was going to be the hardest part. "It took losing my heart to find it, and even then it was in the unlikeliest of places. Because, who thought something real could ever come out of something fake." I huffed a laugh and watched a hesitant, surprised smile start to cross Xander's face.

"Because I think I'm falling in love with the King of the Bows. I told myself I wasn't falling for him for so long. King Douche didn't do dating, he didn't do relationships, he had no-strings hook ups. But Xander does dating, he does relationships, he does more than just hook ups, and he does it all heart-meltingly well. It took a massive social faux pas for me to see the real Xander Bowen, and I still worry how it's going to go. But, I've realised you only really fear losing something that matters, something real."

Xander's smile was closer to his trademark smirk now and his eyes shone.

"What do you say, King Douche?" I asked, looking straight at him. "I'm one hundred per cent in this, if you'll still have me?"

He raised his eyebrows at me teasingly and shrugged with a clear 'eh, I don't know'.

I bit back a laugh and knew we needed to talk in person. "A final word, Maple Ridge. Stop picking sides. Talk to whoever you damn well want. Spread Nutella, not hate. Unless of course you don't like Nutella – though, for all that's holy, how? – then spread the spread of your choice and some love along with it. Don't wonder about that world that doesn't care. Go out and make it for yourself. Get to know someone before you judge them, because how can you judge someone you don't really know? Meet the person you want in the world you live in and stop waiting for a day that's never going to come. Now, if you'll excuse me, I just have to hope I'm not too late to snag the guy of my dreams."

I flicked off the microphone, nodded my thanks to a proud Miss Michaels and rushed out of her office.

Xander was jogging into the building. He stopped in front of me and crossed his arms.

"You expect me to just accept this? To just be ready when you're ready? To not be totally crushed by your behaviour and just open my arms and have you?"

I was about ninety-nine percent sure he was teasing. "I hope. I don't expect."

"You hope?"

"I want. I'd like. I hope everything you said was true. I hope you always knew I'd fallen for you. I hope you know I was just scared and I should have trusted you. I hope you know I'm completely crazy about you in a way I never knew was possible. I hope you know you've somehow become my best friend and you're the first person I felt I could really be myself with." I took a deep breath. "I hope I didn't ruin it."

He looked me over, his face as serious as I'd ever seen it. "I told you I'd never break your heart, Holly…" He sounded apologetic.

"And I still believe that. If you can't forgive me or trust me now, I can accept that. It would hurt like hell, but I'd respect it." Okay, so I was starting to worry I'd royally messed this up.

"I can't keep it up. I'm sorry, doll." He shook his head. "I can't pretend anymore."

My heart trembled in fear. He was right. I'd messed it up. After everything, why would he still want me?

"So that's a no from you?" I asked.

A sparkle shone in his eyes and that hint of a smirk played at his lips. "No, I mean I can't pretend around you. I can't pretend this is all fake. Not anymore. Not in a long time."

I smiled uncertainly. "Is that a yes?"

"Come here." He drew me to him and hugged me close. "Of course it's a yes."

I pulled away to look at him. "I didn't break it? I didn't break us?"

His smile was soft and his eyes were warm and I told my heart to go for it as he ran his fingers down my cheek. "Babe, you shattered every wall I ever built, every illusion I held, every mask I wore. I just had to wait for you to pull your head out of that gorgeous arse. But when you did, it was always going to be yes."

"I'm sorry it took me so long."

"I honestly thought it would take you longer."

"You would have waited?"

"Like I keep telling you, I notice things about you. I just have to wait for you to notice them, too. I had to have faith you'd realise we were right for each other eventually."

"You never rush me."

He smiled, but there was confusion in his eyes. "Rush you?"

"You gave me all those hints, but you never tried to make me see you differently. You let me see it in my own time. And even now, you're not trying to convince me of anything. Even when I hurt you. That's not fair."

"What's not fair is how much I want to kiss you."

I looked around the corridor and finally noticed that the classroom windows were full of people watching us. I'm really not sure why I expected anything different given how public I made this. I felt my face heat and shoved it in his chest as he laughed and held me tighter.

"You should get back to class," I mumbled.

"On one condition."

"What?"

He tipped my face to him and pressed a quick kiss to my lips before he jogged away with that cocky but adorable smirk and a wink.

A cheer rang out in the surrounding classrooms and I let out a half-embarrassed, half-relieved laugh as I looked around. I gave them all a small wave and headed back to the study room, keeping my hair in front of my face.

I walked in to see everyone staring at me. Some people – see: Nancy – were obviously thinking I was an idiot for fake dating a guy I hated to try to make another guy jealous. But, I saw more support on more faces – including Jason's – than I did anything else.

"Welcome back, Holly," the teacher said with a small smile as she went back to her marking.

I nodded as I slid into my seat, avoiding Miranda's look of shock. But, she plucked at my arm and I turned to her with an apology on my lips.

"What happened?" she asked before I could get a word in, her eyes alight the way they always were when we shared gossip. At least, this was the good kind, the friendly kind.

I bit my lip. "He said yes."

She squealed, then snapped her mouth shut quickly as everyone looked at us.

"Quiet please, Miranda," the teacher said pointedly, but she hid a suspecting smile.

When everyone turned back around, Miranda smiled at me and mouthed 'later'. I nodded and she nudged me excitedly.

Later was going to have to wait though as Xander was waiting for me after class, still in his PE uniform. I ran right after my heart and straight into his arms, and he kissed me hard. People around us were talking but I didn't care. I had the guy and I'd done what I could to make everything better. Only time would tell if anyone would listen or if we'd all be the same old teenagers next week as

379

we'd been last week.

As his hand slid over my arse, I pulled away. "Xander!"

He rolled his eyes. "I know. Hands in new places."

I gave him a smirk of my own. "At least at school, okay?"

Understanding flitted across his eyes and his smile grew more rueful. "Does this mean you'll sleep with me now?"

I batted him. "Presumptuous!"

"Can't blame a guy for trying." His grin was sinfully sexy, but I knew he was only teasing.

"Can and will," I answered. "Can and will." I looked him over. "Would you wait?"

"Of course."

"How long?"

"As long as you wanted me to."

And, that was one reason why I might not want to wait for long. "Then maybe if you're a very good boy, you'll get what you want," I answered.

Xander's smile softened. "But, I already have everything I want."

I smiled as my heart soared away with its big balloon. "Rachel was right."

"*Rachel* was right?" he asked sceptically, his eyebrows rising. "About what?"

A lot of things. "That inside the biggest man-whore lives a mushy idiot."

"Only for you."

My heart and my brain were finally on the same page and we were all in on this more than one hundred percent. We finally believed in hope and love and forever. And I knew my fear that it wouldn't work was a good sign, as long as I didn't listen too closely to it. I wasn't a fortune-teller. I couldn't know how long Xander and I were going to last. But, I could control what happened now. I could follow my heart and have faith.

Keeping Up Appearances

Thank you so much for reading this story! Word of mouth is super valuable to authors. So, if you have a few moments to rate/review Holly and Xander's story – or, even just pass it on to a friend – I would be really appreciative. You can find it on Goodreads or Amazon.

Have you looked for my books in your local or school library and can't find them? Just let your friendly librarian know that they can order copies directly from LightningSource/Ingram.

If you want to keep up to date with my new releases, rambles and writing progress, sign up to my newsletter at http://eepurl.com/doBRaX.

You can find the playlist for *Keeping Up Appearances* on Spotify by following this QR code:

Thanks

Oh, wow. So, here we are at the end again.

I feel like I always end up thanking the same people at this point, but I guess it just goes to show that I'm lucky enough to have a whole group of people I know I can always count on. So, thanks go out to the lot of you – you know who you are – as usual.

Thanks too though to my beta readers, who I asked for more help on this little bugger than I have before. Thanks especially to Regina and Renate who talked over ideas with me. I've never had flaws pointed out with such tact and finesse and I loved it. Thanks for helping me work out why the damned thing wasn't working – hopefully the finished product is a lot better.

I want to give a huge shoutout to those of you who pre-ordered. It freaked the hell out of me that I might disappoint you, but your faith and trust made me feel like I could conquer the world. I just hope it was worth it.

And, to all of you who've stuck with me through multiple books; thank you for giving me a chance to keep doing what I love.

No More Maybes

"It would kill the past, and when that was dead he would be free"

Aurora Daniels just wants to get through Year 12 with no distractions.

Then, Cole Fielding comes along.

She is instantly drawn to him but isn't sure he's the sort of guy she should fall for—he smokes, he's unreliable, gets into fights, and just exudes bad boy.

But, Cole hides an intelligence that speaks to her.

As they get closer, so does Cole's harrowing past. Can she believe in someone who can't believe in himself?

Maybe...

Out now.
Companion novel, *Gray's Blade*, coming August 2018.

My books

You can find where to buy all my books in print and ebook at my website; www.elizabethstevens.com.au/books.

About the Author

Born in New Zealand to a Brit and an Australian, I am an emerging writer with a passion for all things storytelling. I love reading, writing, TV and movies, gaming, and spending time with family and friends. I am an avid fan of British comedy, superheroes, and SuperWhoLock. I have too many favourite books, but I fell in love with reading after Isobelle Carmody's *Obernewtyn*. I am obsessed with all things mythological – my current focus being old-style Irish faeries. I live in Adelaide with my long-suffering husband, delirious dog, mad cat, one guinea pig, two chickens, and a lazy turtle.

Where to find me:
Website: www.elizabethstevens.com.au
Facebook: https://www.facebook.com/elizabethstevens88/
Twitter: www.twitter.com/writer_iz
Email: elizabeth.stevens@live.com